Praise for

FIGHTING FOR INFINITY

"5 action-packed, heartbreaking, mindblowingly amazing stars! This series has made me believe in the cosmic power of love, and that the universe has a bigger plan for us than what we imagine."

~MARIANNE ROBLES at *Boricuan Bookworms*

"*Fighting for Infinity* is the polish that makes this stellar paranormal trilogy shine. On par with (if not better than) most of the "big six" paranormal releases out there, I would place this highly romantic series among the best of the best, not to be missed."

~JENNA DETRAPANI at *Bookiemoji*

"What an incredible ending to an absolutely breathtaking series. The truest of all the star-crossed love stories, all of my hopes and expectations were realized in this conclusion to Nathaniel and Maryah's epic love story."

~JENNIFER GREEFF at *Battery Operated Blog*

The Kindrily Series Book 3

FIGHTING
for
INFINITY

KAREN AMANDA HOOPER

FIGHTING FOR INFINITY

Copyright 2014 Karen Amanda Hooper

First Edition

Second Edition cover 2019

ISBN: 978-0-9855899-5-0

Published by Starry Sky Publishing

Starry Sky Publishing

Cover design by Melissa Williams Design
mwbookdesign.com

Edited by Marie Jaskulka
mariejaskulka.com

Visit author Karen Amanda Hooper on the Web
www.karenamandahooper.com

Dedicated to my mom,
the very first reader of *The Kindrily*,
and my first and very best friend.

Dear Reader,

Welcome back...again.

I love writing these notes to you. I imagine us sitting on the Lunas' back deck together while drinking hot chocolate, staring out at the red rocks of Sedona, gazing up at the stars, and chatting about the kindrily and their countless stories.

If you've read books 1 and 2 of this series, you know what I mean (and hopefully you're smiling). If you haven't read books 1 and 2, stop right here because I assure you, you will be lost if you try to read the series out of order.

For those who chose not to read the bonus chapters at the end of *Taking Back Forever*, (kudos to you for having such willpower) now is the time to catch up.

Harmony won't be a narrator in this book, but she covered some important points at the end of *Taking Back Forever*, so I'm including the last couple chapters. Heck, even if you did read them, if it was more than a few days ago, read them again. By now, you know the kindrily and me, and you know there's a lot to keep track of.

Or, if you're impatient like me, feel free to jump ahead to page 18. The perfect page number for *Fighting for Infinity* to begin.

I hope you enjoy the conclusion to Maryah and Nathan's story.

Thank you times infinity,

SKETCHY AT BEST

Harmony

Dakota was in his usual spot, hunched over the desk in the library drawing furiously. I brought him a soda and set it down in front of him, but he didn't look up from his work.

"Take a break," I told him.

He glanced up as if finally realizing I existed. "I can't. I have a lot of work to do."

I worried about him more and more. Since his near-death experience, he'd been obsessed with his comic creating much more so than before. And then there was the issue of him believing he was an Element. He told Faith, Carson, and me that he was a changed person. He claimed he was one of us, and he believed—with all of his dear and hopeful heart—that his ability was creating reality through his comic books. If he drew it, it would happen.

I sighed and reached for his hand to stop him from drawing. "Dakota, you need to stop this."

He tried pulling free, but I kept a tight grip on him. His eyes locked with mine.

"It sucks that you don't believe me. But I know what I'm doing. You guys could help me by telling me what I should draw, but instead you're probably talking behind my back about how nuts I am."

"We'd never talk about you like that."

We had talked about him a lot, but more out of concern for his wellbeing.

"I wish you'd believe me," Dakota pleaded. "I feel it, Harmony. I'm different."

"You almost died, Dakota. Of course you feel different."

"Not different in the way you see people talk about on television documentaries. I didn't see the light and suddenly have a new appreciation for life. Different as in I feel my power coursing through me. I'm part of the kindrily now. I'm meant to help save our members and the world."

Save the world. He'd been saying stuff like that since he woke up. He barely slept. He hardly ate or drank. He was so skinny he looked like he was on drugs.

For years Dakota's only wish was to be an Element. His encounter with almost dying left him feeling invincible. And his damaged brain stem had probably created an alternate reality where his wish came true. No Element in all of time or existence had drawing the future as a supernatural ability.

"I miss spending time with you," I said. "Let's go ride dirt bikes."

He tried pulling his hand away again, but I didn't let go. He squeezed his pencil so tightly it snapped. "You should hang out with Gregory."

"Gregory wants to get to know you. Why don't you hang out with us?"

"After I finish this."

But that was the problem. He never finished. Even when his body did finally run out on him, he'd toss and turn in bed with his pages clutched in his hands. He'd mumble in his sleep about saving the world and needing more pencils. It was disturbing to witness, and I didn't know what to do to help him move past it. Worse, what if he never moved past it? I kept imagining him in a psych hospital, sedated and drooling all over himself.

"Please," I pleaded. "Finish it later. Come hang out with me and get some fresh air and sunshine."

"I can't. Too much work to do and not enough time."

I let go of his hand and sank back in my chair. He immediately started sketching again. His hand swept over the pages with such desperate purpose. I took a deep breath. I hated myself for what I was about to do. "I have a feeling there's something we're supposed to see or find if we go out, something that will help with your comics."

His pencil paused, hovering over the page. Only his eyes lifted. "Really?"

Reluctantly, I nodded. "Really."

"Like an answer from the universe?"

"Yeah, the universe always gives us what we need. But you're making it difficult to reach you because you stay cooped up inside all night and day."

Dakota glanced around the library. "You're right. Okay, where are we going?"

"I'm not sure yet," I said, relieved that as awful as my fake belief was, it worked and he'd get out of the house and back into real life. "We should stay open to wherever the universe wants to take us."

"Sounds good." He stood but grabbed a pad of paper and tucked a pencil behind his ear.

"You're taking those with you?"

"I'm sure I'll need to jot stuff down."

I sighed. My plan wasn't as brilliant as I thought. "Okay, let's go."

"Wait. I need sunglasses." Dakota ran out of the library. I traipsed out into the living room and waited, wondering if my plan would help or only make things worse. He came back wearing Carson's shades. "Don't want to chance the Nefariouns knowing who I am."

"Right." I nodded, putting on my own sunglasses.

We had created a delusional monster.

∞

Riding was uneventful—especially since I was the one who rode while Dakota sat on the ground sketching.

We returned to the house for our usual evening round-table meeting and Dakota dragged in a stool from the kitchen and sat behind Carson. No one questioned his attendance anymore. The whole kindrily was aware of the problem, and since Dakota never said a word during any of the meetings, we allowed him to sit and sketch while we talked.

"The big question is will Dedrick come after any of us again?" I said. "Yes, it's wonderful to live here together as a tightknit group, but it makes us a much easier target."

"My worry is that he'll retaliate," Louise said. "We took Gregory from him."

"No, he took Gregory from us," I clarified. "We took him back."

Gregory squeezed my shoulder. The feel of him being next to me was still surreal at times.

"And we killed one of his valued members in the process," Carson added.

Dakota's head snapped up. He was smiling. I don't know what made him happier, that Carson mentioned what Dakota did, or that he referred to Dakota as one of us. "I doubt he'll just accept that and leave us to live in peace."

"And I still believe he's obsessed with Maryah," Nate added. "I'm worried he'll still come for her."

Maryah took a deep breath. Her confidence had grown leaps and bounds over the last couple of days. I didn't know what she and Nate were doing while they were away together, but whatever it was seemed to be working.

"He knows I erased," Maryah argued. "Therefore, he thinks my ability was erased too. And River will confirm that I was clueless about our way of life and my power. Maybe Dedrick won't care about me anymore."

"Which brings me to my next question," Faith said. "Why did he take River and what does he have planned for him?"

"River never demonstrated any kind of power while you were with him?" Louise asked Maryah. "Not even a hint of something supernatural?"

"Super strength douchiness," Faith huffed.

"No," Maryah said. "But April told me something last week when I went to visit her and her mom. River had been trying to contact me through her. He wanted her to tell me he didn't want to be one of them."

"April knows about us?" Amber asked with concern.

"No," Maryah assured everyone. "I didn't tell her anything. I spilled our secret in the past and created a never-ending chain of problems. I wouldn't make that mistake again. April had no idea what River was talking about. She thinks he's crazy. But obviously River meant he doesn't want to be a Nefarioun."

"He wants you to *think* he doesn't." Faith crossed her arms over her chest. "He tried to kill you. That's as nefarious as it gets."

"But Dedrick made him. We know that. The same way Gregory almost killed Harmony."

"You said his eyes weren't snakelike," Nate pointed out. "His mind wasn't being controlled."

"Yes, but Dedrick had other ways of controlling him." Maryah glanced around the table. "River depended on him for money and a place to live. Dedrick threatened to take all that away."

"Ahh, yes," I quipped. "Murder in exchange for food and shelter. Seems fair."

Krista leaned forward. "Maryah, I know you always want to see the good in people, but River is no good. Now that he's back with Dedrick, he'll be even worse. Let it go. We need to focus on protecting ourselves. River can do the same."

Dakota had stopped sketching. "Maryah," he said. "If you could choose, would you want River to be good or evil?"

We all glanced at each other, not knowing what to do or say.

"Good," Maryah told him. "Of course I'd want him to be good."

Dakota nodded then went back to sketching. If only it were that easy.

RISING TO THE CHALLENGE

Maryah

I woke up in the floating chair of the sensperience room. The stars twinkled all around me.

"Carson?" I called out into the darkness.

No answer.

I had astral traveled again. Only to the garage to watch Nathan work on Anthony's Mustang with him and Dylan, but it was another successful training session. I had astral travelled three more times since the initial time at the cabin, but I must have fallen asleep again because Carson had left the room.

I slid off my chair and walked to the door, squinting at the bright light as I headed for the living room. I pretended to still be blinded by sunlight when I saw Carson and Krista kissing. I cleared my throat, and they pulled apart.

Krista wiped her lips and fiddled with her hair. "How'd it go?"

"Good." I stretched my arms behind my back. "Traveled to the garage and watched the guys work on Anthony's car."

Carson rolled his eyes. "How ambitious of you."

"Hey, we don't all move at rapid speed like you. I'm easing into this traveling thing." I walked to the kitchen to get a drink.

Astral traveling always made me thirsty. I called over my shoulder. "And what's up with leaving me alone in there?"

"There's no way to tell whether you're asleep or traveling. If you were traveling, I didn't want to wake you. But hanging around watching you do absolutely nothing is not how I want to spend my day."

I grabbed a juice from the fridge and rejoined them in the living room. "You mean you just wanted to make out with Krista."

Krista giggled.

"Like I said." Carson smiled. "I had other plans for my day, and every other day."

"Thanks for the support," I chided.

"Whoa, Sparky, don't forget I'm the one who built you the sensperience room that started this whole regaining your ability thing."

"Noted, and thank you," I said. "But don't forget I'm the one who forced you to come up with a way to help me sensperience."

Krista glanced at Carson who was speechless then she smiled. "Oooh, good one, Maryah. That deserves a whole box of chocolates."

"Noted." Carson nodded at me, narrowing his eyes. "But I'm still smarter than you."

I smirked. "I'll catch up soon."

I'd never be as smart as Carson, but my confidence and abilities were strengthening. My intense make-out sessions with Nathan resulted in me remembering a couple more flashes of my past lives. My plans were working.

"Have you tried finding Dedrick when you're traveling?" Krista asked.

I hadn't tried to find Dedrick since the one short moment when I'd seen him and the girl in the window. I wanted to master waking up from my travels at will before I went searching for him. I didn't know why I was so nervous about spying on Dedrick. Maybe because I felt like I was truly *there* when traveling. I wasn't quite ready to be alone with Dedrick. Being around kindrily members felt safe, but it wasn't like I could take anyone with me in my travels. I had already asked Edgar if he thought that was possible, and he assured me it wasn't.

"Not yet," I answered Krista honestly, "but I will try to track him soon. I wanted to wait until I mastered returning to my body. So far my tendency is to fall asleep."

"I'm sure it takes a lot of energy out of you," Krista offered. "Your body probably falls asleep from exhaustion."

"Yes, but the clock is ticking," Carson said. "Time to put on your brave girl panties and try to find Dedrick."

Louise rounded the corner carrying her laptop under one arm. "Hello, all."

"Any news to report?" Carson asked her.

"Nope," Louise said. "Still quiet out there."

Krista and I exchanged worried glances. Most of the kindrily pretended not to be concerned that we hadn't heard one word about the Nefariouns. But I was worried. It had been more than a week since the battle at the airport. I had a gut feeling Dedrick was waiting to make his next big move. Not knowing what or when that move would be had my stomach in knots. Carson was right; I needed to be brave and take the plunge into trying to locate Dedrick again. I was the key to knowing what he was doing and planning.

"I traveled again," I told Louise.

Her face lit up. "You did? Where to?"

"Just the garage," I admitted. "But I'm getting better at it."

"Wonderful." She hugged her laptop to her chest and her lips parted like she was about to say something else, but she stopped. What she probably wanted to say was that it would be helpful to know if Edgar was next on Dedrick's wish list.

"Tomorrow," I told her. I couldn't wait any longer. "Tomorrow I'll attempt to find Dedrick."

The worry lines framing her mouth loosened with relief. "Good. It would be nice to have some clue as to what he's up to."

Krista reached over and squeezed my hand—her unspoken way of telling me she was proud of me for being brave. I squeezed back because the thought of actually locating Dedrick scared me, but I was determined to conquer my fear.

DIVING DEEP

Harmony

Gregory set his sunglasses on the patio table between us. "I'm going to have to meet your parents someday."

"Yes, but not today." I finished the last bite of my sandwich. "Or tomorrow."

As far as my parents knew, Dakota and I were on an educational trip for school that was earning us extra credit. Dylan persuaded them to not only believe it, but also to support my decision to go on the trip, so I was embracing the freedom to stay at the Luna house with Gregory.

"Dakota is going stir crazy being cooped up here," Gregory said. "He needs to go home."

"I know." That was one of my major concerns about us returning to our routine at home. I wouldn't get to spend as much time with Gregory, and my parents would surely notice the change in Dakota's mental state. I could ask Dylan to persuade them to believe Dakota was fine, but that didn't seem fair to anyone.

"What's going through that magnificent mind of yours?" Gregory asked.

"I'm enjoying my time with you. I'm not ready to give that up yet."

"We'll still be together. It will be fun. I can date you and try to impress your parents. Make them wonder if I'm good enough for their daughter."

I grinned. "You're not good enough for me."

"I know that, but the key is getting *them* to believe I am."

"And what about at night? We won't be able to sleep together."

He waved me over to him, and I sat in his lap. "Your bedroom has a window, right? I'll sneak in."

"Ooh, that does sound fun. Real teenage shenanigans."

He pulled me closer and gently bit my lip. "The possibility of getting caught will make it that much more exciting."

"My parents would die if they found you: a towering, muscular, long-haired, Spanish twenty-two-year-old naked in my room."

He wiggled his dark brows. "I look forward to hearing all the shocked expletives running through their head when they catch us."

"That would be a true test of my dad's preaching about remaining peaceful and always acting with love and compassion."

"He sounds like a good man."

"He is." I fed him another potato chip. "Both of them are great."

"Why'd you choose them? And how did Faith become your twin sister?"

I shrugged. "They were close to Louise and Anthony. Mary told us to choose so we'd be close together. Apparently, Faith chose the same parents. She requested to be sent back right after me. The time line was close enough that we could be twins."

"Fascinating."

"Some days I think Maryah is determined to build an army—or Mary was anyway. First Krista and now Mikey."

He squeezed me tighter. "We contributed to the army with Carson."

"Carson is something special," I said. "He probably raised hell in the Higher Realm until they granted him Element status."

"He must have inherited his ability to raise hell from his original mother."

"Or his father."

Gregory's eyes lowered. "I sense it's a bit weird for him. I'm in the same body as I was when I was his father. Sometimes when he looks at me it feels like he's watching a ghost."

"I'm sure it's strange for him, it's strange for me too, but in a good way. Carson will get used to it. Isn't it hard for you too? Physically you're not much older than he is."

"That's not strange. The really disorienting part is my last solid memories of the kindrily—before the day I stabbed you, of course." I squeezed his side where he was ticklish, and he squirmed but continued with his thoughts. "There was Amber and Dylan's wedding. Then things go blurry, and bam, here I am with you, and you're in a different body—hell, almost everyone is in a different body—and I've missed two decades of what's been going on with my own kindrily. The time I was gone is slipping away from my memory more each day. Years of my life have been erased."

My chest tightened at the word *erased*. "Oh, no." I sat up straight. What if Dedrick had the actual power to erase memories? "What if Dedrick erased Maryah's past? What if he's planning to erase all of us? What if you forget our past lives together?"

"That won't happen."

"How do you know? We have no real idea of what kind of power Dedrick has at his disposal."

"I remember everything from all my lives. Just a lot of the time I spent with Dedrick is unclear. And if he has the power to erase all of those memories from my mind then I'll thank him for it."

I traced my fingers around Gregory's obsidian eyes. He knew what I was doing, that I needed to gaze into the windows of his soul and see for myself. That I needed to know every bit of our history was still intact.

He lifted his chin and relaxed back into his seat, knowing it would take a while. "Dive on in. The waters of my soul are fine." I kissed him then went deep beneath the surface. I needed to make sure our history was still there. Every part of it.

Thankfully, nothing had been lost—except almost two decades together. And while losing that time was painful and awful, I had him back—forever. And that's all that mattered.

∞

Gregory and I brought in our lunch dishes from the deck. Louise and Helen were pacing the kitchen.

"Still waiting?" I asked.

Louise nodded. "I hope she locates him. At this point any bit of information is better than nothing. Even members of the other kindrilies are worried about how quiet it's been."

"I'm going to sneak in and see how it's going," I said. "I'll report back in a minute."

I crept down the hall and turned the doorknob to Maryah and Nate's room slowly and soundlessly. Krista looked up as I tiptoed into the room. Already knowing the question on everyone's mind, Krista shook her head.

"She's been under a long time," Nate said.

Krista sat on the bed beside her. "I was just thinking the same thing. But she's been falling asleep after she travels. Maybe she's sleeping."

I stepped closer. "Or maybe she found him and she's finding out a lot of useful information."

Nate looked at me as if considering my reasoning, but then he shook his head. "Something's amiss. I can feel it."

I leaned against one of the branch posts of the bed. Maryah looked peaceful. "She'll be pissed off if you wake her up right before she discovers a plan or something else important."

Nate stood. "That's fine. It wouldn't be the first time I made her angry." He rubbed her arm lovingly. "Maryah, come back. We're concerned." He gave it a few seconds then nudged her shoulder and patted her cheek. "Angel, we need you back here. Time to come home."

Krista glanced at me, then back to Nate as he continued trying to wake up Maryah.

Maryah wasn't budging.

Krista snapped her fingers in front of Maryah's face. "Pudding, wake up." She clapped her hands. "Come on. You're freaking us out."

Nate looked up at me. I shrugged. "Don't ask me."

"Krista," Nate asked, "will you check to make sure she's okay physically?"

Krista held her hands over Maryah's body and closed her eyes, scanning every inch of her. "She's perfectly healthy."

"Where's Carson?" Nate asked. "Perhaps he can figure it out."

Krista sprang up. "I'll go get him."

Nate caressed Maryah's cheek. "Maryah," he pleaded, "wake up."

Carson blurred into the room and halted at the side of the bed. "She's probably asleep."

"We tried waking her," Nate said. "It's not working."

Krista ran in and stood beside him. Carson blurred away again then came back with a glass of water. He dumped it on Maryah's head.

"Carson!" Nate yelled.

"What? It should have worked."

The worry was spreading through all of us. I could feel it filling the room.

Nate dried Maryah's face with a blanket. "Wake up, Maryah. Please, open your eyes."

FIGHTING FOR INFINITY

"People they come together,
people they fall apart.
No one can stop us now,
'cause we are all made of stars."
~Moby, 18

LOST IN THE DARK

Maryah

It was like a dream, a terrible but extremely rewarding dream.

I found him. I found the monster. As terrifying as that was, I kept reminding myself that only my spirit was with him. He wouldn't even know I was there.

I tried to observe and make a mental note of everything. The young girl I'd seen in my other travel session was with him again. They were in the same place. This room was made of stone and had no windows, and it was dimly lit by candlelight.

The raven-haired girl was sitting at a table in front of an old thick book that called to me. I hovered over it, wishing I could open it and scan through its pages, but with no physical form that was impossible.

"Well, hello there." Dedrick looked at the book then sneered. I could almost smell his rotten breath just by looking at his crooked yellow teeth. "We knew you'd be joining us soon."

I scanned the area around me, but no one else had entered the room.

"Yes, Mary," Dedrick said, "or should I say *Maryah*, I'm speaking to you."

If I had a body, it would have gone rigid. He couldn't see me. That was impossible. But Dedrick's eyes penetrated me as if I were flesh and bone standing in front of him.

He walked over to the girl and ran his fingers through her black hair. "She's irresistible, isn't she? Once you've seen her, you're forever drawn to her."

He yanked the girl to her feet and shoved her aside. Her expression was cold and emotionless. "She's my tempting flame, and you're my predictable moth."

Her black eyes met mine as if she could see me too. She didn't have the signature golden irises with black slits like a snake. She wasn't under Dedrick's mind control, but something about her was chilling and eerily familiar.

"Maryah," Dedrick barked, snapping me out of my intense study of her. "Meet Rina. I think you two will become great friends."

I hated that he was speaking to me as if I were really in the room.

I wanted to find out more about where they were, and Rina, but I didn't feel safe with Dedrick speaking directly to me, so I tried returning to my body.

Nothing happened.

I grappled for the cords of energy that usually connected me with my body, but my connection was gone. I tried again and again, getting more anxious and desperate with every attempt.

"Come now, Maryah. You didn't think it could actually be that easy, did you? Didn't Gregory's capture seem a bit too convenient?" Dedrick sat down, kicked his dirty boots up onto the table, and laughed. "All this time, I've thought I needed you—the physical you. But I came to realize your body isn't important. Your soul is what I require. And now I have it."

Rushes of painful energy lashed through me like a lightning storm. I kept opening my awareness, my energy, my soul, trying to reconnect with my body. I stared at the feather on my phantom ring, willing to see its light, pleading to form a bridge back to my body. I pinched my wrist as hard as I could but felt nothing.

"Look at you." Dedrick snickered. "Like a lightning bug trapped in a glass jar."

I darted around the room as if I could fling my spirit into a wall and a secret door would open so I could fly out. I caught a glimpse of light in a glass bookcase, and I slowly moved toward it.

Reflected in the glass was a glow of gold, silver, and green light in the vague shape of me. I moved side to side and so did the light. Around the glow was a translucent bubble.

"Pretty, isn't it, Rina?" Dedrick cooed. "Like our own life-sized snow globe."

She nodded while wringing her hands and keeping her eyes on her bare feet.

Was I really trapped? How was that possible? Harmony's words echoed in my head: *Imagine someone ripped your heart out of your chest and threw it in a cage. Outside the cage, vultures, rats, and coyotes circle, waiting to rip your heart apart and devour it. Worse yet, as they circle, their wicked energy surrounds the cage, tainting the pure and good soul inside. Over time, your heart starts to change; it becomes evil too. Smothered by negativity, it slowly stops beating until it ceases to exist.*

I wanted to cry.

"Let me go!" I shouted.

Dedrick folded his hands behind his head and smiled. "You aren't going anywhere for a very, very long time, Maryah. Might as well make your soul comfortable."

I stared in disbelief. I was trapped. My stomach felt as if it had plunged to the floor and was waiting for the rest of me to catch up. I swallowed down the taste of bile in my throat.

"Can you hear me?" I tentatively asked.

Dedrick watched me but didn't reply. The girl leaned against a wall, biting her fingernails. It was hard to tell where her bare feet ended and the dirt floor began.

"Can you hear me?" I yelled to her, my voice cracking with desperation and fear.

Neither of them flinched.

"I wonder," Dedrick said, "what's going through that mind of yours. Are you wondering how this is possible, or have you already figured it out?" He glanced at Rina and smirked. "If so, she figured it out a teensy bit too late, eh, Rina?"

The girl, Rina, was short, pale, and too thin. She couldn't have been more than twelve, but her obvious lack of nutrition and hygiene made her look as old and gray as the grimy, threadbare scrubs she wore.

"What I'd really love to see is dear Nathaniel's reaction. What will he say?" Dedrick weaved his fingers together, using them as a hammock for his bristly chin, which framed his sadistic grin. "What will he do when he realizes his soul mate, whom he was so recently reunited with, slipped out of his grasp again?"

Dear god. Poor Nathan. As if I hadn't put him through enough already. He would freak out. So would the rest of the kindrily.

Dedrick cackled as he stood. "Let's find out, shall we?"

Dedrick held out his hand to Rina. She shuffled forward, lifting her head just enough that I could see her dark eyes. Were they black, gray, dark blue? It was hard to tell in the dim lighting from the single candle. She blinked quickly then reached out as if she could touch me.

"What are you doing?" I tried to leap back but couldn't move. Somehow she held me in place with only her hand resting against my phantom arm.

"Good girl, Rina," Dedrick said to her. "Don't botch this up or there will be serious consequences."

She bowed her head, and warmth surged through me. For a moment, I could have sworn her skin glowed pale blue, but I refocused, and the light was gone. Dedrick's eyes were closed and so were hers. Neither of them moved or said anything, but I could tell something was happening. Something I didn't understand.

"What are you doing?" My vocal cords shriveled along with any confidence I had in my ability as I whimpered. "Please let go of me."

Rina's hand grew warmer, but she didn't budge or open her eyes. Same with Dedrick—it was almost as if they were no longer in the room.

UNWELCOMING PARTY

Nathaniel

"What if something happened to her?" I asked, pacing beside our bed.

"How could anything happen to her?" Harmony argued. "She's right here."

"She's fine physically," Krista pointed out. "Maybe she's just in a deep travel. Like a deep sleep."

I leaned over her and caressed her cheek. I'd seen her sleep deeply. In previous lives, I'd seen her astral travel a million times to watch countless people or events, but never like this. Something was different in a very worrisome way.

Then I felt it—a shift of energy in the room. My eyes darted up to Carson. He stood across the bed from me, staring at Maryah, tugging on the strings of his sweatshirt. Krista sat beside Maryah, holding her hand. Harmony was leaning against the bedpost. Her eyes met mine.

"What?" Harmony asked me. "You look perplexed. More so than you did ten seconds ago."

I glanced over my shoulder then scanned the room. "Everyone out."

"Nate?" Harmony questioned.

"Just please leave me alone with Maryah for a few minutes."

Carson squinted. "But—"

"Please and thank you," I said firmly.

They exchanged worried glances, but Krista stood. "Let's go see if the others have any ideas." She motioned for Carson and Harmony to follow.

Reluctantly, Harmony turned away but stopped at the door. "Shout if you need anything."

I nodded. "Shut the door behind you, please."

The handle latched behind her. Only Maryah and I were left in our quiet room. I sat on the edge of the bed and cocked my head, listening. No matter how exceptional my hearing was, I wouldn't be able to hear what I had felt. I needed to feel it again.

I lifted my chin and closed my eyes. And there it was—an invisible presence hovering inches away from me, the presence I had felt several times before we confirmed that Maryah still had her gift. She was astral traveling but lurking in our room.

"Why are you watching *me*?" I said out loud. She couldn't physically answer me, but I hoped maybe she'd return to her body once she knew I sensed her. I held her hand, waiting for her to be physically present again.

Did she want to see how we reacted while she traveled? Was she curious about what we said or did when she wasn't around? "I have nothing to hide from you." I spoke to her soul that I sensed hovering across from me. "There's no need to spy on me."

Her body still rested peacefully. I curled up beside her, sliding my arm under her neck and kissing her forehead while suppressing a grin. My fingers trailed along her collarbone. "Return to your body in the next two minutes, and I'll make it worth your while."

Two minutes ticked away and still no movement, but I could feel the energy circling the room. She was watching me.

"Fine then." I adjusted my head against the pillow. "I'll be napping. Wake me when you return."

After a few minutes of listening to Maryah's steady breathing, I dozed off. I have no idea how long I was asleep, but I awoke because of a loud gasp. Louise stood in the doorway with her hands over her mouth.

"What is it?" I sat up, searching the foot of the bed where she was staring. "Louise?"

Maryah hadn't budged.

Louise braced herself against the doorframe. Her facial expression was a mix of anger, shock, and worry. "How?"

"How what?" I climbed out of bed and walked over to her. "What's wrong?"

She yanked my arm, pulling me out of the room while slamming the door shut behind her. "Carson!"

He blurred to us before I could ask why we were standing in the hallway.

"Go in there," Louise told Carson, nodding to our bedroom, "and keep an eye on Maryah."

"Because?" Carson asked, clearly as confused as I was.

"Just do as I say."

He opened the door, and she practically shoved him inside before slamming it closed again. She grabbed my elbow, guiding me down the hall.

"Louise, what in the world has gotten into you?"

Faith was sitting at the island eating pickles out of the jar while Shiloh smeared peanut butter onto toast.

Pickle juice dripped down Faith's chin as she asked, "What's all the commotion about?"

"I could see his aura," Louise said.

"Whose aura?" Faith and I asked at the same time.

"Dedrick's. I'd know that murky evil energy anywhere."

"Dedrick?" I tensed, scanning the kitchen as if he'd actually be in our house. "Where?"

Louise grabbed my wrists, glaring at me over her glasses. "In your room. Not his body, but it sure as hell was his spirit."

Faith gasped as I dissolved from Louise's grip and traversed to the bedroom.

Carson startled. "Everything okay?"

"Where is she?" I yelled, circling the bed. "What have you done to her?"

Carson stood with his hands open in front of him. "I didn't do anything."

"Not you," I barked. "Dedrick."

"Dedrick?"

Louise opened the bedroom door. Faith and Shiloh stood behind her, peering in with wide eyes.

"Where is he?" I asked Louise.

Her jaw shifted and her nostrils flared, but she motioned toward the dresser. I realized, moments too late, that she didn't want him to know she could see his aura. I was so angry I couldn't think straight.

I stomped over to the dresser. "I don't know how you're here, but I swear, if you hurt her, if you do anything to jeopardize Maryah's wellbeing, I will hunt you down like the savage cretin you are, and I will torture you until you beg me to kill you."

Silence. It's not like I expected Dedrick's soul to reply. I knew how this astral traveling system worked, and astral traveling is what he must have been doing. "Louise, is he in front of me?"

"Two steps to your left."

I sidestepped twice. I could feel his putrid energy tainting the room. How could I have mistaken his energy for Maryah's? I should have known it wasn't her, but until now, I wouldn't have believed it was possible for Dedrick to astral travel. I raised my chin as if I could look him in the eye. My voice came out in a snarl. "Mark my words, Dedrick, you will pay dearly for this."

Louise walked up behind me and put her hand on my shoulder. "He's gone."

I opened and closed my fists, which had been clenched at my sides. "For now."

I took a deep breath and turned to face the others. We were all at a loss for words. I stared at Maryah lying motionless on the bed, her soul who knows where, somehow being controlled by Dedrick. It was worse than any nightmare I could have imagined.

"Damn," Carson muttered. "He must be using Maryah's power as his own."

"How do we stop him?" Krista asked quietly.

"Carson," I said, "please tell me your Scion mind has figured out a way to get her soul back into her body."

He opened his mouth then shut it again without saying anything. Even Carson couldn't figure out this one.

"Gather everyone." Louise shooed Carson and Krista out of the room. "Immediately."

HAND THAT ROBS THE CRADLE

Maryah

After what felt like an hour of Rina's silent head-bowing, and neither one of them answering me, Dedrick opened his eyes and stumbled backward. He looked disoriented, but then he focused on Rina. "Well done. That was nothing like I imagined it to be but still quite a rush."

She had let go of me. How she had touched me—my soul—was still a mystery. Keeping her focus on the floor, Rina chewed on her thumb and turned away from us.

"Cuddling, hmm?" Dedrick said. "I never pegged you for the cuddling type."

Cuddling? What was he talking about? I backed as far away from him as I could.

"And Louise," Dedrick continued. "I didn't realize she could see a soul's aura even while astral traveling. Then again—" He picked something out of his teeth with his fingernail. "I didn't know Nathaniel would be able to sense me either."

He had seen Nathan and Louise?

Rina stood in the corner. I watched her for a few seconds before it all clicked together. She had put one hand on each of us. Dedrick had miraculously shut up for a while, and even though she hadn't uttered a word so far, Rina seemed to be doing something while touching me.

I gasped. Dedrick had astral traveled. He stomped over to me, cornering me against the glass cabinet. I wanted to get away from him, but my only escape would be through him, and the thought of my soul passing through Dedrick's body made me feel as if my stomach heaved.

"Quickly." Dedrick waved his hand for Rina to come back to us. "Again, but this time to someone who won't be able to sense or see me."

She hesitated at first, but Dedrick harshly clapped his hands, and she rushed over.

"No!" I begged. "Don't help him."

She kept her head down like a timid, abused animal. Dedrick grabbed her arm but fixed his attention on me.

"Gregory," he sneered. "You know him well enough now, don't you? Your lost kindrily member, Harmony's big strong soul mate, the man who stabbed your brother to death right in front of you. I'm sure you can picture him with precise clarity."

His words sent flashes of memories rushing through my mind. The night Dedrick and Gregory attacked my family and me. When I saw Harmony's old photo of Gregory and realized who he was. The night I walked into the Luna house and saw him restrained on the couch. The loving gleam in his eyes whenever he looked at Harmony.

Rina pressed her hand against me again. Dedrick's eyelids fluttered shut.

I gaped at Rina. "You're using my power to help him astral travel."

She slightly nodded as if answering me.

"Stop it!" I had finally learned to use my own ability, and now some strange little girl was stealing it so Dedrick could spy on my kindrily. I swung at her with my free arm then tried kicking her, but she didn't move. Her hand remained locked on my arm like some kind of supernatural glue keeping me stuck in place. "I swear, if you help him and he hurts any of my kindrily, I will destroy you."

Her eyes flew open, and she stared at me so intensely I felt her eerie darkness seep into my soul. Her lips slightly puckered. She made no other movement or sound but coldly and silently, she told me to *shhh*.

"Like hell, I'll shhh."

She was no longer a scared little girl. She radiated confidence but had the same vehement air as Dedrick. She didn't have the snakelike eyes that were an indicator of Dedrick's mind control, but she obviously had power and let Dedrick use it on demand.

I assessed the room again: no doors, no windows, no rugs on the dirt floor, thick solid stone walls, a flimsy mattress on the floor with one dirty blanket spread across it, and a tattered plastic curtain that hung from the ceiling in the corner. Was it concealing a makeshift bathroom? Did the girl live here in an awful room that felt like the underground ruins of a forgotten basement?

My attention snapped back to Rina, catching onto the fact she had shushed me seconds ago. That meant she heard me—even though I was only in spirit form. "Hey." I leaned closer to her dirt-smudged face. "Can you hear me?"

Her upper lip twitched, and her shoulders rolled, then Dedrick stumbled backward, gasping for air. His hand flew to his chest. Rina fell to her knees, cradling her head in her hands.

"Why are we back so soon?" Dedrick snarled. "I wasn't finished!"

Rina trembled, her arms shielding her head as if she were scared Dedrick might hit her.

Dedrick squatted beside her. "You're weak. You better learn to last a lot longer than that or you'll be of no use to me. And you know what happens when people are of no use to me."

Rina shook more visibly. Dedrick grabbed her hair, yanking her head back until her chin almost touched his. She looked on the verge of tears.

"Do you have anything to say for yourself?" He asked. "Shall I fetch you a notepad?"

She shook her head.

"But you are very sorry, aren't you? You will do better next time."

Rina nodded.

"Good girl." He kissed her cheek then shoved her away. She scurried to the mattress on her hands and knees. Wiping her cheek, she pulled the blanket up to her chin and wouldn't look at him.

I didn't want to imagine what he had done to the poor girl. If he allowed her to live in such a pigsty, he clearly had no regard for her wellbeing. Gregory's stories of how Dedrick had kept me tied to a bed in my last life made me cringe. What had he done to the cowering girl in the corner? I felt guilty for yelling at her.

"We're done here for now." Dedrick leaned over the burning candle. "Lights out."

With one whoosh of breath from his despicable lips, the flame went out. A curtain of black fell around me. I couldn't see anything. I couldn't hear anything. I felt like I was floating in space—a space with no stars or planets, just nothingness.

"Hello?" My voice was absorbed by the stillness. Then as quickly as the dark had enveloped me, it lifted. The candle flickered to life, but Dedrick was gone.

Rina still sat on the mattress in the corner. She wasn't shaking anymore.

I inched toward the glass cabinet, studying my glowing reflection more closely. Every curve and feature of my body— even the curved lines of my lips—were blurry but visible. I looked like a hologram of myself. Turning away, I lifted my hands, spreading my shimmering fingers apart. Through them, I could see the flickering candle on the table.

The candle had remained the same height since I arrived. I floated over to it, noticing the wax never dripped onto its holder. Beads of melting wax ran down the side but then dissolved before gathering on the ring of brass. Where were we, and how was any of this possible?

I could feel Rina watching every move I made.

"We're trapped, aren't we?" I asked her. "You're trapped here too."

She pressed the ends of her tangled hair to her lips. She didn't look at me as she leaned forward and used her finger to write something in the dirt floor. She waved me over and pointed at what she had written. *You have to get out of here.*

SPIRITING AWAY

Nathaniel

Shiloh's brown eyes changed to a lucent copper as he used the recent enhancement of his ability to scan the house, room by room, for any sign of Dedrick. He massaged his temples, blinked hard, and then shook his head. "Nothing. I don't see anything suspicious."

"Did you check outside?" Faith asked him.

"Yes, and Edgar and Helen's cottage. Helen is drying herbs like her usual self."

Louise also assured me she didn't see Dedrick's aura anywhere, but I was still reeling.

"How did he pull this off?" I asked Edgar and Louise.

Edgar tapped his bifocals against his lip while he studied Maryah lying motionless on the bed. "As Carson surmised, it seems he may have harnessed Maryah's ability."

Faith sat at the foot of the bed and rubbed Maryah's foot through the blanket. "How could he use her power? It's unheard of."

"We can't be certain that's what's happening," Edgar said. "But it's the only possibility I can think of. And if that is the case, at least he doesn't have her body. He can't physically harm her."

"He has her soul," I argued. That was as equally disturbing, if not more so. "What if she's trapped? We have no idea where she is, or where Dedrick is. We have to get her back into her body."

"Yes," Edgar agreed. "The looming question is *how* do we do that?"

We all glanced at each other, silent because we had no answers. I expressed my next concern. "How long can her body last without her soul in it?"

Edgar shook his head. "I wish I had an answer for that as well."

My stomach lurched. I felt feverish. Dedrick had Maryah again. He was using her power to spy on us. The nightmare of losing Maryah for nearly two decades had just ended, but a new nightmare had begun.

Krista's hands stopped hovering over Maryah. "The good news is her body is perfectly fine."

"Her body is not fine," I grumbled. "It's missing her soul."

Harmony stomped into the room with Gregory, Carson, and Dakota trailing behind her.

"Carson just told us," Harmony said. "What the hell?"

Gregory hung back, standing in the threshold of the doorway. His odd stance and the way he kept glancing down the hall captured my attention. I jerked my head, motioning for Harmony to look at him.

"What is it, Gregory?" she asked.

His ears pulled back, and he narrowed his eyes. "I think I heard Dedrick."

I stiffened. So did everyone else.

Harmony walked over to Gregory and lowered her voice, but I heard her. "You're hearing his thoughts right now?"

"No, earlier, just before Carson came to get us. He said we were reunited love birds that belong in a cage."

"Is he still here?" I asked Louise.

"I wouldn't have let this conversation continue if he were."

Harmony smacked Gregory's chest. "Why didn't you say something sooner?"

"I thought maybe I imagined it. I was listening to see if I heard him again. If it was real, I didn't want him to know I heard him."

"We have to gather everyone and warn them to be on high alert," Carson said.

"Louise can see his aura," Edgar noted. "That's our safety net."

Louise took a deep breath and stood up straight. "It looks as though our kindrily will be spending plenty of quality time together. Carson, call Dylan and Amber and tell them to pack their bags. Make sure they don't speak a word about any of this until they get here. Dedrick could be spying on any of us at any time."

Carson's cell phone was already pressed to his ear.

Edgar slid his glasses on. "I'll walk down to the cottage and bring Helen back here for the meeting."

Louise sat in the chair beside the bed. "Don't worry, Nathan, we'll be on twenty-four-hour watch until Maryah has safely returned."

As everyone else scrambled around or out of the room, Dakota sat on the floor, hunched over his sketch pad, drawing furiously. Louise and I exchanged worried glances, but Dakota's drawing-the-future delusion was the least of our worries.

∞

The candle chandelier burned brightly above the round table. The only kindrily member not present, besides Maryah, was Krista. She stayed in the bedroom on guard duty.

Twelve sets of eyes had been belting me with pity and concern for over an hour, even Mikey seemed worried. I wanted the meeting to be over. I couldn't think of anything except getting Maryah home, back into her body. She belonged in her seat beside me, far away from Dedrick.

"Amber's right," Louise said to Dylan. "Dedrick doesn't need to see a new baby in the family. God only knows what he might do, especially if he finds out Mikey is an Element. You three will stay at your house. The chances of Dedrick spying on you are slim compared to the chance of him seeing Mikey if you're here."

My gaze lingered on Maryah's empty chair for the hundredth time. I lowered my chin and dug my nails into the table. Where the hell was she and how could we have lost her again?

"Nathan," Dylan asked. "You all right?"

"Nate, we'll get her back," Harmony said.

I exhaled long and purposefully, trying to calm myself, but it didn't help.

"Nathan, please say something," Faith urged.

Pushing my chair backward, I braced my arms on the table while glowering at Gregory. "Where is she?"

"I honestly don't know," Gregory replied.

I slammed my fist against the wood surface between us. "You were with Dedrick for two decades! How can you have no idea, not even a hunch, of where he might be?"

Gregory turned in his seat to face me. Harmony grabbed his arm.

"I'm not going to fight with him," Gregory told her over his shoulder. "You know me better than that."

"Actually," Harmony muttered. "It's him I'm worried about."

I stepped back, shaking my head and trying to regain my composure. "I'm sorry for punching the table. I'm infuriated, but I shouldn't take it out on you."

"We understand," Gregory said. "But truly, Nathaniel, I've been trying my best to remember a location, any hint of where we lived or might have stayed. I can't even remember where I slept. The memories of it all have vanished."

"Even when he first returned," Edgar chimed in, "he couldn't give any specifics of where he had been. I asked every possible trigger question: scenery, smells, sounds, if they'd stayed in a house, a castle, an abandoned warehouse, anything. It was almost as if those details had been purposefully removed from his mind."

I sat down, dropping my head into my hands. "How can Dedrick control her soul? If he can pull this off, what else is he capable of?"

"That's the frightening part," Louise said poignantly. "Maryah was our best chance at figuring out what he was up to, and unfortunately he was up to something more powerful than any of us could have guessed."

"She didn't want to find him," I recalled. "The first time she did, she was terrified. I should have realized her instincts were warning her to stay away from him. This is my fault."

Faith slid into Maryah's empty chair and rubbed my back. "Don't blame yourself. It's not true, and your guilt is so strong it's going to make you sick. We need you to stay strong and healthy."

"Let's brainstorm," Carson suggested. "There has to be something we haven't thought of yet."

If Carson, the superior intelligent Scion of our kindrily hadn't thought of anything, then we had no hope. The kindrily's replies muffled as my temples throbbed. I needed to get away, not run away, I wanted nothing more than to stay by Maryah's side until she woke up, but I needed air—a serious rush of it.

Harmony jumped to her feet when she saw me sit up straight, stiffening and preparing to traverse. She reached for me. "Let me come with you."

I vanished before her hand made contact.

I stood atop one of the tallest mountains in Nepal. The air was so thin it burned my lungs. My face already felt like a sheet of ice. Stepping to the edge, I prepared to jump, craving the rush so badly I felt like a junkie.

Maryah had come with me to the same spot. Kissing her had felt euphoric until I traversed us to this mountain by accident. I was so relieved when I figured out how to safely traverse her home. She could have died that day. Because of me.

Was she in jeopardy of dying again? How long would her body continue existing without her soul in it?

I despised Dedrick and everything he stood for. Someday, if given the chance, I'd tear him apart with my own two hands. I cracked my fingers, realizing they had gone numb from the bitter cold.

And then I had an epiphany. I hadn't been able to consider the option until recently, but now the options were endless. If— *when*—I found Dedrick, I could torture him in ways he couldn't imagine. I could traverse with him.

I glanced around, remembering how fast the cold and altitude affected Maryah. I'd bring him here then watch him suffer until his mind and body were frozen stiff.

That didn't seem like enough. He deserved to suffer much worse than that. I could traverse him to Antarctica, make him run from polar bears then let them rip him to shreds. I could feed him to great white sharks off the coast of Australia. The list of torturous deaths grew so long I didn't know where I'd start first, but I eagerly anticipated that day.

A RIVER RUNS THROUGH ME

Maryah

I wanted to go home.

Rina, the mute ability-stealer, warned me that I needed to get out, and I wholeheartedly agreed. I kept focusing, trying every way I could think of to connect with my body. Rina sat on her mattress watching me but never uttering a sound. The strange black curtain fell around me again. When the dark lifted, Dedrick stood in front of me, beside a woman with snake eyes, and River.

"You've got to be kidding me," I grumbled.

River's faux-hawk had grown out. He had a ten o'clock shadow of facial hair like he hadn't shaved in weeks. I could see the family resemblance between him and his murderous uncle.

"Did you miss us?" Dedrick asked all sing-song.

River's eyes were wide. He stepped closer, cocking his head while studying my transparent light form. A glowing ghostly version of the *me* he used to hang out with. The *friend* he tried to kill. If I could have produced saliva, I would have spit on him.

"Holy shit," he whispered.

"I told you," Dedrick sang. "It was easier than I thought. It took much longer considering the detour and all, but eventually she came around."

"Can she hear us?" River asked.

"I'm quite certain she can."

River reached out, attempting to touch me. I backed away, but he stepped forward. I kept backing up until I was pinned against a wall. If I had a body he would have been pressed against it. His closeness brought back the repulsion I felt at Montezuma Well when he traced a heart on my palm and told me he'd never do something so evil as to throw me into the water alive and let leeches eat me. But he did drug me, and he would have shot me and then thrown me in the water. Now he stood in front of me again, just as evil as his uncle with who knows what disgusting thoughts running through his mind. Even though my voice shook, I wanted them to hear me. "Both of you sicken me."

River whispered too quietly for anyone else to hear. "I'm so sorry."

"Lexie," Dedrick snapped. "Update me."

Lexie, the woman with snake eyes, spoke almost robotically. "She can hear you. Both of you sicken her."

Dedrick chuckled while River's gaze dropped to his feet. Great, Dedrick's drone could hear me. I'd have to be more careful of what I said.

"She plans to be more conscious about what she says," Lexie continued.

She could hear my thoughts too? How could I stop thinking? *Stop right now*, I told myself.

"She's trying to stop herself from thinking."

I snapped at Lexie. "Stay out of my head."

"Not likely," she replied. "It's my job to hear your thoughts."

"This is such fun, isn't it?" Dedrick clapped his hands. "And River?"

River's head jerked up at the mention of his name.

Lexie spewed out her report. "Wondering how Maryah is here. He's intrigued by how her soul could be trapped."

I stared at the table behind River, not wanting to react to anything. *Table, table, table.* If I kept my thoughts boring enough, Lexie would have nothing to report.

"She's diverting her thoughts by repeating "table,'" Lexie said. "River is angry that you asked me to intrude on his thoughts."

I hated her already.

"Maryah hates me."

Dedrick snickered. "Don't take it personally, Lexie. Maryah hates all of us. And River, don't think of it as me intruding. I'm simply acquiring useful data."

Table, table, table.

"She's back to focusing on the table," Lexie said. "He's mentally shouting expletives at me."

"I'm growing bored." Dedrick sighed. "Let me know how Maryah responds to this." He stepped closer, nudging River aside. "I require the use of your ability, my dear, powerful, Maryah." He fanned his bony fingers over Rina's head. "Rina is a pathetic little thing, but she does have one endearing and useful trait—she is a conductor."

I noted the girl was a conductor, but tried not to think anything else.

Dedrick continued, "Rina will connect us so I may use your power to gather the necessary intel to help me acquire the last few things needed to put my master plan into effect. Don't worry, the exceptional beings I'll be spying on aren't any of your kindrily. Amusingly, those hacks aren't nearly as clever or powerful as they think they are." He pulled back his long hair, securing it into a low ponytail. "At least not for my purposes."

He was spying on people more powerful than my kindrily. What kind of powers must those people have? What was he planning?

"She wants to know what you're planning," Lexie said.

Dedrick huffed a half-laugh. Strange as it was, I smelled his sour breath. How could I smell anything without being in my body?

"Nathaniel didn't tell you?" Dedrick asked me. "I'm going to become the gatekeeper of this world."

Nathan had told us that, but we didn't understand what it meant.

"She doesn't know what that means," Lexie reported.

Dedrick stood tall, his chest expanding as if proud of what he was about to say. "I'll control who comes into this world. Some souls should never be allowed reentry." His eyes shifted upward. "*Certain* meddling ones need to be permanently banished. If so, this world would be a much better place and evolve at a faster pace. Reincarnation," he hissed, "is a broken and outdated system, and I plan to update it."

He was a lunatic. No way could Dedrick ever change a universal system that had been in existence longer than anyone knew. Could he?

Lexie started to speak. "She thinks—"

"I know what she's thinking," Dedrick barked. "That it's impossible for me to play God. That I'd never be able to acquire that sort of power, but she's wrong." He leaned close to me, and his foul breath of stale coffee and rotten milk hit me again. "You're wrong, Maryah. I'm not only going to play God. I'm going to *be* God."

"How?" The one word came out breathless because I was shocked and scared. The confidence in his voice, the calm and collected yet steady fire burning in his eyes: it was almost enough to make me believe he could pull it off. And if he did, I didn't want to imagine the state of our world.

River sat on the edge of the table, running his hand over his hairy jaw. Lexie didn't flinch. Rina gnawed her fingers, her head down as if trying to be invisible.

Lexie repeated my question. "How?"

"You'll see soon enough." Dedrick turned to River. "Any parting words, nephew of mine?"

River fidgeted. "Uh, no, not right now, sir."

Dedrick eyed him suspiciously. "Not right now because you have an audience?"

River shrugged.

"I understand," Dedrick said. "I'd allow you alone time with her, but it would be a one-sided conversation without Lexie."

River tapped his knuckles on the table as he seemed to silently plead with his uncle.

Dedrick squinted at him before tossing his hands in the air. "Fine. I'll grant you ten minutes alone with her."

"Thank you." River stood too eagerly. I wanted to shove him back down.

"Let's be on our way, Lexie. We have much to accomplish today."

"Wait." River motioned to Rina. "What about her?"

"My mute?" Dedrick asked. "I can't take her out of this room, but I can see why you wouldn't want anyone eavesdropping. Very well then." He walked over to the cabinet and opened a door. Rina pulled her blanket over her head. Dedrick took out a glass vial and a syringe then filled it with a pale yellow liquid.

"What is that?" River asked.

Dedrick rolled his eyes. "Do you want to be alone with Maryah or not?"

River stuck his hands in his pockets and lowered his head. Dedrick crouched beside Rina's bed. She leaned away, but Dedrick grabbed her arm and stuck her with the needle.

"There," Dedrick said to River. "She'll be out cold. Won't hear a thing. Give it about two minutes to kick in, and then it will be just you and Maryah."

River eyed the blanket covering Rina. "Did you hurt her?"

"Hurt her?" Dedrick cooed as if it was impossible for him to hurt anyone. "I simply put her down for a nap."

"Okay," the gullible idiot muttered. "Thank you again."

I wanted my solid hands so I could grab a syringe and stab both of them.

"Ten minutes," Dedrick warned. "Use it wisely."

River nodded as Dedrick did his "Lights Out" ritual of blowing out the candle. I was hoping when the darkness lifted,

River wouldn't be there, but no such luck. I took some comfort in the fact that my body wasn't in the room with him. He couldn't hurt me again.

"I'm so sorry." River rushed over to me. "You have no idea how sorry I am for all of this."

"Ha! You tried to kill me!" It was pointless to respond since he couldn't hear me, but I couldn't help it.

"I have no idea how he did this to you, but—" He glanced sideways at the heap of blanket where Rina was passed out then lowered his voice. "I'd set you free if I knew how."

That piqued my interest. Would River really help me get out of here if he could? I hated thinking River, of all people, might be my only way out of this mess, but it wasn't like I had a lot of other options.

"I'm sure you don't believe me, or trust me, and I don't blame you, but I swear to you, Maryah, I regret whatever happened at Montezuma Well. I didn't even know what I was doing." He shook his head. His thoughts seemed far away. "I can't remember anything about that night, and when I snapped out of it at the police station and they kept asking me why I tried to kill you, I lost it. I couldn't believe what I'd done. You'd already been through so much, losing your parents and brother, and then I tried to kill you? I've been so messed up over it. I feel like I don't even know myself anymore."

Partly flabbergasted, I wanted to scream at him and call him a liar, but I couldn't do anything except watch him. I analyzed his body language. His hands kept rising limply at his sides. His bloodshot eyes made him look so stressed and upset. It hadn't occurred to me until that moment, but had Dedrick mind-controlled River the same way he did with Gregory and the other Nefariouns?

"No," I muttered, replaying the details of the night River tried to kill me. "You didn't have snake eyes. You knew what you were doing."

"I don't know what the hell is going on anymore. The cops made me take a bunch of psychological tests. They diagnosed me with some mental illness." He glanced away, but not before I saw the shame in his eyes. "I don't understand any of it. I didn't know my uncle was like this."

If only he could have heard me. I would have asked him where he was before they came into this room. Were we in a basement of some kind? A castle? But Dedrick would have never left us alone if River and I were able to effectively communicate.

"I'm locked up too," River said. "If it makes you feel any better."

"What?" Dedrick was keeping his own nephew locked up too?

River reached out to me, but I didn't move this time.

"Can you feel that?" His fingers swiped through my glowing arm. He stared at me, probably waiting for me to nod or shake my head, but I only scowled at him. I couldn't feel him, but I still didn't want him to touch me.

"This is by far the strangest thing I've ever seen," he said. "I keep hoping I'll wake up, and you and I will be back in English class passing notes and laughing about whatever. We could go back to normal." He bit his bottom lip. "I keep thinking about what my uncle said, that you can asteroid travel or whatever. What does that even mean?"

Asteroid travel. What an idiot. He waited as if expecting an answer. I didn't bother thinking of a response. Even if he could hear me, I'd never tell River anything else about me or my kindrily ever again.

"I always knew you were something special, Maryah. April did too. I mean, we didn't know people with supernatural powers existed, but we knew you were different—in a good way." He rubbed his beard again. "I don't understand why my uncle is doing this, but I'm sorry for all of it. I swear I'll do everything I can to help you get out of here."

I wanted to believe him. But I knew better.

QUIET AS A MOUSE

Maryah

Dedrick returned long enough to black-curtain the room again and take River away. Rina remained in a drug-induced nap.

For what felt like forever, but was probably a few hours, I floated around the room. My fear and anger transitioned into worry and disgust.

Behind the moldy plastic curtain were a filthy stained toilet and a bowl filled with dingy water. Not even a sink for the poor girl to wash herself.

"What a monster." Who would let anyone—especially a child—live in such filth? Next, I studied the cabinet in the corner of the room again. The glass shelves were caked with dust and filled with vials of liquid and a box of syringes. I wanted to take all the drugs and dump them down the toilet, but I couldn't touch them. I couldn't do much of anything.

On the table in the center of the room sat the book I'd been drawn to when I first traveled to this dreaded place. I hovered over it, desperately wanting to flip open the leather cover to see what its pages contained. The cracked binding looked super old. There was no title, nothing written on it at all, not even on the spine.

Rina stirred, and I darted to the corner where she hid beneath her dirty blanket. A mouse scurried across the floor then shimmied up onto the mattress and under Rina's covers.

I yelled, "Shoo! Shoo!" while swinging my hands at the blanket. "Wake up! Before that rodent bites you and gives you rabies."

The blanket inched down far enough for her to peer out through her disheveled black hair.

"Get up! There's a mouse in your bed!" Talking made me feel more proactive and less alone.

She pushed the blanket off, and the mouse was sitting on her chest. I expected her to jump up and do a frantic help-there's-a-mouse-in-my-bed dance like I would have done, but she didn't flinch. She reached up and petted the mouse with one scabby finger then opened her other hand. The mouse stepped onto her palm.

"Oh. It's like your pet, isn't it?"

She raised the mouse up to her face, and it rubbed its tiny nose against hers. She smiled and my heart warmed. Considering the way she lived, I wouldn't expect her to ever be happy, but the mouse was clearly her friend. As silly as it was, I was grateful the strange girl had a friend—even if that friend was a rodent.

Rina held up the mouse for me to see. I leaned in, our faces only inches apart. He was sort of cute, brownish gray with big ears, and his whiskers twitched as his pink nose sniffed me. "Hi there, dungeon mouse. So you can see me too?"

The mouse turned, his long tail flicking behind him. He scurried up Rina's arm then sat on her shoulder as if they'd done the same routine a million times. She rested her head on the wall behind her and closed her eyes.

As I watched Rina, who appeared to be sleeping again while sitting up, I realized I wasn't tired at all. Would I ever get tired, or was that only possible if I had a body?

The mouse curled up against Rina's neck and went to sleep. The sight of them together made me miss Eightball—even his snoring. More than that, I missed sleeping beside Nathan, feeling his chest rise and fall against my cheek as I listened to the lullaby of his heartbeat.

I floated in the candlelit room: bored, worried about my kindrily, and feeling completely alone, even with two other living beings just a few feet away from me.

"This is no way to live." I was speaking on Rina's behalf, the mouse's, and mine.

∞

Dedrick returned, hardly saying a word except to announce it was time for him to travel again and ordering Rina to his side.

"No!" I shouted. What if he spied on my kindrily again? What if he used my ability to hurt them or someone else?

I tried pulling away as Rina linked hands with Dedrick and me. "I hate you! My power is not yours to steal."

Dedrick spoke a name as I was yelling. It sounded like Vivian, but I couldn't be sure. I was angry at myself for not staying quiet so I could hear him. Several seconds later, Dedrick went limp.

Rina lifted her head. In a terse and cutting tone, she said, "Hate isn't a strong enough word when it comes to Dedrick."

I gasped. "You can talk?"

"Of course I can."

"And you can hear me?"

"How else would I be answering you?"

"But Dedrick said you were a mute."

"Dedrick is wrong much more often than he's right." She pointed at me. "Don't go spilling my secrets. He can't know that you and I can communicate." She turned away. "Or he'll make me do horrible things."

I cringed at the possibilities of what that meant. "I won't say a word."

Was there anyone who willingly helped Dedrick, or did he have to trap or control everyone? Rina pretended to be a mute. How long had she been fooling him? I was still in shock that she could talk—and hear me. She was a conductor and a faker. "Is there anything else I should know about you?"

She faced me again, looking serious. "I trust very few people. *Very* few."

Fair enough. I didn't blame her for not trusting anyone. I wouldn't either if I was being held prisoner by a madman. "How long have you been here?"

"My whole life."

I couldn't hide my shock. "You were born here?"

She motioned to the corner. "On that very bed."

I turned my nose up, shuddering at the sight of her stained, more-unsanitary-than-I-first-assumed, sad excuse for a mattress. "Where are your parents?"

"I never met my father. All I know about him I learned from my mother's stories."

"And your mom?"

"She had to leave. But she promised to come back for me."

My heart hurt for her. How could any mother leave her child? Mind-controlled or not, I wouldn't be able to stomach it. However, if Rina had lived in this room her entire life, maybe she didn't know how terrible it really was. Maybe she didn't have a sense of family or understand what it meant.

"So this," I said as I motioned to the prison around us, "is all you've ever known?"

"Yes."

"That makes me so sad for you."

She shrugged. "This is where I need to be for now."

She was definitely damaged. No healthy person would take their imprisonment so lightly. "You're okay with being held captive? Being ordered around and used." I had been afraid to ask, but I had to know. "Has Dedrick ever hurt you?"

"Dedrick hurts everyone in one way or another."

"You can't be okay with that."

"What choice do I have? I do what I need to do to survive." She replied so quickly. Sometimes she spoke before I finished speaking. It was almost hard to keep up with her.

"Survive to do what?" I asked. "Live another day like a prisoner in a cage? I would've begged him to kill me and put me out of my misery."

"What good would I be dead?"

"This is a horrible way to live."

"If it's so awful then why are you here?"

"I didn't choose to be here."

"Ah, but that's where you're wrong." She smirked. "You came here of your own free will. Your instincts told you not to go near Dedrick again, but you traveled here anyway. You're here because deep down you chose to be."

I stared at her, bewildered by what a little enigma she was. "How do you know about my instincts?"

She lifted a chunk of hair to her lips. "I've said too much."

"I get the impression you never accidentally say too much."

"You're smart."

"You're peculiar."

"Peculiar. I like that choice of adjective."

"See? Most people wouldn't think being called peculiar is a compliment."

She leaned in so our noses almost touched. "We're not like most people, are we?"

For once I could see the coloring of her eyes. The dim lighting had given the illusion that they were black, but they were actually a striking shade of dark blue.

She backed up suddenly as if she'd been burned or shocked. "He wants to come back. Don't speak a word of this. If you tell him my secrets, you'll ruin everything."

I nodded, panicking a bit. "I won't say anything, I promise."

"Don't think it either."

She was right. I needed to find a way to shut off my thoughts so I didn't accidentally reveal anything to Lexie.

Dedrick stumbled backward, returning from his astral travel. Rina collapsed to the floor and didn't move. Wherever Dedrick had gone, or whomever he had spied on, had him panting and bouncing like an excited hyena. He didn't say a word, just blew out the candle.

When the sorry excuse for light returned, Rina was still on the floor.

"Rina, are you okay?"

She rolled over, alert and not appearing drained at all. She sprang to her feet and brushed the dirt off her.

"You fake it, don't you?" I asked. "Helping him astral travel doesn't drain you at all."

"I told you, I do what's necessary to survive."

She said revealing her secrets to Dedrick might ruin everything. Did she have some sort of plan to break out? "I have a feeling you're hiding a lot of secrets."

One thin brow rose, and she sort of sneered but in a way that hinted she was being playful. "Tip of the iceberg, my glowing lightning bug, tip of the iceberg."

Hearing her call me lightning bug like Dedrick had sent a shiver through me, but my instincts assured me I had no reason to be afraid of her. If anything, I may have just formed a powerful and unexpected alliance.

"How old are you?"

"I don't know."

"Do you know your birthday?"

"We don't celebrate occasions like that here." She tugged at the ends of her frayed hair. "But why does it matter? Why should a person's potential be based on the age of her body? Maybe the soul is older, wiser, capable of more than a much younger body. The age of a person's soul is what's important."

"Okay, Miss Almighty Wise One, how old is your soul?"

She bit her pinky nail. "I lost track."

"You say a soul's age is what matters, but you haven't kept track of how old yours is?"

"I didn't say it was a perfect system."

"Do you think your soul is older than mine?"

"That depends how we're counting. Are we basing it off of your age before or after you erased?"

My voice raised an octave as I tensed. "How do you know I erased?"

"Dedrick just said you did when he was here with River."

"Oh, right." I had almost forgotten she had been in the room because she was so quiet. "Back to who is older. Use my age before I erased. I had lived nineteen lifetimes."

"In that case, I don't know."

"Then why did it matter which option we based it off of?"

She shrugged. "Just wanted to see if you still valued your old self."

"I value all of myself—old and new. And I'm going to remember my past."

"Are you sure about that?"

I hesitated, not sure at all, but really wishing I could. "I'm trying my best."

She turned on her heel and walked over to the table. She ran her fingers over the cover of the book.

"What is that?" I asked her.

"It's my book."

"Obviously, but what kind of book?"

"A storybook."

Man she was frustrating. "What's its title?"

"It doesn't have a title."

"What's it about?"

She looked up at me. "Don't ask so many questions. You won't like the answers."

SECRETS NEVER STAY BURIED

Nathaniel

Edgar had been in a deep trance since sunrise. He was searching the Akashic Records, relentlessly sifting through centuries of important moments in the universal computer, trying to find any hint of how this situation with Maryah could be possible.

While waiting, I traversed from the deck of Helen and Edgar's cottage to Maryah's side dozens of times. I appeared on the deck again and peeked through the window. Edgar was still motionless in his recliner with his eyes closed.

"Nathan," Louise grunted from her deck chair. "Please stop traversing so much. It's like someone endlessly pacing but worse. You're making my blood pressure rise."

"I'm sorry." I tried to stand still, but it was too difficult. "May I pace then?"

Louise nodded. "It would be an improvement."

Every three strides I'd glance through the glass doors at Edgar, but he never moved. His bifocals still rested in his lap. I had worried about Edgar becoming ensnared somewhere like Maryah and not being able to wake up, but he assured all of us that it wasn't remotely close to the same situation. His soul didn't leave his body when he read the Akashic Records. He simply went into a trance from which he could be woken at any time.

"Given the circumstances," I said, "maybe we should wake him."

Helen chuckled, never lowering her sun-basking face. "You know his rule. Never wake him no matter how long he works. That rule has been in place since our first go-round. Not even I have ever broken it."

"Edgar's fine." Louise stood and wrapped her arm around me. "You didn't sleep all night. I'm sure you're exhausted. Let me make you some more of Helen's calming tea."

"I've had a gallon of her tea. It's not helping."

Helen lowered her sunglasses and winked at me. "I could make you my sedative tea."

"No, thank you." I'd seen the results of Helen's sedative tea. I didn't need to be comatose.

Louise leveled me with a concerned stare. "Nathan, how much have you told Maryah about Dedrick?"

"We haven't had an opportunity to discuss him much."

Louise patted my arm. "Not the most enjoyable of topics while you're getting to know each other all over again."

"I should say so."

Helen readjusted in her chair so she was sitting up straight. "There never seems to be enough time. No matter how many meetings we hold or conversations we have with her, there's just too much she needs to know. So much catching up to do."

Louise pressed one hand to her cheek, which meant she was stressed. "I'm worried that her history with Dedrick is one thing we should have told her right away."

"Thank you, Louise." I pulled away from her. "As if I don't feel wretched enough already."

"I didn't mean to make you feel worse, but I am concerned. If he has figured out a way to communicate with her then—" Louise glanced at me then out at the red rocks. "Well, never mind. One thing at a time."

Louise was usually the one making people feel better, but her voicing my concerns out loud—concerns I'd ran through my mind in a million different awful scenarios—made me feel like a daft git.

I should have told Maryah everything about her past with Dedrick, but how was I supposed to delicately deliver so much disturbing information? Maybe I wanted those parts of our past to remain erased.

"Let me know when Edgar is finished," I said. And with that I traversed again.

∞

I stood in the doorway watching Krista switch out Maryah's IV bag. The scene reminded me of all the nights Krista and I had spent at the hospital together while Maryah was in her coma. Only less than a year ago. We'd come so far, yet here I was again, praying with everything I had for Maryah to survive.

"Hey," Krista said to me.

"Hey," I mumbled.

"She's going to be fine. She survived a brutal attack and a coma. This is child's play for her."

I gave a slight nod and walked into the room. "Take a break. Spend some time with Carson doing something normal."

Krista grinned. "Normal? This lifetime taking care of her has become normal for me."

"The old her wouldn't stand for that. She would have thought she should be taking care of you." Mary always wanted to protect everyone.

"I know, but she took care of everyone for so long. It's our turn to look after her."

Krista sat beside Maryah on the bed and held her hand. "I love her, you know. This version of her. The clueless, reckless at times, uncertain person she is now. While we were growing up, so many times she turned to me for advice or help, and it was such a surreal feeling. It was so different to experience her looking up to me for a change." Krista glanced at me and her cheeks blushed. "And with you, she's this lovesick puppy dog experiencing raging hormones—technically for the first time—and the fact that she can't focus on life's bigger issues because she's so twitterpated with you sort of cracks me up."

In spite of everything, that made me smile. "She truly is a teenager this time."

"I know. In so many ways it's cool, and it's fun to watch her experience life with a new perspective and not be insistent and so Mother Superior like she used to be."

I leaned against the bed post, recalling memories of so many instances when Mary wielded her all-knowing upper hand.

"But sometimes," Krista continued quietly. "I miss the old her so much it hurts."

She was gazing at Maryah, lost in reverie of the past. "She was my rock. She taught me so much, and she gave such great advice. She always calmed my fears or worries. Now, all I seem to do is worry or fear for her wellbeing. I wish Mary could sit here with me, wrap me in her strong arms, and tell me that Maryah is going to be fine."

My heart ached for Krista. I knew what it was to adore and love Maryah, to be so endeared by the new her who was experiencing the world anew, but to also miss the old her more than words could express.

"I want them both." Krista's voice cracked as if she was choking back tears. "Is that greedy? That I want my imperfect cousin/best friend and my confident and strong motherly figure?"

"It's not greedy. It's natural."

Krista stroked Maryah's arm. "Mary would have seen this coming. Mary wouldn't have let Dedrick trap Maryah like this."

"Mary is Maryah," I reminded her. Like me, Krista was separating her soul into two different beings too vividly.

"Which means somewhere, deep down, she's going to be strong enough to survive whatever happens." Krista looked up at me with glassy eyes. "Right?"

I spoke with the conviction I wanted so badly to feel. "Right. She always finds a way."

Krista hesitantly nodded as if she didn't quite believe me but wanted to.

"How about a breather?" Carson asked, rubbing Krista's shoulders. I hadn't consciously acknowledged his entrance because lately he and Krista seemed to exist almost as one person. I expected Carson to be wherever Krista was.

After they left the room, I sat on the bed. I lifted Maryah's hand and started massaging it. "Krista misses you."

Talking to her made me feel somewhat better. I kept rubbing her wrist and forearm. "I miss you too. All of you. New and old."

I lifted her arm, moving it in gentle circles, trying to loosen her shoulder joint. I worked her elbow and rotated her wrist. Even if she couldn't do it on her own, her body needed to move. I pulled back the covers and exercised her feet and legs too.

"Good idea." Louise carried in two fresh pillows. "Keeps her blood circulating."

"Not one joint has cracked or popped," I said. "I suspect Krista has already been exercising her."

"Carson suggested it yesterday."

I set Maryah's leg down and pulled the covers over her again. "I never thought of doing it until now."

"You've had infinite worries on your mind."

"Still," I grunted with chagrin. "I should have known what she needed."

"Nathan." Louise's voice softened but sounded stern at the same time. "Please don't throw yourself a pity party right now. We're all much too busy to attend. Be strong, mentally and emotionally. That's what she needs from you."

She kissed her fingers then touched my chin. She shut the door behind her as she left the room.

I stretched out beside Maryah, studying the curves and angles of her innocent face. "I'm so sorry," I whispered. "I keep failing you over and over. I don't know how to fix any of this."

SWEET NOTHINGS

Maryah

"How is she?" Dedrick asked Lexie, keeping his focus on me.

I forced my mind to think about nothing but white noise, like static on a radio station.

"She seems fine," Lexie said.

Dedrick's beady eyes mentally probed me. "What's she thinking?"

"She's not thinking anything."

He squinted until only two black slits framed the bridge of his bony nose. I wanted to sew his lids closed with his greasy hair so he could never look at me again. "Quite clever, aren't you, darling?"

I kept concentrating on my self-created white noise.

He clasped his hands behind his back and strolled around the room like he was enjoying a sunny day at the park. "Rina, how are you today? Are you enjoying your time with Maryah?" She lowered her eyes and chewed on her fingers. "Yes, not much fun to play with when she has no body, hmm?"

Rina still didn't look up at him.

Why didn't Dedrick ever ask Lexie what Rina was thinking? He thought Rina couldn't speak, but surely he'd want to intrude on her thoughts. He opened the glass cabinet again and pulled out a bottle and syringe. Rina hugged her knees to her chest.

"No!" I shouted, rushing to position myself between him and her.

Emotionless Lexie said, "Maryah is yelling 'no.'"

"No?" Dedrick filled the syringe with liquid. "Why not? It does her no harm. Her fear of needles is irrational. It only pricks for a moment." He walked right through me. His energy passing through mine triggered my gag reflex. I turned to see Rina visibly shaking and Dedrick lifting her stained sleeve. "Shh, Rina, you're making Maryah believe I'm hurting you. I'd never do such a thing."

Her head thrashed side to side as Dedrick stuck the needle in her arm. He pulled away and stood up as Rina's eyelids fluttered, then her head fell forward.

"You're a heartless pig."

Lexie repeated me. "You're a heartless pig."

Dedrick sighed as he locked the cabinet. "I'm far from heartless, Maryah. If you only knew."

I played the white noise in my head again. There was no point in arguing with a madman, and I didn't want to give Lexie anything else to report.

"Nothing," Lexie said. "She's gone silent again."

"I expected as much. Lexie, you're free to go." Dedrick licked two fingers then doused the candle flame. The black curtain fell. Much to my disgust, he was still there when the light returned.

He grinned at me like a vulture about to swoop in on its prey. "It's just the two of us now. Time to get reacquainted. I know you view me as some evil monster who murdered your family, but for the record, Gregory did the killing, and I am not a monster." He sat on the corner of the table. "First, I'd like to start by apologizing for Gregory almost killing you that night on your parents' boat dock. I thought you weren't *you*. I thought we had attacked the family of a complete stranger who would be able to describe us to the police. In truth, he shouldn't have killed an innocent girl, but Gregory had just murdered your whole family.

The only humane thing would be to kill you as well. Who would want to live through an ordeal like that after losing her parents and brother?"

"But I did live through it." My eyes stung as if producing real tears. "You left me for dead, but because of Nathan and Krista, I lived."

"I'm still not certain how you survived," Dedrick mused. "I assume Krista stumbled upon you in the nick of time." He lifted a brow while watching me for a reaction I didn't give him. "Hmm, well, perhaps someday you'll enlighten me."

"Never," I growled.

"Next, as if you hadn't suffered enough, jaded and damaged River also attempted to kill you." Dedrick shook his head. "I apologize for his recklessness a million times over. He's a spoiled child. I'm partly to blame for that. He feels entitled to whatever and whomever he wants. He wanted you, and when you rejected him, well, let's just say he gets his temper honestly."

River had told me Dedrick ordered him to kill me or he'd take everything away from him: his car, house, music career. Not that River was excused from almost murdering me, but did Dedrick really think I'd believe he had nothing to do with it?

"I can guess what River told you," Dedrick continued. "He told the police I made him do it, threatened his financial security and such, but I did nothing of the sort. You told him about your kindrily and how they believed you and Nathaniel were destined to be together. The thought sent him into a frenzy, and then you denied his kiss and fell asleep in his bed, calling out for Nathaniel as you dreamed. *That* is what set him off."

Dedrick crossed his arms over his chest. "You most likely don't believe me and that's understandable, but here's something to ponder: Why would I break River out of jail just to lock him up again? I'll tell you why, because he hadn't given up, Maryah. He called me every day, begging me to make sure you were killed. You and Nathaniel."

I stiffened at the thought of anyone trying to kill Nathan.

"Did he try to play it cool during your private visit?" One side of Dedrick's chapped lips lifted into half of a sinister smile. "Still claiming he suffers from temporary insanity? Did he assure you that he'd help you break free if he could? Did he strategically remind you of the friendship you shared?"

Dedrick's brows rose as he waited for me to answer. I stopped myself from nodding. I wasn't telling Dedrick anything.

"Schizophrenia with violent tendencies," Dedrick stated. "That's his diagnosis. He cried to me on the phone from prison. He couldn't bear the thought of you with Nathaniel. I didn't trust that prison to contain him. A heartbroken man will stop at nothing when his mind is hell-bent on a woman." Dedrick stood and walked closer to me. "I'll be honest with you. I intend to always be honest because I want to regain your trust." He reached out to touch me, but dropped his hand when I backed away. "I didn't care about what River might do to Nathaniel, but I couldn't allow you to be harmed again. I'm keeping you safe. From the mentally unstable side of River, and from that group of meddling souls who claim themselves to be your kindrily. Sometimes the true monsters disguise themselves as the good guys, while the unexpected hero stays hidden in the shadows."

Was he freaking kidding me? He was so demented that he thought his creepy speech would make me believe he was a good guy and my kindrily were bad? I almost felt sorry for him. "You're even crazier than I thought."

His eyes softened as he stared at me for several silent blinks. "My, how I wish you hadn't erased. I wish it every day."

I drifted backward again, needing to get away from him. Why would Dedrick care that I erased? If anything he should have been happy that I still had my power for him to steal and use as his own.

He freed the top button of his shirt then rolled his neck. "There's so much you need to know. So, so much. I don't know what lies they've told you, but I fear I'll never be able to convince you of the truth."

I was confused by how forlorn he sounded.

After another long silent moment, he raised his head and much to my shock, his eyes were glassy. He pressed his lips together. "I'm happy you're here. I'm sorry it has to be under these conditions, but please know—" He tapped his fingers against his lips. "I've said enough on that matter for now. The important thing is you're safe." He turned toward the candle. "I'll see you soon."

"Wait!" I wanted to know what he meant, what he almost said. For a brief moment, he seemed sincere and almost human. As the darkness enveloped me, I shook my head at my own moment of stupidity.

Dedrick was not sincere. He was far from human. He was the reason my parents were gone. The reason I no longer had a brother. The reason my heart was breaking for them all over again. A lump swelled in my throat as I thought about how much Dedrick had taken from me. Tears that couldn't be real blurred my vision.

Dedrick was the devil, and I wouldn't fall for his tricks.

A FAR CRY

Nathaniel

"What do you mean you feel nothing?" I asked Faith. She released Maryah's hand. "I mean exactly what I said. I feel nothing. No emotions from her at all."

"How is that possible? Has your ability stopped working?"

She stood and put her hands on her hips. "My ability works just fine. She's astral traveling, Nathan. Her soul isn't here. Emotions radiate from the soul."

"So we have no way of knowing if she's all right." I had hoped Faith could tell me if Maryah was scared, worried, peaceful, anything at all.

"I'm sorry." She touched my hand. "I wish I could have helped confirm that she's okay, but I don't have a bad feeling about this. Even if she is stuck somewhere, I don't think she's in danger."

"You're not psychic. You can't know that."

She crossed her arms over her blaring pink tank top which matched her hair. "I know I'm not psychic. It's woman's intuition."

The slightest movement from the bed pulled my attention away from Faith. I maneuvered around her, rushing to Maryah's side.

A tear ran down Maryah's cheek. I watched it cling to her jaw bone for a moment before it dripped onto the pillow. I sat beside her as another tear trailed down her other cheek.

My heart, which had been struggling to stay whole, cracked and splintered in a dozen different directions. I inhaled a shaky breath. "She's crying."

"What?" Faith moved closer.

I wiped away one tear and then another. My own eyes burned as I imagined what might be happening to her.

"What do I do?" My pulse hammered so hard I could feel it in my knotted throat. "Clearly, she's suffering."

"She can't be," Faith said. "She's not in her body."

I tucked Maryah's hair behind her ears. "You just said emotions radiate from the soul. He's emotionally hurting her. What if he's torturing her in some barbaric way?"

"I don't see how that's possible." Faith walked around the bed, sitting on the other side of Maryah. "Maybe she's upset because she can't figure out how to return to her body."

I shook my head as I held Maryah's soft hand. "No, it's more than that. I know it." I looked up, locking gazes with Faith's blue eyes. "Soul mate's intuition."

THROUGH THE LOOKING GLOBE

Maryah

"I'm glad you don't believe Dedrick," Rina said. "Don't believe anything he says. Ever."

"I won't," I assured her. Dedrick had terrorized me for too long already. Difficult as it would be, I couldn't be scared of him anymore. "While I was waiting for you to wake up, I came up with a plan."

Her eyes glimmered with interest. "A plan?"

"All those needles and drugs are right there in that cabinet. Load up a couple syringes and hide them under your blanket. Next time Dedrick visits, give him a dose of his own medicine."

"He keeps the cabinet locked."

I glanced at the rusted but sturdy padlock. "So shatter the glass."

"And then what?"

"He'll be knocked out."

"And what will I do when he wakes up? I'll still be trapped in this room, and he'll be angrier than ever."

I forgot Rina couldn't come and go as easily as blowing out a candle. "I hadn't thought that far through my plan."

"Trust me, I've been here a long time. I've thought of everything you can think of and more. Besides, those potions don't work on him. He's shielded."

"Shielded?"

She nodded. "From the effects of the magic."

"I don't think he's injecting you with magic sleeping potions. I'm pretty sure he's drugging you."

Rina chewed on her fingers while changing the subject. "River loves you?"

"Huh? Oh, no way. River is as crazy as his uncle."

"I saw the way he looked at you. He was worried about you."

"River tried to murder me. That's a far stretch from caring."

"Dedrick wanted you dead. River didn't."

"I'm not so sure."

"I'm sure. I know Dedrick too well." Rina had an abrupt way of talking. Not one second passed between me saying something and her replying. It was like she never took time to think about anything. She just blurted out the first thing that came to her mind.

"Regardless," I said, "I doubt I'll be seeing River again. Dedrick locked him up because he was obsessed with me. I'm sure he won't arrange anymore visits."

"Silly soul," Rina said.

"What?"

"You. You're a silly soul."

"Why am I silly?"

"Because you should know better."

She was several years younger than I was, but her odd and cryptic way of talking almost made her seem too wise to debate. "I know what it feels like when someone cares about me. Nathan cares about me. My kindrily cares about me. They're probably worried to death."

"Worried because you're here with Dedrick?"

"I doubt they know I'm with Dedrick, but they'll be worried that I'm not waking up from my astral traveling session. I don't even know how long I've been gone. I can't keep track of time."

"What will happen if they worry for too long?"

I tried thinking of an answer, but her question was odd. "I'm not sure. They'll be upset, I suppose. Especially Nathan."

"They love you."

I couldn't tell if it was a statement or if she asked it as a question. "Yes, they love me."

"They shouldn't worry."

Again, I didn't know if she meant they shouldn't worry that I wasn't waking up, like it was no big deal, or they shouldn't be put through the pain of worrying. "I wish they didn't, but they do. And I seem to keep getting myself into situations that make them worry more."

"Then stop doing that."

I huffed. "Easier said than done."

"You make it difficult."

"I don't make it difficult on purpose. Bad things keep happening. Usually because of people like River and Dedrick."

Rina hopped up on the table and ran her fingers over her book. "You attract those bad things and people."

I was offended by her incorrect assumption and bluntness. "I do not."

"Yes, you do."

"No, I don't." My defensiveness peppered each of my words. "I just have really bad luck."

"The universe doesn't operate with luck; it operates with energy and laws of attraction. You attracted the bad people and negative events in your life."

The nerve of her. "If that's true, then it's your fault you live here like this, and it's your fault Dedrick treats you so horribly."

"That is true."

"How can you say that? You didn't ask to be imprisoned here your entire life. You're a victim of circumstance."

"No one is a victim."

"Rina."

"Maryah."

I let out a frustrated sigh.

"You attracted the good people too," Rina said, trying to backpedal. "Your kindrily shouldn't worry."

"I wish I could find a way to tell them I'm okay."

She slid off the table then poked me in the stomach as if I had a real body. "Stop wishing and start doing."

"I can't do anything!" I was almost shouting. "I'm trapped here."

Her lips pursed inward like she didn't believe me. She could see that I was trapped in my invisible cage. What did she expect me to do?

"You act like I have any control over being stuck here," I said. "I'm helpless."

"No one is helpless."

"So what do you suggest I do?"

She flapped her hands at her sides like wings. "Break out of the jar, my narrow-minded lightning bug."

"Break out? And how do you suggest I do that?"

She mocked my earlier words. "Shatter the glass."

I pretended to knock on the air between us. "I would if there were glass to break, but there isn't."

"Even easier. Glass is energy turned solid. There's nothing solid about the energy confining you. It should be easier to break."

"I've tried reconnecting to the energy cords that link me to my body. They've been erased."

She giggled while shaking her head. "Energy can't be erased. Energy moves and changes, but it never vanishes." She giggled again then muttered, "silly, silly soul."

I still felt defensive, but also sort of ignorant. I should've paid more attention in science classes so I understood energy better. "If you know how I can return to my body, please tell me."

Her lips straightened into an unreadable expression. "You already know the answers to all of your questions. You just have to open your eyes."

Open your eyes. Those words had been haunting me since the night Dedrick and Gregory almost killed me. "I'm trying, but I don't see anything."

Her midnight blue gaze pinned me in place. She leaned in and whispered, "Look closer."

I looked much more closely at Rina. Clearly, she wasn't the scared, helpless soul she first pretended to be.

M IS FOR MYSTERIOUS

Maryah

Sometimes hours passed without Rina and I speaking to each other. She slept a lot, and I didn't have many reasons to wake her. While sleeping, she'd twitch and make sounds like she was trying to talk with her lips sealed shut.

Did she dream of beautiful places, people who loved her, maybe even a knight in shining armor who would rescue her and take her someplace safe where she'd live happily ever after? Or was she reliving nightmares and imagining new ones?

I watched her, curled on her side, asleep on her dingy bed. Even though she was helping Dedrick—hopefully not by choice—I wanted to help her break free. She was so young. She had her whole life ahead of her. If she got out now, maybe she'd still have a chance of living a normal life and escaping from Dedrick's world of darkness and corruption.

The black curtain fell.

When it lifted, a woman with a long black ponytail and the signature Nefarioun snake eyes stood across from me. She held a tray in her hands that contained a dictionary, bowl of water, washcloth, glass of milk, a couple slices of bread, and a container of what looked like some sort of chocolate and vanilla spread. My mouth watered.

I pressed my invisible hand to my invisible lips, amazed how real the sensation of my mouth watering felt. I could have sworn my stomach growled.

The woman set the tray on the table. She soaked the washcloth in the water and wrung it out then walked over to Rina and knelt down beside her. Then, much to my surprise, as she wiped one of Rina's hands with the washcloth, the woman sang.

Wake up, darling girl,
A new day is dawning.
Wake up, starry eyes,
the future is calling...

Rina bolted upright and ran to the table. Like a starved monkey, she attacked the tray, plowing her fingers into the container of chocolate and vanilla spread and shoveling it into her mouth. The woman rose from the mattress as she folded the washcloth into a perfect triangle and set it beside Rina. "Remember to breathe, darling."

Rina continued licking the spread from her fingers. The woman stood behind Rina, smoothing down her tangled hair. "I heard about our guest, but seeing her for myself, it's almost unbelievable."

Rina nodded while inhaling a bite of bread.

"How are you doing with it?" the woman asked. Rina shrugged then chugged her milk. The woman nodded as she wiped Rina's mouth with one corner of the washcloth. The two of them interacting so comfortably reminded me of the bond I once shared with my mother.

They had the same black hair, pale skin, petite frame. The woman even walked with the same slight hitch in her left side as Rina. She easily could have been her mother. Had Rina lied to me? Was this woman her mom? Or had Dedrick fabricated a story to make Rina think her mom was gone, but in reality she was right here taking care of Rina even while being mind-controlled by Dedrick? I wouldn't put it past him.

But then again, I barely knew Rina. Was she lying to me to help Dedrick?

Rina lapped up the last of the spread with her bread crust while the woman flitted around the room trying to tidy up, but failing given the impossible conditions. She wore the same type of outfit as Rina and Lexie. Loose gray pants with the same type of shirt. Not one speck of color in Dedrick's godforsaken world.

Rina finished the last of her milk and wiped her mouth with her forearm. The woman tsked her then used another corner of the washcloth to dab her mouth and wipe her arm.

"Come." The woman pulled out the chair. "Reading time."

Rina grabbed the timeworn dictionary from the tray and sat down. "Which letter did we leave off at last time?"

My eyes flew open wide. Rina spoke to her.

I don't know why I assumed I was the only one who knew Rina could talk, but hearing her speak to someone else, even, possibly, her own mother, shocked me. Judging from the woman's snake eyes, she was under Dedrick's control. What if she told him Rina's secret?

"We had just finished with L," the woman said.

"Good." Rina thumbed through the dog-eared pages. "M words are my favorite."

"Yes, darling, I'm aware. Start with the first word."

"Ma," Rina read out loud. "A female human parent. See mother." Rina lifted her eyes from the page. "Maryah, this is Evelyn."

Was that an unconscious slip of revealing that Evelyn was her mother? Was Rina playing along with some script Dedrick had given her to fool me?

Evelyn nodded in my direction. "Charmed."

"Can she hear me?" I asked Rina.

Rina subtly shook her head. "Macabre." Rina continued with the next word. "Extremely disturbing or repellent. See Dedrick."

Evelyn grinned, but it was empty and sort of sad. "It doesn't say that."

"It should," Rina said.

Evelyn stood behind Rina, brushing her hair as Rina read the next word. "Machiavellian. Not guided by or showing a concern for what is right. See unprincipled." Rina mumbled, "or Dedrick."

"Rina," Evelyn scolded.

"I can't help it. Some definitions just suit him."

Evelyn delicately separated matted sections of Rina's hair, making sure she didn't yank Rina's head as she tamed each one. "Next word please."

"Machinate. To engage in a secret plan to accomplish evil or unlawful ends. See—"

"Don't say Dedrick." Evelyn playfully tugged on Rina's hair.

Rina slid back in her seat and pulled her legs in, planting her dirty bare feet on the chair and resting the dictionary against her thighs. "I'm skipping ahead to my favorites. Macrocosm. The whole body of things observed or assumed. See universe." She tilted her head back and winked at Evelyn. "And your favorite. Magic. The power to control natural forces through supernatural means. See us."

"Shh. Remember the rules." Evelyn finished detangling Rina's last section of hair. "Your clothes are filthy. I'll bring you a clean set tomorrow."

Rina turned in her chair to face Evelyn. "I have a favor to ask."

"Anything, darling."

"Tonight, keep Dedrick from coming here."

"I suspect that will be impossible. He'll want to check on Maryah."

"After that. Keep him occupied for a few hours. No matter what, don't let him come back here a second time."

Evelyn tensed. "That is asking a lot of me."

"I know. I'm sorry, but please."

Evelyn bowed her head as if thinking. She tightened the drawstring waist of her pants then replied, "Anything for you, but what are you up to?"

"I can't say. Not yet."

Evelyn licked her thumb then wiped a smudge of something from Rina's chin. My own mother used to do that, and I always hated it. Judging from Rina's scrunched up face, she hated it too. But now, I missed my mother so much that I'd happily let her spit-shine my face a dozen times a day if it meant she'd be alive again.

"Be careful," Evelyn warned. "You know how Dedrick gets."

"I'm always careful," Rina assured her.

Evelyn seemed a little too willing to grant Rina's request. The whole interaction was a bit too Hallmark moment-ish considering they were both Dedrick's prisoners.

Mistrustful. See Rina and Evelyn.

Manipulated. *Antonym:* Maryah.

∞

Rina wouldn't tell me anything about her plan. She barely spoke to me at all from the time Evelyn left until the time she returned much later with another tray. Rina's dinner wasn't much better than what I assumed was her breakfast earlier.

Just like after breakfast, as soon as Evelyn left, Rina's mouse friend scurried across the floor, and she scooped him up.

"You and Evelyn look a lot alike." I tested Rina's story, watching her carefully for any indicators that she had lied to me. "So much alike that she could easily pass as your mom."

Rina's face remained relaxed as she fed the mouse a few saved cracker crumbs. "Evelyn is pretty, so thank you for the compliment."

"You don't see the resemblance?"

"We both have black hair. We've both been defiled and treated like scum. We're both pale because we never see the sun. If that's what you mean, then sure, I see resemblances."

She didn't rapidly blink, or fidget, or talk fast, no sign whatsoever that she had lied. Maybe it really was just the prisoner lifestyle that made them look so much alike. After thinking about it, River had the same dark and dejected look as Rina and Evelyn.

Rina scratched the mouse's head.

I hoped Nathan was taking good care of Eightball while I was gone. I had to find a way back to my kindrily. I had already put them through so much grief and worry, and now this.

"What's wrong?" Rina asked me.

"I miss Nathan. I miss all of my family. I keep messing up and ruining lives." Or lives ended because of me. I swallowed down the never-ending guilt of being the reason my parents were killed.

Rina cupped her mouse in her hands and hugged him to her chest. We were silent for a long time. She had her mouse, and I had no one.

Dedrick didn't visit us after dinner like Evelyn said he would. Even after the mouse scurried into a crack in the corner, Rina sat on her mattress, waiting for what felt like two more hours.

The silence became unbearable. "Maybe he's not coming."

"He'll want to check on you." Rina sneezed.

"Bless you."

She wiped her nose on her wrist. "Why do I need to be blessed?"

"I don't know. It's what you say after someone sneezes."

Rina's forehead wrinkled. "Why do you say that?"

"It's not just me. It's everyone." I shrugged. "It's good manners. Evelyn has never blessed you after you sneezed?"

"When one of us sneezes we say, 'Jupiter adsit.'"

I'd never heard that one before. "What does that mean?"

"We ask Jupiter to preserve the soul, so no one's spirit can jump into your body during that brief moment between expelling your soul and breathing it back in."

I laughed. "That's almost as bad as the one my dad told me. He said demons rush out of you when you sneeze and someone has to bless you before they crawl back in."

"Sounds like a different version of ours." Rina rubbed her nose. "Too bad yours is wrong."

Neither theory was realistic, but who was I to argue that her Jupiter saying was weirder than my "bless you" tradition. At least her version sounded more interesting than fighting snot demons.

Again, I asked Rina what she was planning to do, but she wouldn't tell me. She said if she couldn't tell Evelyn she definitely couldn't tell me.

After another hour or so of waiting in silence, Rina stood. She walked over to the table and sat in the chair. "I don't think he's coming."

"Doesn't seem like it."

Rina leaned forward, resting her head on top of her forearms. "I'm tired. I think I'll take a nap."

A nap sounded wonderful, but I couldn't even sleep without my body. I'd never been a prisoner before—at least not in this lifetime, or that I could remember from other lifetimes—but I assumed regular imprisonment would be much easier than soul imprisonment.

"Enjoy your nap," I told Rina. Her torso rose and fell as her steady breaths became slower. She murmured, "Jupiter adsit."

I quietly obsessed about her top secret plan.

BODY SNATCHING

Nathaniel

"I'm terrified of what might be happening to her," I admitted to Carson and Krista. "Tears fell from her eyes earlier."

"Are you serious?" Carson waved his hand. "Rhetorical question. Ignore me."

"Why would her eyes tear up?" Krista opened the curtains, allowing sunlight to spill into the bedroom. Beams of colored light bounced off the walls as the crystal hanging in the window swung side to side.

"Maybe it's just her body's natural response." Carson stretched his arms behind him. "Like how muscles jerk even while we're asleep."

"No. She's hurting. Emotionally." I wanted to punch something. Not something—Dedrick. I wanted to rip him into pieces. I sat beside Maryah, watching her chest rise and fall as her body continued breathing without its soul. Her leg twitched so hard, it bounced the mattress.

"See?" Carson presented his hand. "Case in point. Muscles jerk even though her soul isn't here."

Maryah turned toward Krista and Carson. She cleared her throat, and my heart rebounded from the pit of worry where it had been struggling to beat. "Maryah! Thank god!"

I threw my arms around her and pulled her close.

"Oh, Pudding." Krista hugged both of us. "We were so worried!"

"Welcome home, Sparky," Carson said.

I pulled back to look at her, and my heart plummeted back into its empty pit. My hands tightened around her arms.

Krista rubbed Maryah's leg through the sheet. "Where were you all this time?"

Maryah's eyes floated in every direction until they landed on me. "How long has it been?"

I let go of her and stood, slowly backing away.

"Two days," Krista told her. "Where did you go? What happened? Do you feel okay?"

"Easy with all the questions," Carson said. "Let her catch her breath. She's probably tired and disoriented."

I was still backing away from the bed. I watched them as if it were taking place on a movie screen. I wished it were a movie, a terrible film I could stop and eject from existence.

"Nathan?" Krista looked up at me. "What's wrong?"

"It's not her," I said. "That's not Maryah."

"What?" Krista laughed. Carson pulled Krista to her feet, distancing them from whomever inhabited Maryah's body.

Krista, Carson, and I stood on either side of the bed, watching Maryah's impostor. She pulled the sheet up over her chest, clutching it in her fists, not taking her attention off me.

"Who are you?" I had no idea who or what we were up against.

"I'm me," she answered.

"And whom are you referring to when you say 'me?'"

"I'm here to help."

"I'm going to ask you one more time, and I want a straight answer." My fists balled. "Who are you?"

Carson had moved Krista behind him. His arms were low at his sides, ready to protect her. I didn't know what to do. We couldn't threaten or hurt the uninvited guest because they were encased in Maryah's body.

"My name is Rina."

"Where is Maryah?" I asked.

"She's safe. I came to tell you not to worry."

"Not worry? You're a stranger inside of my soul mate's body. We haven't heard from her in days. Worrying is an understatement."

She adjusted to sit more upright. "Maryah is fine."

"Well, Rina, if that's your real name, you are here in the most invasive manner I can imagine, but you're still possessing the body of someone I cherish, so I ask that you inhabit it respectfully and please, tell me if she feels weak."

The imposter looked down, holding Maryah's hands out in front of her. "She feels much stronger than me."

"She should eat and drink something," Krista told me.

Not that I wanted to be hospitable to a body snatcher, but considering it was Maryah's body, it needed to be taken care of. "Any special requests?"

The stranger, Rina, eyed the room and everything in it. "What does Maryah like?"

"Cereal," I replied, "different kinds mixed together in one bowl." Seeing Maryah's body move as if she were in it, but knowing it wasn't her, was extremely hard to process.

Rina spoke in a voice that resembled Maryah's but with a hint of an undetermined accent. "I've never had cereal."

Carson, Krista, and I glanced at each other.

"Well then." Krista's voice shook. She was trying, and failing, to hide her consternation. "You should try it. I'll be right back."

After Krista rushed out of the room, Rina blurted out, "She misses you."

I stiffened. "Where is she?"

"A room with no doors or windows. Her spirit is trapped in a bubble."

"A bubble?"

She nodded. "Dedrick keeps her locked in an energy bubble."

"I don't understand what you mean."

"I don't understand it either, but you asked where she is so I'm telling you."

"Can you see her?"

"Yes."

"How?"

"She's a light form."

Like how Louise sees auras. Could this Rina person see auras too? "Is there a way to free her from the bubble?"

"She's trying to figure that out."

Maryah was astral traveling. That meant—as far as I knew—she couldn't talk, but until Louise saw Dedrick's aura, I also assumed a soul couldn't be seen while traveling. Yet Rina claimed she was visible, so anything was possible. "Do you communicate with her?"

"Yes."

Maryah was without her body which meant she had no actual voice. "You can hear her thoughts?"

"Yes."

"So you're a mind reader."

"No."

She had used Maryah's ability to astral travel and take possession of her body. Perhaps she stole mind-reading from someone as well. "Do you steal other peoples' powers?"

"I borrow their power. I never take it away from them. They still have it."

"How is that possible?"

She stroked Maryah's hair. "You ask a lot of questions."

"You're in Maryah's body while she's being held captive by the most evil man I've ever encountered." I crossed my arms over my chest. "I'm entitled to ask as many questions as I want."

Maryah's green eyes had been replaced with a dark blue that momentarily glimmered. "I like you."

"I'm not sure what to make of you."

"No one ever does."

"Understandably so."

She looked away. "I'm very thirsty."

I spoke my words deliberately slow so Carson would understand my intention. "Carson, walk to the kitchen and fetch our guest some water."

I didn't want this stranger to know anything about our abilities. I especially didn't want her in Maryah's body, but it seemed I had no say in that matter. Carson backed out of the room. His footsteps faded down the hallway at a normal pace.

"Where is he keeping her?" I asked. "The actual location."

"Dedrick has her trapped in my room."

My jaw clenched at the mention of his name. "So you work with him."

"Not exactly."

"What does that mean?"

"I've been his prisoner since I was born."

I didn't know whether or not to believe her. Anyone associated with Dedrick couldn't be trusted. "How old are you?"

"I'm not sure." She answered every question quickly, an indication that she was telling the truth, but I still didn't trust her.

Carson returned holding two large glasses of water. He handed one to her, and she clutched it with both hands, gulping it down. When she finished, she wiped her mouth and peered into the empty glass. "Feels strange being in her body. It's very different from mine."

Krista rushed in, sloshing milk on the floor from the overfilled cereal bowl. "Are you an astral traveler too?"

"No," Rina replied.

"Then how is your soul here in Maryah's body?" Carson was holding the second glass of water, but when Rina tried to take it, he held it out of her reach. "Answer the question first."

"I'm a conductor," Rina explained. "I borrowed her power to travel here and tell you she's okay and not to worry."

Carson glanced at me, and I nodded. He handed her the drink, and she gulped that one down faster than the first.

"Where is your home?" I asked. "Where does Dedrick have you and Maryah trapped?"

"I don't know. I've never known."

"What do you mean?" Krista offered her the bowl of cereal, but Rina eyed it then scrunched her nose.

"I'm kept in a room with no windows or doors. I never know when it's day or night. I've never been anywhere except that room. Until now."

If that was the truth, it was a crime which made me despise Dedrick even more. No one should be subjected to that sort of confinement.

Before any of us could react or reply to her shocking claim, Rina threw the covers off of her. "I need to use the bathroom." Deep pink spread across Maryah's chest. "This is awkward. I've never had to pee using someone else's body."

We all glanced uncomfortably at each other. Awkward indeed.

∞

When Rina stepped out of the bathroom, we were all waiting for her, including Louise and Anthony. Carson, Krista, and I had updated them on the body snatcher situation.

"Hello," Rina said, wiping her hands on Maryah's shorts, "I'm Rina."

Anthony's eyes narrowed. Eightball whined and backed into the corner.

Louise pushed her glasses to the top of her head. "Fascinating."

Judging from Louise's smile, she didn't see any indication that Rina's aura was malevolent. "My name is—"

"No." I stopped Louise from introducing herself. "No names. We can't trust anyone associated with Dedrick."

Louise glared at me. "My cover was already blown when Dedrick visited us, so it doesn't matter if she knows my name. She extended her hand. "I'm Louise."

Rina stared at Louise's hand. Clearly she wasn't familiar with that form of greeting. She leaned forward, examining Louise's bangle bracelets. "What are those?"

"My bracelets?" She jingled them, and Rina's eyes lit up. Louise removed a few beaded ones and handed them to Rina. "Here, try them on. They're jewelry."

Rina slid them onto Maryah's wrist and held them up in front of her, admiring them. "They make a lovely sound." Her attention switched to something beyond her bracelets. She lowered her arm and walked toward the windows then touched the glass. "These are unusual. What are they?"

"She claims to have never seen a window," I explained. "Or been outside." We had failed to mention that part of Rina's story.

"What?" Louise gasped. "How horrible. Here, come have a look." Louise opened the balcony door. "Step outside and enjoy the fresh desert air."

Rina peered up at me from beneath Maryah's long lashes. "Will you go with me?"

"Me?" I was the most leery of her, and I had made it clear that I didn't trust her. "There's nothing to be afraid of. It's a small private balcony."

"Nathan, go with her," Louise urged. "This is all new to her."

Reluctantly, I walked forward and motioned for Rina to step outside. She did, but timidly. Reaching forward, she ran one finger over the balcony railing. She scanned the sky and ground then took a deep breath and closed her eyes. "It tastes heavenly."

Could she taste the energy around her the way most of our kindrily could? Before I had the chance to ask if she sensperienced, a bird landed on the railing, flapping its wings. Eightball ran toward us barking as Rina jumped sideways, hugging me and burying her face in my chest.

I don't know if it was because she was startled or because she was in Maryah's body, but I couldn't push her away.

GRASS IS ALWAYS GREENER

Maryah

Rina jerked awake so hard that her chair scooted backward. She sat up, wiping her eyes.

"What?" I asked after a period of her staring at me and blinking, but not saying anything. "Did you have a nightmare?"

"I'm not sure how much to tell you."

"How much to tell me about what?"

Rina wrung her hands together. "I told them you were okay."

"Told who I was okay?"

"Some of your kindrily."

I was confused. "Some of my kindrily?" The possibility hit me like a truck. "Did you travel to them?"

She nodded.

"You stole my ability to spy on my family?"

"I didn't spy. I told them who I was and that you were fine and not to worry."

My mind reeled. "But how? I can't talk to people when I astral travel. How can you be sure they heard you?"

Her fingers fumbled around themselves faster. "Don't be angry."

"Angry about what?"

"I borrowed your body to interact with them."

She spoke clearly, but I struggled to process her words. To comprehend what she meant. She borrowed my body? "You *what?*"

"It's a secret. No one can know I am able to do it. If Dedrick found out—"

"Forget Dedrick!" I shouted. "You had no right to use my body as your own!" The room was spinning. Or maybe I was. I pressed my hands against the sides my head, trying to make the dizziness stop. "How is that even possible? What did you do as me? Who did you see? Who did you talk to?" I rushed toward her, fuming, as she protectively raised her hands. "Was Nathan there?"

She nodded. "Nathaniel, Krista, Carson, Louise, and Anthony."

I was trying to catch my breath, but I had no lungs so a cold void kept tugging at the center of my chest. "You actually talked to them?"

"I told them I was me. I told them you were safe. I wasn't trying to be sneaky or do anything bad. You said they were probably worried sick, and I didn't want them to worry, and I didn't want you to be upset so I went there so everyone would feel better."

"You had no right!"

"I was careful. I made sure not to harm your body in any way. I even drank a lot of water because you were thirsty."

Anger, confusion, and the overwhelming sense of being violated twisted and turned around me like a tornado. "Tell me everything. Every word you said. Every step you took. And most importantly, tell me how the hell you invaded my body."

∞

Rina's story and her ability were so far-fetched, but she described mine and Nathan's bedroom in perfect detail. And

Louise's bracelets. Even the scent of Nathan when he held her. He held *her*. A stranger in my body.

I asked for the third time. "You swear you told them the truth about who you were?"

"Of course I did."

"I still don't understand how your soul was able to exist in my body."

"You don't understand a lot of things, Maryah."

It's a good thing I didn't have a tongue or I might have bitten it off while trying to keep my cool. "Then why don't you educate me?"

"You're limited by your beliefs." Her tone was gentle, almost like she pitied me. "I can't educate you if you don't open your mind and expand your awareness."

This coming from the girl who had been trapped by Dedrick since birth.

If what Rina told me about her visit with my kindrily was true—which it seemed to be—then Rina had temporarily escaped from her cell for the first time. She had tasted freedom. In my body. She hadn't needed or even asked for my permission. What would she do with the ability to be free now that she had experienced it? What if next time she stayed in my body, stole my life, and never gave a second thought to my soul being trapped here with Dedrick? The possibility terrified me.

I'd have to be more careful. I'd have to be extremely cautious about what information I shared. If I made my life sound too enticing, she might steal it. I needed to know how she felt about her time away, but I was nervous to ask. If she enjoyed it, and I made her relive those positive feelings again, it could make matters worse. Then again, maybe she'd be one of those kidnap victims who stayed with her captor for so long that she wouldn't leave even if she could.

I scanned her from her dirty bare feet to her greasy disheveled hair. Wanting to stay here with Dedrick was a long, long shot.

I had to find out how she felt about being me. "How was it?"

"How was what?" Rina asked.

"Your experience with them, and being outside for the first time."

A light flickered in her eyes. "It was wonderful. Louise is so nice. I think she sort of liked me. I wish I could have kept the bracelets she let me try on."

She did like it. Of course she did. Who wouldn't? "And Nathan?"

"He doesn't trust me."

"Can you blame him?"

She tickled her lips with the ends of her hair, but disappointment lurked in her frown. "He should know I'm trustworthy."

I had to say or do something to keep her from wanting to spend more time with them. If that happened, she might never come back. "He uses you, you know."

"Who?"

"Dedrick."

Rina started doing an awkwardly sloppy version of jumping jacks. "He uses everyone."

"He's using our abilities to spy on people so he can execute evil plans, but you're capable of doing powerful things by yourself, so why don't we use your power to stop him?"

She stopped jumping. "What do you mean?"

Rina knew more than she revealed to me. I could tell from her remarks about power, energy, and the ease of seemingly impossible feats. Sure, I was sort of manipulating her into helping me, but I didn't feel guilty about it. The girl had inhabited my body without even asking. "If we can figure out a way to free my soul so it can travel, I can see what Dedrick is up to. He won't ever suspect I'm spying on him because he'll assume I'm still trapped here. I could figure out where we are and how to get you out of here permanently."

"Permanently," she repeated. She restarted her jumping jacks. "Where would I go?"

"Wherever you wanted."

"With you?"

"What do you mean with me?"

Dirt stirred every time her feet slid across the floor. "Could I live with you and your kindrily?"

I hesitated. "I'd have to ask them."

"That means no."

"I didn't say that." I felt guilty for lying before the words even came out of my mouth. "But it's Louise and Anthony's house so they'd have to decide."

She was still flailing her arms and legs, and she was becoming winded, but I was almost certain she mumbled, "liar."

"If you left here," she said, "you'd never come back."

"Of course I'd come back."

Her breathless words were choppy. "I wouldn't want you to. No one should be stuck here."

"Exactly. No one, including you. But I wouldn't be trapped anymore. Dedrick would just think I was. And we'd figure out a way to free you too."

"It's too risky."

"It's your only chance of getting out of here. Why is it okay for you to be trapped here forever?"

She stopped jumping and bent over, trying to catch her breath. "It's not forever."

"You've already been here much too long."

She was panting. "It hasn't been long enough."

"What does that mean?"

"We need more."

"More what?"

She leaned against the wall. "More time."

"Time for what?"

"To grow stronger."

"Is that why you're doing jumping jacks?"

She rubbed her thighs then sat on the floor. "Evelyn taught me some exercises a long time ago, but I didn't enjoy them. Being in your body, I felt so strong. When I squatted over your toilet, your leg muscles were so much firmer than mine."

"Gross. I don't want to hear about your bathroom adventures in my body."

"Sorry." She attempted to do a push-up. "I want to have muscles like yours, so I'm going to exercise."

On the positive side, she was working out to build muscles in her own body, which meant she wasn't considering trading it in for a new one. On the alarming side, she wanted to be stronger. What if results from exercise took too long and she decided to steal my body?

STATING THE OBVIOUS

Nathaniel

R ina had left Maryah's body so abruptly. She crumbled into a
lifeless heap in my arms, so I carried her from the balcony to
the bed. Krista scanned her for any health issues but didn't detect
anything.

Eightball kept barking, which I suspected was the reason
Rina left without a goodbye.

"Eightball, enough," I said.

Krista picked him up, and Carson hushed him while rubbing
his ears. "I'm sure he sensed the stranger. I'll call Amber and
have her come over to talk to him."

I tended to Maryah as Carson pulled out his cell phone.

"I'll be in the library," Louise said, seeming distracted but
rightfully so.

"Louise?" I called before she exited the bedroom.

She turned and lifted her chin.

"What is it?" I knew Louise too well. She'd be in the library
because she had something to research or someone to contact, and
I was certain it was related to our unexpected visitor.

"Nothing to get excited over or worry about. I'll keep you
posted if it turns into anything."

"What did you—"

"Here." Carson shoved his phone in my face. "Amber wants
to talk to you."

I pressed the phone to my ear. "Evening, Amber."

"Never a dull moment over there, hmm?" Mikey was cooing in the background.

"So it seems."

"Carson tells me Eightball is upset about a body snatcher encounter?"

"We all are, but Eightball isn't suppressing his opinions as well as the rest of us."

Eightball growled long and deep then barked in the direction of Maryah's body again.

"I'm trying to put Mikey to sleep, and Dylan isn't here, so I'd rather not come over to have a conversation with Eightball that you can easily manage yourself."

"Me? I can't talk to animals."

"Anyone can talk to animals. You just can't hear them reply, but they're great at understanding tone and body language. You'll do fine."

Eightball's eyes met mine, and his growling eased into a soft whimper.

"Assure him Maryah is all right," Amber said. "Explain the stranger meant her no harm."

"You want me to lie to him?"

"It's not a lie."

"I can't be certain it's the truth."

Amber sighed. "Have you been spending any quality time with him?"

"Quality time with Eightball? I've been sort of occupied with the Maryah crisis."

"You two should be comforting each other right now."

I couldn't believe I was having a conversation about our dog while Maryah's body had so recently been invaded by a stranger. "Look, I love Eightball, truly, but I can't communicate with him like you do, and I don't have the same bond with him that Maryah does."

"You could work on strengthening your bond with him. Take him for a walk. Play catch with him."

"Catch?" I laughed. "Somehow I suspect Eightball wouldn't have the slightest idea what to do if I threw a ball for him to fetch."

"He would. Just try it. Some playtime will be good for you both."

I agreed to it simply to end the absurd conversation. "Fine."

I hung up and handed Carson his phone. Krista held out a stuffed alligator toy. It was so faded that the color could no longer be declared green, and it was missing an eye.

"It's his favorite toy," Krista explained.

Relenting, I took it from her. "It's damp."

"He loves when you throw it in the pond."

"The pond? We have koi in the pond."

"He never bothers the fish." Carson winked then nodded at the slobber-covered toy I was holding. "He prefers gator."

It seemed everyone else had made time for living their lives except for me. "Maybe a break would do me some good."

Krista set Eightball down at my feet. He sat up, ears at attention, eyes locked on his wet, cyclops gator. "My, how quickly you forgot about your mother's soul being in peril."

He pawed at my leg then laid down. I tossed the gator toward the door, and his short stubby legs scrambled to chase after it.

"He just needs to know she's going to be okay," Krista told me.

Eightball turned and stared at me, the gator sandwiched between his teeth.

"We both need that reassurance."

∞

After a thirty-minute play session, Eightball passed out in the living room, snoring before his eyes even closed.

I made my way to the library and tapped on the door before pushing it open. Louise was so engrossed with whatever she was reading from a book that she didn't notice me until I spoke.

"Care to fill me in?"

She stood then walked around the desk and sat on the edge of it. She motioned to the two chairs in front of her. "Sit. Let's chat."

I couldn't take another conversation of her staring down her glasses at me with worry, so I sat beside her on the corner of the desk. I inhaled a preparatory breath. Insisting that I sit meant she was about to tell me bad news.

"Rina's aura," she began. She stared at the spinning ceiling fan, trying to find her words. "Her light is galactic."

"Galactic," I repeated. "As in from the stars? Every human is made from the stars."

"That's not what I mean. The colors, energy field, and light that humans give off are complex but defined. I thought I had seen it all in my many centuries of living, but Rina's light is nothing I've seen while in human form or while in between lifetimes. She's recondite. I can't mentally process what her aura means. Whatever her energy is, it's beyond my understanding."

I stared at her at a loss for words. Auras were never beyond Louise's understanding. "Could she be dangerous?"

"I honestly don't know. I see nothing negative in her aura. Clearly she's powerful, but judging from the unique spectrum of her light, her vitality may be more powerful than we can comprehend. I assume she is unaware of it, or she wouldn't be controlled by Dedrick."

"Or she does know how powerful she is, and so does Dedrick, and she's his secret weapon."

"Could you paint her aura?" Carson's voice surprised me. He stood in the doorway, his hands hidden in the front pocket of his sweatshirt.

Louise drummed her fingers on the desk. "I could try. I'm not sure any of the paints I have could adequately portray what I see."

Curious, I asked, "What colors do you see in her aura?"

"That's just it, I see every color of the spectrum and colors I didn't know existed."

"All at once?" Carson asked.

"No, she constantly flickers as if her being isn't sure of who and what it is."

Carson sat in the chair in front of me. "Maybe it's some sort of force field Dedrick created so you can't see her real aura."

"I don't like this," I grumbled. "We need to find a way to get Maryah away from her."

"Or," Carson mused. "Maybe she's exactly what Maryah needs to help her remember who she is."

I stood. "How could she help Maryah with that?"

"Louise said Rina's energy flickers like she's trying to decide who she is. I can't help but notice the similarity. Maryah does the same thing with her memories. They come and go, and as much as she wants to remember who she was, something is preventing it. Maybe Rina struggles in the same way with her power. What if the universe crossed their paths so they could help each other?"

Louise tucked her fist under her chin as we both considered Carson's suggestion.

I had to consider any suggestion of Carson's because his intelligence, as young as he was, far outweighed mine, but this theory felt like a stretch. "I'm not sure I understand how you made such a huge leap to connect Rina's flickering aura with Maryah's struggle to retrieve her memories. What aren't you telling us, exceptionally wise little brother of mine?"

He tugged at the strings hanging from his hood while his knee bounced. "I might have been influenced by one of Dakota's comics."

I rolled my eyes.

"His story made sense," Carson argued. "And it was pretty badass too. This shooting star turned into a girl as she fell to

Earth, and her energy was so powerful she gave Maryah back all of her memories."

"Carson," I chided.

"I like that story," Louise said happily. "I hope our shooting star stranger visits again soon."

"What?" I gawked at her. "Return in Maryah's body again? Are you mad?" I stood, staring down at Carson. "And stop encouraging Dakota with his comic nonsense."

"You should read more comics. Maybe some hero mojo would rub off on you." Carson slid forward, bumping his foot against mine. "Look, I've been waiting for someone to suggest my next idea because I feel bad being the *only* one to state the obvious, but I'll be nice and dismiss it to everyone being too distracted or worried to see it." Carson raised his brows at me. "Want to take a stab at our next big move before I take the credit?"

I had no idea what he was talking about. "I give credit when it's due. Go on."

"Rina *visited* us. You *saw* the difference between her and Maryah." He glanced expectantly at me and Louise. "Come on, really? Still no clue what I'm about to say?"

I shook my head.

Carson sighed. "You saw Rina's soul. Rina is with Maryah. Stop sitting around here and traverse to them."

Louise straightened.

"I saw Rina's soul through Maryah's eyes," I argued.

"But you saw distinct differences, right?"

"Of course." I stared at him, contemplating whether something so obvious and easy could work.

"You could traverse to where they are," Carson continued. "You could see for yourself where they're being kept. You could even traverse the girl back here, although I wouldn't recommend it until we know for sure she isn't working with Dedrick."

"That might actually work," Louise said. "But what if Nathan appears when Dedrick is there?"

"Then he traverses back home."

"It's worth a try," Louise urged.

My heart was racing at the possibility. I most certainly wouldn't traverse Rina back here and put everyone in danger, but knowing more about Maryah's location and how her soul was being trapped would help us figure out a way to free her.

I closed my eyes, opened my energy field, and pictured the windows to Rina's soul. I vanished from the library.

I materialized in black space. I wasn't standing, but I wasn't floating. There was no sound, nothing to see or touch. I waited, hoping it was a transition to somewhere, but nothing happened.

I visualized Carson's eyes and traversed back.

"Well?" Carson asked. Louise was anticipating my report as well.

"That's never happened before," I said. "I ended up in darkness. Pure, empty darkness."

"Try again," Carson insisted.

"Why? There was nothing. No Maryah, no Rina, no sound, or anything else."

"But there was darkness," Carson said.

"So?"

Louise held my hand. "Without light, there can be no dark. You need to keep searching until you find a light."

"Rina said darkness falls over the room before anyone comes or goes." Carson grabbed my shoulders and stared directly into my eyes. "You were halfway there. Keep searching until you find a way in."

FRIENDS IN LONELY PLACES

Maryah

R ina and I were mid-conversation when the candle went out.
When the light returned, Evelyn and River stood behind
Rina.

Rina glanced over her shoulder, and when she faced me her
eyes were wide.

"Hi, Maryah," River said quietly.

"What do you want?"

Rina sidestepped to the table and sat down. Evelyn set the
tray of food in front of her, but Rina didn't inhale her makeshift
meal like usual. She reached for the slice of bread while watching
River.

"He needed to speak to Maryah," Evelyn explained.
"Dedrick doesn't know. He can't know, do you understand?"

Rina nodded then tore her crust into small pieces.

River crept toward me, and I backed away. He put his hands
up in front of him as if his empty hands would prove he was
incapable of harm.

"I don't expect you to trust me. Hell, I wouldn't trust me, but
I'm telling the truth when I say I don't want to see you trapped
here. I want to help you. Or at least try." He stuck his hands in the
pockets of his gray prisoner pants. "I'm still locked up most of the
time, but my uncle has been sending in some quack to discuss my
schizophrenia. I'm convincing him that I believe I'm crazy, and

that I want to get better. I'm cheeking my meds but acting like a zombie around my uncle. The more I go along with the mental patient act, the more I get let out of my cell."

Evelyn busied herself by tidying up the hopelessly dirty room. She didn't seem the least bit interested in what River was saying, which seemed weird considering how worried she was about Dedrick in her prior conversation with Rina.

"I won't betray you," River told me. "I'm not like them. I don't want to live like this, doing whatever he tells me, hurting people, killing people." He glanced at Rina. "Watching people suffer. I want to get away from him too, but I'll never be able to do it on my own, and you and your kindrily are the only people I know who might be powerful enough to help me." His eyelids looked heavy and his mouth was weighed down with a permanent frown. "I know that might sound like I'm using you, and maybe I am in a way, but it's not like I'm asking you to help make me popular or something shallow. I'm asking you to help me escape and have some sort of normal life. I'll help you break free if you promise to come back for me."

"Are you kidding me?" I gawked at him. "I don't care if you have mental problems. You tried to kill me! And now you want my kindrily and me to help you? Why? So you can try to kill Nathan? Or me again? How stupid do you think I am?"

"He's being genuine," Rina said.

"Rina!" How could she blow her cover with River around?

River whirled around to look at her. "You can talk?"

Rina nodded. Evelyn didn't even look up from wiping the table.

River glanced at me then back at Rina. "I guess I'm not the only one keeping secrets."

Keeping secrets. He even admitted it. He was probably keeping diabolical secrets from everyone, especially me.

"I know you won't tell anyone." Rina stood, pinning him in place with her candlelit glare. "You're not that stupid."

Had Dedrick instructed River to do this? To try to get close to me again and gain my trust? Dedrick had me right where he needed me, trapped with a conductor who allowed him to use my ability for whatever spying he needed to do. I couldn't see what Dedrick had to gain by tricking me into teaming up with River— he knew I hated him—but there was no way River was being genuine. I had to be missing something.

"I don't know how often I'll be able to sneak in here to see you," River said, "but whenever I find out something that might help us, I'll visit as soon as possible to tell you."

"Where are we?" I asked urgently. "Rina, ask him where we are."

"Maryah wants to know if you know where we are."

"I don't know yet," River answered. "The room where I'm being kept looks a lot like this, but Dedrick let me out yesterday to help Evelyn with chores. We walked down long dirt hallways. One tiny room with no door had light pouring in from the ceiling. I could only see sky. I'm guessing we're pretty secluded."

I saved every detail to memory. "How did he get here? Ask him if he flew in a plane, or drove, or what?"

"How did you get here?" Rina asked.

"I wish I knew. Dedrick had a private plane waiting in Sedona after he took me from jail. There was a fight with some of your family at the airport." River searched my face like he was wondering if I knew about it. Of course I knew about it. They had almost killed Harmony and Dakota that night. "The plane took off, and then Dedrick knocked me out. I woke up here in my newest prison cell."

"How did he get into this room?" I asked Rina. She repeated my question.

"Evelyn helped me."

"And now we need to leave," Evelyn said. "We've already stayed too long. We can't risk being caught."

"Wait!" I shouted. "A couple more questions."

Rina shoved food in her face as Evelyn and River stood by the candle on the table.

"Rina," I said, "Ask him if he saw other people."

But Rina didn't ask.

"I'll be back as soon as I can," River told me.

Evelyn blew out the candle before I could say another word.

"If Evelyn can get River in and out of this room," I said to Rina, "Why doesn't she let you out?"

"She can't." Rina licked the leftover spread from her fingers. "I'm locked in the same way you are."

"Have you tried using her power to let yourself out?"

"Dedrick and Evelyn are shielded. Most of the people here are. I can't access their powers." She shrugged. "Besides, I need to be here."

I ignored her brainwashed-victim comment and focused on the powers issue. My kindrily told me Dedrick's Element status and privileges had been taken away long ago, so how was he accomplishing so much? "What kind of ability does Dedrick have?"

"He doesn't have any natural abilities. He uses spells and magic."

Louise and Helen had informed me about witches, some they knew personally, but hearing about spells from a girl who had been locked in a dungeon all her life confirmed I was stuck in a real-life, twisted fairy tale.

"His most valued spell is controlling minds," Rina said.

"Why doesn't he control your mind?"

She grinned. "My mother protected me from it."

"How?"

"I'm not sure."

"What about Evelyn? She has snake eyes so I thought she was mind-controlled, but she seems to sneak around doing whatever she wants."

"Evelyn is brilliant."

"That doesn't answer my question."

She held up one finger and lackadaisically waved it. "You didn't ask a specific question, but even if you did, I'm not permitted to discuss what Evelyn does."

"Why not?"

"It's a rule."

"Her rule?'

Rina's brow furrowed as she wiped her hands on the thighs of her pants. "Wouldn't you rather find out answers to more pertinent questions such as how is Dedrick protected from the abilities of the people he's mind-controlling?"

"How is he protected?"

"A man named Thomas has a shielding ability." She turned up her nose. "He's ugly and smells bad. He shields the others too."

"Thomas shields all the Nefariouns?"

"Nuh-what?"

"We call them Nefariouns. Dedrick and his evil gang."

Rina sounded out each syllable. "Nuh-far-ee-uns. Like nefarious."

"Exactly."

"Fitting."

I needed to find out more about this shielding thing. "Back to this Thomas person. How long has he been working for Dedrick?"

"Since before I was born." She stared at the ceiling, pondering. "But it wasn't that long ago that Dedrick made him shield the others."

"He didn't always do that?"

"Evelyn said it was recent."

"Did you conduct his power so the others could be shielded?"

"No, Evelyn told me they used a spell."

Shielding the others must have been a very recent addition to their defense, because Nathan told me about the encounter in London with several of the Nefariouns. Dedrick's goons weren't shielded from anything that night, or during the fight at the airport when one of his people was killed.

Evelyn seemed to tell Rina a lot of valuable information. I could use that to work in my favor. "Has Evelyn explained how the candle thing works? How she can come and go from this room?"

"It's one of the many tricks Evelyn can perform."

"I wish I could come and go that easily."

Rina sighed. "Maryah, you're not even physically here like the rest of us. Stop being so inert. If you want to leave then do it."

"It's not that easy."

"It is that easy. Or it's that hard. It's whatever you believe."

"Okay, smarty-pants. If believing something into reality is so easy, then *believe* you can direct me on how to free myself."

"Use your energy."

"I tried. It doesn't work!"

She threw her hands up. "You should discuss this with Louise. She could give you better instructions."

"What do you mean? Why Louise?"

"She knows a lot about soul energy and the universe."

"Well, I'd love to speak to Louise, or any of my kindrily for that matter, but that doesn't seem likely anytime soon, does it?"

She grunted. "Only because you choose to be stuck here."

If I were in physical form, I would have had to restrain myself from smacking her.

READY FOR HER CLOSE-UP

Nathaniel

Traversing to a shrouded destination required an immense amount of energy. I had tried so many times to traverse to Rina, but I only ended up searching the void until I barely had enough strength to return home.

I hadn't slept much since Maryah left. Even when I did manage to sneak in a few minutes of rest, I dreamed about past events I never wanted to think about again: arguments with Mary, the horrors of wars, our deaths throughout the centuries, the time England suffered the plague and we watched our town dwindle to five percent of its population. My mind was spiraling into negativity, my thoughts darker than the black hole I had been searching.

I had to keep reminding myself that we weren't living in the past. We weren't hiding children to protect them from gas chambers or barbaric medical experiments. Our friends and family weren't covered in boils and vomiting blood. We had lived through worse—much worse. So why did it feel like surviving the Black Death would be easier than freeing Maryah from Dedrick?

Maryah's hand twitched, startling me from my trance-like staring at the ring on her thumb. Her eyelids fluttered open.

Rina had returned for another visit.

"Hi," she said, rubbing Maryah's nose.

Of all the strange things I'd seen throughout my existence, seeing a soul inhabit Maryah's body took the prize of most bizarre. "How is Maryah?"

She sat up and stretched. "She's stubborn and naive."

I tried to keep my tone pleasant, despite my indignation. "That's not a nice thing to say about someone you hardly know."

"I know her well enough."

She knew nothing about Maryah as far as I was concerned. "And to what do we owe this visit?"

"I enjoyed being outside." She glanced at the balcony. "I was hoping to try it again."

I had to figure out a way to barter with Rina for information. If she wanted simple experiences such as being outside then so be it. "That balcony is small. You should expand your horizons and venture to the back deck. The view is beautiful."

She enthusiastically agreed so I guided her out of the bedroom and down the hall. She paused, staring at Louise's paintings lining the walls. I waited for questions or a reaction, but after a few moments of studying them, she sniffed the air. "What's that smell?"

"Eggs and bacon. Louise is cooking breakfast."

"I like Louise."

"Would you care to say hello and eat something before we go outside?"

"That would be lovely. Thank you."

For being trapped in a so-called dungeon with limited interaction with the world and people, she had exceptional manners.

We rounded the corner into the kitchen. Louise finished tossing eggshells into the garbage bin then smiled at us. "Welcome back, Rina."

Rina waved while eying the sizzling eggs and bacon.

"Would you like some breakfast?" Louise asked.

"I'm not sure. I've never had those things before." Rina leaned over the stovetop. The bacon grease popped, and she jumped back, wiping Maryah's neck. "Ouch. It bit me."

"Bacon is a bit dangerous." Louise wet a dish towel and pressed it to Maryah's neck. "We'll stick with eggs for now. Sit and I'll make you a plate."

Louise waved her spatula at me, so I pulled out a stool, motioning for Rina to sit down. She clumsily climbed into her seat, appearing to not quite be in control of Maryah's limbs. Licking Maryah's lips, she watched Louise butter a slice of toast then began biting her nails.

"Please stop chewing Maryah's fingers," I said.

"I'm sorry. It's a bad habit."

"They aren't yours to mutilate."

She clasped Maryah's hands in her lap. "I'll try not to from now on."

"I'm sure Maryah would appreciate that."

Louise served Rina an egg sandwich, and Rina attacked it ravenously. The entire time she ate, I pondered what her true motives were for visiting us again.

∞

I tossed Eightball's gator into the pond. He bounded after it then belly-flopped into the water. Rina giggled as he chomped hold of his toy and paddled his way out.

"I like him." She seemed to like everyone—or at least claimed to.

"I suspect he likes you as well."

"Only because I'm in Maryah's body."

"He knows the difference between the two of you."

I stayed silent for a few moments, contemplating whether or not to reveal my failed attempts at traversing to wherever she and Maryah were being imprisoned. "The darkness that you spoke of when visitors come and go from the place you live, how long does it last?"

"A few seconds."

"Do you know how or why it's needed to enter and exit the room?"

"Because there are no doors or windows."

"Do you know how it works? How others travel in and out?"

Maryah's forehead wrinkled with suspicion. "Why are you asking?"

I needed to obtain more information. I didn't know how long I had before she'd disappear again. "I'm wondering if there's a way for me to visit you."

"You mean visit Maryah."

Why lie to her? The girl seemed intelligent. "She is my first priority, but you would be there as well."

"You can't visit us."

"Why not?"

"Because it's too dangerous."

She didn't say it was impossible. She didn't question how I would travel there, or how I'd even figure out where *there* was. Did she know I could traverse? "I'm willing to risk the danger."

She spoke softly. "I'm not."

"Why should my safety matter to you?"

"Because you're too important." She pressed Maryah's hair to her lips. "You're too important to Maryah."

The fidgeting of her hands and feet suggested she was either lying or uncomfortable. I couldn't figure out her angle. Was she working with Dedrick or not?

"Is Dedrick the only one who controls who comes and goes?" I asked.

"Stop it."

"Stop what?"

"Stop trying to find a way in. Let her find the way out."

Every muscle in my body went rigid. "Is there a way out?"

"There's always a way, but if you don't let her embrace her own power, you will enable her to remain weak."

I gaped at her. "You know how she can free her soul?"

She bit Maryah's thumb and stepped back.

"Rina!" I advanced on her, matching each of her steps backward. "If you know how she can free herself, you must help her."

Her voice quivered as subtly as the breeze that blew Maryah's hair across her face. "I can't interfere."

She did know. She knew how to free Maryah. My pulse pounded in every cell of my skin. "Interfere with what?"

"The plan."

"Whose plan?"

She just stared at me, not uttering a word. I wanted to shake her until every last bit of what she knew came spilling out, but I worried I'd scare her away and I couldn't risk that. I spoke gingerly. "Rina, please, you have no idea how precious she is to me. If you know how to help her—"

"I do know how precious she is." The wispy hint of fondness in her voice was gone with her next cutting words. "You're not there. You don't know what I know. You haven't seen what I've seen. You have to let me do what needs to be done or none of it will have mattered."

Questions raced through my mind. "Please tell me what you know. What needs to be done? None of what will have mattered? Rina, let us help you."

"Not yet!" She pressed her palms over Maryah's face as she groaned. "You can't rush it. Please stop trying or you'll ruin everything!"

"Rush what? Ruin what?"

Her eyes widened like my questions were angering her more. She knew more than we suspected. I could feel it as sure as the sunlight beating down on us. Louise was right. She was more powerful than she seemed. I put my hands up in surrender. "All right, all right, no more questions. Just tell me what you need me to do to help Maryah help herself."

She took two deep breaths before speaking again. "I need you to trust me."

"I don't want to lie to you. Do you understand how difficult it is for me to trust you?"

Pain flashed in her eyes. In *her* eyes, *her* soul, not Maryah's. "Why? I've never done anything to make you suspect I'm not trustworthy."

"You're in Maryah's body with knowledge of how she can return to it, yet you won't tell me or her how, or everything you know about Dedrick."

Maryah's bottom lip quivered. "Because I can't."

"But I don't understand why you can't. You speak in vague circles. I'm sorry, but that leads me to suspect you might be in cahoots with Dedrick."

"Cahoots." She stepped forward. A fierce darkness bubbled beneath the surface. "Nathaniel, some day you will know what I know, and you will understand why I couldn't tell you, and it will all make sense, just as everything always does, and you will be very, *very* sorry that you ever doubted me, and that you ever accused me of being in *cahoots* with Dedrick."

A bead of sweat trickled down my spine. Her personality seemed almost bipolar with how she switched from childlike to confident. "I look forward to that day."

"Me too, but until then, please let me do what I'm destined to do when I'm meant to do it."

Destined? Who was this girl? "I'll stop asking questions if you promise me one thing."

She tilted Maryah's head inquisitively.

"Help free Maryah. If you do, we will do everything in our power to find you and help you escape."

"It's not about escaping. It's about fighting."

"Fighting Dedrick?"

"It's so much more than that."

"Then fighting for what?" I asked.

She leaned closer. "The answer to that question is infinite."

"I sense this is bigger than you and me. Whatever you're trying to accomplish, we'll help you. All I ask in exchange is that you help Maryah free her soul."

She bowed her head and snorted. "That's what I've been doing. She can't grasp how simple it is."

"She has had to absorb an impossible amount of knowledge in a very short time. She can't do this alone. Please, help her." I touched Maryah's arm.

Rina flinched. Her soul stared back at me.

She placed her hand on top of mine, slowly, as if she were afraid to touch me. She pursed Maryah's lips then gazed out at the horizon of red rocks. What felt like an eternity passed before she spoke. "If I do free her, do you swear on your life that you'll help us fight?"

No vow had ever been so easy to make. "I swear on all my lives, past, present, and future."

"I will hold you to that." She squeezed my index finger before letting go.

Rina stepped to the railing of the deck and lifted Maryah's face toward the sun. Would she keep her word and help Maryah? Did she truly intend to fight Dedrick? If so, what were the infinite reasons she had mentioned? I needed answers, but couldn't chance pushing her too far too soon.

Rina lifted Maryah's hands, delicately weaving them through the air in front of her as if she could feel the sunshine the way evolved Elements could.

The patio door opened, and Dakota walked out.

He stared at Rina for a few seconds, watching her bask in the sunlight, but then he focused on me. "Harmony told me, but I wanted to see for myself."

Rina was in her own world. She paid no attention to us. Her eyes were still closed, and her smile had grown wider.

Dakota stood beside me and whispered, "Can we trust her?"

I shook my head.

"How long is she staying?"

I shrugged.

"What is she doing?"

"Basking in the sun."

He rubbed the eraser of his pencil against his temple. "I feel the need to draw her."

"Be my guest."

Dakota sat at the patio table and started sketching. For a few minutes, I wondered how long Rina would continue her sun worshiping. I tried imagining what it must be like for her, living with no natural light. She eventually stopped and opened her eyes.

"It's so magnificent." Rina spotted Dakota and froze in place. "Oh."

Dakota had stopped sketching to watch her, but when they looked at each other, Dakota rose to his feet and crept toward her.

"Rina," I said, "this is our friend Dakota."

"Duh-koh-ta." She enunciated each syllable in a hushed voice.

Dakota stopped with only inches between them. "You look familiar."

Harmony joined us. "Of course she looks familiar. She's in Maryah's body."

"That's not what I mean." Dakota shook his head. "Her eyes look familiar."

Energy prickled at the back of my neck. Dakota had been at the airport and helped fight a few of the Nefariouns. Faith said two were women, but they had worn sunglasses most of the time. *Most* of the time. Had Dakota glimpsed one of their souls? Did he recognize her?

"I feel like I know you," Dakota said to Rina.

"Damn," Harmony muttered beside me. "If only Sheila were alive. She could read her and tell us who she was in her past lives."

I almost hushed Harmony, still in protective mode of our kindrily's abilities, but revealing Sheila's ability couldn't hurt anything, considering she was no longer with us. My own heart ached at the reminder.

Dakota stepped closer to her. "It's sort of weird meeting you like this, you being in Maryah's body and all."

Rina looked down as if she'd forgotten she wasn't completely herself. "I don't look anything like this."

"I figured." Dakota pushed his bangs off his forehead. "What do you look like?"

Rina studied Harmony. "My hair is the color of hers, but only the black parts. And much longer."

Dakota perked up. "Sit down and describe details so I can draw you."

"Draw me?"

He grabbed his sketch of her enjoying the sun and handed it to her. "Like this, a picture. Except I'd draw you instead of Maryah."

"This is very good. Much better than the pictures in my dictionary."

"Thank you." Dakota pulled out a chair for Rina.

Harmony and I stood side by side, arms crossed over our chests, never taking our eyes off them. Rina explained her physical features and Dakota drew them. She'd tell him if it was correct or not, that her nose was smaller, her eyes bigger, her hair longer.

"Rina," I interrupted, "How do you know what you look like? Is there a mirror where you live?"

"I see my reflection in the glass cabinet in my room."

Dakota stopped sketching. He held his pad out in front of him, squinting at it. Turning semi-pale, he dropped the pad. "I'll be right back."

As he ran inside the house, I glanced at Harmony and she shrugged.

Rina twiddled Maryah's thumbs while frowning. "He didn't like how I look."

It was as if Maryah had returned. The lack of self-confidence combined with Maryah's face and body language oozing disappointment made me rush to her side.

"I'm sure that's not why he ran off." I touched her shoulder and she startled.

"I have to go."

"No!" Harmony and I both said in unison.

Rina's eyes closed. I caught her head as Maryah's body went limp and collapsed forward.

"Rina?" I said softly, but I felt the absence of her. No soul existed in Maryah's body.

Dakota ran back out onto the deck holding a comic book. "What happened?"

I picked a piece of egg from her shirt. "She's gone."

"What? I told her I'd be right back."

"I'm not certain, but I got the impression she was scared." I pushed Maryah's hair from her face and gathered her in my arms.

"I didn't mean to scare her," Dakota said. "I swear."

"I don't think it was you." Harmony ruffled his hair. "My guess is something, or someone, was pulling her back to her body."

Dakota's hands fell at his side, still clutching his rolled-up comic book. "I wanted to show her one of my stories." He thumbed through a few pages and held it up for Harmony to see. "I think she might be this girl."

Harmony bit her lip, the doubt etched all over her face. Instead of telling Dakota his drawings weren't real, she forced a smile and said, "She's pretty."

I eased past them, carrying Maryah's body to the bedroom.

Dakota sounded like he'd just lost his best friend. "I hope she comes back soon."

Several of us had gathered in the dining room, but it wasn't an official meeting.

"This isn't fair!" Dakota slammed his comic book on the table. "You guys need to start taking me seriously. Look at it." He pointed to an open page. "I drew that Maryah was encased in a snow globe and now that's what's going on. Okay, so it might not be a snow globe exactly, but Rina said it's a bubble. Close enough."

Faith popped her chewing gum. "I read it, but I figured you drew Maryah in a snow globe because Carson made one for his school project."

Carson was leaning against the back of Krista's chair. "Actually, the snow globe was Dakota's idea first. I was inspired by his drawing."

Gregory flipped through the pages. He held up a drawing of a girl draping her long black hair out of a tall castle window like Rapunzel. "Who is this girl?"

"That's Rina!" Dakota said, exasperated.

"How do you know that's her?" Faith asked.

"She described what she looked like, and it sounds exactly like her."

"You drew the castle nestled into the side of a mountain." Carson pointed at the comic. "Do you have any idea where the castle might be?"

"No." Dakota lowered his eyes and shrugged. "That's just what came to me when I drew it."

Krista looked up at me. "What if he really is drawing some sort of psychic interpretation of what's going on?"

Exhaling, I shook my head.

"Krista," Harmony stretched her name, warning her not to encourage the issue.

"Stop shutting down the idea," Carson argued. "Dakota has drawn some stuff that is actually happening. Of all the things this kindrily is capable of, and considering how badly Dakota wanted to be one of us, why is it so far-fetched that he might have developed a supernatural ability after his near-death experience?"

Everyone was silent. Yes, Carson was Dakota's best friend, but he wouldn't argue on his behalf unless he truly believed it might be possible.

"I told you," Dakota said, glancing around at all of us. "I feel different." He raked his fingers through his hair. "It's like I see story lines in my head sometimes, and I can't think about anything else until I draw them. I drew Harmony finding Gregory. That fight at the airport? I drew that!"

"You did?" I asked, shocked no one had mentioned it.

Dakota grunted and tugged at his bangs. "Does anyone ever read any of my comics?"

"I do," Carson said.

"Where is that comic?" Gregory asked.

"I gave it to Harmony as a gift before you came back."

Everyone glared at Harmony. She guiltily spun her eyebrow ring. "There's been a lot going on. I didn't have a chance to read the whole thing."

"Good grief, Harmony." Faith cracked her bubblegum. "Let me borrow your boots so I can give you a swift kick in the—"

"Faith," Louise chided. "Save the sibling bickering for another time. Harmony, where is the comic book right now?"

"In my room," Harmony said.

"Where exactly?" I asked.

"Top desk drawer."

I traversed to Harmony's room, grabbed the comic from the drawer, and returned to the meeting.

Dakota snatched it from my hand. He flipped to the end then slapped the book onto the table and pointed to a cartoon drawing of Harmony and Gregory surrounded by flames, reuniting in front of a spaceship. I raised my brows. Not exactly a clear depiction of what happened at the airport.

Dakota saw my reaction and sighed. "Okay, so a few details were wrong. It was a plane instead of a spaceship, and the laser guns were regular guns, but there was fire."

Gregory sat forward, snickering as he read the dialogue bubbles. "Your theory was that I had been abducted by aliens?"

Dakota shrugged. "Close enough."

We were back where we started. Dakota was a skilled artist, but he wasn't psychic, and his stories weren't predicting the future. However, I was convinced that he and Rina had seen each other before—possibly at the airport. If we could discern who she was, it might help us know whether or not to trust her.

NOTHING COMES FREE

Maryah

I felt like I was getting weaker, but how could that be possible without a body?

"If your soul were free to travel—" Rina chewed her fingers. "You would really spy on Dedrick?"

"Of course."

"And?"

"And what?" Having a conversation with her was so difficult.

"Where else would you go? Honestly."

Lying to her seemed pointless. I needed her to trust me and this one seemed like a given. "Honestly, I'd visit my kindrily. Because I miss them, but also because they are super wise and could help us."

"Nathaniel said he would help stop Dedrick."

"Obviously. He despises Dedrick. We all do."

Rina's face was emotionless. She didn't look away or even blink. After what felt like a long time, she quietly said, "Okay."

Hope pulsed through me. "Okay what?"

"I'll release you."

"*You* can release me?"

She tentatively nodded.

"Just like that? You've had the ability to release me this whole time, but you kept me trapped here? Why? Does Dedrick know?"

"So many questions," Rina mumbled.

"Um, you think?" I was furious. My suspicions had just risen tenfold. "What's your part in all this? How could you hide so much from Dedrick for so long? Maybe he does know how powerful you are and you're helping him, and all this time you've been trying to act like we can trust each other, but in reality you might be the most evil Nefarioun of them all."

She lurched forward. "I am not evil!"

"Then why would you keep me here like a prisoner?"

"I was hoping you'd figure out how to set yourself free."

"Why would I need to figure it out if you could do it for me?"

Her eyes widened. "Listen to yourself. Me do it for you? Is that how you want to live your life? Counting on others to fix your mistakes? Everyone else should figure out how to get you out of trouble? Wouldn't it be more dignified if you learned how to do it yourself?"

She made me sound like some lazy leech who wanted to sit around eating ice cream all day while everyone else worked for me. "I can handle my own problems, but I didn't ask to be trapped here. This isn't my mistake to fix."

She snorted a laugh. "You traveled here, Maryah. It is your mistake." She walked to the table and ran her fingers over the old book. "You have a lot of mistakes to fix, and I can only help you so much."

I screamed with frustration. "Stop talking in riddles! You act like you know so much, but you never actually say or do anything helpful."

She lifted her gaze, her eyes reflecting some emotion I hadn't seen before, maybe part sadness but with an accusatory heat burning somewhere deep within her. Her pained voice was almost a whisper. "I never do anything helpful?"

I could tell I hurt her feelings, and I considered apologizing, but for what? For speaking the truth? I wasn't sorry for that. She was frustrating, and she hadn't done anything to help. All she had done was use my body without my consent.

She stood straight and cleared her throat. "I'll do what you've asked. Like I always do." She held her hands out at her sides, closed her eyes, and bowed her head.

"Rina, wait. I'm sorry I lost my temper."

She didn't acknowledge me. She stayed in place, unmoving.

"Rina?"

I felt different—stronger. The invisible cloud around me had dissipated. I searched my mind's eye for the cords of light that allowed me to astral travel—the cords I hadn't been able to see or feel since I arrived in this dreaded place.

I found them, glowing brightly, more visible than they'd ever been. Rina did it. She was setting me free.

"Rina?" I couldn't leave like this. As frustrating as she was, she didn't deserve to be hurt. She had already suffered more than one person ever should. "Please answer me."

She still didn't move, open her eyes, or say a word.

"I won't be gone more than an hour or two," I told her. "I promise I'll be back."

As scary as those words sounded, I knew I meant them.

KEEPING IN TOUCH

Nathaniel

Everyone had gone to bed for the evening, but I couldn't sleep. One of Maryah's favorite songs played for the third time. I lay beside her, singing along with Ella. The same song that played as Mary passed away two lifetimes ago, so peaceful and undramatic. Just she and I at home, our bodies aged and exhausted, waiting for the curtain to fall and allow us to start all over again. She passed quietly, drifting to sleep in my arms while Ella sang on our record player. I couldn't hear it because I was deaf, but I felt the music in the air.

I passed two days later, looking forward to the next time I'd hold her and wondering what my new life and body would be like.

A trumpet played a soft, slow riff as the song came to an end. Unlike two lifetimes ago, I was grateful to hear the music. Being deaf enhanced many of my senses, but I had missed music immensely.

Maryah thrashed violently then choked in a deep breath. Eightball barked and sprang out of his bed, his nubby tail wagging uncontrollably.

"Nathan!" She sat up and threw her arms around me in one burst of motion.

I pulled back to confirm it was her.

"Maryah." I kissed her. "You have no idea how worried I've been."

Her fingertips pressed into my pecs as if trying to clutch onto the heart that already belonged to her. I held her hands and kissed them then pressed my forehead against hers. "I'm here. I'm right here, and so are you. You're safe."

She touched my face, staring into my eyes as if I might not be real. "I missed you so much."

"I missed you infinitely more." I caressed her cheek. "How do you feel?"

"I'm okay." Eightball whined and pawed at the bed. I lifted him up to join us, and he tackled Maryah, covering her with kisses.

After their reunion had calmed down, she hugged him and said, "I'm shook up and thirsty, but relieved to be back here."

I wrapped my arms around both of them and traversed us to the kitchen. I set them down on the counter, letting go of Maryah long enough to grab a bottle of juice. She gulped it down as I stood and watched her in the glow of the light from the refrigerator.

Eightball snorted happily. His whole back end wagged as he squirmed in her arms, licking her chin. She giggled, and my heart overflowed.

She took a long swig of juice then lowered the bottle and wiped her lips. "Thank you."

I nodded then kissed her again, tasting the fruit punch she just drank and assuring myself this was really happening. She was back in her body. She was safe. "Never again," I said. "I'm so sorry."

She pulled away. "Why are you sorry? You didn't do anything wrong."

"I felt so helpless knowing you were trapped with Dedrick and there was nothing I could do. Never again will you astral travel to him. None of us will ever ask you to."

"Nathan," Maryah said, "I'm going back."

"Absolutely not," I argued. "We'll figure out another way to stop Dedrick without putting you in danger."

"Dedrick can't know I left. I came here to tell you I was fine, and to relay everything I know, but then I have to go back."

"That wasn't part of the deal."

"Deal? What deal?"

"I promised Rina we'd help her fight Dedrick if she set you free. I never agreed that you'd return to his lair."

"He'll kill Rina if he finds out I'm gone. Or torture her. Then he'll come after us." Her voice hitched with concern. "All of us."

Krista and Carson hurried into the kitchen wearing their pajamas. "Pudding!" Krista exclaimed. "It's really you. Thank goodness!"

I stepped aside so Krista could hug Maryah, but I was still trying to absorb the fact that Maryah would voluntarily go back to Dedrick. Louise and Anthony rushed in too.

"Thank the heavens!" Louise said, taking her turn to hug Maryah. "What happened? Tell us everything."

"You look exhausted," Anthony told Maryah. "Do you need to sleep first?"

Maryah shook her head then her eyes found mine. "I have to update you then I have to go back."

My heart sank again.

"Go back?" Louise and Krista asked at the same time.

"The girl who visited you; her name is Rina, and Dedrick is keeping her prisoner. It's so awful. You can't even imagine. I have to help her, and if Dedrick finds out that she helped me escape then who knows what he'll do to her."

Carson moved to Maryah's side. "Where is he? Do you know where he was keeping you?"

"No," Maryah answered. "We're locked in some room with no doors or windows."

"At least Rina was telling the truth," Carson said.

"She had never left that room until she traveled here and met all of you. If you could see it for yourself, you'd understand how horrible her life is and that I need to help her." Maryah sat up so tall and fast it looked like she'd been whipped. "Wait, Rina was here! Nathan, you saw her soul through her eyes, right? You could traverse to her and bring her here."

"Sorry, Sparky," Carson said. "We've been trying that already, and it hasn't worked."

"Why?" Maryah asked me. "Can you not picture her eyes in detail because it's my body?"

"That's not it," I explained. "Every time I try, I find myself in darkness. I don't end up anywhere."

Her forehead wrinkled. "What does that mean?"

"We're not sure yet," Louise said. "But we're working on it."

We all stood around as Carson asked the necessary questions for his exceptional mind to figure out as much as he could.

I wanted to argue that Maryah's safety came first, and she shouldn't astral travel anywhere until we had more helpful information, but Maryah was still Mary. The deepest, truest part of her would always be dedicated to helping others. No one would convince her to turn her back on Rina. As much as I wanted Maryah home safe with us, I couldn't in good conscience ask her not to help Rina.

"What if it is a trap?" Carson asked. "What if Dedrick is using this girl to get to you somehow?"

Maryah hugged Eightball tighter, petting his head. "Rina hates him. She's not mind-controlled. And I think she's an Element. She has gifts like us."

"We know she's a conductor," Louise said, "and that she traveled here using your ability, but can she do anything else?"

"I think so, but I'm not sure what exactly. Somehow she freed my soul. She's sort of secretive about everything."

"Secretive indeed," I agreed. "This whole time she was able to free you, but she didn't until I promised her I'd help her fight Dedrick."

"Like kill him?" Carson sounded a little too excited about the idea.

"How can we trust that's her real intention in all of this?" Krista asked.

"You all met her," Maryah said. "Sort of. Did you get the impression she was bad?"

"Her soul was luminescent," Louise said. "Not one trace of malicious intent."

"She could have been emanating a false aura," I pointed out.

Louise glared at me over her glasses. "No one can fake their aura."

"We didn't think a soul's energy could be trapped," I argued, "but obviously Dedrick is capable of more than we thought." I placed my hand on top of Maryah's. "We have to be overly cautious of everyone and everything given the circumstances."

"I feel the same way, but why would Rina release my soul?" Maryah held my hand as Eightball licked it. "She helped me. I have to help her too."

Anthony chimed in. "It would be beneficial to know what else she knows about Dedrick and what he's been doing these past two decades."

"Which is one of the many reasons I have to return," Maryah said. "I need to find out a lot more if we have any hope of stopping Dedrick."

"Stop him from what?" Krista asked.

Maryah slid off the counter and stood, setting Eightball on the floor. "He's going to *be* God. He's going to control who comes into this world." Louise and Anthony glanced at each other. Maryah squeezed my hand. "What does that mean?"

"It means you're right," Louise said. "You have to spy on him so we can see what he's planning."

Everyone stared at Maryah, but she kept her focus on me. "Nathan, please try to understand. I need your support now more than ever."

As much as I wanted to shelter her and keep her locked safe in my arms, I knew her spirit couldn't be caged. Especially not by Dedrick. "Then as always, you have it."

WEIGHT OF HER WORLD

Maryah

I finished showering and stepped out of the bathroom, towel drying my hair. Nathan stood on the balcony staring out at the night sky. The door was open, so I snuck up behind him, wrapping my arms around him and resting my head against his strong back. He already carried centuries of pain and worry, and without meaning to, I kept adding more. I prayed he wouldn't break under the weight of it all.

He turned to hold me in his arms. I breathed in his nectar-of-the-gods scent and from the deepest trenches of my memory came a deluge of déjà vu. Skin tingling, sheets rustling, the sensation of being blissfully sated, body and soul. My guttural sigh brought me back to the present.

In a perfect world, I could stay wrapped up in him forever, but our life was far from perfect. "My time is almost up. I promised Rina no more than two hours."

Nathan lifted my chin. The stars shone behind him, but they dulled in comparison to the love in his eyes. "When will you be back?"

"I'm not sure. We didn't discuss that yet. This was a test. Hopefully she'll let me leave more frequently." An all too familiar wave of pain spread up the back of my neck. The beginning of a headache. I didn't want to worry Nathan even more, so I did my best to ignore it.

"What if Dedrick finds out you're able to travel?"

"We have to make sure he doesn't."

"I hate that you're enduring this type of stress and danger."

"I'll be fine."

"I wish I could believe that." He stroked my face while looking at me with so much worry it made me wish I could erase emotions instead of memories. "Find out where you are. That's crucial. If we know where he's keeping Rina, we can rescue her."

"I have a feeling Dedrick has that place well-guarded. Wherever it is."

"We will get her out." He sounded so confident. "Just do your best to find out where it is. Pay attention to details, even the smallest ones."

"I will, but not much happens unless someone visits."

"Visits?"

I stayed focused on the facts instead of my brewing migraine. "So far there's a woman, Evelyn, who brings Rina meals and is sort of a mother figure to her, but her eyes are snakelike so she's being controlled. Dedrick has also brought in Lexie, the mind reader, and River."

Nathan's biceps and forearms flexed as he scowled. "River?"

"Don't worry. He never stays long, and I don't believe a word he says. He claims Dedrick is keeping him locked up too. Dedrick wants me to believe he's protecting me from River, but they're probably working together."

"I don't like this, Maryah. What if River tries to kill you again?"

Despite my headache, I grinned. "Nathan, he can't kill me if I'm not in my body."

Nathan blinked rapidly, as if that fact had momentarily escaped him. "Right, but still. Be careful. Dedrick is a master manipulator. Be on high alert for any way he could be deceiving you or using someone against you. Especially River."

"I'm alert as can be."

Nathan's Adam's apple bobbed as worry lines framed his mouth. "Louise swears she saw no negativity in Rina's aura, but I'm suspicious of her as well. Dedrick leaves you alone with her for long stretches of time. He must have a reason, and I suspect that reason is so you'll become friends with her."

"I'd know if she were up to something, but she's not." I was surprised to hear the lie tumble so easily from my lips. I was confused by Rina's words and questioned her intentions almost every time she spoke, but I couldn't worry Nathan or the rest of our kindrily. Deep down, I really believed Rina had a good heart, but my instincts also screamed that she was hiding something big.

A shooting pain forced me to squeeze my eyes shut. I was looking forward to checking out of my body again. The pain had spread behind my ears, which meant this headache would be a bad one.

"What's wrong?" Nathan asked. He leaned so close his minty breath cooled my cheek. "Is it a headache?"

I tried acting like it was no big deal. "Good timing. At least I won't be in my body to suffer through it."

"I'm not sure if that's good or bad."

"Trust me. It's good."

"Please be careful," Nathan said, concern dripping from his voice. "Don't share any information about us with Rina. Don't give her anything she could use against you later."

I almost told Nathan about my fear that she'd travel to my body and never return to her own. That she'd realize she could break free forever by living as me, but if I expressed that possibility out loud, he'd never support me going back. And I wouldn't blame him.

"I'll be careful," I promised.

"Maryah." His next words were laced with sadness. "We need to discuss a lot about our past, but I'm not sure where to start."

My two hours were up, and my headache was getting worse. "We'll discuss everything, but it has to wait. I can't break my promise to Rina the first time she let me out."

He somberly nodded, holding my hand as we walked inside. I crawled into bed, and he leaned over me, kissing me with such tenderness that it almost made me change my mind about leaving him. "I love you. Come home soon."

His worried green eyes were the last thing I saw before I closed my own and focused on the cords of light that would return me to Rina.

∞

Rina sat up on her bed, brushing her hair out of her face. "You came back."

"I promised you I would."

"People have promised me a lot of things that weren't true."

"I'm not one of those people."

She smirked. "That's refreshing to know."

"We're safe, right? Dedrick didn't stop by while I was gone?"

"No one visited except Manny."

"Who?"

She gathered her hair and draped it over one shoulder. Her mouse poked its head out from behind her neck. "Manny the mouse."

"Ah, I didn't realize he had a name."

"I assume your trip was a success?" Rina asked. "You look happier."

"As successful as it could be in such a short time. I feel stronger, better. I feel less lost and desperate."

Rina crossed her legs and picked at the dirty, frayed cuff of her pants. "So what now?"

"When do you think Evelyn will visit again?"

"I'm never sure. She visits whenever she can."

"Ask her if Dedrick will be visiting anytime soon. If not, I'd like to astral travel again so I can see what he's up to. I also plan on figuring out where we are."

She perked up. "I like that plan."

I wasn't sure whether I was relieved or worried that Rina liked my plan. "I've been thinking. Dedrick knows you're a conductor, so wouldn't he worry that you would use my power to astral travel?"

"He believes I can conduct, but not use anyone's power as my own. I need it to stay that way."

"That's an awfully big secret to keep hidden from Dedrick for so many years."

A mischievous grin cracked her dry lips. "I've kept much bigger."

"Will I ever get let in on all of your big secrets?"

"I tell you what you need to know when you need to know it." She had barely finished her last word when the candle snuffed out, leaving us both in the dark.

TELLING IT ON THE MOUNTAIN

Maryah

Conveniently, as if on cue, Evelyn visited.

Evelyn told Rina that Dedrick had been gone since yesterday and he wasn't scheduled back until tomorrow. She didn't ask Rina why she wanted information on his whereabouts or what she was planning, which seemed suspicious.

Then again, maybe Evelyn wasn't worried because Dedrick wasn't around to catch Rina doing anything wrong. I was so back and forth on who and what to trust. It's like my instincts were short-circuiting and giving me no strong indicator either way.

After Evelyn left us, Rina offered to let me travel without me even asking. It seemed too easy. She was almost too eager. I would spy on Dedrick just like I said, but maybe I also needed to spy on Rina.

I focused on Dedrick's morally dead eyes, cringing at first, but then giving into the flow of energy connecting me to him. Like being pulled along by a current, I rushed through a tunnel of light until it dumped me into the cesspool of Dedrick's energy.

We were outside at what appeared to be the base of a mountain. No one else was around. Dedrick's hair was pulled back in a ponytail, whipping against the hood of his heavy coat due to the wind. I couldn't feel temperature in soul form, but based on the snow on the ground and Dedrick's heavy clothes and boots, I would have guessed he was hiking through Alaska or somewhere just as cold and remote.

He walked for a long time. The only sound he made was a sniffle of his runny nose.

"What in the world are you doing out here?" Even though I whispered the question, I worried he might hear me. I couldn't assume anything about what he could or couldn't do.

He reached a place I wouldn't have recognized as much different from the rest of the ground he had been trekking across, except that he fell to his knees, pressed his hands and forehead to the snow and chanted. He repeated the process so many times I lost count.

He lifted his face and palms skyward and then—I couldn't believe it—he unzipped his coat and removed it, followed by his sweater and thermal shirt.

I glanced away, repulsed by the sight of his hairy chest. The last person in the world I wanted to see half naked was Dedrick, but I had to look again because scars and cuts covered his arms, chest, and stomach.

He started reciting prayers about guidance and enlightenment. Every deity in the universe was probably laughing at the irony.

Finishing his prayer, he said, "I have completed my one hundred and seventh circle of your sacred temple. Please accept this as a demonstration of my loyalty."

He pulled something out of his pocket that looked like a curved blade made from ivory or—I hated considering the possibility—bone. Without even flinching or showing any discomfort at all, he cut a deep gash into a non-scarred area of his stomach. "My next and final lap will complete my pledge. I shall be a vessel for you to fill with your power."

His blood dripped onto the snow as he shivered and spoke to the sky. I knew he was a sicko, but this was too much. I'd heard rumors about a few kids being cutters in school, but self-mutilation as part of a spiritual ritual was a whole new level of crazy.

Dedrick stood, gathering his clothes, and then continued walking. After several minutes, we reached a lake that was so serene I wanted to sleep on its glistening, perfectly still surface.

I gasped when Dedrick jumped in, pants, boots, and all. He disappeared under the water for only a second before bursting through the surface and gasping for breath. It sounded like his lungs were already frozen. Was he trying to kill himself?

He crawled out, shaking and shivering so hard I could hear his teeth banging together. He sprawled out on the snow-covered ground wheezing and convulsing.

I wanted to tell him he was certifiable. I also wanted to tie an anchor to his feet and shove him back in the lake, but I couldn't do anything, so I just watched and said my own prayer. "Please, *please* let this be the death of you."

He lay curled in a fetal position. I saw nothing and no one around anywhere. How would he get away from here and into someplace warm? Dedrick was too strategic to die of hypothermia.

When I looked down at him again, he was pulling a large stone from his bag. It almost looked like a giant ruby, but not as shiny. He held it above his head and uttered words in a language I didn't recognize. The stone lit up, glowing bright red and orange.

He clutched it to his chest, and within moments his shivering subsided. The stone was warming him.

Dedrick muttered "thank you" over and over again. His words grew stronger and louder as the stone warmed him and he regained his strength. He dressed, and as he zipped up his coat he stared out over the lake. "Help her to see the truth. Help her remember."

"Holy Fruit Loops, you better not be talking about me," I said. "I don't want any part of your maniacal mountain ritual."

A thwacking noise hummed faintly in the distance. As it grew louder, a helicopter rounded the mountain peak. Dedrick put on sunglasses and walked to the stretch of flat land where the helicopter landed.

I stared through the windshield at the female pilot, silently cursing the familiar face looking through me. I had just seen her. She said Dedrick wouldn't be back until tomorrow, but she never said she would be with him.

"Evelyn," I grumbled as Dedrick climbed in beside her.

I officially added her to my *Can't Be Trusted* list. I moved closer, penetrating the helicopter's exterior like a ghost. Inside, I stared at the back of both of their heads, anxious to see where they were going, or perhaps overhear Evelyn mention their location. As the chopper lifted, the sky grew brighter until everything, including Dedrick and Evelyn, transformed to pure white. Even the sound of the blades cutting through the air faded to silence.

I floated there, searching the white void around me. No mountains, no wind, nothing at all.

I had lost them.

∞

I no longer trusted Evelyn or her relationship with Rina.

When I returned, I told Rina about Dedrick's cutting ceremony and his dip in the lake. I explained how he used the glowing stone to warm himself, but then I altered the story. She couldn't know that I saw Evelyn helping him, just in case Rina was in on it somehow. I finished the abbreviated version of what happened. "After he put his clothes on, I felt so weak and tired that I came back."

"Your soul felt weak?" Rina asked.

I had just updated her on Dedrick's walkabout in the arctic, slicing open his skin, diving into a frozen lake, and a magic stone warming him like a space heater, but her first question was about my soul being tired?

"Yes," I lied. "I felt like my ability to travel back here might be in jeopardy."

She narrowed her eyes as she scanned me up and down. "Hmm."

"What?"

She bit her nails and after several tense seconds said, "No clues as to where he was, or where we are?"

"Only that there were snow and mountains."

"I wonder how he got there."

A helicopter flown by your beloved Auntie Evelyn, who you're either working with or shouldn't be trusting. I wanted to say that, but instead I went with, "I'll have to spy on him again next time Evelyn assures us it's safe."

Rina stopped biting her nails, but she kept her hand over her lips. Creases formed around her eyes. She looked as skeptical of me as I was of Evelyn.

"Time to rest." Rina walked over to her mattress, bending down to arrange her blanket.

"Actually, I was hoping to visit my kindrily and tell them about Dedrick's strange adventure before I forget the details."

She kept her back to me, snapping her blanket and smoothing out the wrinkles. "I thought your soul was tired."

I offered a quick save. "Right, but checking into my body might restore some of my strength."

Turning, she glared at me. "I trusted *you*. Now how do I gain your trust?"

She knew I was hiding something from her. I didn't want to keep lying to her. "I'm trusting you as much as I can given the circumstances."

She crawled onto her mattress and pulled her blanket over her head, but the energy cords that allowed me to reconnect with my body appeared, glowing brightly.

"Thank you, Rina."

She didn't answer.

HIGHER EXISTING

Nathaniel

I stood on our cliffs—the place where Maryah and I shared our first kiss of this lifetime, where we had so many meaningful conversations, where I had tried to teach her how to sensperience, where I wished she were standing beside me, her hand in mine.

I reminisced about the first time we stood atop these same red rocks in our last life. Mary had said Sedona was a place of positive energy, that settling here would make her (and the rest of our kindrily) stronger mentally, emotionally, and spiritually.

We had hiked to the top just in time to see our first breathtaking sunset over Sedona. Construction on our home began the next week, delayed for so long because Mary couldn't decide if she wanted the front door to face the northeast or south. She hadn't been able to determine for certain which would be more harmonious. It was too important to guess, Mary had said. Guessing left too much to chance. She never left anything to chance.

She walked our property every day—every sunrise and every sunset. Many nights we slept under the stars in a sleeping bag surrounded by construction materials and Mary's notebook filled with ever-changing ideas and sketches of what must be added to our new home.

I never fought her on one idea or detail. After spending hundreds of years with her, I knew arguing about anything from tile color to the need for an underground weapon room was pointless. She would get whatever she envisioned, because nothing was more important to me than seeing her happy.

Eightball snorted at my feet. I glanced down at him, and he turned his big head inquisitively, probably curious about my sudden smile. "Yes, old boy. I'm daydreaming about your mother."

He head-butted my shin as I squatted down to rub his ears. My phone rang, and I fumbled to pull it from my back pocket. When I saw *Home* on the screen, I traversed Eightball back to the house with me.

I appeared in the kitchen, facing Louise as she hung up the phone.

"There they are," Maryah said from behind me. "My two favorite boys."

It was a close race for which of us reached Maryah first.

∞

After Maryah finished reporting Dedrick's recent whereabouts and fielded questions from a few members, the meeting fell silent as we processed it all.

I exchanged concerned glances with Edgar, Helen, and Louise.

Louise pushed her glasses to the top of her head and rubbed the bridge of her nose. "Let's not beat around the bush. Dedrick is completing the 108 laps around Mount Meru with hopes of obtaining otherworldly powers and enlightenment."

"Meru doesn't physically exist in our plane of being," Helen pointed out.

"True," Louise agreed, "but he's circling a real mountain somewhere, perhaps Mount Kailash, with the belief that it is Mount Meru. Belief can be a powerful thing."

"If we could confirm that's where he was," I said, "we could be there when he completes his final lap. Maryah said he was alone. We could overpower him, make him take us to wherever he's keeping Rina. We could figure out how to free everyone he has mind-controlled."

"Final lap?" Maryah asked me. "I'm lost. What is Mount Meru?"

I motioned to Edgar. "Edgar is better at explaining such matters."

Edgar leaned forward and summarized the legends. "Meru is claimed by some to be the center of the universe, the energy axis of the cosmos, a sacred mountain, if you will, that connects our plane of existence with others. It descends so deep that it reaches the oceans of other realms, and it extends so high that even the stars must look up to see its peak. Its foothills in hell, its summit in the heavens: it serves as the bridge to an existence of perfection and transcendence."

"Is it real?" Maryah looked stunned and shaken as if she'd been hit by a spiritual truck. "Could Dedrick be obtaining some kind of power from the mountain?"

"Honestly." Louise exchanged a confirming look with Edgar and Helen. "We don't know. This will require more research."

"What about the glowing rock?" Maryah asked.

"From what you described, and what we know about it, it sounds like Dedrick has the Firestone."

"Firestone," Maryah repeated. She stared at the middle of the table. I could almost see how hard she was thinking. "There are other stones, aren't there? Earth, Air, and Water."

"Did you remember that?" Helen asked.

"I'm not sure." Maryah rubbed the back of her neck, a sign that she was either tired or a headache was starting. "I'm learning that any mention of one element usually means the others are connected."

"*Connected* being the key word," Edgar said. "An ancient story was passed down that the element stones, while each extremely powerful on its own, could be used together as a key of sorts. Each stone would be placed on its designated face of the mountain: north, south, east and west. Four elements, four directions. Together they open a doorway to Meru."

I studied Maryah, watching for a hint of recognition. Hoping this conversation might be the metaphysical slap in the face she needed to wake up and remember. "There's also legend of an Aetherstone," I added, trying to fuel the fire. "A starstone."

Maryah blinked several times. Her head tilted. She closed her eyes for a moment, and I held my breath, praying, pleading, *please remember.*

"Can the Firestone be used to control minds?" she asked.

No big epiphany. Mention of a starstone hadn't had any effect. But at least she was asking questions. She was trying, and so would I.

Gregory elaborated on Maryah's question. "Or can it stop bodies from aging?"

"I don't know," Louise said. "But you can bet I'll be searching near and far for an answer. Louise pushed back her chair. "We'll update those who aren't here and find out as much as we can." She made her way to us and placed her hand on Maryah's shoulder. "You, my dear, must keep watching Dedrick. Listen for mention of a mountain name or location, and find out if he has any of the other stones."

Maryah's eyes widened. "You think he might have more?"

"I wouldn't put it past him."

Everyone dispersed from the meeting except for Maryah and me.

"How long before you have to return?" I asked her.

"Maybe an hour or so. I can't be gone for long."

"Will you come with me to the cliffs?"

"Nathan, this is hardly the time for a romantic moonlit stroll."

"As tempting as that sounds, that wasn't my intention. I'd like to explain something that might better help you understand some things."

"And we need to go to the cliffs for you to explain?"

"I think it would help."

"Okay then. I'd love to."

WILL POWER

Maryah

Nathan spread out a blanket and we sat down.

"I know you don't remember it," he said, "but in our last life, when we first moved to Sedona, we slept here under the stars."

"Like we camped out?"

"Here, and on the ground where our bedroom now sits." He leaned back, lying flat with his hands behind his head. His T-shirt rose just enough to reveal a peek at his toned abs. God, I missed him. I missed touching him, kissing him, being touched and kissed by him. I ached for more of the delicious quality time we had spent together before this most recent Dedrick crisis ensued. The carefree happiness of getting lost in Nathan seemed light-years away.

I shoved my hormones back where they belonged and curled up against him, resting my head on his chest. "Can we camp out here again? When all of this is over?"

He ran his hand through my hair. "It's a date."

Countless thoughts and questions whirled through my mind. I started with the most persistent one. "I'm curious about the starstone. What is it?"

His heartbeat quickened against my ear. My head rose as he took a huge breath. "I'm so glad you asked. A couple souls throughout history have claimed they have knowledge of it, but its whereabouts were never proven."

"Maybe we could find those people and talk to them."

He gently pushed me up to a sitting position. He searched my face while tucking my hair behind my ears. "The only one we would trust to tell us the truth can no longer discuss the matter with us."

"Why not?"

He pressed his fingers so tightly against his lips that he looked like he was trying to keep his words from spilling out. That's when I knew. I knew what he was about to say before his words escaped. "Because that person was you."

I didn't stiffen. I didn't gasp. My heart didn't even race. I was vaguely aware that my hands were squeezing the blanket on either side of me. Nathan stared at me and I stared back, neither of us saying a word.

My eyes dipped down, my focus landing on the peacock feather in my thumb ring. The truth hovered thick around me, waiting for me to snatch it and store it in my consciousness, but actually doing so was like trying to catch moonlight and stuff it in a jar.

Nathan rubbed my forearm "Are you all right?"

I looked up at him again. "It's part of it. I don't know how or why, but as soon as you spoke those words I knew the starstone is part of why I erased."

He held my hand as pity unexpectedly darkened his eyes. "The stone wasn't important to you. You mentioned it in passing, an afterthought. If I recall, you said something like starstones existed and they conducted energy to provide power to Meru. *They*," Nathan repeated. "As in more than one. A starstone isn't some coveted mystical gem protected by secret societies like the other stones. According to you, starstones aren't even stones, or as rare as the legends led us to believe. Starstones are to Meru what oxygen is to Earth. They aren't tangible, but they're vital."

I hardly heard anything after Meru. "You said Meru. Are you saying I knew something about the mythical mountain place?"

He gave me one of his ah-ha-you're-finally-catching-up smiles. "You visited Meru. You communicated with souls who lived there."

This time I did stiffen. And gasp. My heart beat so fast my vision blurred. "What?" I rocked backward, but Nathan kept a tight grip on me. "The center of the universe, the mountain in the heavens place Edgar just told us about?"

Nathan nodded. "I know it's a lot to take in. We told you that you were by far our most powerful member. You were always leaps and bounds ahead of us as far as enlightenment and universal dynamics."

I opened my mouth, expecting all my questions about Meru and the universe to pour out as fast as they formed in my head. But all that came out was, "What?"

"You described it as seeing a colorful sunset for the first time after living in a monotone world. You said the beauty and energy of it couldn't be described with any human words that could ever do it justice. You told me it was the most awe-inspiring moment of your existence."

"Did you believe me?"

"Did I believe how beautiful it was?"

"No, did you believe I really visited this Meru place?"

"Of course. You wouldn't have lied about something like that."

He believed I had somehow visited an otherworldly paradise with no proof. We must have had one heck of a relationship. "It sounds too good to be true."

"Which is precisely why you said you'd never want to live there."

"I said that?" If such a wondrous place existed why would I have never wanted to go back? "Why?"

"You said it was too perfect. The energy level was too pure. You said it was like a sky filled with stars so big and bright that there left no space for darkness. I told you it sounded beautiful, but you reminded me that stars are most appreciated when they shine in the dark."

His words, my words, echoed through my mind. "Mary was so much deeper than I am."

He laughed. "Your depth knows no limits. Then and now." He held my other hand, rubbing his thumbs across my wrists. "You said you had too much to do here. That Meru would always be there, perfect and glorious, but you enjoyed the imperfections and challenges of our world. You did go back once. You said you needed something but wouldn't tell me what."

"You have no idea how much I want to remember the past. Each new thing I learn just leaves me more lost. How could I have erased so many magical experiences and memories?"

"After Rina's last visit, I felt closer to an answer. I still couldn't grasp onto it, but it felt within reach. Then you came back and told us about Dedrick and Meru. All of our conversations about Meru came rushing back to me. Toward the end of the meeting a possible answer finally came to me."

"An answer to why I erased?" I perked up. "Tell me."

"I think you had peaked. What if last time, after you died, there wasn't a choice of who and where you wanted to be reborn? What if because of your experiences at Meru, you had become too enlightened to live a human existence again? Perhaps your only other option was starting over—wiping your soul's slate clean of all the knowledge and power you had acquired."

I couldn't wrap my head around what it all meant. All of this magic, otherworldly stuff was still brand new to my wiped-out hard drive. I rubbed my temples as if that might help me compartmentalize the surge of information. "You mentioned souls who lived there. Who are they? Angels?"

"Higher-vibrating beings."

"Oh god." I glanced at the sky then pressed my palms over my eyes. "Please don't say aliens. My brain might spontaneously combust."

He laughed and pulled my hands into his lap. "You referred to them as akin. Souls who operated with a different awareness and type of existence. You said they were light and energy. No skin and bones."

"Why didn't you tell me any of this before now?"

"Like you said moments ago, I didn't want your brain to spontaneously combust." He caressed my cheek. "You erased everything. Weeks ago you struggled to believe that reincarnation was real. You were just getting used to the fact that supernatural abilities were a reality and that I was your soul mate." He dipped his head, peering up at me from beneath his dark lashes. "When would have been a good time for us to tell you that you communicated with beings from other planes, that your soul traveled through energy portals and acquired knowledge that even our eldest members couldn't fathom?"

Definite mental overload. But I had to suck it up. I had to prove I could handle anything. Nathan couldn't be afraid to tell me anything anymore.

"Your first Meru visit was two lifetimes ago," Nathan continued. "After that you sprang into action, steadfast with an intricate plan for the rest of that life and our last one. You insisted we all needed to live near each other and that we relocate to Sedona. You convinced our kindrily to blindly follow your lead many times. It's like you were positioning everyone where they needed to be."

"And then I erased. I just gave up on you guys. Chickened out."

"Don't say it like that. The reason will reveal itself in time. Maybe this is all still part of your plan. Perhaps these ups and downs were necessary to achieve a happy ending."

"Ending?"

"Metaphorically speaking."

"I don't know. What if I realized I really messed up? All the bad history with Dedrick, getting everyone killed at the wedding, what if I had screwed up to the point nothing was fixable so I decided to just throw it all away?"

"You believed you could fix anything."

"Maybe the second time, when I went back to Meru, I saw some tragic destiny that couldn't be changed."

Nathan stared up at the sky. "My old friend Wil used to say, 'It is not in the stars to hold our destiny, but in ourselves.'"

I grabbed Nathan's knee. "I'm having déjà vu. Maybe I'm remembering Wil from a previous life. No, wait, maybe not. I think that's a Shakespeare quote."

"Right. He was famous for his writing in that life."

My eyes bugged. "You knew William Shakespeare?"

He smugly winked. "Still do."

I gaped at him and tugged his shirt. "Who is he now?"

"I'm not at liberty to say, but he's been in a few movies and on television. One of his series even had *star* in the name. Funny how our origins stay connected with us no matter how different each lifetime is. He's still sharing stories with the world, just in a different way than when he was Shakespeare. You'd be surprised how many gifted souls there are roaming this world."

William Shakespeare reincarnated. My father would have been beside himself. "Does he have a soul mate?"

"He and Anne have been together through thick and thin."

"That's so cool. In a way Shakespeare is still alive."

Nathan leaned back on his elbows. "Yes, older and wiser."

"I miss this." I traced my fingers over his thigh, feeling the solid muscle through his jeans. "I miss being here with you and hearing about our past. I don't want to go back."

"Then don't."

"I have to."

He lifted my hand then kissed each of my knuckles. "I know."

"You aren't putting up much of a fight."

"Because I know you too well. You'll return no matter what I say. Because that's what has to be done." Apathetic encouragement coated his words. "The villain must be fought. The innocent girl must be saved. The story must end happily."

I returned his bittersweet grin. "In order for that to happen you can't hold back anymore. I can handle the revelations. You might need to use small words so my immature soul can understand, but I need to know everything."

"Maryah, it will take me lifetimes to tell you everything."

"That works for me." I pushed him onto his back and cuddled up against him.

We lay there together gazing at the stars. One streaked across the sky so fast I thought I might have imagined it.

"Did you see that?" I asked.

"I did."

"I used to wish on every shooting star I'd see, but now that I know it's a soul resetting, it feels wrong." I swallowed down my guilt and disappointment in myself. "Someone out there just erased. They chose to burn out, like I did."

Nathan rolled over, leaning over me and pinning me in place with his fervid gaze. He didn't touch me. He didn't need to. The loving flames in his eyes warmed me to my core. "You never have, nor will you ever burn out. You are the light of all of my lives. Then, now, and eternally."

THICKER THAN WATER

Nathaniel

After Maryah returned to Rina, I visited the library to talk with Louise.

I didn't bother knocking. "That's how he trapped her soul, isn't it? He has the Airstone."

Louise glanced up from her computer, pressing a pen to her lips. "Perhaps."

"What if he obtains all of them?" I collapsed into the chair across from her, rubbing my hand over my jaw and already missing the feel of Maryah's lips against mine.

"I sincerely doubt he could find all of them."

"But if he does, and if the legends are true—"

"He will never possess a starstone. Mary said they don't exist in our plane of existence. And Dedrick won't be able to link the other stones together without one."

"Louise, this is so much bigger than we thought."

"Don't presume anything. He may have only the Firestone."

"Each one has incredible power, and in Dedrick's hands each of them is a deadly weapon."

"No argument there." Edgar walked up behind me and clutched my shoulder. "Would you be willing to visit the keepers of the Waterstone?"

"Me? I haven't visited them since the 1600s. I'm sure the guardianship has changed hands by now. I'd have no idea how to find them, and the ocean is too big to search haphazardly."

Edgar sat in the chair beside me. "You met two of their kind two lifetimes ago, a dear friend of mine and his late wife. She offered to restore your hearing. He is directly connected to one of the guardians and would gladly help us."

I remembered the couple. Mary and I were well along in years. I declined the kind woman's offer because of how finely attuned my other senses became due to my loss of hearing. A quiet cycle of life had its benefits. "Her husband is still alive?"

"Yes. I already sent notice that you'd be visiting. A change of scenery would do you good."

"What if they tell me their stone is missing?"

Louise finished jotting something on her notepad then tossed down her pen. "If so, we'll retrieve it and give it back to those who can protect it just like we plan to do with the Firestone."

"Clearly the Firestone keepers failed to protect it from Dedrick," I said. "Why would we return it to them?"

Louise sat back in her chair and folded her hands across her stomach. "Because with them is where the Firestone belongs. The same way Maryah was returned to us. All great power needs the support and protection of those who have known it the longest and treasure it the most."

I stood. "Let's hope the Waterstone guardians did a better job at protecting their treasure than we did."

∞

Edgar's old friend Lloyd stared shamefully into his coffee cup.

"You're positive?" I asked. "One hundred percent certain the stone is gone?"

"Sadly yes." His son sat between us on the edge of the kitchen table, kicking the table leg with his bare foot and causing my cup to rattle in its saucer. "The team assigned to guard it was distracted by a tangled mess of recent events."

"Distracted." I rose from my chair and stared out the patio door. Beyond the sandy beach was an azure ocean that appeared to go on forever—the ocean where the Waterstone was supposed to be hidden away from people like Dedrick. "Distracted from protecting one of the world's most powerful energy sources?"

"We're not saying it's a good excuse," Lloyd grumbled, "but it's the truth."

His son stood and moved to my side. "We will get it back. That I assure you."

I studied his face. He had physical features from both of his parents. Hopefully he inherited their wisdom and bravery as well. "Pardon my manners," I said, "You told me your name when your father introduced us, but with all my worrying I've forgotten it."

"Treygan." His dark blue eyes resembled the color of Alaskan water. "And no apology necessary. I wish we had better news for you. I feel somewhat responsible."

"Stop blaming yourself for everything that goes wrong," Lloyd told him. "You can't save everyone and everything. The Waterstone wasn't your sole responsibility."

Treygan ignored his father. "You have my word. We will retrieve it and then we will greatly improve our system for guarding it."

"The man who has it," I explained, "Dedrick, he's very powerful and dangerous."

Treygan crossed his arms over his bare chest. "So are we."

As much as I loved our home in Sedona, I admired the island lifestyle he and Lloyd lived. I had heard stories of what their kind were capable of, but considering their stone was stolen without anyone noticing, I didn't have much faith in them. Dedrick had yet another piece for his evil puzzle.

I checked my phone for missed calls.

"Hope you're not waiting to hear from anyone important," Lloyd said. "Those things don't work way out here."

Why hadn't I realized that earlier? We were on a remote island south of the Florida Keys and I expected to have cell service? Treygan and his people weren't the only ones distracted and not thinking straight.

"I should be getting back," I said. "Thank you for the hospitality and for your honesty."

"I'm sorry we didn't have better news for you." Treygan shook my hand.

"It was a pleasure meeting you. And Lloyd, it was great seeing you again."

Treygan's father didn't seem to be in the best shape. Returning the favor his wife once offered me was the least I could do. "Lloyd, as promised, I'll be back with someone who might be able to help with your health."

He waved me off dismissively. "I told you I'm fine. Her ability probably won't work on someone like me."

"It doesn't hurt to try, and I know Krista would be glad to help."

"Thank you," Treygan said. "That would mean a lot to us."

I said goodbye then opened the patio door.

"What's with the door?" Lloyd called. "Figured you'd exit by vanishing into thin air."

Pulling off my shirt, I told him, "I couldn't visit your island and not swim in that beautiful water."

"I'll join you," Treygan said. "I was heading home anyway."

We walked out onto the sparkling sand then dove into the waves. As blissful as it was to be swimming in a sunlit paradise, I had to return in case the kindrily needed me.

I said farewell to Treygan then traversed home.

I called out for Louise several times, but she wasn't anywhere in the house. I needed to dry off, so I walked down the sunny path to Edgar and Helen's cottage with Eightball trotting behind me. Louise and Mikey were on the back deck. Helen was potting plants.

No need for me to hem and haw. "Dedrick has the Waterstone."

Helen dropped her shovel and looked up at me, shielding her eyes from the sun. "Does he also have your shirt?"

I shook the water from my hair. "I went swimming."

"I'm envious. We could all use a trip to the islands."

Louise stopped bouncing Mikey on her lap. "Lloyd is certain Dedrick has it?"

"They're certain it's gone. Who else would have taken it?"

Helen brushed dirt from her hands. "This does not bode well."

I sat on the end of a lounge chair. "Have we confirmed who the keepers of the Earthstone are yet?"

Helen shook her head. "Edgar has been searching the records, but their identity is veiled more thoroughly than any of the others."

"If only the other groups had done as well as them," I said. "Then we might not be in this situation."

"We'll keep searching." Louise bounced Mikey again. "Someone out there knows more than they're admitting."

TWO-FACED

Maryah

"What do you mean Evelyn came while I was gone?" I was panicking. Evelyn found out I wasn't trapped. She knew I could return to my body. She would tell Dedrick.

"She promised she wouldn't tell," Rina snapped.

"She's lying!"

"Evelyn would never lie to me."

I couldn't think. I couldn't breathe. Thankfully my soul didn't need to breathe, but I was still feeling the physical sensations of real panic. Rina didn't know I had seen Evelyn piloting Dedrick's helicopter. She didn't know Evelyn was helping him.

Think, Maryah, think. What now? I had no idea. Dedrick would find out that Rina helped me escape and he would separate us. Then he'd do who knows what to punish us. I didn't know how much time we had.

"There's no reason to be so scared," Rina said.

"I'm not scared," I lied.

"Yes, you are. I can see it in your aura. You're pulsing with fear."

I tried planning my next move, but I didn't know what to do. I needed more information. So much more information. "He'll visit soon."

"Evelyn said he was delayed. He won't be back until tonight."

We couldn't trust Evelyn anymore. That much I knew for sure, but could I still trust Rina? Maybe I had been wrong in thinking I needed to help this girl. What if I was putting myself in jeopardy to help a stranger who might be Dedrick's manipulative weapon against my kindrily and me?

I needed to leave—travel back to my body and stay in it. The kindrily could figure out Dedrick's plan some other way. I felt the need to sit down, but that was impossible.

"Please stop," Rina said calmly.

"Stop what?"

"Stop reacting so dramatically and losing control of yourself."

"I'm fine."

"And stop lying to me."

I almost denied I was lying, but that would be another lie, so I stayed quiet.

"We're supposed to be working together," Rina said, "you and me."

"We are working together."

"Not for long if you can't trust me."

"I already told you, I trust you as much as I can. I hardly know you."

She stepped closer. "Part of trusting me is communicating with me. You assume too much, and you keep information from me."

"I tell you what I think you need to know."

She smirked. "That should be the other way around."

"Because you know so much more than I do?"

"Yes, I do."

It was my turn to smirk. I couldn't expect her to know any differently. She'd been trapped in this room her whole life. She didn't know what Evelyn did when she wasn't in this room. "Rina, maybe you don't know as much as you think you do."

"Or maybe *you* don't."

We were at a stalemate. We'd have to agree to disagree.

Rina tossed her hair behind her shoulders. "I'm about to offer you a sliver of knowledge—a sliver you could have already known and not been stressing about if you had simply communicated with me instead of suspecting I'm the enemy."

I felt guilty yet defensive at the same time.

Rina continued before I could say a word. "Evelyn loves me. She does not lie to me. Just because you think you saw her somewhere doing something you think she wasn't supposed to be doing, that doesn't make her guilty."

How did she know?

Rina stood on her tiptoes, trying to raise her face so it was level with mine. "You *assume* you saw Evelyn piloting Dedrick's helicopter. You should have considered other possibilities. Given your family history, it's amusing that it never crossed your mind. You actually saw Vivian, Evelyn's twin sister."

Mikey's sky-blue eyes flashed in front of me. How had I not thought of that possibility? Evelyn had a twin sister? They looked absolutely identical. But then again, how well had I really studied Evelyn's features in detail?

"Oh," was all I could mutter.

"Still believe you know more than I do?"

My guard went up again. "Maybe we're just knowledgeable about different things."

She smirked, but there was something cocky, almost sneaky behind it. "It's bad enough you lie to me. Don't lie to yourself. You've wasted a lot of time. Dedrick is progressing faster than expected. I need to take care of some important matters."

"What do you mean? Progressing with what faster? And what matters do you need to take care of?"

She turned away. "I see. *Now* you want me to share all I know. Suddenly I might know more than you?"

"I honestly don't know." My voice screeched with frustration. "I don't know how to process everything that's happening. It's just so much to take in. I'm trying my best."

Her glare softened. "I know. I forget that sometimes. I'm sorry for all you've lost, but I'm doing the best I can too. I just thought you'd be more helpful."

"I want to help." I leaned forward. "Tell me what to do."

"Rest. I'll be back soon." She sat on her mattress, bowed her head, and closed her eyes.

"Rina?"

She was gone. And I had an unnerving hunch that her destination was my body.

∞

The panic I felt when Rina told me Evelyn had visited while I was gone was child's play compared to what I felt when the lights went out.

The candle flamed to life, and Dedrick stood before me. A whole new level of panic fought to overtake me.

But I couldn't let Dedrick see it. He couldn't find out that Rina was astral traveling. I stood perfectly still even though my body wanted to tremble. My legs weakened, but then I reminded myself those sensations weren't possible.

Rina's body was still on her mattress, collapsed on her side with no soul inside.

Dedrick said hello to me then eyed Rina. "Sorry to intrude in the middle of the night like this." Middle of the night. I tried doing the math. How long had I been back? What would the time difference be from Sedona to wherever the middle of the night would be? As I tried calculating, Dedrick continued. "I was moved by a powerful need to see you."

I could tell he was speaking only to me. He surveyed the glass cabinet then glanced down at Rina again and walked back over to me. He assumed she was sleeping. Maybe we'd get away with it. Unless she came back while he was here. No, even if she did, she'd play it off.

"I had an epiphany," Dedrick said, "a nudge from my spirit guides, you might say. They informed me that you're ready to know more. You're ready to know the truth."

The truth. As if Dedrick was capable of speaking truth. Why hadn't he brought Lexie so he could hear my thoughts?

"My plan is phenomenal." Dedrick clasped his hands behind his back. "Even I'm impressed with how far I've come and what I will soon accomplish." He turned to stare at me. "Long ago, I would have shared the details with you. Long, long ago, when you and I were...closer."

I had never been close to Dedrick. No freaking way.

"But now," Dedrick continued. "Our trust in each other is gone along with your memories." He lifted his hand as if he was trying to touch my face. I darted sideways out of his reach.

"I'm still not sure how or when we became enemies, Mary, or Maryah, whatever name it is you're calling yourself these days. I told you I'd do this with or without you, and I am almost there. It is going to happen."

I kept gliding sideways, distancing myself from him.

"You're acting as if I'm a contagious disease you don't want to catch. Would you like me to educate you? Would you like to know some of the many truths that are being kept from you?"

I looked away. I wasn't interested in anything he had to say.

"You only know what your kindrily has told you about me. You used to know so much more. You knew I wasn't evil like they wanted you to believe. You doubted your allegiance to them. You believed in me and understood my mission."

His words were lies that I refused to consider.

"Are you feeling tired?" He strolled around the room, circling the table. "Do you feel as if you're losing your grip on your own being? I'm sure that's how you're feeling. It's what happens when a soul is away from its body too long. To prove I have no intention of harming you, I'm going to revive you, give you a bit of strength back." He pressed his hand to his chest. "I ask nothing in return. I simply want you to know that contradictory to what you may think of me, I do care very much about your wellbeing."

I couldn't help but sneer. How stupid did he think I was?

He opened a velvet bag attached to his belt then removed a beautiful blue stone. "You're a water sign this time. I'm not sure how that's possible, but who am I to question the mechanics of the universe?" He silently laughed as if he had said something amusing.

I didn't find the humor in it. I cursed under my breath. He had the Waterstone too.

He spoke in a foreign language that sounded similar to the one he used when I spied on him. A dull light grew brighter inside of the stone. A stream of shimmering water poured out of it and encircled me. Blue light swirled around me in sparkling, rippling waves. I felt like the figurine in Carson's snow globe.

I couldn't hear Dedrick through the wall of water surrounding me, but his wavy image stood in front of me with his hands held out at his sides. It was hard to tell, but his lips looked like they were still moving. After several minutes, the water receded back into the stone.

The room was so silent I heard only Dedrick's labored breath.

"You're welcome," he said much too kindly. He wiped sweat from his brow. "I will always do whatever I can to help you."

He licked his fingers, squeezed out the candle flame, and he was gone.

I did feel better, but I was far from grateful. If Dedrick wasn't keeping me as his prisoner then I wouldn't need to feel better.

And the only other person who could free me was using my ability to sneak away.

PLANTING DOUBTS

Maryah

Rina had been back only a few minutes. She hadn't stopped asking me questions about Dedrick's visit long enough for me to ask her where she went.

"Please, Rina. I'll tell you every single detail as soon as I come back. I won't be gone long, but I need to tell them he has the Waterstone. It's urgent."

"It's not safe yet." She spoke even faster than usual. "We don't know when he'll return."

"I'll travel to him first to see where he is. If needed I'll zip right back here." Now that Dedrick had strengthened me, I'd spy on him as much as possible. We needed to know how many of the stones he had. Seeing Dedrick conjure power from two of the stones so easily was beyond alarming.

"Don't you want to know where—" Rina didn't finish because the room went black. When the candle re-lit, I was surprised to see River and Evelyn.

"I have some information," River said excitedly. "I think this place, wherever we are, might be in Ireland."

"Why Ireland?" Rina asked, matching my own question before I could ask it.

"Earlier today, Dedrick walked past my room. He was talking to a man with an Irish accent. I heard only part of the conversation, but the man said—"

Evelyn sprang forward. "He's coming. Quick!" She shoved River toward the makeshift bathroom and yanked the tattered curtain closed to conceal him. "Don't move a muscle. Don't utter a breath, or we'll both pay dearly."

I couldn't see River behind the curtain, but the fear in the room—Evelyn's, River's, Rina's and mine—was palpable.

The black curtain fell and lifted too quickly.

Dedrick stood before me holding a large, thick book. He eyed Evelyn who was fidgeting with dishes from the meal Rina hadn't touched yet, then he turned his attention back to me. "Are you feeling better?"

Lexie was with him. She would hear River's thoughts. We'd all be busted. He'd never let River out of his cell again. Maybe he'd even kill him. And what would he do to Evelyn? Would he punish Rina even though she wasn't directly involved? Was there anything worse he could do to me? He could revive my soul, so could he also harm it?

He followed me as I drifted to the wall farthest away from River. "As you can see, I trust Rina, Evelyn, and Lexie. That's what we have here in our home, a circle of trust with no secrets. It strengthens our bond and allows us to function as a family unit. We would like you to be part of that, Maryah. Now that you're feeling better, now that you've seen that I sincerely care about your wellbeing, it's time to tell you what everyone else here already knows." Dedrick's dark eyes penetrated me. "You were torn between those outdated kindrily members and me. That is why you erased."

"No," I said, unfazed. "That can't be why I erased. I don't believe you."

"She doesn't believe you," Lexie said.

"Rina!" Dedrick snapped, waving her over without taking his eyes off me. She scurried over, and he grabbed her hand.

"Lexie," Dedrick called. Lexie stepped to his side.

Rina grasped Lexie's hand, but not before glaring at me and shaking her head in such a slight way it wouldn't have been seen by anyone else.

Dedrick would use Rina's conducting power to hear me with Lexie's mind-reading ability. He would be able to hear my thoughts. Surely he'd hear River's thoughts too, and it wouldn't take much searching to find him. If I listened hard enough I could have sworn I heard him breathing. *Don't think about River. White noise, white noise.*

Dedrick clutched Rina's hand tighter, and she closed her eyes.

I focused intently on the veins in his hairy forearms and my self-created white noise.

"It's true," Dedrick insisted. "I can answer so many questions you have about your past. I can help you remember again."

"You're a liar," I hissed.

"I'm not lying. You and Nathaniel had your share of problems throughout your lifetimes. You and I had our moments too. Some lives you and I were friends; sometimes we were more than that. I was more powerful than him. I had much more ambition. You had outgrown him and wanted bigger and better."

I cringed at the thought of being with Dedrick. "No," I said firmly. "He's my soul mate."

"People evolve," Dedrick said. "They change. Their needs and desires change too. Three lifetimes ago, you reached a higher level. You wanted more. You and I both did." His eyes softened. There was a gentleness I'd never seen, and never expected to see in someone so evil. "I loved you so much"

Dedrick? Capable of loving anyone? Impossible.

"We ran away together. We discovered so much about ourselves and metaphysics. Our powers strengthened. That's when you started developing your ability to see omens, to know things about the future."

He knew about me seeing omens? I didn't want Dedrick to know anything about me.

"That kindrily of yours," Dedrick continued, "They made you feel guilty about ending things with Nathaniel to be with me. They banned together and convinced you that the rare love we shared was wrong, but it wasn't." He leaned closer. Keeping linked to Rina and Lexie, he placed their connected hands against his chest. "I have missed you every single day. No one has ever affected me the way you did. Everything I have, all the power, the control, it feels like such a waste without you to share it with me. You helped me reach this level, and you should be here to enjoy it with me."

I shook my head. Lies. "They would have told me all of this."

"*They* would have told you? Your kindrily?" He almost laughed. "*They* are the reason you erased, my love. They wouldn't let you choose for yourself. They wouldn't let you live the way you wanted. They ruined you, and me, and our future together. They won't tell you that's why you erased because they loathe me. But you told me you would choose erasure if it became too much. Your pain was too much to bear. You lived with the guilt and heartache too long."

"No. I slit my own throat to get away from you."

He tilted his head. "That was the plan. *Your* plan. We made it look like you were part of the massacre. I had a healer on hand so you wouldn't die, but your kindrily would think you did. By the time they were reborn and questioned why you didn't return to them, they'd assume your guilt for causing the deaths of so many would be too much so you erased. You even suggested kidnapping Gregory to lure Harmony away from you so she wouldn't see that your spirit didn't cross over."

My mind whirled. Harmony was lured away by Gregory. She did assume I crossed over. But Gregory said Dedrick kept me trapped, that I was so miserable I cried all the time.

"Then why did you treat me like a prisoner? You kept me strapped to a bed."

"Strapped to a bed?" He looked genuinely surprised.

"Gregory told me I was strapped to a bed and crying."

"Never," Dedrick guffawed. "He's remembering it wrong. My healer had difficulties stabilizing you. We had to give you blood transfusions and IV fluids. You were sick and upset, but never did I restrain you in any way. You were helpless. You weren't able to get out of bed for weeks."

"This is all lies!" I yelled. "I wouldn't be with you. Ever."

"No?" He let go of Lexie's and Rina's hands then opened the book he'd brought. He flipped through the pages then slid it to the edge of the table. "Do you recognize her?" His finger landed on a dark, curly-haired girl I had seen in so many other photos. Mary. Me from my previous life. "That's you last lifetime. I don't look much different due to my manipulation of aging."

In the photo, with his arms wrapped around Mary, stood a smiling Dedrick. His hair was shorter, less greasy, and he looked happy. Not like the bitter, villain who stood before me. He and Mary stood on bright green grass in front of a castle. They looked like a couple. I cringed, realizing I had been one half of that couple.

I rocked backward. The stone walls threatened to crumble in and suffocate me. My lungs wouldn't work.

Breathe, Maryah. The feeling of having a body with its physical reactions was all in my mind. I needed to pull myself together. I wanted to slam the book closed so I didn't have to see Dedrick and me together.

"I don't know what they've told you," Dedrick said quietly, "but it wasn't the truth."

∞

After the curtain lifted, and Dedrick and Lexie were gone, Evelyn collapsed into a chair, sighing with relief that Dedrick didn't discover River.

I hovered in front of Rina. "Did you hear what Dedrick said? Did you hear our conversation?"

River stepped out from behind the curtain. "It all makes sense!"

Rina answered me, ignoring River. "Don't believe a word Dedrick says. Ever."

The revelations, or lies, had left me shaken to my core. I wanted to believe everything my kindrily had told me was the truth, but what if it wasn't? They wouldn't have lied to hurt me. They would have thought they were protecting me, but what if I really had seen good in Dedrick in previous lives? Everyone kept telling me I had amazing instincts, that I saw omens and knew things about the future. Maybe I saw good in Dedrick that others couldn't.

Or maybe I was a naive idiot who was letting Dedrick manipulate me.

"That was much too close," Evelyn said.

"Why didn't Lexie tell on us?" I asked. "She must have heard River's thoughts. She had to have known he was here."

Rina asked Evelyn my question.

"Lexie is like me," Evelyn explained. "We can disarm ourselves from Dedrick's mind control while appearing to still be under the spell. He trusts her and keeps her at his side full-time." She lowered her voice. "We keep our friends close and our enemies closer."

Her snake eyes flickered to a soft, normal shade of brown. They were just a disguise.

"Are there others who pretend to be under this spell?"

Rina repeated my question verbatim.

Evelyn looked away. "I'm not at liberty to say."

"Rina," I probed. "We need to know who we can trust. It's important."

Evelyn looked appalled as Rina translated for me.

"*We*?" Evelyn drawled. "We don't even know if we can trust you."

"Fair enough. Why didn't Dedrick hear River's thoughts while he was using Lexie's power?"

Rina squinted then asked Evelyn my question, sounding concerned herself.

"I wondered the same thing," Evelyn said. "Perhaps Lexie prevented it somehow."

"I tried not to think," River confessed. "Like I blanked out the best I could."

I knew how difficult it was to think about nothing. He would have made some kind of mental noise.

"Besides," River continued. "There's no time for bickering. We need to discuss this giant revelation that my crazy ass uncle is in love with Maryah."

I agreed with River. "I need to talk to my kindrily."

"Right now?" Rina asked, shocked.

"It's crucial."

"But Dedrick might come back," she argued.

"He won't come back anytime soon. I have a feeling he'd want me to be alone with my thoughts for a while. He'd want me to process everything he just told me." He'd want me to believe him.

"We can't risk it."

"Rina, please. I'm begging you. I won't be long. Maybe an hour at most. He won't be back that soon, I know it."

She chewed on her fingers while staring at me. "If he does come back—"

"He won't." Evelyn stood, fidgeting with the sleeves of her shirt. "I'll make sure of it."

Rina swallowed hard and hesitantly stepped forward. Her hands lifted at her sides.

"Don't forget to tell them that I think we're in Ireland," River reminded me. "And be sure to tell them I'm the one who told you. Maybe they won't hate me if they know I'm helping."

It would take more than that to change their opinion of River.

"Thank you," I told Rina. "I promise no more than an hour. Don't worry."

She nodded then a pale blue light formed around her hands. The welcomed sensation of my soul sinking into my skin ended with me staring up at Krista reading a book beside me.

I coughed like I had bronchitis as I reconnected with the auto-functions of my body.

"You were right," Krista said, still reading without even a glance in my direction. "I am swooning over Jamie. In my next life, I want to be Claire."

I sat up on my elbows, clearing my throat of its last cough. "You're not the least bit excited I'm back."

She bit her lip, her eyes scrolling, still distracted by the words on the page. "It's a really good part."

I pushed the book away. "How'd you even know it was me? It could have been Rina."

"You always gasp or cough. Rina fidgets."

"Was she here earlier?"

"Not that I'm aware of." She finally lowered the book. "Why?"

"She astral travelled but wouldn't tell me where she went."

"I don't think Faith would have slacked off during her shift, but we can review the recording."

"Recording?"

Krista pointed to my dresser. Hanging on the top of the mirror was a tiny camera. "Carson set it up for Nathan so he can check in on you with his cell phone, but the feed also records and automatically saves to a computer in Carson's room."

"Seriously?" I smoothed my hair down, worried Nathan could see me.

"I told Carson you wouldn't be a fan of the idea, but Nathan was exhausting himself traversing to you every other minute. Carson programmed a motion detector so that anytime you move it alerts Nathan's phone."

"I'm moving right now." I waved my hand. "Is he watching us?"

Krista grinned. "I disable the camera during my shifts. It creeps me out too."

She knew me so well. "We need to talk. Preferably somewhere that doesn't have a camera pointing at us."

∞

She scanned through an hour of boring video footage. As we watched Faith sit beside my motionless body while talking or texting on her cell phone, I finished filling in Krista on everything Dedrick had told me.

"It's all crazy talk," Krista said. "I don't believe any of it. Not for one second. You've always loved Nathan."

"Right now, you know more about my life back then than I do. Did I ever mention anything about Dedrick?"

She sat back in Carson's desk chair. One of her tank tops was draped over the arm, and she fiddled with the straps as she thought about my question.

I glanced around, noticing a few more pieces of her clothing in his hamper. What if they were sleeping together already? I cringed at the thought. I was happy for her, but I still couldn't think of them together in that way.

"You want the truth so I'm giving it to you." Krista pressed her hands together in her signature prayer position. She was about to tell me something important, but I had a feeling it was something bad. "My first life, when I met you in the orphanage, you saw me heal one of Sheila's injuries."

"Right. I remember you telling me that."

"After that you were convinced I was an Element, or if not, that I was destined to be one, but you wanted confirmation."

"Confirmation?"

Krista nodded. "One day you took me to see a woman who read tarot cards. You said she was the best tarot reader in existence, and she'd be able to confirm what you already knew. Sheila went with us. The lady read my cards and without any information from you, she knew I was a healer. She predicted me staying connected to you for many lifetimes to come. Then she read Sheila's cards and said Sheila was similar to her, that she had 'the sight.' It's what sparked Sheila's interest in reading palms and tea leaves. The tarot reader told her those were the two areas where she'd excel."

"Great, but what does that have to do with Dedrick?"

Krista sighed. "You took us to his house afterward."

I almost fell over. "What?"

"I was young, so the memories are only bits and pieces, but I remember he gave us hot chocolate while you told him about Sheila and me."

"Why would I do that?"

"Apparently, you trusted him." She leaned forward. "But that doesn't mean you loved him. Or that you were unfaithful to Nathan. Like I said, I don't believe you loved Dedrick. You never lit up around him the way you did around Nathaniel. There was never any hint of flirting that I can remember. You considered him a friend—if that—until later when he betrayed you."

"Betrayed me? How?"

"He stole a bunch of your journals."

"Journals?" I'd never been much of a writer. My mom had given me a journal on my thirteenth birthday, but the only things I ever wrote in it were song lyrics, favorite quotes, or birthday and Christmas lists. "Like a diary?"

"Research notes, your thoughts and recollections of your travels and experiments, visions or messages that came to you through meditations and visualizations, that sort of stuff."

"Do you remember anything specific that I had written?"

"I never read any of it. You were very protective of them, which is why you were so upset when Dedrick stole them."

"How did he steal them? Did he break into our house or something?"

"No." Krista's eyes shifted sideways, watching the computer screen as she tried recalling details. "I don't remember that part. Maybe Nathan remembers? You could ask him."

I took a deep breath. "My conversation with Nathan is going to be—"

"Hey." Krista grabbed the mouse and started clicking. The screen was frozen on Dakota sitting by my bed with his sketch pad on his lap. "Great. It's stuck."

"Gotta love technology."

"All this video is probably taking up too much of the computer's memory. I'll have Carson fix it." She pushed the keyboard away. "What were you saying?"

"I was saying I need to have a really uncomfortable conversation with Nathan."

TAKING A VOW

Nathaniel

I was surprised to receive a text message from Maryah. *Can u come home? We need to talk.*

I was in our living room before I finished sliding my phone into my pocket. "You returned sooner than planned." I kissed Maryah's cheek, but she pulled away.

If there was any question that the look in Krista's eyes was worry, her listless tone confirmed it. "I'll leave you two alone."

As Krista left the room, I kept my focus on Maryah. She looked irritable, almost nervous.

"What is it?" I asked. "Did something happen?"

"I need to know the truth about Dedrick. All of it."

I sat on the arm of the sofa. "As I told you, it would take lifetimes to tell you everything about Dedrick."

"No, you said it would take lifetimes to tell me everything about everything. I'm specifically asking about Dedrick."

"That would still take a great deal of time."

"So there are things you haven't told me?"

"Maryah, we are on our twentieth cycle of life. You erased all knowledge of the nineteen before this one. Dedrick made appearances in more than I care to count. There are volumes I haven't told you about our past because we haven't had time. It will take me a dozen more lifetimes to recap everything we've been through, which is why I'd much rather we figure out a way to restore your memories."

She paced. "Were we ever together?"

"We were always together."

"Not you and me." She pivoted to face me. "Dedrick and me."

My heart skipped at least five beats. My eyes narrowed. "Together how?"

"Together, together. Like a couple."

I was sure blood no longer pumped through my veins—only rage. "Of course not."

"I need to know the truth, Nathan. No matter how hard it might be, I need to know."

"That is the truth!" I leaned forward, bracing my hands on my knees. "What did he tell you? That you two were involved romantically?"

She pressed her palm to her forehead. "He had a picture."

"A picture? Of what?"

"Of me as Mary, and him, we were standing in front of a castle. He had his arms around me, and we looked happy."

My jaw shifted so hard that I probably stripped the enamel off of my clenched teeth. "He's trying to manipulate you. To get closer to you and make you trust him."

"Explain the picture to me. Tell me how it could—"

"It's a photograph!" I stood and turned away, aghast that we were having this conversation. "He's mind-controlling an army of people. He figured out how to trap your soul in some ethereal prison." I whirled around to look in her eyes. "Do you honestly think simple photo manipulation would be difficult for him? The photo isn't *real*, Maryah."

"What's going on?" Louise asked, easing into the room.

"Dedrick is feeding Maryah lies and trying to make her doubt us," I snapped. "And very sadly, it seems to be working."

"I didn't say I believed him," Maryah argued. "I just want answers."

"To be honest," Louise said, "I overheard the last bit of your conversation, and I feel it's time we told Maryah how deep her past runs with Dedrick."

I blew out the breath I'd been holding in an attempt to calm myself. I despised Dedrick with everything inside of me. I despised him for making us have this conversation.

"How deep my past runs with him." Maryah glanced between Louise and me. "What does that mean?"

"Have a seat." Louise patted the couch.

"I'd rather stand."

"All right then." Louise turned to me. "Would you like to do the honors, or should I?"

Maryah would think I had kept this information from her on purpose. She was going to throw a fit, and we didn't have time for one of her fits. I plowed right in, wanting to get the train wreck over as soon as possible.

"He was obsessed with you," I said. "Not just your power, but you."

"He loved you," Louise added.

Maryah gasped. "What?"

"He did not and does not love her," I argued. "He is not capable of love."

"He loved her in his own way." Louise's head bobbed. "Twisted as his way might be."

"Why didn't you tell me?" Maryah gaped at us.

I parted my lips to say I had lived with his vile, psychotic obsession with her for several lifetimes, that I had already endured it too long and it was infuriating that he still found her even after she erased, but I settled for, "The time never seemed right."

"The time never seemed right?" Maryah's voice grew shrill. "The maniac who killed my family and tried to kill me was obsessed with me in my previous lives and supposedly loved me, but you didn't think I should know about it?" She advanced on me with anger flaring in her eyes. "How about the time I astral traveled to him and was terrified? Or when I told you I was going to spy on him even though it felt dangerous? Neither of those seemed like good times to enlighten me?"

"I never would have guessed he could confine your soul. I thought you were safe."

"Well, I wasn't safe. And now he has me, Nathan." Her words hurt worse than being nailed to the pillory by my ears.

"He doesn't have you. You're right here. You don't have to go back there."

"It's not just me he's keeping prisoner." Her hands flailed in every direction. "I can't leave Rina."

"You're risking your soul for a stranger who could very well be a Nefarioun!"

She shook her head. "You aren't there. You don't see or hear them. That poor girl. Dedrick hurts her and uses her, and who knows what he'd do to her if I escaped. I've gotten to know her. I feel a strong connection with her. How could I ever live with myself if I don't help her?"

I could never stop her from trying to save someone. I had never been able to in the past, and it wouldn't change in the present.

"Start with Emily," Louise suggested, attempting to refocus the conversation.

Maryah's head snapped around to Louise like she forgot she was in the room. "Emily?"

My mind raced with so many thoughts and emotions that I wouldn't have known where to start. I sat down and rested my elbows on my knees, clasping my hands together. Some knowledge would be better left erased, but just because Maryah didn't remember it, that didn't stop it from being true. "Emily was Dedrick's soul mate. Keep in mind, Dedrick used to be an Element, but he abused his power so he became an outcast."

Maryah nodded. "That part I know."

"Emily did not abuse her ability," I continued. "She grew more powerful than him, and he resented her for it. Emily was a seer. She could see the future. She also developed the ability to astral travel."

Maryah's chin lifted. "Like me."

I glanced at Louise. She nodded for me to proceed. As much as I didn't want to, there was no way around it. "The Akashic Records state that Emily foresaw Dedrick's downward spiral. She didn't want to live to see him become something so ugly. She blamed herself for not being able to stop him, so she abandoned the cycle of reincarnation and resigned from our world."

"Where did she go?"

"Wherever it is that souls go when they choose to stop living a human existence."

"Did she go to Meru?"

"As infinite as this universe is," Louise said, "we can only assume there are countless possibilities of where Emily might have gone."

Maryah turned and looked out the windows. She was silent, but I could see her contemplating what might exist beyond our world. "So what happened after Emily left?"

I raked my hands through my hair. "You and I came into existence almost one year after he lost Emily. He didn't know that when he first heard about you, but he figured it out later." The full version of the story would take hours. I tried to summarize. The quicker I dropped the bomb, the sooner I could clean up the debris. "Long story short, his deranged mind believed, and may still believe, that you are his Emily."

Maryah swayed then stepped sideways. "Me? Dedrick's soul mate? That's disgusting."

"I couldn't agree more."

"He came to that conclusion," Louise explained, "based on your creation date. Your birthday has always been on the eighteenth of a month—so was Emily's. Plus, you have the same abilities that Emily had. You and Dedrick were introduced by happenstance, but he believes it was fate bringing Emily back to him in the form of you. He believed Emily erased so they could have a fresh start and she reincarnated as you."

"How do you know all this?" Maryah sat beside me.

I touched her shaking knee and let Louise answer her question.

"Because he told you. And you told us. Long, long ago."

I knew more due to other circumstances, but I had vowed to keep a secret, and I couldn't break my word.

Maryah clamped her hand over mine. "It's not possible, right? There's no way this Emily person could have erased, and I'm reincarnated as her?"

"Not that anyone has ever been able to determine," Louise said.

"No," I insisted, hating that Louise's response left room for doubt. "It's not possible."

But Maryah didn't look convinced.

RUNNING AWAY SOLVES EVERYTHING

Maryah

Louise excused herself to check on Mikey while Nathan and I started another round of questions I didn't want to ask.

"Did I ever—" I hesitated, hating myself for needing to be assured. "Did I ever have doubts about us?"

"No. You were mine, Maryah. And I was yours. Always. We're soul mates."

"I know what we are, but every couple has problems. You cheated on me, so—"

"I can't believe you're bringing that up, much less comparing that meaningless mistake to this. That was *hundreds* of years ago." Nathan stood with such force the couch cushion bounced. He clasped his hands behind his head as he walked away from me. "Dedrick, of all people, is making you doubt us."

"I'm not doubting us right now—the *us* in this lifetime. I know how I currently feel about you, but I don't remember my past and so many other people do. You have no idea how frustrating that is. I'm entitled to ask questions about my own past, and you knew me better than anyone, so I'm sorry, but I need to ask about this crappy, horrifying, makes-my-skin-crawl, Dedrick stuff." I hung my head, rubbing my stiff neck. "I need to know the truth so I know where to go from here."

"Where to go from here?" He spun to face me. "What does that mean?"

"Everyone claims to have no idea why I erased." I didn't want to upset Nathan even more, but I wanted answers. "Everyone except Dedrick."

Nathan's nostrils flared. "What did he say?"

I swallowed hard, knowing my words would sting both of us. "He says I erased because I wanted to be with him, but you and the kindrily wouldn't allow it."

Nathan stepped back. He looked disoriented for a moment, but then he shook his head and walked away from me.

I followed him into the kitchen, spitting out the rest as fast as I could like ripping off a Band-Aid to avoid prolonging the pain. "He said you and I had problems, that he was more ambitious than you, that he and I grew more powerful together. He said that's when I developed my ability to see omens. He said I planned everything on the beach to make it look like I died so I could run away and be with him."

Nathan braced himself on the kitchen counter. He looked down, up, out the window. He looked everywhere except at me. He collapsed forward, dropping his head into his hands. He didn't move or say anything for what felt like forever.

I stepped closer to him, reaching my hand out but then pulling it away. "Nathan?"

He lifted his head and stared at me. "I failed you once already in this life. I didn't have faith that you would remember who you were. I let my heartache consume me. Just weeks ago, after the miracle of holding you in my arms and feeling your lips against mine, I vowed to never fail you again. I will not break that vow." He stood up straight. His voice was stern. "Dedrick is a liar. He is smart, cunning, and manipulative, and he's twisting facts, but I swear to you on all my lives that it was you and me since the very beginning up until right now at this very moment." He held my hands and pressed them to his chest. "*Only* you and me—always. Deep down, you know that's the truth."

Did I know that was the truth? My world felt so upside down. I wanted Dedrick's story to not make sense. I wanted there to be a different explanation. "Then why did I erase?"

Nathan's confidence crumbled. "I wish with all my being that I could give you that answer." The pain in his voice made me want to retract my question, but it was already out there, tormenting us like always. "But *I* truly love you, Maryah; therefore, I don't pretend to know why. I don't lie to you, or manipulate you, or create fictitious stories. Dedrick does that. Not me. *I* am your twin flame. Not him."

I kissed him. Because I loved him. Because I was so sorry for all the suffering I caused him and kept causing him. I kissed him to remind myself what his kisses did to me. No one—in this lifetime or any other—could ever give me the earth-shattering, stars-igniting, souls-colliding, warming-every-fiber-of-my-being kisses that Nathaniel Luna gave me.

And he knew it.

He returned my kiss so confidently and passionately, but with a natural ease that only my soul mate of twenty lifetimes could pull off. He lifted my legs and I wrapped them around his waist. My back pressed against the refrigerator as we devoured each other. I was a fool for ever thinking I could have strayed from the one person meant for only me.

His lips trailed down my jaw and neck. "Let's leave."

"Leave?"

"Leave all of this," he said, his voice raspy. "Leave it all behind us."

The cloud I'd been floating on fell out from under me. "Leave our kindrily?"

"They'll understand."

I pressed against his chest, pushing him back so I could read his facial expression. I planted my feet on the floor. "Where would we go?"

"Anywhere." He was serious. "Somewhere Dedrick would never look for us."

"We can't just abandon them."

"Everyone has been so focused on you regaining your memories. Even me. But all of this—Dedrick trapping you, almost losing you again—it made me realize that the past is just that, the past. I want to focus on the present." He cupped my face in his hands. "I love you. The *you* who you are right now. I don't want to change you or trade you in for the previous model. You should be free to live this life exactly as you are without others expecting you to act a certain way. No one should expect you to know everything. I want to be with *you*. And if you'll have me, we can start a new chapter and see where it leads us."

I shook my head. "But knowing we lived so many lives together, I'll always want to remember. I can't just ignore that."

"Why not? There is so much you're better off not remembering. So many illnesses, wars, deaths of people we loved. Billions of people on this planet can't remember anything from their past lives for good reason. Those that erase are relieved of so many painful memories. Allow yourself to be washed clean of all of it."

"But there were good times too. I want to remember all the people we knew and loved."

"Please, I'm begging you." He held my hand and kissed my wrist. "Don't go back to Dedrick's torture chamber. Every minute you spend with him is tainting you and us."

"I have to—"

"I know you want to help Rina. And we will. We'll figure out where she is, and we'll help her break free."

"How?"

"We'll figure out a way."

I almost told him about River suspecting we were in Ireland, but I stopped myself. What happened with Dedrick and Lexie had me perplexed. Dedrick must have known River was hiding in that room. He had to have heard his thoughts. But Dedrick didn't do anything about it, which led me to suspect that River was helping set a trap. If I told Nathan about Ireland, the whole kindrily would come running to the rescue. And what if the Nefariouns were waiting? I couldn't chance it. Not until I did more investigating.

"You said you have faith in me," I reminded him. "Have faith that I can do this. Believe that I'm strong enough and smart enough to bring down Dedrick and save Rina."

Nathan's eyes glistened with sadness but also love as he studied my face. He touched my cheek. "I do believe in you. But you can't do this alone. You have to let us help you."

I pressed my hand over his. "You are helping."

"We're sitting around here not doing much of anything while you voluntarily subject yourself to Dedrick's mind games and risk your soul."

"I'm sure everyone's abilities will be put to good use but only when the time is right."

Gregory opened the kitchen door, letting in a warm breeze. "Maryah, may I speak with you for a moment?"

I peered up at Nathan, silently asking if we were okay. I didn't want to desert him during such an important conversation.

He kissed my forehead. "Gregory doesn't ask to speak with anyone unless it's important."

I was still a little uncomfortable around Gregory. The physical similarities between Dedrick and him rattled me. They both had dark shoulder-length hair they'd sometimes wear in a ponytail, they were both over six feet tall, and let's face facts, they killed my parents. Mind-controlled or not, Gregory stabbed Mikey while I watched, and then Dedrick ordered him to beat me to death.

"Maybe you should come with me," I whispered to Nathan.

He glanced at Gregory then smiled. He leaned down, pressing his warm lips to my ear. "Whispering is useless. Gregory can hear your thoughts."

Warmth flooded my cheeks. Gregory shut the door, and I watched through the window as he sat on a deck chair across from Harmony. His lips moved, and she burst out laughing. Most likely he had told her about my whispering blunder.

I was getting used to embarrassing myself in front of kindrily members. My recovery time was improving. "Guess I'll go see what he wants."

Nathan nodded, still grinning.

I stepped out onto the deck, and Harmony stood. I stared at her bare feet, shocked to see her not wearing her combat boots. "You have feet."

She lowered her sunglasses and squinted at me. "Did you think I had hooves?"

"No, it's just I've never seen you without boots, and your feet, they're so pretty."

All three of us looked down. Harmony really did have pretty feet: high arches, toes that weren't too long or too short, even purple-painted nails.

"I agree," Gregory said.

Harmony's black eyebrow ring lifted as she smiled. "I'll leave you and Gregory alone to talk."

I practically stuttered. "Uh, no, you don't have to."

She either sensed my nervousness or Gregory had read my thoughts and told her I wasn't comfortable around him, because she nudged my arm and said, "Don't be afraid. He only bites me, and that's because I like it."

She giggled then went inside.

Gregory's head was bowed, his sunglasses dangled from his fingers. His eyes lifted to meet mine. "Harmony and the others have been catching me up on all I've missed, but the one detail I'd like to discuss with you is how most everyone's ability seems to be strengthening."

I nodded and sat down.

"Well." He cleared his throat. "Evidently mine is strengthening too, but it seems to be specific to you."

"What do you mean?"

"I read minds by making eye contact with a person. At times, I still hear some thoughts even if the person looks away, but that only lasts for a couple seconds at most, like their thoughts are smoke that quickly dissipates. Out of respect for our members, I never listen to anyone's thoughts without permission unless it's an emergency of some sort."

"I remember. Very noble of you."

He slid to the front of his chair. "Recently, it seems no matter what I do to block you out of my head, your thoughts are leaking in."

"Leaking in?"

"Yes, which wouldn't be a problem if my usual method of not looking at you worked in this situation, but it doesn't." His broad shoulders slumped forward. "I'm embarrassed to admit this, but I've overheard some of your thoughts in the last few days."

I was taken aback. It was hard enough getting used to the idea that Gregory could hear my thoughts when he intended to, but now he had no control over it? "What thoughts of mine have you heard?"

His tan cheeks blushed, and he smoothed back his ponytail. "Please know that no matter what I've heard, I don't judge in the slightest. Trust me, I've heard things you wouldn't believe throughout my lifetimes. None of your thoughts were shocking or ultra-personal. I'll try my best to gain control over this new development, but until then I wanted you to be aware of it."

What if Gregory's ability wasn't getting stronger? What if he was losing control over it?

"No, it's not like that," he said. I flinched at him responding to my thoughts, but he continued. "It's more like my range with you has expanded. Twice now, I've known your soul was back in your body before you or anyone else came out of your room. Your thoughts invaded my mind."

"When?"

"Once I was out here eating breakfast with Harmony and Carson. The second time I was showering."

I fidgeted, uncomfortable with the mental image of Gregory naked while hearing my thoughts.

He laughed. "It was awkward for me too, but as I said, this is all new to me, and I haven't figured out how to manage it yet."

"You're saying you could be listening in on my thoughts or conversations at any given time no matter where I am in the house?"

"You don't have to be in the house. My range seems to extend pretty far."

"How far?"

"One day, you and Nathaniel went for a walk. I overheard you talking about Meru and William Shakespeare."

"What?" I gasped. "We had that conversation out on the cliffs. That's like a mile from here."

"As I said, my range with you has increased significantly."

I sat back, gripping the plastic arms of my chair. "This is so intrusive."

"I'm sorry. I don't like it any more than you do. I don't like not having total control of my ability."

I thought of Rina and how easily she could control whether or not I astral traveled, how she could use my ability as her own without my permission. "I know the feeling."

∞

When I went back inside, Krista and Louise were in the kitchen making cookies. I didn't expect everyone to put their lives on hold because of all the drama with Rina and Dedrick, but I was a little surprised to see Louise baking like it was just another day.

"Everything okay?" Louise asked.

I sat at the island across from her, tracing the veins of the granite countertop. "Just the usual. Dealing with psycho mind tricks and finding out life-altering secrets from past lives that make me fight with my boyfriend of nine hundred or so years. Oh, and dealing with the fact that I'm being video monitored, and my parents' killer can hear my thoughts at any given time. You know, the usual teen drama."

Krista sympathetically grunted.

Louise grinned. "You're coping exceptionally well, all things considered."

Nathan stood on the deck talking to Gregory. We were separated by nothing but glass windows, but he felt so far away. Why couldn't I be a normal girl with normal boyfriend problems? "I'm looking into joining a support group tomorrow so I can meet others going through the same thing."

Louise poured sugar into measuring cups. "Sarcasm and humor to mask your true feelings, I like it. Carson is rubbing off on you."

Krista giggled as she grabbed a handful of chocolate chips.

I stole a couple from her before she swatted me away. "I figured sarcasm would be a nice change from stress, worry, and wanting to throw myself off of the highest cliff in Sedona."

"Oh, stop." Krista pinched my arm. "You'd just be back in nine months or so, and you'd still have to deal with the mess you left behind. Why prolong it?"

She had a valid point. Even death wouldn't end my problems.

"Anything you'd like to talk to me about?" Louise asked me.

"How many centuries do you have?"

"As far as I know, my time is unlimited."

I watched Nathan again. He was absorbed in his conversation with Gregory. He ran his hand over his hair and then over his jaw. He stared at the ground then Gregory stood and clasped his shoulder. Gregory's lips moved enough to say only a few words. Nathan turned, and our eyes met. He grimaced, and I expected him to come inside and talk to me about whatever was bothering him, but then he vanished.

I sighed. "I worry Nathan isn't telling me everything."

Louise reached across the counter and held my hand. "He's telling you what you need to know."

"He shouldn't get to decide what I need to know. I should know everything about my past."

"I'm not saying this to hurt you," Louise said, "but you erased all knowledge of your past. That could only mean there were things you didn't want to remember. None of us know as much about your past as Nathan. He can't tell you volumes of history all at once, so he's picking and choosing as the situations call for certain information."

"He'd never intentionally keep anything from you," Krista agreed, "especially about Dedrick."

I spun my ring around my thumb. "Dedrick claims to know so much about me. He has all these stories, and he pretends we were so close."

Krista sat beside me. "Never trust a psycho."

"Look at all the people he has doing his dirty work." Louise cracked a couple eggs into a bowl. "And as you've seen with Gregory, they aren't working with him of their own free will."

My lips parted, preparing to tell them about Evelyn and Lexie, how Evelyn was only pretending to be mind-controlled, but then Louise said something that shifted the conversation. "The best advice I can give is to trust Nathan."

Even Nathan had told me things that were hard for me to believe. "He told me I claimed to have visited Meru."

Louise set her spoon down and smiled up at the ceiling. "Ah, I remember that so well. We were so proud and a bit envious."

"So you believe it too?"

"How could I not?"

"Because it's a mythical place, and I claimed to meet beings called akin."

"Oooh!" Krista rocked happily in her seat. "The alien people. I remember hearing about them. They always fascinated me."

I refused to picture an encounter with little green men with antennae on their heads. "No. Nathan said I described them as light and energy."

Krista nodded. "But they live in outer space."

"Not exactly," Louise said. "They come from the stars. The stars are where everything and everyone begins and ends, and begins again."

"Right," Krista confirmed. "But I remember her describing them as living among the stars, so that had to be somewhere in space, right?"

"I'm not sure of their specific location. Mary—" Louise pointed at me. "*You* explained it as a different plane of existence. Not a specific destination."

"How did I get there?" I asked. "How does one travel to a different plane of existence?"

"How do you astral travel?" Louise asked.

"I'm still not sure I understand the ins and outs of that either."

"You travel using energy. Every living thing, every planet and star, every energy source: we're all different parts of the same universal puzzle. We're kindred. Whether good, bad, light, dark, past, future, existing on Earth or in some other galaxy, or even vibrating on a different plane, we're all connected by the same energy. Once you tap into that energy, the possibilities are infinite."

"That's why my soul can travel anywhere," I clarified, "because of energy?"

Louise pinched a finger full of flour and held it in her palm for me to see. "We're all made of recycled stardust." She flung it above her head, and a white cloud formed, but then it froze in place. My jaw went slack as I watched the flour hang in mid-air. Then it swirled and dipped around us as if being controlled by Louise's words. "You travel like light, fly through the air, swirl with the wind, ride on waves, glisten in the sun, and though you may settle in one place for a short period of time." The flour trails stopped then gently joined together and fell into a pile in her open hand. She blew on the flour, and it burst into a cloud. "You will always rise again."

"Oooh," Krista cooed. "That was cool."

"How did you do that?" I stared at Louise's powdery fingers.

Louise tossed the flour into the sink and wiped her hands on her apron. "Come now. As old as my soul is, I've learned a bit of magic throughout my journeys."

"Sure, but you just controlled that flour like it was nothing."

"It is nothing. And it's everything. It's energy."

"What other kind of energy can you control?"

"Small doses mostly. Nothing as impressive as you or Nathaniel." She clicked a beater into her mixer. "And nothing nearly as exciting as how Anthony can freeze time. I still think it was a cruel joke of the universe to give me a partner with such a powerful ability."

I smirked. "You can see people's auras. That's pretty powerful."

She bobbed her head. "It has come in handy from time to time."

Dakota barreled through the back door. He was focused on his sketch pad. "I did what you said, and it worked!"

He slapped the pad on the counter in front of me. "Check it out." He looked up at me, and his smile fell. He pulled back his pad. "Sorry. I thought you were Rina."

I hadn't asked Dakota about Rina visiting because I hadn't seen him since I arrived. "Why would you think that? Was she here today?"

Dakota hugged his pad to his chest. "Yes."

"Why didn't you tell us?" Louise asked him.

"I thought she was still here. She taught me a new way to draw then said she'd be back to check on me. I've been busy working on a new story ever since." He eyed the cookie ingredients and licked his lips. "I guess I lost track of time."

Why would Rina visit Dakota? I held out my hands. "Can I see what you drew?"

Dakota's cheeks blushed. "You probably won't be able to."

"Why not?"

"Because you're still learning how to sensperience."

Louise, Krista, and I shot each other questioning looks.

"And *you* can suddenly sensperience?" Krista asked him.

"Not exactly," Dakota said, "But I can draw with stardust, and those who can sensperience can see it."

Dakota mentioning stardust right after Louise's magical flour lesson gave me goose bumps.

"May I see it?" Louise asked. Dakota handed her his pad.

I leaned forward, stealing a peek at the blank page. Louise flipped through a few pages then looked at Dakota over the rim of her glasses. "Rina taught you how to do this?"

Krista moved beside her to look at it too. "It's blank." Krista hummed. "Oh wait, I see traces of something, but I can't make out any details."

"What?" I grabbed the pad from Louise and held it close to my face. "There's nothing there." I set it on the counter. "Are you guys messing with me?"

Louise's serious expression answered my question. She dipped her head, making eye contact with Dakota. "Why was Rina teaching you to draw this way?"

"So Maryah can learn to see it."

"So I can learn to see what?" I asked.

Louise pressed her hand to her necklace and calmly said, "What's written in the stars."

FOR CRYING OUT LOUD

Maryah

I returned to my invisible cage, more fuddled and lost than ever. "Why didn't you tell me you visited Dakota?"

"I was going to," Rina said, "but we were interrupted."

"He told me to tell you that it worked. He drew with stardust, and Louise could see it."

"Good."

I had asked Louise a dozen questions but somehow forgot to ask an obvious one. "Where would someone even acquire stardust?"

"Stardust is everywhere. Rub some dead skin from your hands, and you'll have stardust." She cocked her head. "Did anyone else see Dakota's drawing?"

Louise had explained one of the drawings as two hands clasped together. Another was a peacock feather surrounded by black feathers. Krista told me she saw blurs of lines but nothing more. "Almost every kindrily member could see it."

Her head tilted. "Almost every member?"

"Obviously I can't." As if I needed another reminder of how inadequate my abilities were. "And Krista can see only hints of something."

"Keep trying."

"How can I keep trying when I have to be stuck here?"

She rubbed at one of the many dirt spots on her pants. "Try whenever you go back to your body."

"The short spurts of time I do have in my body aren't going to be spent staring at a sketch pad, hoping to see a magical drawing."

"If you want to free us, you'll practice. When you're there, you practice with Dakota's drawings. When you're here, practice with that." She pointed to her prized blank book.

"Rina, you have to—"

The candle went out.

Dedrick had returned with Lexie.

I had been back mere minutes. That was way too close.

Dedrick leaned down and whispered something to Rina. She kept her focus straight ahead at the wall but nodded then walked over to Lexie. Darkness cloaked the room again, and when the light returned, Dedrick and I were alone.

"How are you, Maryah? Are you adapting to not having a body or do you miss yours?"

Conversation was pointless considering he couldn't hear me without Lexie. What did he expect me to do, blink my light-beam eyes once for yes and twice for no?

"I know you can't answer me. I'm certain you feel incomplete. Hopefully we can come to some sort of agreement." He paused as if waiting for me to react, but I refused to give him the satisfaction.

"I'd like to bring your body here so you can feel whole again."

It was hard to show no emotion. What did he mean bring my body here? Was he planning to kidnap me? The kindrily's safety was my main concern. What if he hurt them—or worse? I shook my head.

"No?" His brows arched. "You don't want to be back in your body?" He rubbed his beard. "Ahh, I see. You're worried what lengths I will go to make that happen. You're worried about your precious Nathaniel."

"No!" I shook my head again, trying to convince him it had nothing to do with Nathan. If Dedrick thought Nathan was the reason I refused his offer, he might try to eliminate him all together. Dedrick turned away from me.

"He's not good enough for you. Never has been." He rested his fingertips on the table, slowly moving them as if playing an invisible piano. "You told me that yourself three or four lifetimes ago."

Again with the lies. I activated my mental white noise to drown out his words. It worked for a few minutes, but then he held up a photograph. He shoved it so close to me that I drifted backward.

It was a black-and-white image of a newborn baby wearing only a diaper. He flipped to another photo of a toddler smiling big for the camera. Dedrick pointed to a lady in the background, sitting cross-legged on the floor. I recognized her from old photos Faith had shown me. It was me from two lifetimes ago. "That was you, my love. I'm sure you can see the father-son resemblance. We had a child together."

The baby had dark features like Dedrick, and my nose, but I refused to believe I had ever slept with Dedrick, much less had a child with him.

He flipped to another photo of me holding the child while Dedrick leaned in to kiss the boy's cheek. "This was our lifetime before last. Have you seen photos of yourself from that cycle yet?"

I reminded myself what Nathan had said. Photoshop, mind tricks: Dedrick was capable of much more impossible things than doctoring photos. He was getting desperate, and this was just another one of his elaborate lies.

"You can keep looking away, but it doesn't change what's true, Maryah. You loved me once, and you loved our son. But of course your precious Nathaniel would never reveal that dirty little secret. How convenient that you erased your past so he and that kindrily of yours could pick and choose which parts of your history to disclose." He set the photos on the table. "I'm not like them, Maryah. I will always tell you the truth. The whole truth—whether you want to hear it or not."

∞

Rina returned not long after Dedrick had left.

"Where'd you go?" I asked.

"Dedrick needed me to conduct someone's power for him."

"Whose power?"

"I don't want to talk about it."

"It will help if I know what kind of abilities the Nefariouns have. I can warn my kindrily."

"What's wrong?" Rina asked, changing the subject. "Your light is much dimmer than when I left."

I was too upset to deny or mask my feelings. Dedrick talked for at least thirty minutes, telling me stories about our make-believe son. His first word, his first day at school, his favorite foods, the woman he married, how he died too young and sadly wasn't an Element. "Dedrick's lies are draining me."

"What did he say?"

"He said we had a child together."

Rina's brow creased. "If you don't believe it, why do you seem so affected?"

"It's another reminder of how much I don't know about my past. Dedrick showed me photos of the previous me with a baby—a baby who looked like me. What if he really was mine? I never even thought to ask Nathan about our children because, well, I don't know, it's so weird to think about."

Rina chewed her fingers, spitting out tiny bits of skin onto the floor. "Go ask him."

"Ask Nathan about our children?"

"Just remember what I told you. You won't like the answers."

"What do you mean?"

She turned away. She knew information on that subject too?

"Rina." I steeled my voice. "Tell me what you know."

"I'm not allowed."

"Says who?"

"This is a conversation you should be having with Nathan."

"Why are you always pawning off these conversations on other people? Why can't you just give me a straight answer?"

One impassive shrug was her only reply.

A big secret loomed thick in the air. Was I wrong to so quickly dismiss Dedrick's illegitimate child story? Could it be true and my betrayal is what caused me to erase? There was only one way to find out. "Will you free me so I can talk to Nathan?"

"I was wondering why you were taking so long to ask."

She was right. I had procrastinated. Part of me was afraid to ask Nathan because I was afraid to hear the truth.

∞

Nathan agreed to my request to talk in private, but instead of going to a different room, he politely suggested everyone should leave the house and catch up on errands. The news report on the television revealed the date and time. I doubted that anyone had errands to run on a Sunday night, but Anthony, Louise, Gregory, Harmony, Krista, Carson, and Dakota filed out the front door, like they all knew that whatever I was about to say would spread through the house like a virus, and they didn't want to be infected.

I sat on the couch. Nathan clicked off the TV with the remote and stood in front of me, waiting. The shadows cradling his eyes had deepened.

"You look exhausted," I said. "You need more rest."

"I don't sleep much without you next to me." He sat down and rubbed my knee.

"My body has been here the whole time."

He attempted to grin, but didn't seem to have enough strength. "You're right, let me clarify, I don't sleep much when your soul isn't with me."

I tugged at my fingers, staring at him as I rehearsed a dozen different ways to approach my heinous question. Finally, I eeked out the words. "Did I ever have a child with Dedrick?"

His eyes flamed with a fire I'd never seen before. I didn't even know what emotion to call it. "Never."

"How can you be sure?"

"How can you ask me that?"

"I hate to say this, but every couple has problems. I'm sure we must have too." I tucked my hands under my legs to keep from fidgeting. "Did we ever go through a really rough patch where I might have strayed?"

He hung his head. "After our last discussion, I can't believe you're even suggesting that as a possibility."

"No relationship is perfect," I said weakly. "Nothing lasts forever."

"That's a blatant lie." He swiveled to kneel in front of me. One of his hands braced my thigh while the other lifted my chin so our eyes met. "My love for you is forever. Even through awful, nightmarish times when we both wanted to give up, even the rare moments when we couldn't stand to look at each other, even when you deleted every precious moment of our history together, when you erased all knowledge of me and *us,* I never stopped loving you. Despite your best efforts, the universe led us back together. Do you know why?" His gaze pierced me like a lightning bolt connecting my heart with his. "Because *we* are forever. There's no changing it, no erasing it, and no one will ever come between us. There is one thing in this unpredictable merry-go-round called life that is certain: Our souls belong together. Forever."

I inhaled as he exhaled. Slowly, and silently, we breathed each other in and out. Just like our first kiss, just like every time he allowed me to enjoy the calm before a perfect storm of our souls connecting. I closed my eyes, overwhelmed in the best way by his downpour of devotion.

The energy radiating from his lips warmed my own as he leaned closer. His bottom lip brushed against mine, just long enough to offer an invitation I could never decline. My mouth closed over his and a whirlwind of passion erupted.

Eventually, when I came up for air, I was on top of him. We had somehow ended up on the living room rug. "I'm so sorry," I said between kisses. "I hate having to ask you such ridiculous questions."

"It's all right." He shifted beneath me, his fingers still kneading my scalp and making the rest of me ache for more. "My answers keep earning me kisses that make the aggravation well worth it."

We both smiled.

"You're absolutely certain," I said, trying to refocus. "Maybe by trickery or some other awful soap opera plot twist, that none of our children could have been his, right?"

Nathan's body tensed against mine, and then his gaze dropped, but not before I saw his eyes flood with sadness.

"What?" I pushed myself away from him and kneeled on the floor, staring down at him. "Nathan, what's wrong?"

He sat up and shifted a couple times. Keeping his head down, he held my hand. His voice sounded grim. "We never had children."

A rush of air escaped my throat as I almost laughed at the absurdity of it. "Over the course of nineteen lifetimes, we never had any children?"

"Krista and Sheila, but they were adopted."

It didn't make any sense. "You're kidding, right? I had to have given birth at some point."

He shook his head with a serious and somber look on his face.

"Why?" I asked quietly, somehow already knowing the reason but needing to hear it out loud for confirmation.

A long silence stretched between us before ending with his wistful words. "We were never physically able."

"We?" I questioned, but my instincts knew differently. "You mean me. *I* was never physically able."

He squeezed my hand. "This isn't a matter we need to discuss right now."

"Yes, it is." I stood, stepping backward until the couch hit the back of my legs and forced me to sit. "I need to know about our past to help me understand who I was. Now tell me, Nathan. Never, not in any of my lives was I ever pregnant?"

His shoulders buckled under the weight of my question. A sudden twinge of pain tugged at my heart. "I was, wasn't I? I was pregnant at least once. Probably more than once."

"You never did anything wrong." He closed the distance separating us in one swift movement. Kneeling between my legs, he softly braced my waist. A flash of a memory hit me—him from two lifetimes ago, resting his hand on my round belly as we both felt a firm kick from inside.

My hands gripped my stomach as if the kick happened in the present. A bolt of pain shot up the back of my head.

Nathan noticed it. He knew I had just experienced a memory flash. "You did everything you could every time."

Every time. "How many?" I asked, tentative and breathless. "How many did I lose?"

"Please, don't." He was trying to protect me, but I needed to know. Some part of me needed to know, no matter how painful the answer.

"How many?" I repeated.

He stared over my shoulder, into some past I couldn't see or remember the way he could.

"Nathan, how many?"

He inhaled. His hands tightened on my waist. "Twenty-seven."

A wrecking ball swung full force into my chest. I swayed backward then clutched his forearms to steady myself. For several long blinks we stared at each other, silent, until I found my voice again. "Twenty-seven?"

His reply was almost too quiet for me to hear over the whooshing of the blood in my ears. "Keep in mind that was over nineteen lifetimes."

"How—why would we—my god, how could you bear it?"

"We mourned for each one, but we remained hopeful. You weren't a quitter, and you wanted a child more than anything. Each lifetime you prayed for your body to be strong enough."

"How did I endure that kind of suffering and loss? I can't even imagine what that must have been like for us. For you." My stomach wrenched. "You still remember every one of them?"

Nineteen lifetimes of sadness seeped from his lips. "Every precious one."

I fought back the tears pooling in my eyes. "What was wrong with me that out of all the bodies I had, none of them were ever able to—"

"Stop." He pulled me closer to him. "Don't blame yourself. Those types of things are beyond our control."

The front door opened and Faith came barreling in, obliviously dancing around. "You guys, I have exciting news." Faith paused. "Hey, where is everyone?"

Nathan and I didn't reply. I stared out the windows at the back deck, feeling so broken.

"Maryah, what's wrong?" Tears rolled down my cheeks.

Nathan brushed them away with his thumbs.

Faith sat beside me on the couch, wrapping her arm around me. "Why the tears, Ma-Ma?"

Faith's awful nickname for me sent me over the edge. "Don't call me that anymore!"

"Faith," Nathan said. "We were just discussing Maryah's past childbearing situation."

"Oh. Oh, no." Faith pulled my hair from my face and rested her head on my shoulder. "Maryah, I'm so sorry."

HOWLITING AT THE MOON

Nathaniel

Maryah left, and this time I couldn't push away the empty feeling of not being there with her as she processed such a jarring, emotional blow.

I sat by her side, staring at her closed eyes, waiting for her to return so I could defend myself against the next preposterous lie Dedrick conjured up. He was trying to wear her down and break our bond, but instead, as we addressed the painful wounds of our past, we grew closer. That closeness caused my heart to ache that much more whenever she wasn't with me.

Carson finished rehanging the fixed camera and leaned against the dresser. I didn't look at him, but I could feel him watching me.

"You look like crap," he said, "worse than crap, actually."

"Thanks. Matches how I feel."

"Maybe you should shave. And use some Visine. Your bloodshot eyes are scary."

I tucked the blanket around Maryah's arms. "I don't care about my appearance right now, Carson."

"It might make you feel better."

"Having Maryah safely and permanently back in her body, and knowing Dedrick's dead with no chance of reincarnating, are the only things that will make me feel better."

He sighed. "This is some messed up stuff."

"I know." I rubbed my tired eyes. "And when does it end?"

"It ends after she remembers her past."

"Which could be never."

He walked over to me and leaned against one of the branch bedposts, running his fingers along the wood. "I had an idea this morning, but I need your help. Could you take me somewhere?"

"Where?"

"Iona, Nova Scotia."

"Why do you want to go there?"

"Helen says it's the best place to find Howlite." He thumbed his own Howlite necklace.

I grinned, knowing the answer to my question before I asked it. "And you want more Howlite for Maryah?"

"She needs all the help she can get remembering her past."

I glanced up at the Howlite stone in the center of the dream catcher hanging above our bed. Louise and Helen had stuffed tiny nodules of Howlite into Maryah's pillows days before she arrived in Sedona. Faith attached fragments to the sunglasses she gave Maryah. All with hope that the power from the crystals would help her remember her past lives.

"I know what you're thinking," Carson said. "We already scattered lots of Howlite pieces around the house and in her car. That's great and all, but it's not the same as her wearing a big hunk of it at all times."

"You're right. And I think she'd treasure a gift like that from you."

Carson held up his hands. "Whoa, let's not make this into some sappy grand gesture. I just want to make life a little easier on both of you."

A hint of blush tinted his cheeks. He could deny it all he wanted, but for Carson, this was most definitely a sappy grand gesture. "When would you like to go to Iona?"

"I'm ready whenever you are. Helen says to get the most powerful stuff, we'll have to climb down the cliffs and search the shoreline."

"It's been a while since we've been rock climbing together."

"Too long." He smacked my shoulder and excitement tinged his words. "It will be fun."

"If it's windy or raining, it will be miserable and impossible to locate anything of substance."

Carson chuckled.

"What?" I asked, unsure of what was so amusing.

"Miserable and lacking substance. Like Maryah."

I glared at him. "Carson."

"Kidding." He murmured, "sort of" as he turned to leave. "I'll tell the others we'll be gone for a few hours so they can reschedule their stalking-Maryah shifts."

"Is Krista coming with us?"

He kept walking, but replied over his shoulder. "Nah, just you and me."

Brotherly bonding and a gesture to prove Carson had grown fond of Maryah—it was an expected ray of sunshine in my dreary day.

∞

We materialized farther from the cliffs than I had planned. I looked around, unsure of where we were at first.

"This is it?" Carson asked me.

My gaze followed the railroad tracks. "I think it's that way. Maybe a mile or so."

"A mile? Is your supernatural compass malfunctioning?"

"I've only been here one other time and this is the only spot I could envision in detail."

He stood straight and rolled his shoulders. "Want me to carry you so we get there quicker?"

"Beg your pardon?" I hopped backward.

"No one's around. I could warp speed us there, but I'll have to carry you." He stepped toward me, lifting his hands, but I pushed on his forearms and stopped him.

"No, we'll walk at regular pace."

"Oh, it's okay for you to hug everyone and traverse them around the world, but I can't carry you a mile down the road?" He slipped one hand free from my grip and tried playfully smacking my face, but I dodged it.

"Exactly."

"Evolve much?"

I started walking. "I'm a slow evolver. It's why I've reincarnated so many times."

Carson shoved me in the back then walked beside me. "At least it's not windy or raining."

The lake was sapphire blue, the waves were calm, and the sky was painted with wispy clouds. Maryah would have loved the view. Someday I'd bring her here to visit.

We followed the railroad tracks along the sea cliffs. As we neared the outcrop of rocks that would most likely contain Howlite, my skin started tingling from the raw power of the crystals.

"Do you feel that?" Carson asked.

I leaned out and peeked over the edge. A jagged jut of rocks rose out of the water not far ahead. "We're almost there."

"That's some crazy powerful energy to affect us that way."

"It's in its raw form," I explained. "And still absorbing energy from all the elements. Look around: Earth, Water, Air." I pointed toward the sun shining bright in the sky. "Even Fire."

"Duh," Carson said.

I smirked. "Smart ass."

"Exactly. That's why we're here, because of my brilliant idea." He rubbed his hands together. "Let's go Howlite hunting!"

We found the most strategic place to begin our climb down. We managed the descent with no trouble at all. The weather couldn't have been more cooperative. Carson waded into the water first.

"I don't even have to hunt for it," he said. "I felt it getting stronger as we climbed down."

"Seems your sensperiencing has strengthened too."

"Or the crystals are just that awesome. They're bound to help Maryah."

I followed as he made a direct path to a group of rocks still damp and glistening from the waves. Carson crouched down. "Clear as can be! Not even a tint of brown like mine."

"Very pristine," I agreed, looking over his shoulder.

"With all the recent drama about the element stones, I almost feel bad taking it away from here." He looked out over the water then down at the Howlite. "It's like the elements worked so hard to create it. What right do I have to take it away from where it belongs?"

"You don't have to take any if you don't feel it's appropriate."

"But it could help Maryah."

"True."

"What should I do?" Carson asked me.

"You're the exceptionally intelligent one, not me."

"Maybe I could borrow a piece then bring it back once Maryah is whole again." He pushed damp strands of his hair from his forehead. "Return it to where it belongs."

"Or, if it does help Maryah remember the past, then perhaps it's meant to be with her."

He smiled at me. "You don't give yourself enough credit for being smart."

I gave him an appreciative nod then motioned at the pack on his back. "Did you bring tools to harvest a piece?"

"Yup, the tool is my hand." With hardly any effort, he used two fingers to snap off a large chunk of flawless Howlite.

I grinned. "Showoff."

HOLY KILLING

Maryah

I kept astral spying on Dedrick. We needed to know if he had more than the two stones.

My soul connected with his just as he and a snake-eyed Nefarioun strutted into an elaborate church or temple of some kind. The walls were covered in ornate carvings of symbols and scrolls. Long wooden beams stretched across the arched ceiling, but far above them was the sky.

A white-haired man in gorgeous gold robes stepped down from the vine-covered altar. A younger man and woman flanked him on either side. They also wore robes, but they looked more like brown burlap.

"To what do we owe this return visit?" The old man in gold asked.

"You know where it is," Dedrick snarled. "I'm gifting you with the opportunity to stay alive by giving it to me."

"Death does not scare me. It does not scare any of us."

"It should." Dedrick lumbered forward and leaned close to the man's face. "Because you won't return this time."

The old man demonstrated complete calm. "If that is the path fate has planned, I will travel it willingly."

"All of your meditating has your head buried in the sand. Your existence in this world will be over. For good."

The man clasped his hands behind him and turned his back to Dedrick, looking up at the blue sky. His two sidekicks remained silent but did the same. "Look up there. So much exists beyond our fragile grain of sand called Earth. We protect it as well as we can, but we can't protect it from everything. If you succeed, it will be because the source deemed it time for such an event to occur. If you must kill me during your quest, then I will be grateful to pass on so that I am not forced to witness what becomes of our beloved planet." He turned and leveled Dedrick with a sagely gaze. "With no new life there is only decay. No balance means dark will flush out the light. I do not wish to ever exist in a place such as that."

Something the man said ignited a deep anger in Dedrick. His face cracked with lines of fury. "Tell me where the sodding stone is."

"I'm a simple man. I am not gifted with such knowledge."

"Someone here knows where it is, and you are the prime candidate. You're the highest rank they give around here."

"Yet I haven't been entrusted with its location, so it seems, my friend," he opened his hands, palms up, "you have come to a dead end."

"A dead end for many if you don't take me to the Earthstone immediately."

The man folded his hands over the tassels of his roped belt. "It appears we have reached an impasse."

Dedrick's eyes bounced side to side, studying the three robed people in front of him. He motioned to his sidekick, and the mind-controlled monster rushed forward.

I screamed as the Nefarioun plunged a dagger into the chest of the woman. The old man in the middle, the leader, lowered his head, quietly saying a prayer as the younger robed man rushed to the injured woman's side.

I put my invisible hand over my mouth as if that would help the sickness I felt from watching the horror happening in front of me.

Dedrick's goon ripped his dagger free from the woman's chest as she gasped for breath and collapsed into the younger man's arms. He recited the same prayer the old man was chanting.

"You're a monster!" I shouted at Dedrick, hovering so close I could have spit on him. These people were peaceful and spiritual, and he was a ruthless murderer.

"That was strike one," Dedrick said, "two more strikes and you're all out." I tried knocking the bloody dagger from the murderer's hand, swiping and punching over and over, but my ethereal form was useless.

The robed men didn't acknowledge Dedrick or his goon. The leader kept his head bowed as he continued praying, and the younger man smoothed the woman's hair from her face. She took a couple ragged breaths as her eyelids fluttered, and then, like the rest of her body, her eyes stilled with a finality that left me numb.

Dedrick was murdering more innocent people the same way he had murdered my parents and brother. It tore open a wound that would never heal.

"Strike two coming up soon unless you start talking," Dedrick threatened.

"No!" I yelled, positioning myself in front of Dedrick's sidekick to shield the robed men.

Behind me, the older man said, "Forgive these souls of their evil and let them find peace."

"Your precious community will be next," Dedrick hissed. "I'll burn it to the ground along with everyone who lives here."

It was the first time the old man flinched. Worry lines creased his brow. "I do not know the stone's location. Please don't harm our people."

Dedrick waved his hand, and his goon plowed through me. I cried out, wishing I could take the hit instead of the man behind me. The elderly leader gasped as I turned to see him being stabbed. The younger man kept praying, catching the man in gold as he knelt in a puddle of the woman's blood.

I felt like I was going to puke. All the sensations of it were real. I dry-heaved, not wanting to see anymore, but I couldn't leave. Dedrick was here for something important—so important these people were willing to die and let each other be killed to protect it.

"Two down," Dedrick told the only survivor. "Tell me where the stone is or you will join them, and your death won't be so swift. You'll be burned alive with the rest of your community."

The man finished his prayer, closed the leader's eyelids, laid him gently on the ground, then stood. He held open his hands in front of him. "I do not know the answer you are seeking. No one here does."

Dedrick waved to his murdering minion. "Take him outside and wait for me."

He snatched up the survivor and dragged him along the cement pathway. The man tripped over his robes as he thrashed, trying to fight free of the Nefarioun's grip.

They left the temple, and Dedrick assessed the two dead bodies. He squatted beside the woman and placed her hands over her chest. Then he did the same to the older man. "I'm sorry it had to be this way," Dedrick said quietly. "Forgive me."

"What?" I gaped at him. "Forgive you? You will never be forgiven for any of this!"

Dedrick stood, crossed himself, then pulled out a gold cross from under his shirt and kissed it. He walked through the double doors where a woman waited, another Nefarioun. Dedrick grumbled something to her, and she strolled toward me. With a flick of her fingers, fire shot out from her hands and ignited the robes of the two deceased people. I turned away, horrified.

Dedrick was really going to burn down everything. I had to get help. I desperately searched for my energy cords. Light swirled all around me. I couldn't travel fast enough.

When I reached my body, I practically leapt from my bed, gasping for breath. "Help!" I screamed.

Krista burst through the doorway with wide eyes. "What's wrong?"

"Where's Nathan? I ran toward the door, yelling, "Nathan!"

He materialized in the hall. We collided into each other. "What is it?"

My words rushed out of me. "It's Dedrick. He's killing people. He's going to burn down everything. We have to stop him!"

"Where?"

"I—I—" I didn't know where he was. I didn't know where those holy people were. "Oh god, I don't know."

"Details." Carson grabbed both of my shoulders and turned me to face him. "What can you tell us about the place where you saw him?"

I spoke as fast as I could. "It was a church or temple. There were three people dressed in gold and brown robes. Dedrick demanded they give him the Earthstone. He stabbed them and said he'd burn down the whole village, or community. I can't remember his exact words. He has a woman who shoots fire from her hands."

"What else did you see?" Nathan asked. "Mountains, ocean, landmarks?"

"I never went outside."

"We don't have enough to know where he is," Carson said.

"I'll go back." I ran for the bed. I had to figure it out. We had to stop him. I pictured Dedrick's menacing eyes, searched for the cords of light to connect me to him. My heart raced too fast. I struggled to breathe.

"Try to lie still," Krista said above me. "You're freaking out. You need to relax in order for it to work."

I tried to stop trembling, but I was panicking. Why didn't I go outside? Why didn't I look for an address or something definitive so I'd know where they were? I messed up big time. "I have to go back. We have to help them."

"We will, we will." Nathan lay beside me, sliding one arm under my neck. "But Krista's right, you have to calm down and focus."

His touch helped. I took deep breaths and closed my eyes. Every passing second felt painful. I was taking too long.

Finally, I felt a cord and rode it as fast as I could.

Dedrick stood in front of me, talking to the man who had done the stabbing. We were outside, surrounded by trees. I turned, scanning the rolling green landscape, trying to find any indicator of where we were.

Black smoke billowed in the distance. I rushed toward it, determined to save anyone. I didn't know how, but I had to try.

Flames poured from the windows of a cluster of stone houses. I heard screaming—terrified, earth-shaking, life-ending screams. The smell of burning flesh gagged me, but I kept racing forward.

A little girl, no more than four years old, leaned out of a second-story window, waving her teddy bear as she cried and choked on the smoke rising around her. I flew toward her, my arms outstretched. I was so close.

She looked up at me with swollen, watering, puppy dog eyes, but she saw me.

She *saw* me.

She reached forward, stretching farther out the window, her teddy bear clutched in her tiny hand. My fingers grazed hers at the same time a deafening crack made her brown eyes fly open wide. The floor buckled beneath her. Her dark curls flew up around her face as the raging flames swallowed her from my view.

"No!" I screamed, diving into the fire, but the flames burned so big and bright that I couldn't see anything. Her screaming faded in volume but not intensity.

Everything blended into a burst of orange light.

My soul cried for her. I rubbed my eyes, trying to find the girl again, but I found myself back in my body. I couldn't breathe. It felt as if the smoke had really charred my lungs.

"What did you see?" Nathan asked.

I squeezed my eyes shut, trying to rush back to her. I hadn't seen any addresses, no clear way to determine where the village was. Tears stung the corners of my eyelids. Whoever those people were, whomever's daughter that little girl was, they were being burned to death. My voice cracked. "We have to save them."

"Where?" Carson pleaded. "Did you figure out where you were?"

I shook my head.

"It's all right," Nathan said gently, pulling me against him.

"Their homes are on fire." I cried into his chest as he stroked my hair. "People are inside. A little girl." Her teary, terrified brown eyes would haunt me until my dying day.

"There's nothing we can do," Krista said, petting my leg. "It's too late."

I sobbed and clutched Nathan tighter. The echoes of innocent people screaming still rang in my ears. I was sure I would hear them forever. "I hate him. I hate Dedrick so much."

"I know," Nathan whispered. "We all do."

ROCKY ROADS

Maryah

Helen brewed a special tea to calm me. No matter how powerful Helen's tea was, it wouldn't ever erase what I had witnessed.

I continued sipping my tea, trying to come up with a plan to stop Dedrick and his Nefariouns from killing more people. The roundtable meeting would begin soon, and I had no ideas or suggestions. I felt so useless.

Carson slid into the seat beside me. "I have something for you."

"For me?"

"Here." He handed me a silky cloth. I opened it and found a beautiful white rock in the shape of a teardrop. "What is this?"

"It's Howlite. It's supposed to help with remembering past lives."

"Where did it come from?"

"Nova Scotia."

"How did you get it?"

Carson sighed. "Sparky, you ask a lot of questions."

"You're a Scion who is multi-gifted. You should easily be able to answer simple questions."

"Nathan and I went there. It's not a big deal."

Krista was grinning so big behind him I thought her lips would get stuck.

"When did you go there?" I asked.

"Earlier today."

"Why did you go there?"

Carson rolled his eyes. "To get the stupid Howlite. Seriously, enough with the questions."

He stood and turned to walk away, but I followed him. "You and Nathan went to Nova Scotia specifically to get me Howlite?"

"Yes, but stop acting like it's a big deal."

"I never said it was a big deal." I quickened my pace to keep up with him. "But you've said it twice so maybe it's a big deal to you."

"I was just trying to help."

"That was amazingly sweet of you."

He halted to a stop in the hallway and faced me. "I was *not* being sweet. I'm just trying to help you remember your past so we can straighten out this mess and Nathan can stop being so miserable."

"Deny it all you want," I said. "You made a special trip across the world to find a beautiful stone for me. That is sweet."

"Good grief, stop acting like such a noob." He held out his hand. "Give it back. I changed my mind."

I clutched the rock to my chest. "No way. It's mine."

"Then shut up about it." He stormed into his room and slammed the door.

"Can you believe it?" I asked Krista as she walked up behind me.

"Of course I can. He's super thoughtful, and he worries about you constantly."

My eyes bugged. "He does?"

"You know I'd never date a guy who didn't like you."

"You do realize how drastically different our conversations about dating have changed in the last few months, right?"

Krista shrugged. "I'm just glad you're finally catching up. The supernatural life is much more interesting than regular life."

I examined the Howlite. "He made it into a necklace."

"He's crafty."

"I still can't believe he did this. I'll treasure it forever."

"Good." She shouldered me. "He'll pretend it annoys the crap out of him, but in reality he'll be touched. Especially if it works."

I draped the cord over my head, admiring the stone resting against my chest. "You mean *when* it works."

∞

When Dylan and Amber arrived with Mikey, I knew the meeting wasn't just about me seeing Dedrick kill the possible keepers of the Earthstone. Dylan and Amber hadn't attended the last couple of impromptu meetings. Louise said they'd be updated, but their attendance wasn't necessary. All hands on deck meant we were meeting about something of utmost importance.

Amber set Mikey's carrier on the table beside Carson, his proper place in the alignment. Dakota carried a stool in from the kitchen and squeezed in to the right of Mikey, left of Edgar, completing the circle. All members—official and unofficial— were in attendance.

I gulped down the rest of my tea.

"What's going on?" I asked Nathan as he sat beside me.

He rested his arm on the back of my chair. "Nothing you can't handle."

"Let's begin, shall we?" Louise's bracelets jingled as she rested her hands on the table. "We already know that Dedrick is trying to acquire all the stones. When used together, the stones feed off each other and connect all energy on this planet. They could potentially control or destroy creation."

Control or destroy creation? I glanced around, assessing reactions. I didn't want to be the one to ask stupid questions, but what exactly did that mean?

"An Aetherstone," Louise continued. "Or a starstone connects the other four. A starstone would enable the other four to be used together."

"But the starstones aren't located on Earth, right?" I asked, confirming what Nathan and I had discussed.

"Right. And based on what you told us from your travels to Meru, we know there were many of them, but—" Louise shifted in her seat.

"Ahh, there it is," Carson said, "the big *but* that can't be ignored."

Nathan gripped my shoulder in a supportive way. "I'll tell her."

My head snapped left, wondering what exactly Nathan was about to tell me and why he waited until the meeting to spring it on me.

"There are many starstones, but whether there's one or one billion," he whispered, "we think you may have brought one back."

I leaned toward him. "Me? I brought back a starstone? From Meru?"

"That's our best educated guess."

"Maryah," Edgar said my name gingerly. "I found it buried deep within the Akashic Records. Last life, you performed a ritual that vibrated you to such a high energy level that you were no longer a blip on our earthly radar. The Akashic Records couldn't record you for the short time you were at Meru. Then you reappeared with a much stronger signal than before. At first and second glance, I couldn't find anything unusual. Your energy had strengthened but with good reason. However, I searched again, more closely, and I glimpsed a patch on the screen, as if you tried to hide your thoughts and actions from being recorded." He grinned at me. "I must say, the fact that you accomplished such a feat is impressive. It's also somewhat disturbing that you manipulated our universal record-keeping system, but impressive nonetheless."

"Why would I hide anything?"

"Perhaps you knew Dedrick had a reader like me. Josephine was being mind-controlled by him. She could have read the records and traced your actions."

"But I don't understand how a patch on the screen would mean I had a starstone."

"I tried removing the patch," Edgar said. "To help you understand, it's like trying to watch a scrambled television station. I could make out parts of what I was seeing, but without the whole picture, my interpretation becomes muddied."

"I figured it out," Nathan said. "Based on what Edgar told me he saw in the records combined with things you did and said during the weeks before we were killed, I'm almost certain you had a starstone and were protecting it."

I shook my head. "That's too vague. What did I do and say?"

"It's all the stuff that didn't make sense until now," Nathan explained. "You insisted all our members live near each other, that we had to live in Sedona due to the powerful elemental energy here. Building the weapon room and bunker under the house, you were preparing for a war. Us versus them. You knew Dedrick would come for it. I don't understand why you wouldn't tell me you had it, but I think you were concealing the starstone and equipping us to protect it at any cost."

"Concealing it where?"

His focus dropped to my hand. "Your ring."

My fingers wrapped around my thumb ring. I pressed my fist in my lap and stared down. Peeling back my fingers, I rubbed the small glass dome with my other hand. "My peacock ring?"

"That's the thing. It didn't always have that feather jewel inside of it. And you weren't wearing it when we were attacked at the beach. You had given the ring to Sheila. You told me she had a friend who made jewelry and you were having a peacock feather embedded inside."

Sheila told me we used to share secrets. That Krista used to get upset because I confided in her so much.

Nathan held my hand. "Your ring is the one possession that has stayed with you every lifetime. What if you found a way to put the stone inside of the ring and disguise it as that feather?"

I stared at him, then at my ring, then back at him. Was it possible?

"Sheila kept the ring with her for many years," Louise said. "She refused to give it to us until recently when you returned to Sedona. It has always been your wedding ring, so we assumed it was her way of holding onto you, believing that you and Nathan would be together again. Now we think she might have known the ring contained the starstone."

"No, she would have told us." Krista's on-edge voice startled me. "She wouldn't have taken such important information to the grave with her."

"Maybe it's true," I murmured, spinning the ring around my thumb. "There is something magical about it. The peacock feather inside, I've seen it move or glisten a few times. It's been a trigger object to me astral traveling or remembering things."

All eyes were on me. Even the tiny eye of the peacock feather, suspended in its glass globe, seemed to be watching me. "What do I do? How do I keep it safe?"

Louise hugged herself, rubbing her own arms as if she felt the same chill that had just given me goose bumps. "We were hoping you'd instinctively have an answer to that question."

"It's a big part of why I gave you that Howlite," Carson said. "You have to remember why you took a starstone from Meru and how to give it back—before Dedrick steals it and uses it to connect the other stones."

"What would happen?" I licked my lips, dreading the answer to my question. "If he did connect the stones?"

"It's not pretty." Carson tugged his hoodie strings.

"Again, we can only speculate," Edgar said.

"Tell her, Car," Dakota insisted.

"Edgar fills me in on what he discovers while he's trancing out doing his thing. I've been making mental notes, trying to figure out what all the bits add up to. My conclusion—" Carson rapped the table with his knuckles. "It's sort of out there. Like, part of my brain insists I'm right, but the other part thinks I've read too many comic books, and I'm jumping to irrational conclusions."

"Spit it out, Carson," Harmony said.

He cleared his throat. "It would mean Dedrick could do what he threatened. He could control the energy portals to this world. Shut them down if he chose to."

"How is that even possible?" Faith asked.

Carson tucked his hair behind his ears. "Given what I've learned about the stones, I think Dedrick could use them to disconnect the power that connects Earth's ley lines."

"Ley lines?" I asked.

"Think of them as veins that run through our planet," Carson explained. "If they were shut off, it would be like a body with no blood running through it. You can imagine the results."

"Good god." I gasped. Nathan wrapped his arm around me again.

"We can stop him," Dakota said. "The good guys always save the world. It's like a universal law that evil never wins."

Dylan sighed. "This isn't a comic book, Dakota. This is real life. And real evil."

Dakota crossed his arms over his chest. "And we're real life superheroes, so what's the problem?"

Everyone exchanged glances, communicating dozens of silent worrisome thoughts.

I stared at my ring resting in my lap. I don't know where my confidence came from. It was almost like having an out-of-body experience when I heard myself say, "Dakota is right. Dedrick can't win, so let's figure out how stop him. Permanently."

LEAD TO BELIEVE

Maryah

"Did I miss anything?" I asked Rina. She was reading pages near the end of her book. "Nothing worth mentioning."

I hovered behind her and focused on the blank pages. "What do you see when you look at those pages?"

"Stories. A song. A letter."

"All written with stardust like Dakota said?"

"Yes."

"Can you read it out loud to me?"

"No."

"Why not?"

She placed her fingertip on the page and dragged it left to right as if keeping track of each line as she silently read. "Because."

"Because why?"

"The author forbade it to be read out loud." Her finger stopped moving. "Those who are meant to know the story will read it on their own."

"Can you at least tell me what the story is about?"

She spun in her chair and glared at me. "Don't be lazy. Read the book if you want to know what it's about."

"I'd love to read it." At least it would give me a way to pass the painful time of being trapped in this place with nothing to do. "But I can't."

"You haven't even tried."

"I'm going to," I conceded. "If you say it's important, I believe you. I'll start right now."

"Really?"

"Yes, scoot out of the way so I can see it."

She hopped out of her chair, staring at me as I studied the two blank pages.

"What are you doing? No one starts at the end of a story."

"Oh, sorry. Could you flip to the beginning for me?"

She closed the book, rested her hand on the cover, and took a breath. "Remember, all you have to do is open your eyes."

My eyes were open, at least my spiritual eyes were, but nothing was visible. She opened to the first page and stepped away slowly as if she had just presented me with a gift. I focused on the ivory page, imagining words glittering the way my ring did.

My ring. Eyes. Duh. Why did it take me so long to make the connection? If what the kindrily suspected was true, if the starstone was in my ring, and my ring contained the eye of a peacock feather, I was certain the ring would help me read the story written in stardust. Out of habit, I reached for my thumb, but of course my ring wasn't physically with me, so I doubted it would work.

"What's wrong?" Rina asked.

"Nothing." She couldn't know about the starstone. If that information leaked out to Dedrick, the whole world could suffer.

If my soul could communicate with Rina, maybe my ring could help me sensperience enough to see something in the book. I pictured the tiny feather in vivid detail, and then stared at the pages, squinting until my head ached.

I couldn't have been more shocked when Nathan materialized in front of me.

Rina leapt up from her place on the floor. "What are you doing here?"

"I did it?" Nathan looked surprised too. He glanced down at the table he was sitting on. I moved back as he stood and pulled the book out from under him. "I found you."

"How?" I asked, forgetting he couldn't hear me.

"Leave," Rina demanded. "Dedrick could come here any second and catch you."

"Take her!" I was so excited I couldn't stop myself from yelling. "Rina, tell him to traverse you to our house right now. He can get you out of here!"

Rina looked dumbfounded. Nathan was still examining my glowing form.

"Holy heavenly light," he uttered. "It's even more awe-inspiring than I imagined." He leaned forward, trying to touch me. "How did Dedrick manage this?"

"Rina," I urged. "Tell him! Tell him to traverse you out of here."

Rina tentatively stepped closer. "Maryah wants you to traverse me to your house."

Nathan turned to face her. He stared at her, his head craning sideways. He sucked in a breath and his lips parted, but he said nothing. His fingers flexed at his sides. He swayed forward then back again and rubbed his hand over his face.

"Enough with the awkward meeting!" I shouted. "Tell him to traverse you out of here!"

"She's yelling at you," Rina said meekly, "to traverse with me."

I realized this was Nathan's first time actually seeing Rina in her own body instead of mine, but we couldn't waste any more time.

"Yes, of course." Nathan shook his head, snapping himself out of his rude staring, and then he scanned the room. "I lost my head for a minute."

Rina reached toward me. "You'll follow us, right? You'll return to your body."

"Yes, I'll be right behind you."

"We're not coming back?" she asked.

"Never."

Nathan watched us, understanding we were communicating even though he could hear only Rina's side of the conversation.

"Then I'll need to get my things." She clutched the book to her chest. "Okay, I'm ready."

Nathan looked as sad as I felt. One book was the only possession she had.

I placed my hands on the back of her shoulders and eased her toward Nathan. "Take her to her new home."

"My new home," Rina said longingly.

Nathan stepped closer to her. He spoke gentler than I'd ever heard him or any other man speak. "I'm going to put my arms around you."

"Okay," she whispered.

Looking over her shoulder, she smiled at me. Her smile was so bright the room seemed to acquire windows, allowing light and joy to shine through for the first time. Nathan hugged her to him and closed his eyes. Then he vanished.

Rina still stood there, hugging her book.

Nathan reappeared.

"What happened?" My light energy pulsed rapidly.

"It didn't work," Rina said.

"It felt like I had you," Nathan told her, "but you didn't go anywhere."

"Again," I insisted.

"Maryah says try again."

He hugged her a second time, pressing her cheek against his chest, then he disappeared, leaving her behind.

"No!" I wanted to punch something.

"It won't work," Rina said. The room was dim again, her inner light gone. "I'm still trapped."

Nathan returned. "I don't understand why it's not working."

"It wasn't meant to be this way," Rina told him. "I should have known. You have to leave before someone sees you."

He moved so close to me our faces were touching. "At least we know I can traverse here. I'll tell the others and we'll figure out what to do next."

"Rina, tell him not to traverse back here until I come home and discuss it."

She repeated what I said and Nathan agreed.

He raised his hand, touching my soul. "You're so beautiful."

"Go. Now," Rina commanded.

Nathan turned, bent forward and kissed the top of her messy-haired head. "We'll find a way to get you out of here, I promise."

She halfheartedly nodded, and then Nathan was gone. Now we both had the same promise to keep.

"Go," Rina said.

"Go where?"

"To talk to him. I'm sure you want to discuss what happened."

Her disappointment mirrored mine. We had glimpsed hope for a few brief moments, but it had been snuffed out. I couldn't leave her so soon.

"I'll go in a little while. Maybe by then the kindrily will have figured out a solution." I struggled to find something else to say, something to comfort her. "I'm so sorry it didn't work."

"It's okay." She sat in the chair, her hands hanging limp at her sides. "It was one of the happiest moments of my life."

"But you didn't go anywhere."

"Still, for a few seconds..." She folded her hands in her lap and stared at the flickering candle flame. "I was going home."

My heart ached even more. I wanted nothing more than to set her free, to help her find her place in this world.

"That's what you said." Rina shifted in her chair. "You said my new home."

"I figured you could stay with us." The Luna house was always filled with people. One more wouldn't make a difference.

She spoke softly. "Before you said you'd have to check with Louise and Anthony for permission."

"You were a stranger when I said that. Now I'm sure everyone would welcome you."

Even in the dim lighting, I saw her cheeks blush. It was the first trace of color I'd ever seen on her face besides food or dirt.

"I hope Nathaniel is okay," she said.

"You know a lot about how things work around here. Do you have any guesses as to why Nathan couldn't traverse with you?"

Rina shook her head. "Nothing for certain."

"Maybe Dedrick shielded you?"

"From one power in particular but not the others? Not likely."

"Hopefully Carson will think of something." I reached for my Howlite necklace. The real version was still back in Sedona with my body—where I wished Rina and I could have safely escaped to. But even if we did, Dedrick would have come looking for us. We would have lived every moment looking over our shoulders, waiting for him to strike again.

"Escaping won't be enough," I told her. "We have to stop Dedrick for good."

"Do you mean kill him?"

Did I mean that? Was I capable of ending a human life? "I haven't figured out that part yet."

Manny scurried out of a crack in the wall then crawled up Rina's leg and sat in her lap.

She scratched his head. "Probably best it didn't work. I wouldn't have said good-bye to Manny, and he would have been upset."

"True." I grinned at the sight of them. "Maybe we could bring Manny home too. And hope Eightball doesn't try to eat him." I snapped to attention. "Oh my gosh! Manny!"

"What's wrong?" Rina asked.

"He could help us."

"Manny could help us?"

"Yes! Maybe. I'm not sure. How intelligent are mice?"

Rina scowled as if I'd offended him. "Manny is brilliant."

"Let's hope so." A glimmer of optimism had returned. It was a long shot, but it was worth a try. "I need to see my kindrily. When I get back we might have a new plan."

"What is it?" Rina asked, excitement simmering beneath her confusion.

"Don't get your hopes up again. Just give me a few minutes, and then I can explain more."

She agreed then effortlessly allowed me to travel home.

As soon as I reconnected to my body, I threw back my covers. Helen startled as objects flew off my bed. "Maryah?"

I eyed the array of rocks and plants I had just flung all over the floor. "What's all that stuff?"

"Herbs and gemstones I used to increase the frequency of your energy so Nathan could locate your soul."

"Awesome. It worked." I sprang out of bed and grabbed Helen's hand, dragging her behind me. "Come on, I have an idea."

As Helen followed me down the hall, I heard Nathan discussing his failed traversing attempt.

I rounded the corner, sliding across the tile floor due to my fuzzy socks. "Come back and get Manny."

Nathan, Louise, Carson, and Krista all stared at me.

"Who?" Nathan asked.

"Rina's mouse."

"Ohh, I like it." Carson rubbed his hands together. "Dr. Doolittle meets James Bond."

Nathan's face relaxed the moment it registered. "Yes. Dedrick wouldn't have thought to put a spell on a mouse to keep him trapped there." Nathan kissed my forehead. "You're brilliant."

Krista raised her hand. "I hate that I haven't caught on yet, but please fill me in."

Carson wrapped his arm around her. "I'll explain it to her. Louise, you call Amber. Nathan, go catch yourself a mouse."

Nathan wrapped his arms around me then jerked away like I burned him. "What am I doing?"

We both stared at each other, somewhat in shock that he almost traversed my body to Dedrick's dungeon.

"Probably not a good idea," I said.

"Awful idea. What if I couldn't traverse you out of there?"

"I'll astral travel back. Give me a few minutes lead time so I can explain why you need to take Manny."

Nathan nodded. "I'll be there soon."

∞

"Rina." She and Manny were still sitting in the chair. "Nathan is coming back, and he's going to take Manny with him for a little while."

She cupped her hand over him. "Why?"

"He might be able to help us figure out where we are."

Rina squinted at me then at Manny. "How?"

"One of our members can communicate with animals."

Understanding swept over her eyes, but then she glanced at Manny with concern. Nathan materialized, looking much more optimistic than when he left a short while ago.

"What if traversing hurts him?" Rina asked.

"He'll be fine," Nathan assured her.

I hoped he was right. Manny was so small. What if it made him really sick? Or heaven forbid he died. Rina would be devastated if she lost her only friend.

Nathan held out his hands and Rina lifted her arm, offering Manny a bridge to scurry down. Manny followed her silent command and hopped onto Nathan's open palm.

"Manny," Nathan said his name so tenderly that I wanted to kiss him. "You're going on a journey to meet some of my family. They'll be very kind to you."

Manny's whiskers twitched. Rina grinned.

"I'm speaking to a mouse as if he understands me," Nathan said, "but according to Amber, animals understand most of what we say."

Rina tugged his shirt. "Please be careful with him."

"Of course." Nathan cupped Manny. "I must say, this is a first. Let's hope my ability works with animals."

"He likes bread and crackers." Rina petted Manny's head poking out of Nathan's hands. Her voice strained with sadness. "And whatever happens, don't bring him back here."

"Are you sure?" Nathan asked.

Rina's shoulders sagged as she nodded.

"You'll see him again soon. In a place much better than this." Nathan closed his concerned eyes, and then he evaporated.

"That was very selfless," I said, "letting go of your only friend."

"He deserves better than this."

"So do you." I bent down, trying to get her to look at me. "Nathan's right. You'll see Manny soon. When we go home."

She peered up at me with bleary eyes. "Do you really believe that?"

"I do."

GREAT THINGS COME IN SMALL PACKAGES

Nathaniel

I materialized in Amber and Dylan's bathroom, practically standing on Amber's feet and falling backward into the sink as I tried to gain my footing.

"Nathan!" She pulled her towel tighter around her.

"I apologize for the unannounced visit." The tickling of tiny claws and a tail confirmed I had indeed traversed with the mouse. I opened my hands. "This is Manny."

"Carson told me you were coming, but I didn't think you'd be here so soon."

"Amber, you okay?" Dylan rushed into the bathroom. "Oh, Nathan, that was quick."

"Let me get dressed," Amber said. "Dyl, be a good host and get our guest some cheese from the fridge."

"Pretty ingenious idea." Dylan elbowed me as I walked out of the bathroom.

"I can't take credit. It was Maryah's suggestion."

Dylan lifted Mikey out of his playpen and set him on the floor. Mikey crawled behind us, following us into the kitchen. I watched him with amazement. "He's crawling already?"

Dylan grinned. "Amber and I are fairly certain he's a Scion. He has so many of the same characteristics as Carson. His muscle control is developing abnormally fast, and he's already making noises that almost sound like words."

Dylan opened the refrigerator then set a block of cheese on the counter. "The other day he tugged on my pant leg to get my attention."

"Impressive," I noted. "I'm eager to see what abilities he develops."

Dylan's lip curled, and pride shone in his eyes. "I have a hunch of what it might be." He broke off a corner of cheese and handed it to me. "But Amber won't allow me to say anything until we're sure."

"Let's focus on our task, shall we?" Amber said, walking up behind me. "Maybe this mouse can tell us where Dedrick is."

As interested as I was in Mikey's ability, I was much more interested in finding out where Dedrick had Rina living in such dismal conditions. Maryah was right. We had to get her out of there. Now that I'd seen Rina—the real Rina—with my own eyes, my reasons were mounting.

Amber took the mouse from me. "I'll speak out loud so you guys can feel involved." She smiled down at our furry guest. "Hello, Manny. Do you know where you came from? The name of the place, or its location?" She subtly shook her head as if mirroring the mouse's thoughts. "Anything you can share would be most helpful. Details of the inside or the outside, names you may have overheard."

After a couple of silent minutes, Amber's chin bobbed up and down. She stood then backed up, swaying a moment before turning. She tried to sit again, but missed her chair and landed on the floor, her hands clutched to her chest with Manny still inside.

Dylan and I were by her side in an instant, offering her help, but she seemed unaware of us. Her head kept twitching left to right.

"Amber?" I knelt in front of her. "Look at her eyes. They're darting around like she's having a seizure."

Dylan shoved me aside and held her face. "Amber, what's wrong? Can you hear me?"

She jerked hard, snapping out of it. She opened her hands to make sure Manny was all right then glanced up at us. "Well, it seems my ability has strengthened too."

"What happened?" Dylan asked.

"He didn't *tell* me any details. He showed them to me."

"Showed them to you?" I repeated.

Amber pushed her glasses up her nose. "It was fascinating. From his perspective, I traveled dirt hallways. I was low to the ground, squeezing between cracks and behind walls. I saw bugs, cobwebs, even mouse droppings."

"Do you have any idea where it was?" I asked.

"Not yet, but he's willing to show me more. I wanted to tell you guys what was happening so you wouldn't worry, but I was so fascinated by what I was experiencing. He doesn't understand when I ask for the name of a town, but that's the mentality of a mouse. They can follow and retrace paths exceptionally well, but they don't have geographical awareness like we do. He'll show me memories of everywhere he's ever been, but I don't know how long that might take."

"While you investigate, I'll tell Rina her mouse is safe. She was worried something might happen to him."

"We'll be here," Dylan said. Amber had already turned her attention back to Manny.

That wasn't my only reason for needing to see Rina again. I wasn't ready to alarm anyone else yet without more information, but I was fairly certain I had solved the mystery of Rina's identity.

∞

I didn't want to admit it, even to myself, but I was exhausted.

Finding my way to the room where Rina and Maryah's soul were being kept took more energy than usual while traversing. Helen's idea had worked, but it still required intense focus to find Maryah's soul.

I splayed my hands in front of me, pushing against the tunnel of darkness. I needed to find the opening quickly. The longer I searched, the weaker I felt. I moved faster, urging my hands to find the pocket of warmth again. Finally, my fingers buzzed with a familiar electrical current. I pushed through, parting the invisible curtain.

Rina tried yanking him away so he didn't see me, but it was too late.

"Nathan?" River gawked at me.

My fists balled. Maryah's light form darted toward me. The faint outline of her lips moved, but I couldn't hear her.

Rina positioned herself between River and me, facing him.

"You can't utter a word about Nathan," Rina told him. She stood on her tiptoes and poked River's chest. "Not a word. Not to anyone."

River kept his focus on me. "How long has he been coming here?"

"None of your bloody business," I snarled.

Rina snapped around and glared at me. "Stop it. River is trying to help."

"*He* is trying to help? He tried to kill Maryah and me."

Maryah's glowing figure kept swiping at me as if trying to grab my arm or face. I couldn't concentrate on anything except the fact that River now knew I could traverse here. Surely, he'd tell Dedrick, and he'd find a way to make his protective force field stronger.

"Like I've told Maryah," River said, "I swear, I don't remember anything at Montezuma Well. I just want to get out of this hellhole and far, far away from Dedrick."

"Right." I sneered. "As if I will ever believe a word spewed from your mouth."

He stepped forward and so did I, but Rina put her hands on our chests, keeping us separated. "I don't care how you two feel about each other. Wouldn't our odds of surviving this, of Maryah surviving this, be much better if we all worked together?"

"I will never work with him on anything," I growled. "Not in this lifetime or any other."

He puffed up his chest as if that would intimidate me. "If we don't stop Dedrick soon, there won't be any other lifetimes."

"Boys," Rina said sternly. Her head whipped back and forth as she spoke to us. "You both need to get out of here. Evelyn said Dedrick was coming to visit this evening. He can't catch one of you here much less both of you."

"He leaves first," I insisted. I wanted to see if I could figure out how he left the room without a door.

"Please!" Rina clutched River's shirt. "Maryah and I are both begging you. You need to leave."

"Fine," River agreed, "but I'll be back as soon as I can." He turned to Maryah and said, "See you soon."

I wanted to cut his tongue out so he could never speak to her again. The woman who had been standing in the corner of the room, in the shadows, still as a statue and never uttering a word, stepped forward and held onto River's arm. She blew out the candle and darkness engulfed the room. I couldn't see anything, not even Maryah's glowing form.

When the candle flickered back to life, Rina was the only physical body in the room with me. Maryah's light pulsed in different shades of purple, green, and blue.

"Dedrick could be here any second," Rina warned me.

Part of me wanted to stay and beat him senseless when he arrived. I could kill him now and end it all. But considering I felt exhausted enough to pass out at Rina's feet, and I had no idea what abilities Dedrick had working to his advantage, or how to physically get in and out of the room, me staying would only make matters worse.

I smoothed down Rina's messy hair. "I wanted to tell you that Manny is fine. Amber is taking good care of him."

A grin tugged at her lips. "Make sure he eats."

"He's feasting like a king."

Her smile brightened ten shades, but then shadows darkened her eyes again. "You need to go. Don't come back again until Maryah tells you it's safe."

I nodded then turned to Maryah. "Don't trust River. Come home as soon as you can so we can discuss this. I love you."

Her light pulsed, and her lips moved.

"She loves you too," Rina said.

I used the last bit of strength I had to traverse to Dylan and Amber's house.

As hard as I tried to stay upright, the journey drained my body of the limited strength it had left. My head whacked against the coffee table as I collapsed on their living-room floor.

Molokai sat a few feet away. Her tail wagged as she pawed at a baby rattle hovering in mid-air. Mikey appeared in front of her. He dropped his rattle and crawled toward me. His body flickered in and out of existence as his blue eyes became a tunnel of light.

"Baby," I murmured, and then I passed out.

SPITTING IT OUT

Nathaniel

I sat up in bed beside Maryah.

Krista glanced up from her book. "Hello, Sleeping Beauty."

"How long was I out?"

"Almost twenty-four hours."

I rolled my stiff neck. "Bollocks. What have I missed?"

"Surprisingly, not much."

"Has Maryah been here?"

"No, but Rina visited and told us to let you sleep as long as you needed while she and Maryah worked on her training."

"Training?"

Krista shrugged. "We asked. She wouldn't explain. As usual."

I stood. "I need to talk to them."

"No!" Krista closed her book and set it on the nightstand. "Rina said you couldn't traverse there again until she or Maryah gave you clearance. She was adamant about that."

I felt slightly out of it, weak and light-headed. Perhaps it would be wise to wait until I felt better. "I'm famished. I need to eat."

"I'll go with you." Krista helped me out of bed. "I'm supposed to tell the others when you're awake so we can have a meeting."

I stopped. Did they already know what I suspected? "A meeting about what?"

Krista flashed an impish smile. "Oh, did I forget to mention that Amber knows the location of Dedrick's lair?"

"Krista! Where is it?"

"I don't know yet. Amber said she'd tell us as a group, and we'd figure out the next step from there."

"Where is Amber?"

"Probably feeding Mikey. It's dinnertime."

I traversed to the kitchen. Amber sat on the living-room floor, playing with Mikey. "Where are they?"

Amber handed Mikey a teething toy. "Good evening to you too, Nathan."

I forced my tired legs to move forward until I stood over her. "Amber, where are they?"

"I'm not discussing it until we have a proper roundtable with everyone present. And after you promise not to traverse there."

My voice was almost a growl. "Amber."

"Back off, Nathan." Dylan unloaded the dishwasher. "It's for everyone's safety. If she told you their location right now, you'd impulsively traverse there and put yourself and Maryah in jeopardy."

I took a deep breath, watching Amber. She knew where they were. She knew Dedrick's location, and yet she sat there cooing at Mikey and playing with him as if the information she possessed wasn't life and universe-altering.

"For crying out loud," I said, "When is the blasted meeting?"

"I'm already calling everyone," Krista shouted from the kitchen.

∞

Less than an hour passed before all members arrived for the meeting, but it felt like ages. I paced around the table, waiting for everyone to sit down so I could find out Dedrick's location.

Faith and Shiloh were the last to arrive, but Faith announced she had to use the restroom.

"Is Maryah here?" Harmony asked.

I sat down. "No."

"Actually," Louise said, strolling into the kitchen with Maryah behind her. "Maryah's body will be present for the meeting."

Dakota sprang up from his seat. "Hi, Rina."

"Hello, Dakota," Rina replied politely.

I rose from my chair. "Impeccable timing. Did you know we were about to have a meeting?"

Rina started to chew Maryah's fingers but then clasped her hands behind her back. "I had a feeling that one of us needed to be here for an important discussion."

"And why did you come instead of Maryah?" I asked.

"She's practicing."

My interest piqued. "Practicing what?"

"Connecting strings."

"Strings?" Dakota asked. "How can she handle strings without her hands?"

"They're special strings," Rina said.

Faith sashayed into the room. "Maryah! You're back."

Rina turned, and Faith's smile wavered, but didn't fade. "Oh, sorry, Rina. Hello again."

Rina touched Faith's stomach. "You're pregnant."

Faith beamed. "How'd you know?"

"Faith!" Louise exclaimed. "Why didn't you tell us?"

Amber and Krista squealed and rushed to Faith's side to congratulate her. Shiloh received handshakes and celebratory slaps on the back. I donned a smile to show my support, but my feet stayed rooted in place.

Faith's sparkling eyes drifted to me. "With all this soul-stealing madness going on, it never seemed like an appropriate time to announce it."

"You're having a baby," Helen squealed while clapping. "We can always use that kind of good news."

Faith walked over to me and touched my arm. I flinched because I didn't want her to feel my emotions, but she had probably already seen them written all over my face. "I'm sorry you're upset. I know the timing is awful. I didn't want you to find out yet."

She didn't know the half of it.

"It's fine," I assured her. The kindrily tip-toed around the issue of pregnancy for my sake. Mary and I had always been the last to know when one of our members was expecting a child. We were always happy for them, of course, but after so many failed attempts, so many heartbreaking losses, we couldn't help but be envious of those who could have children. "Despite my initial reaction, I am genuinely happy for you."

She hugged me, but over her shoulder my eyes locked with Rina's. Did she know? Was it one of the many secrets she hid from us, or was her history kept in the dark and locked away just like she had been for so many years?

"Okay," Faith said, turning back to the group. "We can celebrate the baby news later. Let's find out where Maryah and Rina are being kept so we can get them out of there."

Everyone took their seats, but Rina kept still. Only one chair remained empty, so it was obvious where she should have sat. Gregory pulled out the chair between us. "Rina, you can sit in Maryah's place."

She stroked Maryah's hair, eying everyone gathered around the table. "I feel like that would be wrong."

"Rina, please," I said, "I insist and so would Maryah."

She crept forward and slowly sat down.

"Nathan—" Louise glared at me over her glasses. "You must solemnly swear to stay put once Amber discloses Maryah's location. We will discuss our strategy as a group and not make a move until we weigh all of our options. It's getting late so we will all take a solid night's sleep to think on this. If we have any chance of proceeding and being successful, we will need a well-thought-out plan. Do you understand and agree?"

As difficult as it would be to not act impulsively, Louise was right. "I understand and agree."

"All right then." Amber leaned forward and pushed her glasses up her nose. "Thanks to Manny, I think I know where Rina and Maryah are being imprisoned."

Their location couldn't spill from Amber's lips fast enough.

FATE LINES

Maryah

When Rina returned, I was hovering in front of the glass cabinet, watching my light change colors as I focused on different kindrily members and my feelings for them.

"You're a great teacher," I told her. "It works—especially when I use your Connect the Dots method." I had been practicing on my ties with Krista. "It's fascinating how many different shades of color and textures there are for each person."

"I told you. No soul's energy looks or feels exactly the same."

I turned in a circle, still watching my reflection. "Louise says the same thing. Her paintings around the house are her interpretation of our auras. Now I see why she paints some to look metallic, sparkling, smooth, grainy, or whatever. You can see and feel so many differences."

"Have you practiced with every member yet?"

"Almost. I started with Edgar since he's the oldest and worked my way down. I still need to study Carson and Mikey."

"What about Dakota?"

Dakota wanted to be an Element so badly. Rina probably assumed he was a kindrily member since he was staying at our house and attended every roundtable meeting. "Dakota isn't an official kindrily member, but we think of him as one."

"Have you seen his comics?"

"One of them."

"He's gifted."

"Yes, very talented." I tore my focus away from my colorful reflection. "So, who did you see while you visited this time? Any news to report?"

"I saw everyone."

"Everyone?" My brows rose. "Like the whole kindrily?"

"Every member except you."

My pulse quickened. "Did something important happen?"

"Amber announced our location."

I couldn't have heard her right. "Our location? You and me? This dungeon?"

"Yes," she confirmed nonchalantly.

"Rina! How are you so calm about this? Why didn't you tell me as soon as you came back? Where are we?"

She sat in her chair, scooting it close to the table. "An abandoned subterranean kingdom in the Himalayas."

My shock hung in the air for a moment before my limited geography knowledge surfaced. "The Himalayas are massive. They extend across multiple countries. You're saying we could be buried inside of one of hundreds of mountains?"

"They narrowed it down to a couple."

I floated over to the table, hovering across from her. "How will they search the inside of two huge mountains?"

"Not two mountains. Two mountain ranges."

"*Ranges*? How many ranges are there?"

"Carson said seven, I think." She opened her book. "I'm not sure. It was a lot of information to absorb."

"Seven ranges? That means each range has..." I had no idea how many mountains were in the Himalayas. A broad math equation would have to do. "...tons of mountains!" My heart sank. "They'll never find us."

"Yes, they will because we'll help them."

"How?"

She tapped her lip. "I'm not sure yet. It's all happening much sooner than expected, which is why you need to master connecting with the kindrily's energy quicker than we thought. Also, if you could tap into your power to alter the future, that would be beneficial."

"What?" I guffawed. "I wouldn't even know where to begin."

She spun the book around and pushed it toward me. "Begin here."

I finally understood. She didn't want me to read the book; she wanted me to use it to create a story. She had spent too much time with Dakota. "You want me to write a story and predict a happy ending for us?"

"You already wrote the story." She jabbed the blank page. "We need you to read it and finish where you left off."

"I haven't written anything in that book."

She slammed her palms on the table. "You did in your previous life. You just need to open your eyes and read it."

I lowered my voice in an attempt to keep her from getting more angry or frustrated. "Rina, I erased all memories of my previous life. Even if I had written in that book, it has clearly been erased from the pages just like my memories were erased from my soul."

"You didn't erase them forever. Energy has no beginning and no end. It can change form, but it can't be erased."

"Well then, I have changed into a weaker and less knowledgeable version of myself, so any story you think I may have written has been deleted."

"That's not true. Look at your fate lines."

I glanced down at my ghostly hands, wanting to look at the parallel lines on my palms that Sheila had discussed with me before she passed away. I couldn't make out the details of my skin through the blur of light. "How do you know about my fate lines?"

"I know a lot of things."

My voice rose with agitation. "Can you ever answer a question directly?"

"Yes."

"Then tell me how you know about my fate lines."

"That wasn't a question."

"Rina!" I wanted to shake her.

"Sheila told me."

"Sheila?" I gasped. Shelia had passed away. Harmony assured us her spirit crossed over. There was no way Rina met Sheila while spending time with the kindrily. "How did—when did you ever meet Sheila?"

"I met her today."

"Today? That's impossible."

Rina moaned. "Stop saying things are impossible. Most everything is possible, and you of all people should know that!"

"Tell me how and where you met Sheila."

"She was with Faith."

"But Sheila is dead."

"Not anymore."

The truth hit me like a thumb jab to my third eye. The words spilled out of me in a whisper. "Faith is pregnant, and the baby is Sheila."

"Correct. If we have any hopes of surviving, you'll need to have epiphanies like that much more frequently."

"But how could you talk to Sheila? She just passed away. Even if Faith is pregnant with her, Sheila would barely be developed."

She slumped back in her chair as if the inconceivable—no pun intended—conversation was boring her. "Her body isn't developed, but her soul is an entirely different matter."

"Her soul told you about my fate lines?"

"Nobody told me anything about you. I read it all."

"You read it?"

"Sheila knew things about people's past. I looked for what she knew about you. The important stuff. Anything that might help us."

"But how? She's an embryo in Faith's uterus. How did you communicate with her?"

Rina looked at me as if I were the most oblivious person in the world. "I touched Faith's stomach to make the connection, and then I borrowed Sheila's reading ability to search her soul for what I needed."

"That's amazing." I shook my head. "Unbelievable, but amazing."

Rina snorted.

"What's so funny?"

"You astral travel," she said. "Nathan traverses around the world. I can leave my body and inhabit yours. But you think me connecting to a soul's energy and gathering intelligence is amazing."

"I guess I'm in shock that Sheila is coming back to join us. Good shock, of course." I paused, thinking of how happy Krista would be. I couldn't contain my enthusiasm as the realization hit me. "This means Sheila is an Element, right?"

Rina's dark brows furrowed. "Was there ever any doubt?"

"None of us knew if she would be. We weren't even sure if she was going to retain. She said she planned to erase."

"But you made her an Element."

"Me? I didn't do anything."

"It's part of the story." Rina pointed to the book.

I wasn't straying into another argument with Rina about the stardust story. "Faith must be ecstatic. And Krista is probably over the moon that Sheila is coming back so soon." I stared at my palms again, trying to recall my conversation with Sheila. "What did you find out about my fate lines?"

"Two parallel lines mean you've created double energy influencing your fate. It also means you're twice as strong because of the duality."

"You're saying I'm stronger than I was in my previous life?" Rina nodded.

"Um, have we met? I erased. I just recently learned to astral travel, I still can't sensperience, and I can't predict the future or whatever I used to do. How does that make me *more* powerful?"

"It's like Rock Paper Scissors. If you play with only those three tools, too much is left to chance. You must play with rocks, paper, scissors, strings, and glue."

"What in the world are you talking about?"

"You've never heard of the game Rock Paper Scissors?"

"Sure I have. Back when Mikey was my brother, we played it to decide who sat shotgun or who'd do the dishes." It was still awkward to think of Mikey my brother as Mikey, Dylan and Amber's baby. "I'm surprised you know about games like that."

She ran her finger across a page, talking to me while supposedly reading. "When you played with only rock, paper, and scissors, you lost a lot, right?"

"It was hit or miss."

"Exactly. Because you didn't use strings and glue."

"Rina, I really need you to get to the point."

"The rock, the paper, the scissors—they're all useful, but if you connected them with string and used glue to unite them together, they'd be unbeatable."

"Well sure, because you'd have all the tools instead of one."

She pointed at me and dipped her head. "Now you're getting it."

"But what does that have to do with anything?"

She closed the book. "Dedrick has rocks, paper, and scissors, but we have string and glue."

Rocks. Glue. The starstone was used to connect the other four stones. Could Rina know about that? Was she speaking in some silly code trying to tell me that Dedrick had three of the stones: rock, paper, scissors, and we had the other two stones: strings and glue?

"Where are they?" I asked.

She pointed to me. "String." Then she pointed to herself. "Glue."

She knew I had the starstone.

"Do you know where the last stone is?" I asked.

"No, but I know what we need to do next. It's time to teach you some important skills, but there's one crucial thing we need to make all of this work."

"And that one crucial thing is?"

Her dark blue eyes gleamed in the candlelight. "Your body."

RINGING TRUE

Maryah

I reconnected with my body, ready to tell Nathan about Rina's plan.

Nathan shook me awake. "Are you aware of what's going on in the world?"

"What?" I rubbed my eyes. Our room was different. The curtains were blue instead of green and the bed was facing the balcony door.

"No births have occurred in over twenty-four hours. Anywhere. Worldwide. Dedrick has all of the stones. He's more dangerous than ever." The panic in his voice made my pulse race. I sprang out of bed and pushed past him, rushing toward the open door to our balcony.

In front of me towered a wall of flat red rock being used as a screen. All the kindrily members stood in front of it, watching a breaking news report in their pajamas. The reporter talked as a headline of *World Crisis* scrolled across the top of the screen.

"Over three-hundred-thousand births occur each day in this world, but yesterday zero took place. Researchers have investigated far and wide for evidence of one birth anywhere on our planet, but shockingly none has been discovered. Officials aren't commenting, but online groups and social media feeds are erupting with predictions that this is the beginning of the world's end.

Amber called my name, but it sounded as if she had whispered in my ear. She pointed to the sky, and when I looked up, ravens fell all around us like rain.

I turned to run back inside, but the door and house were gone. I stood on a snowy mountain, dead birds still pouring down all around me, but none of them hitting me. I reached out, catching a raven in my hands.

The black bird lay still, not breathing. I leaned forward blowing on her chest, her inky feathers fluttering from my breath. Her wings flapped, and she rose in front of me. Her eyes opened, glowing dark blue. She squawked, and then with Rina's voice said, "He has all of the stones."

Harmony's voice echoed through the mountains. "If no souls are entering the world that means none are leaving either. Do you realize how many souls will be in limbo?"

I couldn't answer. I tried, but my lips wouldn't part.

Faith rose out of the snowy ground. Her eyelashes were covered in icicles. Scarab beetles crawled across her round stomach. "My baby will never be born."

Rina screamed.

Gregory was dragging the human form of her by her hair. He lifted her, holding her over the edge, about to drop her in the sea of flames below. I yelled for him to stop, but hands grabbed my waist and yanked me backward.

I turned and found Dedrick bleeding from his mouth. We flew over mountains, over Sedona's red rocks, through the balcony door to my bedroom, and down the hallway. The floor to ceiling picture windows in the living room transformed into one of Louise's paintings.

Beams of light rushed forward like a river, surrounding us and filling the room. We were floating, or falling, through a pool of endless swirling colors.

Dedrick spoke to me in gargled words I couldn't understand.

One black feather floated behind him, drifting back and forth as it fell toward a ground that no longer existed.

"Up here," Rina shouted.

She peered down at me through an open manhole cover. She reached through the small hole, stretching her hand until it connected with mine. She pulled me up, and up, and up, and just when I thought I'd never make it out, she lifted me through the round opening and into a starry sky.

We stood there together, riding a slow-moving comet, holding hands, and staring down at Earth.

"How do we save it?" I asked her.

The sphere of blue and green started spinning faster until it blurred and became the eye of a peacock feather floating in space. Its quills turned to thin rays of light, extending through the sky and connecting the billions of stars surrounding us like a universal game of Connect The Dots.

"Are we too late?" I asked.

She squeezed my hand so tightly it hurt, but when I looked down, Rina was gone, and Nathan's hand was gripping mine.

"Please remember." He let go and clutched my shoulders. His voice caused all the stars to brighten. "Open your eyes."

He shook me. Then shook me again.

I jolted up in bed. Nathan sat in front of me, concern etched on his face. "That must have been some nightmare."

Our room was normal. The curtains were green. The bed hadn't moved. The balcony door was closed. "The news. Have there been news reports about no babies being born?"

"Beg your pardon?"

I rubbed my clammy forehead. "Nothing. You're right. It was a nightmare."

Except it wasn't just a nightmare. I had seen what could happen if Dedrick acquired all of the stones. It was a strange, psychedelic version of it, but still real enough to convince me that I had to proceed with Rina's plan.

"I need you to traverse me to the dungeon."

Nathan look appalled. "I most certainly will not. It's too dangerous."

Anger bubbled inside me. "You promised you'd have faith in me. That you'd help me when I needed it."

"I do have faith in you, and I will help, but not like this. Not until we figure out how Dedrick has made Rina immune to my traversing ability."

I shoved him. "Take my body back there right now!"

He caught my hands and held them against his chest. "And what if Dedrick does the same thing to you? Casts a spell or whatever it is he did to Rina, and then I can't traverse your body out of there either? You can't ask me to put you in jeopardy like that. I won't."

"I'm not asking you, Nathan. I'm telling you."

He grimaced then dropped my hands. He stood and turned to walk away from me.

I followed him out of the room and down the hall, my voice getting louder with every step we took. "If you don't take my body to her right now, and something happens where we can't free her from Dedrick, I'll never forgive you."

The tension poured into the house like wet cement, hardening with each passing second of silence. My pulse pounded in my ears.

We stood in the kitchen, Nathan leaning against the island and me staring at his back, waiting for him to reply. Finally, he said, "That's a risk I'll have to take."

I had to make him agree. What could I threaten him with? "If you don't traverse me back there right now, I'm breaking up with you."

He slowly turned around. I could tell he was fighting back a laugh. "Then I'm very sorry. It's not me. It's you."

I lunged forward to grab a piece of fruit from the bowl I knew was behind him. He stepped aside, but the bowl was gone. Seething, I turned, realizing he was holding it behind his back.

"I really want to throw something at you."

"I know. That's why I moved the ammunition. And why I'm strategically standing in front of the toaster."

The only thing left within reach was a dish towel. I balled it up and threw it at him, but it wasn't at all satisfying.

He set the bowl of fruit on the counter behind him and closed the space between us, wrapping his arms around my waist. "Just breathe. The anger will pass. If breaking up with me will help you feel better, go ahead. Winning you back will be enjoyable for both of us."

"This is no time for jokes."

"I'm not joking."

"Rina said in order for us to stop Dedrick, I need to be there body and soul."

"I will take you when the time is right, but not now."

Carson walked into the kitchen carrying a packed duffel bag. "He's right, Maryah. It's for your own protection."

I pushed Nathan away from me. "I can't even look at you right now."

I stormed off down the hall and into the bathroom.

"Maryah?" Nathan called gently from the other side of the closed door. "Please, let me in."

"Go away."

"I'm not going away. Please try to consider my side of this argument."

I huffed and shook my head, kicking the linen closet door.

"Maryah?" he called again. "I won't intrude on your privacy by traversing in there, but I wish you would come out so we can discuss this."

"There's nothing to discuss. When you're ready to traverse me to Rina, let me know. Until then, I'm not coming out."

"Maryah, don't be daft."

That did it. I was tired of everyone else thinking they knew what was best for me. I lay on the bathroom rug, breathed deep, and pictured Rina's eyes.

Nathan's voice sounded further away. "Maryah?"

Drifting like a feather, I became weightless. I wouldn't return again until Nathan brought me my body.

I found myself staring at Rina's dirt-smudged face. Her eyes widened, and she shook her head furiously.

"Well, well, well," Dedrick said from behind me.

I whirled around.

He held a syringe in his hands. "It seems I should have been using the stronger tranquilizer all along."

"Don't touch her!" I threw my arms out, trying to protect Rina. I lunged for the candle, wanting to grab it and burn him. But I had no body. No way to protect Rina. I couldn't think straight.

Dedrick inched closer, taking his time as he circled us like a vulture, enjoying the fear he must have seen in Rina and me. "This calls for a permanent separation of you two."

Just when I thought it couldn't get any worse, Nathan materialized.

"No!" I yelled so loud the room quivered. I caught one fleeting glance of Dedrick's sneer before Nathan spun around, his arm already cocked behind him.

Nathan's fist connected with Dedrick's jaw, and Dedrick's head snapped sideways, but other than that, it barely fazed him.

Nathan grabbed the book from the table. He swung and hit Dedrick in the head so hard that the candle almost blew out. Dedrick fell to the floor.

"Get out of here!" I shouted at Nathan. "Rina, tell him about the tranquilizer!"

Eyes wide, jaw clenched, Rina waved her hands at Nathan, but didn't say a word. Nathan glanced down at her, and in that split second, Dedrick jammed the needle into Nathan's calf.

Nathan staggered backward. Dedrick stood, holding the side of his head.

Nathan threw another punch, but whatever Dedrick injected into him was working fast.

Dedrick dodged his fist and laughed. "Nathaniel, you fool. I never imagined you'd be so easy to trap."

I pounced on Dedrick, kicking and clawing, my pulsing light filling the room as my emotions raged out of control. I roared like a lion attacking.

No one but Rina could hear me, and she seemed paralyzed with fear or shock.

Nathan crumbled to the floor. I tried catching him, but he fell through my useless arms.

Dedrick hooked his hands under Nathan's shoulders. I tried shoving him away, but Dedrick blew out the candle, and the black curtain fell.

When the darkness lifted, Dedrick was gone, but so was Nathan.

"Oh god!" I choked back a sob. "What did I do?"

"Get out of here!" Rina shrieked. "Return to your body before he comes back!"

"I'm not leaving you."

She spoke so fast she tripped over her words. "He's coming back, and when he does, he'll take me away, and I won't be able to free you. You'll never see Nathan or me again."

I opened my mouth to argue, but the candle went out. All I could see was a faint blue glow and energy cords. It might have been my last chance at freedom, so I took it.

I gasped for air, choking back tears as my soul reconnected with my body. The bathroom lights above me were blindingly bright.

"Maryah?" Krista tried grabbing my hands, but I was flailing.

"We screwed up!" I yelled. "I screwed up. Dedrick has Nathan."

"What?"

"He knows Rina helped me." My voice trembled. "What do I do? I don't know what to do!"

Carson blurred into the bathroom.

"What happened?" Louise asked from the doorway. Gregory and Harmony stood behind her.

I spewed out everything in a rushed, crazed voice. My worst nightmare was coming true. My actions had caused Nathan to be captured by Dedrick.

"Don't worry," Krista tried assuring me. "We'll figure it out. We'll get him back."

I clutched the bathroom rug I was sitting on and bent forward, expecting to throw up. Choking and dry heaving, I asked, "What if he kills them?"

Speaking the possibility out loud sent me into convulsions. Carson eased Krista aside.

"What are you doing?" she asked.

Carson lifted me into his arms. "Helping her."

HER OWN BIGGEST SECRET

Maryah

I sat curled up on the couch, staring out the windows. They might die. They might already be dead. Because of me. How many more people would Dedrick kill because of their connection to me? Because of my stupid decisions.

Helen took my mug of cold tea from me and handed me a new one. The steam rose in front of me, but I couldn't feel its warmth. I couldn't feel anything.

Louise watched me from the kitchen. Her worried eyes bore down on me every time I made the slightest movement. I ached to astral travel back there and find out what was going on, but Rina's warning kept my soul crazy-glued to my body.

She said I'd never see Nathan or her again. I couldn't take that risk. I prayed for them to be alive.

Krista sat beside me. She didn't make me false promises that it would be okay. She didn't fuss like Helen and keep urging me to drink tea. She just stayed beside me. I needed her there more than anything. If she left me I was sure I'd come unglued and fall apart.

Anthony walked in and squatted down in front of me. "Maryah, we're preparing the plane. You're welcome to come with us or you can stay here with Faith, Amber, and Mikey. It's your choice."

I stared at him. His big brown eyes looked so much like Carson's, except less smartass and more sympathetic. Biologically, Nathan was his son, but they'd known each other for centuries. Dedrick had captured his son, his friend. What lengths would Anthony go to save him?

I licked my dry lips. "How do you freeze time?"

He contemplated my question then shrugged. "How do any of us do any of the things we do? The universe gifts us with the ability."

He was the biggest challenge. When Rina taught me to how to tune into each member's energy, Anthony was the toughest for me to read. He was the most closed off. His power was just like his personality, astoundingly strong but guarded.

"If someone asked you to describe how you do it, could you?" I asked. "Could you teach them to stop time if they had that ability?"

"I don't know. I've never tried to teach it to anyone. What are you getting at?"

I sat forward, lowering my voice. "Everyone's ability seems to be getting stronger. Maybe yours is too. What if you couldn't just freeze time? What if you could rewind it?"

"Maryah," Krista said. "This isn't the Outlander series. No one can travel back in time."

"How do we know that for sure?"

Anthony touched my knee. "If it were possible, where would you travel to?"

My mind raced at all the possible points: before I caused Nathan to traverse to me and be trapped by Dedrick, the night my parents and Mikey were killed, before I erased. "I'm not sure yet. Maybe back to the lifetime when I told my so-called-friend about my ability. Then Nathan and I wouldn't have been punished on the pillory. Dedrick would have never known about me or any of us."

"Do you realize how much you'd be altering our history?" Anthony asked. "Besides this strife with Dedrick, we've had countless great times since then."

"We could relive the good parts."

"You don't know that. You don't know what traveling back in time would do. Every choice and action has a consequence. It's like throwing a pebble into a lake. It will cause ripples."

"Could you try?" I begged. "Just far back enough that I can stop Nathan from traversing to me and being tranquilized by Dedrick."

"We don't move backward, Maryah. We never have. Just like always, we play with the cards life deals us and we march forward like we're about to do now. If we have to, we'll search every mountain until we find Nathaniel."

I hung my head. Impossible as it seemed, rewinding time was my only idea.

"Besides," Anthony said, "I'm not capable of that level of time manipulation. Nor would I ever want to be." He stood and touched the side of my face like a concerned parent. "Plane leaves in less than an hour."

He walked away, and I handed Krista my mug. My hands were too weak to hold it any longer. She took it with no questions asked and sipped it then leaned her head against my shoulder.

We stayed like that for several minutes while others flitted around the house talking in hushed whispers.

Krista's head bobbed forward, and she dropped the mug of tea. Even with the splash of liquid on my feet and the crashing of ceramic on the tile floor, I didn't flinch.

It was the cymbal crash before the bittersweet symphony.

Her fingers fluttered. Her head twitched. I knew before she even turned to look at me. Krista's brown eyes had been replaced with a deep blue.

In one shifting bounce I kneeled beside her. "Rina, are you okay? Where are you and Nathan?"

"I don't know where Nathan is, but I'm okay. For now."

The sob that had been stuck in my throat escaped in a gargled, "I'm so sorry."

"I need you to travel to me. Hurry."

Krista's body went limp. I caught her and gently laid her back, tucking a throw pillow behind her head. I leaned back and visualized Rina's eyes. My soul traveled at record speed.

She was sitting on the floor of her room, her knees to her chest and her head down. The candle burned near her feet.

"Rina?"

She lifted her head. Her swollen cheek was smeared with blood, and a bruise was forming.

I moved closer. "He hit you?"

"No, he ordered one of his slaves to do it." One side of her lips lifted. The half that didn't lift had been split open. "I expected much worse."

Anger and guilt rippled through me. "This is all my fault."

Rina nodded like her head weighed a thousand pounds. "Yes."

"Thanks for your honesty."

She smirked then flinched. Her hand flew to her split lip. "You had no choice. You did whatever it took to protect us."

"Protect you? You're worse off than ever. And I have no idea what Dedrick has done with Nathan, but I'm sick over it. I haven't protected anyone. I've made everything a million times worse."

"It's time to tell you." Her hand dropped to her side like dead weight. "I'm pretty sure both of us have what we need."

"Tell me what? What do we need?"

"You said this was the only way we'd survive—if we accumulated enough power and knew how to use it." She sounded so tired. Some of her words slurred together. "I thought you'd have more time to practice, but we'll work with what we have."

She was either fighting the effects of a drug Dedrick had injected into her, or she was just recovering from it.

"Please, Rina," I pleaded. "No more riddles."

"I wasn't allowed to tell you. No matter how badly I wanted to, you forbade me to tell you."

"Tell me what?"

She leaned her head back against the wall. "The big secret."

"Which is what?"

"I'm not the powerful one. I was the glue you needed to connect your strings. It took time for me to become what you needed, but I'm not the one who can save us." She sucked in a labored breath. "You are."

"Me? Compared to what you can do—"

She held up her hand, cutting me off. "Deep down, you know the truth. You've known the whole time. Your mind just couldn't process it."

"Known what?"

Her heavy eyelids fluttered until she forced them open. "Look at me. Really look at me. You know who I am."

She reached forward, fumbling for the candle, then lifted it to her face. She didn't blink. Her pupils dilated. The candle flame danced, and I stared deeper as a ring of green formed around her dark blue irises, like a peacock feather but more beautiful. Almost hypnotic.

The room went hazy in my peripheral vision.

I was swept away.

Rina and I stood together in a tunnel of blue and green light. I reached out, running my fingers through the clouds of swirling colors around us as they shifted into different shapes. I had experienced this before during the couple of precious times I had truly seen into Nathan's soul.

My breath caught. I was seeing into Rina's soul. Reading her story.

Information flooded through me. I watched, unable to peel my gaze away. I saw her past and how she came to be. I felt her emotions as if they were my own.

So much joy, so much love, so many experiences had been stripped away from her. A normal life had been stolen from her—and me.

One gorgeous cord of light connected her heart and mine. The miraculous, stupefying truth rushed through me until I could no longer breathe.

"No." I stumbled backward, out of the tunnel of light, unable to absorb anymore. "That can't be true."

My shimmering hands trembled. My soul blazed so hot with sadness and regret that I felt like I was actually sweating. Shame kept me from looking up at Rina for several excruciating seconds. Had part of me known all along?

I hated myself for what I had done, so I buried it as deep as I could.

I erased it.

I erased her.

"You." I lifted my head. My eyes met hers again. My voice was breathless as my heart plummeted. "You were my daughter."

She reached forward, holding my hand. "You erased to protect me. To protect the kindrily and the world. To protect him."

"Nathan," I whispered. How could I do that to him? To her?

"He didn't know about me. No one did. You were only a couple months pregnant when Dedrick kidnapped you."

My head involuntarily shook like a bobble head doll. I didn't want to believe it. Any of it. Even though part of me knew without a doubt that it was true. "But you're so young. Younger than me. It doesn't add up."

"I've been like this since Dedrick stopped me from aging."

My fists clenched. Of course. He stopped himself and Gregory from aging, why didn't I suspect he'd done the same with Rina? He deprived her of becoming an adult. He deprived her of so, so much.

She inhaled a sharp breath then blew it out through her teeth. "Dedrick's healer kept you alive so I could be born, and then he took me away from you. He tried using me as leverage so you would help him find the stones."

"You were a baby. How could you possibly know any of that?"

"You secretly wrote the book to leave me with knowledge of who I was and why you had to leave. You gave it to Evelyn before you killed yourself. She gave it to me when I was old enough to read it."

I wanted to cry. "What kind of person gives up like that? Leaves her own daughter with someone like him? And then erases all knowledge of it."

"You had to or we wouldn't have made it this far." She was still wincing with every move, but her speech was no longer slurred. "If you remembered me, if you knew Dedrick had me, you would have tried saving me too early. I wouldn't have been powerful enough. The kindrily wouldn't have been powerful enough. Dedrick's plan would have worked. The whole world would have suffered. He would have won."

"But he did win. He has you and Nathan."

"You planned accordingly. Now you're more powerful than him. You wrote pages and pages, predicting how our story would unfold, and promising to come back for me when the time was right. I memorized that book by heart and soul. And now it's time for my favorite part."

I croaked out my words, still fighting back tears and struggling with the shock of what I had done. "How could you have a favorite part of such an ugly, tragic story?"

She leaned forward. Somehow through her suffering, fervent hope shone in her eyes. "Because it's the part where you save me."

The lump in my throat grew bigger until I couldn't swallow. "But I don't know how."

"Yes, you do." She traced a figure eight around my eyes. "I'll be waiting."

She dissolved like starlight.

I reached out, stunned that she had vanished. "Rina?"

The candle still sat where she had set it on the floor, but I was alone. I tried reconnecting with my body, but the energy cords were nowhere to be found.

And Rina wasn't there to help me.

My despicable soul was back in its cage, and I had no idea how to save her or Nathan.

GHOSTS FROM THE PAST

Nathaniel

"Nathan?" Someone gruffly called my name.

I woke up slowly, blinking away the fuzzy feeling in my head and limbs.

I was in a dim room even smaller than Rina's. Dirt floor to ceiling, it couldn't have been more than six feet. My hands and feet were shackled together. I opened every cell in my body, ready to return home.

Nothing happened.

I couldn't traverse.

I should have killed Dedrick. I should have taken the one chair in the dirty room and beat him with it until not one iota of life force remained in him.

A burning candle moved closer, warming my face. I squinted, unable to lift my arms high enough to shield my eyes from its light.

"You okay, man?" River asked.

I thrashed, impulsively trying to leap up so I could strangle him, forgetting my hands and feet were chained together. I toppled over, landing on my side again.

On his knees, River inched closer to me. "I get it. You're beyond pissed. You think I'm one of them, but I'm not. I want to help Maryah and—"

"Bite your tongue or I swear, once I'm free I'll cut it from your mouth."

He held up one hand. "Fair enough. I wouldn't want to talk to me either if I were you." He stared down at me as if he pitied me.

I tugged against my shackles, hoping to break them with the strength of my hatred.

"Nathan, stop. That rusty iron hurts like a bitch once it rubs your skin raw. I know because I tried fighting my way out of them when I woke up trapped in this room."

How did I let myself end up here? Where were Maryah and Rina?

He reached behind his back and then held up a bottle of liquid. "You need to drink this. It will temporarily override the stuff Dedrick injected in you. Evelyn said she doesn't know how long it will work. Make sure you only traverse home, or someplace safe. She said she's not sure if it's strong enough to work twice."

I thrashed again, trying to kick my feet high enough to knock it from his hands. He moved out of the way just in time.

"Come on, don't screw up your only chance of getting out of here." He spoke in a hushed but frustrated voice. "Evelyn warned me not to spill it or lose it. It's the only one she has."

Whatever was in the bottle would most likely kill me. "I'm not accepting anything from you."

"You don't have much of a choice. Dedrick will be back any minute, and I promise he's not coming to chat. He'll kill you, Nathan. Evelyn said if he does, and if Dedrick succeeds with his plan, you might be separated from Maryah for eternity."

"He'll never succeed."

"Won't he? From what I've heard, the only chance at stopping all of this was Maryah and Rina. Together. They had to be together. Don't ask me why because I don't understand half of what these people talk about, but Evelyn insisted they had to be together or there was no hope. And as of right now, there's no hope."

I hated that I was asking River to elaborate. "Where are they?"

"Dedrick separated them. He found out Rina was helping Maryah so he took her away."

"Took her where?" I asked.

"We don't know."

"Where's Maryah?"

"Her soul is still trapped in that room. Evelyn says she'll never be free unless you bring her body here."

"And why should I believe Evelyn? A person I've never met."

"She said you'd ask that. She told me to tell you that you did meet her. In your first lifetime. She said you knew her by a different name, but that if I described how you met you'd understand and drink the elixir."

"Then proceed because so far I don't believe any of the dribble sputtering from your mouth."

"Let me remember exactly what she said." He rubbed his jaw. "It was a lot to remember."

I shook my head in disgust. Clearly this Evelyn person couldn't be very intelligent if she sent River, the imbecile, to do her dirty work.

"Okay," River said. "I'm pretty sure this is it. You and Maryah had a fight."

Idiot. Her name wasn't Maryah back then.

River continued. "She threw a rock at you, and your head was bleeding. Evelyn tried helping you by putting some leaf against your cut." My jaw went slack. "And then she kissed you."

The room spun. River watched me. "Do you remember that? Does that make sense?"

It was the only time I had ever cheated on Mary. I regretted the kiss the moment our lips touched. The instant our lips parted, she told me who she was. Her story was more grandiose than anything I could have imagined. I hadn't believed her at the time—her claims of eternal life, Elements, and soul mates.

I had always worried that my mistake started the chain reaction of our ongoing problems with Dedrick. I didn't even know who he was at the time—the man she said she abandoned to save her own soul—but many years later, the woman's name haunted me again. I had always wondered if the woman I kissed had been Dedrick's forsaken twin flame.

"Emily," I whispered.

"What?" River asked.

Emily never erased like Dedrick claimed. She never moved on, never progressed to a higher level, never chose a different form of existence like we suspected. She stayed and hid her identity. She hid in plain sight—as close to the enemy as she could.

I didn't trust River, but I did trust Emily wholeheartedly. "Pour half of the elixir into my mouth."

"She said you'd need to drink all of it."

"Just pour half in and shut up."

River did what I said then stood and backed away. I licked my lips, wondering what the horrendous tasting liquid really contained. I half-expected to seize and die right there on the spot, but if Evelyn truly was the Emily I had met long ago then I was in good hands.

River leaned over me. "Well, how do you feel?"

I waited for the sensation of having control over my cells again, but it was too weak. "Nothing so far."

"I'm telling you, she said to drink the whole thing."

Light glistened in my peripheral vision, but it wasn't in the room. It was my energy strengthening. "It's working."

The connection clicked on like a light switch.

I traversed out of my constraints and reappeared in front of River. "Tell her I'm grateful beyond words."

I snatched the bottle out of his hand and traversed to Sedona.

Krista and Louise told me what happened, but it didn't make sense.

I covered Maryah with the quilt and sat beside her on our bed. "She didn't say one word before she went back?"

Louise shook her head, worried. "We thought she and Krista fell asleep. They'd both been drinking Helen's tea."

"And you don't remember anything?" I asked Krista again.

"She asked Anthony if he could rewind time. He told her no, said the plane would be leaving soon, and then I fell asleep." She pressed her hand to her forehead. "But I do feel kind of spacey."

"Come." Louise helped Krista out of the bedside chair. "You haven't had much to eat."

Louise guided Krista out of the bedroom while I tried making sense of everything.

Several minutes later, Maryah's foot bounced, then her nose twitched. Her eyes opened, but I was staring into the soul of the enemy.

My body shook, not out of fear, but rage. Eightball growled.

"Hello, Nathaniel." The scratchy words were spoken with Maryah's voice, but it wasn't her or Rina.

"Dedrick," I snarled.

Eightball barked ferociously and lunged at him. Awkwardly, kicking off balance, Maryah's foot clipped Eightball in the face. He yelped, and I scooped him up.

I had never struggled so hard to keep my composure. I tried not to speak, not to give him the satisfaction, but I failed. "Get out of her body or I swear, when I kill you, I will make it extra excruciatingly painful."

Dedrick smiled using Maryah's lips. It was the most conflicting feeling I'd ever experienced, wanting to rip him to shreds, to somehow squelch his soul from this earth, but not being able to lay a finger on him because he possessed Maryah's body.

"How did you manage to traverse back here? I'm quite intrigued."

I kept my mouth shut. The muscles in my jaw and neck were so tense I thought they'd snap.

"Not revealing your secret? Fine then, how about another question? How does it feel to know I'm *inside* of her?"

I balled my fists tighter.

He walked away, flexing Maryah's fingers and running her hands down her waist. "Such subtle curves and soft skin." He looked up at me and laughed. "You really should work on your poker face, Nathaniel. If you keep bottling up all that anger, you'll give yourself an aneurysm."

"I will savor torturing you, Dedrick."

"You'll never touch me. Don't you see how much smarter I am than you? How much more powerful I am and always have been? I'm right here, Nathaniel, using her body as my own, and there's nothing you can do about it. There is nothing you will ever be able to do about anything I do because you have always been inferior to me."

"We'll see about that."

"Yes, we will see. At least *I* will see. You won't live to see Maryah and me live happily ever after because you'll be banished from this planet forever. Your soul won't be allowed reentry. And do you know why? Because I won't allow it."

"She's not Emily."

"You have your beliefs, and I have mine."

I wanted to tell him about Evelyn, but I had made a vow long, long ago. Revealing her identity would cause me to lose everyone I loved. I had never forgotten her words, and given the circumstances, her warning could come true too easily if I didn't keep my promise.

Eightball kept struggling to leap out of my arms so I set him in the hallway and shut the door. He barked and pawed, but I returned my attention to Dedrick. "Maryah will never love you whether I exist or not. She will never, *ever* love you."

"Ah, but you're wrong. Mary did love me, and so will Maryah."

"You're delusional."

"Interesting. Her actions said otherwise, considering how many times she passionately made love to me."

I lurched forward, fists clenched. "That never happened."

"And yet your body language reflects that you believe it, and it clearly upsets you." He sat on the bed, crossing Maryah's legs and looking down at them. "Such a young, tight little body she has." He used her hands to touch her thighs. "I eagerly look forward to ravishing every inch of it."

I yanked her hands away. He was violating her, and I wanted to kill him for it. I gripped her wrists and shook him. "I'll find a way to permanently end your existence if it's the last thing I do."

"Oww," he cooed. "You're hurting Maryah. I didn't peg you for the abusive boyfriend type."

I released my grip, cursing him and myself. "Set her free before you make things much harder for yourself."

"Set her free?" He chuckled. "Why would I do that? And even if I did, which I won't, admit it, you'd never be able to look at her the same." Her fingers trailed across her breasts. Even masked with Maryah's innocent face, his wickedness shone through. "Now that I've been inside of her."

I wanted to break his fingers, but they were her fingers. "If you think possessing her body as a temporary vessel for your dejected soul is in any way an act of intimacy, you're a bigger fool than I thought."

"And yet she feels so delectable." He stood and ambled to the mirror. "Could you please leave the room so I can properly enjoy exploring every inch of her?" He traced her reflection. "I assume you wouldn't enjoy watching. Or maybe you would?"

Anthony was in the hangar, so I yelled for Carson. He blurred into the room a second later.

"Get Anthony," I demanded.

Carson asked no questions. He was gone as quickly as he came.

Maryah's head tilted. "Ahh, so you can't traverse after all. The mystery deepens."

"Your drugs will wear off soon, and when they do, fair warning, I'm coming for you." I stepped closer, staring past Maryah's face and into the hellish abyss of Dedrick's soul. "And I will be merciless."

Carson returned, setting Anthony down beside me.

"Freeze time," I demanded, "including Maryah."

Maryah's lips parted to say something. Anthony barely waved his hand, and her body froze.

"What's going on?" Anthony asked me.

"Dedrick," I hissed. "He's in Maryah's body."

"What?" Anthony circled her, running his hand through his hair. "This takes bedeviling to a new level."

"Wait here." I ran to the guest room and shook Dylan awake from his nap. "I need you to come with me."

He rubbed his eyes while scrambling to his feet. "Time to go already?"

On our way to the bedroom, I updated him.

"This might work to our advantage," I explained. "Persuade him to stop all of this. To return the stones, to leave Maryah alone, and to free Rina."

Dylan squinted at Maryah's frozen form. "What makes you think it will work this time? I tried to stop him last lifetime at our wedding, and it didn't work."

"He was in his own body then. Maybe he was protected. Now he's in Maryah's body. Please try."

Dylan nodded at Anthony to release his hold on time.

Maryah stumbled forward, but Dylan was already speaking in his distinctive, persuasive tone. "Dedrick, you are finished with this battle now and forever. You will free Rina and never speak to or think about Maryah or any member of our kindrily or any other

~ 266 ~

ever again. You will return all the element stones and cease and desist with any and all plans you had to control people or energy."

Maryah's lips curled upward, but it was Dedrick's darkness staring back at us. "For a moment, I contemplated pretending your useless power worked on me, but I simply couldn't keep a straight face." He spoke in a low grumble that didn't sound anything like Maryah. "I am so far above you pathetic Elements that I need a telescope to see down to your level."

Anthony froze time again, and Maryah's legs stopped mid-stride.

"Go get Louise," Anthony said. "She can tell us when his soul leaves her body."

Dylan sunk into the chair. "How can his soul travel anywhere if you're freezing time?"

"He might be immune to our powers," Anthony explained, "but Maryah's body is not. Eventually he'll grow bored and go back to where he came from."

Or he'll inhabit someone else. I didn't express that concern out loud because I didn't want to give Dedrick any ideas. Dedrick's body-snatching power meant he could be anyone. We had to be extremely cautious.

∞

Dedrick grew bored of our stalemate within minutes. Louise verified that his filthy aura had departed. She didn't see any trace of him anywhere, in anyone.

"If Maryah's soul were in her body," I asked Carson, "Do you think Dedrick would be able to possess it?"

"I'm not sure. I'm still unclear on how he and Rina accomplished that feat to begin with."

"Are you thinking of agreeing to Maryah's plan?" Krista asked. "Traversing her body to where her soul is?"

"Maybe. I couldn't ignore River's warning—or rather Evelyn's—that Maryah needed her body to survive this. "Dedrick might keep possessing her. Eventually, Anthony won't have enough strength to keep time frozen."

"What if he traps her body there too?" Carson asked.

"Maryah said she and Rina had a plan. I need to trust that she knows what she's doing."

I stared down at her. Maryah told me this needed to happen in order to save everyone and stop Dedrick. If it were Mary, I wouldn't have had a choice but to follow her demands. But this was inexperienced and vulnerable Maryah. She was asking me to directly put her in harm's way.

I breathed deeply and caressed her cheek. She was asking me to have faith in her.

Krista touched my arm. "Go with your gut."

Carson tucked his hair behind his ears. "Don't look at me. Even I don't have the answer to this one."

I walked to the dresser and pulled out a pair of leggings, a fleece, and socks then selected the most durable shoes in her closet. Krista helped me dress her. I was sliding her shoe onto her foot when Harmony tapped my shoulder.

"Screw sneakers. She can borrow these." She shoved her combat boots at me. "We're nothing alike except for our foot size."

I looked down at her black socks. "Won't you need them?"

"I have several pair."

"Thank you, Harmony."

Krista and I finagled Maryah's feet into Harmony's boots and laced them tight.

I removed Evelyn's potion from my pocket. I hoped half of the elixir would be enough to travel there and back again. I swallowed the last of it then scooped Maryah's body into my arms.

Harmony gave an approving nod, but then her eyes flew open wide. "Nate, wait!"

We were already gone.

I landed less than a foot away from Maryah's radiant soul. She pulsed brightly when she saw me, even brighter when she realized her body was in my arms.

"You said you needed to physically be here, so here you are."

For a moment she stared down at herself like she wasn't sure how to join herself together, but then her light spiraled into her body. She took in a deep breath, and when I was sure she was whole again, I set her down on her feet.

"It worked." She patted her chest and face. "I'm here."

"I hope we're doing the right thing."

"Nathan." She clutched my forearms. "I need to tell you something, but I don't know how much time we have. Dedrick could come in at any second. If he does, traverse immediately. No matter what we're talking about. No matter how shocking or unbelievable it is. "

"No."

"What?"

"I'm staying."

She squeezed my arms tighter. "You can't!"

"I can and I am. I'm not leaving you."

"That's not how it works. Rina said you can't be here."

I rolled my shoulders and stood up straight. "*Rina* is part of the reason I need to be here."

She stepped back and searched my eyes. I wasn't certain of my suspicion until Maryah's mouth twisted, struggling to find words for such a difficult conversation. Her shoulders slumped with shame, but then she stood tall, already accepting her new responsibility. "You know, don't you?"

"I didn't know when she was visiting us in your body, but the moment I traversed here and saw her for the first time." I exhaled. I'd been trying to keep my emotions tamed, not knowing whether I wanted it to be true or not. Complications, heartache, blame: Rina's existence raised so many questions and opened so many old scars. "She's so much like you. Like you were last lifetime."

"You'd do anything to protect her, right?"

"Of course."

"Then go. I'm begging you. It's the one thing I know has to happen. It's not that you can't be here. It's that we're going to need you to be somewhere else."

"Where?"

"I don't know. That part of my intuition isn't clear."

"I won't be able to traverse to you again. Whatever Dedrick injected me with, it prevents me from traversing. I came here on a limited ticket. I'm not even sure I can traverse again."

"Go. Now. Please. Before it's too late. For Rina."

"Do whatever it is you need to do to get out of here." I stepped closer, staring into her eyes. "We're on our way. We won't stop searching until we find you." She laced her fingers with mine. "I believe in you, Maryah. I'll see you soon."

I used my depleting energy to traverse back to our kindrily.

They all stood in the weapon room, gathered around the oblong table as if awaiting my return.

Harmony was sharpening a knife. "We should have hidden a couple of these in my boots for her. I thought of it at the last second."

I rubbed my head, cursing myself for not thinking of it myself. I left her there unarmed, and she didn't need to be. "Maybe I have enough time left to get back to her."

Harmony handed me the knife. I clutched it to my chest and closed my eyes. A few sparks of light momentarily blurred my vision, but I didn't go anywhere.

"Damn it." I tossed the knife on the table. "Is the plane ready?"

Anthony gave one firm nod and handed me my bulletproof vest. I pulled it over my head and tightened the side straps.

"Weapons are packed too," Gregory said.

I glanced at the cabinets lining each wall. The doors had already been closed, but through the fogged glass, I saw silhouettes of guns. I placed my hand in the reader on the wall, and after a few beeps, the fog turned to clear glass, and the locks clicked open. Each cabinet was only half empty.

"Is the plane at maximum weight capacity?" I asked Anthony.

"She could hold another few hundred pounds."

I threw open the cabinet doors. "Take all you can carry."

"Now we're talking." Carson rubbed his hands together and grabbed two more guns.

Faith opened the adjacent cabinet and removed her wind-and-fire wheels from their pegs. "Here." She handed them to Shiloh. "Take these."

"Those are your favorite." He held up his hands, stepping away from her. "You told me I'm never allowed to touch them."

"This is a special occasion."

"Uh uh, no way. This is just your hormones causing a generous moment. I might lose them, and then I'll never hear the end of it."

Faith grinned. "If you lose them while slicing open Dedrick's jugular, you will be excused."

I loaded a shoulder harness with a Swiss dagger and throwing knife. "I take it you won't be joining us, Faith?"

She patted her stomach. "Not with baby Sheila on board."

Helen handed me a bottle of cloudy brown water. I didn't ask what it was, just took a gulp and screwed the cap back on.

Dylan opened the door to the hangar tunnel.

"Let's go, "I said. "One way or another, this ends today."

SHATTERING THE GLASS

Maryah

It was a confusing thing to hate a part of myself I could barely remember existed, but the self-loathing was still there. I had a child. And I abandoned her, knowing she'd be a prisoner. I wanted to travel back to my previous life and beat some sense into myself.

I circled the room—my anger, confusion, and regret building with every step.

I stopped in front of the cabinet, bracing my hands against the frame. I stared at my reflection. "You did this," I growled. "You got everyone into this mess so you get them out."

I felt a little schizo, talking to myself as if I were two people, but whether I was addressing past me or present me, it was still me.

"Fix it!" I shouted while trying to shake the cabinet, but it was anchored in place. I punched my own palm. I refused to cry. Crying would not help save Rina. Or myself.

I turned away from my reflection and stared at Harmony's boots, kicking my heel into the floor over and over. *Think, think, come up with something.*

And finally, an idea hit me.

I tugged on the padlock attached to the cabinet of drugs, but it was thick and solidly locked.

I grabbed Rina's book from the table, lifted it over my head, took three strides toward the cabinet, and shattered the glass.

∞

Dedrick would return. He had to.

I was pretty sure I had thought of everything, right down to erasing my shoeprints from the dirt floor. My back ached form being scrunched up in the corner, and I really had to pee. I glanced at the science experiment of a toilet less than a foot away from me and clenched my thighs together. I could hold it.

While sitting there, staring at the shower curtain and waiting, I replayed everything over and over, trying to self-induce an epiphany. How did Rina traverse? Did it have something to do with her being Nathan's daughter?

Eventually, the room went dark. I tried to steady my nerves. I flexed my fingers. I felt like a caged animal ready to attack.

Instead of Dedrick's voice, I heard River's. "Where is she?"

"I'll be back soon," Evelyn said.

The room went dark again, and when the candle glow returned, I stood and stepped out from behind the curtain.

River's eyes bugged. "You're here. All of you."

Not all of me. I desperately needed the old me's memories so I could figure out how to get us out of here. "So it seems."

"Where's Rina?" River asked.

My voice came out defeated. "I don't know. Dedrick took her away."

Part of me wanted to tell him how important Rina was to me. I wanted to tell him the revelation that had just rocked every fiber of my being. But it was too complicated to explain.

"Nathan traversed you here?" River asked.

"Yeah."

"You're here because of me, you know. I helped him escape."

"You did?" I couldn't picture Nathan willingly accepting help from River. "How?"

"Evelyn had some magic potion that allowed him to traverse. I snuck it to him."

"Magic potion." The words felt so unnatural on my lips. "Thanks for helping him."

"No problem."

I leaned against the wall. "Did you ever think we'd be discussing magic potions and traversing while being held captive in some hidden underworld?"

"Never. It's still unnerving. All of it."

I glanced at the shattered glass cabinet. None of the bottles had been labeled. All I knew was Dedrick used the pale yellow one to put Rina to sleep. "Can Evelyn get us more of that potion?"

"That was all she had. She said she'd been saving it for a long time, and she was insistent that I could not spill a drop."

"Figures." I slid down the wall and sat on Rina's mattress.

"Aren't you worried your body will be stuck here too?"

"It doesn't matter. I need to be here, body and soul, if we have any chance of breaking out."

"We?"

"Rina, me, and you."

"You're still willing to help me?"

"I promised you I would."

He sat next to me but at a respectful distance. "I figured Nathan would have talked you out of it by now."

"Nathan doesn't make decisions for me. Besides, you helped him get out of here. I'd say he owes you one. A big one."

River raised a brow then nodded. "If we do escape, if this nightmare with Dedrick ever ends, I really hope we can stay friends."

I snorted with surprise. "That's asking a little too much of me. When we get out of here, we go our separate ways, and you leave me and my kindrily alone. Forever."

"Right." His shoulders slumped forward. "I understand. I'll stay away."

I pulled my knees to my chest. What if he truly didn't remember the night at Montezuma Well? I knew firsthand how frustrating it was to not remember things I had done. Nineteen lifetimes worth. I couldn't even remember having a daughter and abandoning her.

"We did have some good times though, right?" he asked. "Before the night in question."

"Yeah." I picked at a loose thread on the mattress. "I guess so."

"I still remember the look on your face when I sang you that song on Valentine's Day."

"That was so embarrassing."

River leaned his head back against the wall. "Tell me about it. I felt like such a loser when you ran out of there almost throwing up."

"That wasn't the only time I almost threw up. How about on my birthday when you tried kissing me right after that slutty redhead left your house?"

His smile vanished and he squinted. "What redhead?"

"You know, the day I came over and confided in you about my kindrily. You were hungover but not that hungover."

He studied the section of blanket between us then his eyes lifted to meet mine. "Maryah, I have never tried to kiss you."

"Liar. You tried the day we ditched school too. In your car, you said you wanted to spoil me rotten. And the morning after your drunk escapade with Little Red Riding Whore, your lips actually made contact." I shoved his shoulder. "You tasted like beer. It was right before I fell asleep, and when I woke up, you took me to..." I gulped. "Montezuma Well."

River stared at me, biting his lip. He shifted so he was facing me. "No."

"You're denying it?"

"I'm telling you I never tried to kiss you."

"Is this part of your mental problems? I thought you said you were just playing along with the doctor." The serious look on his face made me stop smiling. "Okay, if it wasn't you, who was it?"

His eyes blazed with anger. "Exactly."

My breath caught in my throat. "You're saying you think it could have been Dedrick?"

"It all makes sense!" River jumped to his feet. "That's why I don't remember anything the cops told me. If you asked me to swear on a Bible, I'd swear that I wasn't at Montezuma Well with you that night. I have no memory of any of it, Maryah. None. And shouldn't I? I mean, even if I totally snapped like that doctor said, wouldn't almost killing one of my best friends stick in my mind at least a tiny bit?" He paced, but he paused to look at me. "And I can tell you another thing. If we had ever kissed, I would remember it."

"You think Dedrick took over your body?" Dedrick used River's body the same way Rina used mine. Why hadn't I thought of it sooner?

"It's the only explanation. I knew it!" River clasped his hands behind his head and sighed with relief. "While I was in jail, I mentally tortured myself wondering how I could have ever hurt you. But it wasn't me!"

So many conversations and events with River poured through my mind. Which parts were River and which were Dedrick?

"April," I murmured, "Why did you break up with April?"

Sadness glistened in his eyes. "That's another thing. I could never remember actually breaking up with her. I called her on New Year's Day, thinking everything was fine, and she yelled at me. I drank a lot the night before, and I was really hungover. I told her I didn't remember breaking up. She asked how I could have forgotten that I told her I was in love with you. I was so confused."

"He broke up with her. Dedrick. It wasn't you?"

River's head dropped into his hands. "What a mess. I felt so insane. I was almost convinced I was losing it. I'd have spells where people swore I had said or done something that I didn't remember. Like the thing about you. I thought maybe it was one of those times where the truth comes out because you're drunk. Like maybe I really did have feelings for you, but I didn't admit it until I was wasted." He lifted his head. "Please don't take this the wrong way, but I don't think I ever wanted anything more than a friendship with you."

"But that song you sang to me on Valentine's Day. You remember that. That was you at the restaurant, right?"

"I do remember that, but—" He paused. "I don't remember writing that song, which has always freaked me out, because I don't forget anything when it comes to my music."

More moments with River popped into my head. "The first day of school. In music class. You sat in front of me and told me something about how my eyes haunted you or something like that."

River nodded. "I saw a video clip of it."

"You or him?"

River took a ragged breath. "That's when it started. That's when I assumed the drinking and drugs had finally killed too many brain cells. I couldn't remember anything that happened in that video. I even searched the Internet to see if too much tequila caused long-term memory loss."

I was dumbfounded. How many times had I been with Dedrick when I thought it was River?

My head snapped up. "The night you came to my house. Nathan and I were in my driveway. He had just given me my Desoto. You kicked the candles away and were really possessive of me and rude to him."

River was silent for only a moment, but that moment seemed to stretch out like poisoned taffy. "Not me."

I felt dizzy. Dedrick had stood face to face with Nathan. He clutched his shoulder at one point, asked him to carry my roses into the house. Dedrick had been there, right in front of him, interacting with both of us, and Nathan didn't know it.

"Why didn't he know?" I mumbled, still shook up by how deceived we had been. He was so close to us so many times, and none of us knew it. "Nathan said they can tell who a soul is by looking into their eyes. It's why we wear sunglasses everywhere. He looked right at you—at Dedrick. Why didn't he know it wasn't your soul in your body?"

River touched his temples. "My contacts."

"Contacts? That shouldn't make a difference."

River's gaze met mine. "They'd make a difference if they were supplied to me by Dedrick."

"You wear them all the time?"

He nodded. "I have to. I'm practically blind without them."

"Holy hell," I said.

River nodded in agreement.

"Dedrick could be anyone." I had to warn the others. Dedrick might possess someone else's body, throw in some soul-shielding contacts, and pretend to be them. Or worse yet, physically harm them. "I have to tell my kindrily."

I stretched out on the mattress. River stood above me, his head tilting as his brow wrinkled. "How will you tell them?"

"I'll only be a few minutes."

"But—?"

I envisioned Nathan's green eyes and ended up on the plane. I glanced around. Almost everyone was on board. I was practically sitting on Gregory's lap. Nathan sat across from us. "Nathan, Dedrick can possess other people's bodies."

He stared out the window, not acknowledging me at all.

He couldn't hear me. No one could. I had left my body.

What was I doing? I had become so used to astral traveling back to my body to relay messages that I confused the two.

I sailed through the cabin toward the front of the plane where Louise was sitting. Her hands were folded in her lap, and her eyes were closed. "Louise?" I waved my hands in front of her. "Open your eyes. See my aura. Realize something is wrong."

I tried shoving her, patting her cheek, but my efforts had no effect. "This sucks so bad."

I went back to Nathan and yelled his name as loud as I could. My voice was swallowed by the roar of the jet's engines. I turned around to face Gregory. He said he could hear my thoughts from a distance; maybe he could hear my soul too.

I leaned down, almost butting my nose against his. "Gregory! Can you hear me?"

He reached next to him and held Harmony's hand but showed no sign of hearing me.

I'd have to figure out another way to tell them. I reconnected to my body and traveled back to River.

He was squatting over me, shaking my arm. "About time! Come on. We only have a few minutes."

"A few minutes for what?"

He yanked me to my feet. "To find Rina and get out of here."

"Rina? Where is she?" I froze when a wooden door opened to a hallway. "Where did the door come from?"

"Apparently, it's been there the whole time. Evelyn creates illusions."

He ran ahead, practically dragging me behind him at first, but then my adrenaline pumped to full blast, and my feet wouldn't move fast enough.

"Where's Rina?" I whispered as we raced down a dim hall.

"There's a steel cage down this corridor and to the left."

"A cage?" A real cage?

We turned left and continued down an even darker hallway. There was a cage—with Rina passed out inside. Just weeks ago

Harmony had described how she felt about Dedrick having Gregory as his prisoner. Now I understood what she meant.

"How will we get her out?"

River pulled out an old key and grinned.

"Wow," I said. "Evelyn thought of everything."

His brows furrowed like maybe he was upset that I was giving Evelyn all the credit instead of him.

"Go on," I urged. "Unlock it."

STICKS AND STONES

Maryah

The lock opened with a deafening click. I swung the steel door open and ran inside, struggling to lift her limp body into my arms.

"This way." River waved me down a hall. "It's the only way out."

Rina was heavier than she looked, or maybe my muscles weren't as strong because I hadn't been using my body much. I had trouble keeping up with River.

"Let me take her."

"No." I adjusted my arms to shift her weight. "I've got her."

He turned and proceeded down the hall. We came to a wooden door, and he pushed it open. "In there."

He practically shoved me inside. I stumbled, but regained my footing and set Rina on the floor as he pulled the door closed behind us. The room was too dark to see anything.

"I thought you said this was the way out."

"It is, but shhh," River hushed me. "I heard someone coming down the hall."

My heart sped up at the thought of getting caught. We couldn't get caught. This was our only chance to escape. If Dedrick found out we'd come this close, he'd figure out a way to trap us with an even tighter rein.

A small light clicked on, illuminating the room. River pointed a flashlight at me, and I swatted it away. "Are you trying to blind me?"

"Sorry."

I adjusted Rina so her head was resting on my thighs and smoothed her hair from her face.

"Is someone out there?" I asked River. My pulse hammered so loud in my ears I wouldn't have been able to hear a parade outside.

He pressed his ear to the door. "I can't hear anything, but we should wait a minute or two to be safe."

I gazed down at poor Rina. She was breathing, thank the heavens, but how long would she be out? She told me we needed to work together to escape, and working together would be tough with her unconscious.

"What else did Evelyn say?" River shined the flashlight in my face.

I shielded my eyes. "How would I know? She told you way more than she ever told me."

"But she didn't tell me everything." He crouched beside me. "This has been stressful, hasn't it? All this drama and not knowing who to trust."

"Stressful doesn't even begin to describe it."

"May I point out an obvious fact that you may not have considered?"

"Sure."

"Nathaniel isn't here. He's not coming to your rescue like a real man would."

"What?" I gaped at him. "He tried to be here. I made him leave."

He hesitated then brushed something off my shoulder. "Have you asked yourself why you didn't want him here?"

I leaned away as far as I could while still watching Rina for any signs of waking up. "Because I didn't want him to get hurt or trapped again."

River took my hand then flipped it over. "I can give you so much more than he ever could." He traced a heart on my palm.

The bottom dropped out of my stomach. Flashbacks of the all too familiar night at Montezuma Well washed over me. River had traced a heart on my palm. Only it wasn't River then, and it wasn't River now. The walls closed in around me as I struggled to breathe. "Dedrick."

"Why such contempt when you speak my name?"

"Because I despise you."

He gripped my hand so hard it hurt. "I've explained our history. You've seen the lengths I have gone to be with you. All of your animosity for me is built on lies your kindrily told you. Long ago, I was your true love, and I always will be."

I yanked my hand free. "You are delusional."

"I don't care how many times you erase, or what name you go by, my soul recognizes and loves your soul as it always has. This—" He motioned to River's body. "It's just a vessel. I realize it's hard for you to look at me and not see the man who was present the night your parents were killed. I can continue inhabiting River's body to make it easier on you."

"Are you insane? You can't just steal people's bodies. And you tried to kill me while in River's body too." I squinted, trying to see any difference in River's eyes now that Dedrick's soul was present. "You claim you love me, that you believe I'm Emily reincarnated, so why did you try to kill me at Montezuma Well."

Pure evil stared back at me. "I told you, I realized I no longer needed your body. If you kept running back to your pathetic Nathaniel it would only make using your power more difficult. I was so close to capturing your soul that night. Your irksome kindrily would have believed you were dead and left us alone, but as always, Nathaniel ruined everything." He waved his hand dismissively. "Once you came to your senses, we would have found you a new body, preferably one taller and darker. I always did prefer brunettes."

I shook my head, disgusted. "You're a monster no matter what form you take."

"Monster is a term mistakenly given to unique and powerful beings. Can't you see how powerful I am? The world was mine for the taking, and I took it."

I scooted backward, carefully resting Rina's head on the floor. I had to lure him away from her without making it obvious. "You stole the stones. They aren't yours to use."

"Possession is more than nine tenths of universal law. I have them, and I am enlightened enough to use them."

"Enlightened?" I stood and backed up. "You kill innocent people. You destroy lives. You want to use precious ancient stones to shut down our planet. You're not enlightened. You're the greediest and most egotistical person I've ever known or heard of."

He followed me. "I understand how it must look from your perspective, but once I bridge the two worlds together and you see the great things that await us, you'll understand and be grateful that I lifted you into a higher state of existence with me."

My back pressed against the wall. "You're kidding yourself. You hiked around a mountain a hundred times and jumped into a lake. That does not mean you'll ever live a higher existence."

He grinned wickedly. "I suspected you were with me on my final lap but confirming it warms my heart."

A primal part of me spoke my next words without analyzing or second-guessing myself. "I've been to Meru, and you couldn't be more wrong with your translation of how to connect or use the stones."

"Don't kid yourself." He scoffed. "You are the one who taught me how to use them."

"I never taught you anything. You stole my journals."

"You left them for me to find." He matched me step for step, so I kept creeping along the wall. I didn't want Rina getting trampled on or hurt. "If the secrets you had learned were so precious, why record them onto a page, documented for anyone to stumble upon? You weren't that foolish, my love. You wanted me to find them."

Every kindrily member said I had been so powerful, that I foresaw future events lifetimes before they occurred. I wouldn't have been foolish enough to leave such a sacred treasure map to be snatched up by a morally deprived pirate.

Whatever I had written in the journal he stole was a decoy to lead him the wrong way.

I knew what I was doing then, and I would do what needed to be done now. I inhaled all my fear and apprehension then I blew it out until only courage remained.

I knocked the flashlight from his hand. It flew across the room, bouncing off a wall before landing on the floor and shutting off. It was the few seconds of distraction I needed.

I had anticipated a fight with Dedrick, not Dedrick in River's body, but there was nothing I could do to change the circumstances. I reached into my boot and pulled out the loaded syringe.

Now he'd get a dose of his own wretched sleeping medicine. I cocked my arm, thumb ready and waiting on the plunger for Dedrick to make his move.

The room was pitch black, but I heard Dedrick chuckle using River's voice. "Don't make this so difficult, Maryah. I am not the enemy."

He stepped toward me, his feet shuffling like the rat he was. I lunged forward, stabbing the needle into what felt like River's shoulder. He sucked in a quick breath as I pulled out the needle and shoved him away from me. I stepped back, hoping to stay out of his reach as the drugs took effect.

"Stupid girl," he uttered before River's body collapsed onto the ground.

I crawled around on my hands and knees, searching for the flashlight. I needed to figure out how to get Rina and River out of the room before Dedrick came back in his own body—or someone else's.

I found the flashlight and clicked it on, shining the beam on Rina then River. Both were passed out. I ran to the door and pulled on the steel latch, but it was locked.

I pounded my fists against the door and, as loud as I could, yelled for help.

STRINGS AND GLUE

Maryah

The door opened.

Evelyn stood backlit by the torchlight from the hallway. She glanced down at Rina and River. "Oh dear."

I eyed her suspiciously. I had to suspect everyone and anyone could be Dedrick at this point. She stepped inside, and I positioned myself in the doorway. No way would we be locked in again.

She felt River's neck. "I know what happened to Rina, but why is River unconscious?"

"You already know the answer to that."

Evelyn looked up at me. Her tone was terse. "No, I don't. That's why I'm asking you."

"You're not fooling me. I know it's you."

She squinted and sat up straight. "And who precisely are you referring to when you say *you*?"

"Dedrick."

"Oh." She looked at River again. "I see." She stood and brushed her hands on the front of her shirt. "Maryah, Dedrick has not taken possession of my body, I assure you."

I didn't reply. Of course he'd say that.

"Come with me." She waved her hands over her snake eyes, and they changed to normal. "I think I know how to help you."

"I'm not going anywhere with you," I said. "Even if you really are Evelyn, I can't leave Rina and River."

"Dedrick will return fairly soon, and when he does, what will you do? It seems I'm the only conscious ally you have at the moment."

I glanced at Rina, not wanting to leave her. "Where would you take me?"

"To the prayer room. It's your best chance at being able to read the book. Rina and River will be fine. I'll come back for them."

Reluctantly, I followed her down the hallways. They weren't really hallways. They were more like dirt tunnels.

Evelyn had a torch so I could see better than during my rushed travels with River/Dedrick. She led me to a tiny room with rounded walls and no corners. It was more like an alcove carved into the hallway. Light poured in from above, flooding the round room with a glow that made the dirt sparkle.

I leaned in and looked up. A long, narrow, vertical tunnel stretched stories above me. At the end was daylight. The circle of blue sky looked so out of place given the dark and dreary tunnel system of windowless cave-rooms.

Evelyn handed me Rina's book. "Sit and read."

I hesitantly took it from her. "What if I can't read it?"

Her gaze drifted down to my ring. "You can."

Had everyone known about my ring except me? "How did you do all of this?"

"All of what?"

"Help free Nathan, get me out of that locked room, bring me here. Where is everyone else? Why aren't other Nefariouns chasing us and trying to kill me right now?"

"Dedrick keeps them separated from this area. This small section of caves is our home."

"Home? Who lives like this?"

"Someone who has many secrets to keep hidden. Someone who has lost touch with reality in order to obtain power to which he was never entitled. Someone like Dedrick."

I clutched the book to my chest. "Do you know my big secret?"

Her lashes batted then she sighed. "I do. And it's nice to see you now know it too."

"How do you know so much?"

"Because I was your caretaker. Before, during, and after Rina's birth. You used to have a great deal of trust in me. Before you *departed* from here, you entrusted me with the book. I taught her how to read it by the time she was five."

How could I not remember any of that? "Why did you help me back then, and why are you helping me now?"

"I'm obligated."

"Obligated by what?"

"My conscience."

"Is anyone else involved?"

"Lexie." She said it freely as if she had nothing to hide.

"The Lexie who reported all of my private thoughts to Dedrick?"

"She didn't tell him anything that would have led to the plan failing. For nearly two decades she has put on a constant show around him just like I have."

"Who else here is involved?"

"Rina."

"Why doesn't Dedrick's mind control work on her?"

"She was immune to it since birth, which is why he kept her secluded here. He knew she was gifted. He tried controlling her in other ways, but she's too intelligent. His biggest mistake was keeping her here. In the end it will be the cause of his demise. And I have been anxiously awaiting that day for so long."

I peered down at the book with no title. "So if I can read this, what happens when I'm done?"

"I don't know. That's the part we've been waiting for."

"The part? What do you mean?"

"To see if the prophecy can be changed."

"Dedrick's plan to shut down the energy vortexes of this world?"

She nodded.

"How am I supposed to change anything? He's more powerful than I can even begin to understand."

"My best advice—my only advice—is read the book. I'll be back with Rina when she wakes. And then the two of you must go."

"Go where?"

"Away from here."

"Why?"

"Because he has obtained the last stone. Rina can't be here any longer."

"What about River?"

"He must stay with me."

A shiver crept up my spine. I'd make the kindrily come back to help free River. Getting Rina out was my top priority. "How would we escape?"

"By helicopter."

My eyes bugged. "That's it? Easy as that? You have access to the helicopter?"

"Yes."

"This whole time, you could have freed Rina! You could have escaped with her. Why didn't you?"

"It wasn't part of the plan. I had strict orders to follow the plan."

"Whose plan?"

She leveled me with her eyes. "Yours."

∞

I sat on the dirt floor, staring up at the small pool of sky far above me. It represented freedom, or at least the possibility of it, and it was so close, yet lifetimes away.

As I thumbed through the book, a ray of sunlight glimmered against the page. For a moment I thought I saw a diagram of some sort, so I flipped back, trying to find it again, but I found nothing.

I opened to the first page, angling it in every possible direction, searching for even a faint outline of ink. Still nothing.

I thought back to my sensperience sessions in the room Carson created, the starlight practice sessions with Nathan, and our time at the lodge where I first understood what it felt like to open every cell in my body and feel the energy around me.

My hand wrapped around the Howlite hanging over my heart. I bowed my head, focusing on the peacock feather in my ring. I gripped the Howlite tighter and pressed my lips against the cool smooth dome of my ring while begging for the ability to read the book.

At first, it was like trying to see a shimmering coin through ocean waves. I squinted and craned my neck forward. *Please,* I begged. *Come into focus.*

I closed my eyes and saw Rina's smile—the one that lit up the room when she thought she was going home. Her dark blue eyes—ringed with the same green as her father's—had glimmered in those few precious moments of possibility. "Help me save her."

My lids fluttered open, and glistening silver words appeared on the page.

To my dearest and cherished Marina, you are the star I have been wishing upon all of my lives.

Guilt plowed through me all over again. How could a mother leave her daughter? How could I have left Rina with an evil person like Dedrick?

I turned the page and saw the answer to my question.

Leaving you is the most difficult decision I've made in my hundreds of years of existence. I would move Heaven and Earth to keep you safe, to give you the beautiful life you deserve. According to the prophecy, you will live one extremely short human life before everything is gone. Before everyone is gone. Your father and I will be separated forever, and you will never know what it means to have a family.

I can't accept that.

I WILL move Heaven and Earth. I will do the impossible.

Burn bright, my shooting star, because together you and I will rewrite the story of this world.

My eternal, inerasable love, M.

I would have lost her and Nathan. Countless lives would have ended. I was beginning to forgive myself, or at least understand why I did what I did.

I'd read a paragraph and hate myself. I'd hate Mary for deserting her own flesh and blood. A paragraph later I would be amazed by her strength and foresight of what might be possible.

She was so brave. And then I reminded myself that *she* was me, and I needed to believe in the words I had written. I needed to follow my own plan and manifest a miracle into reality.

I found the diagram and ran my finger over the many circles. All of them were labeled with powers: traversing, freezing time, reading minds, and so on. Several of the circles contained only a question mark. On the center of the page, each circle was connected to a star.

"How could anyone ever predict such a thing?" I whispered.

Rina's voice was quiet but confident. "Evelyn said you were the most gifted seer she had ever known."

My head snapped up. Rina peeked out from behind the wall to the opening. The sight of her forced my lips together as I held back tears. I reached out and motioned for her to come to me.

She moved fast, nestling in beside me as I wrapped one arm around her. "I'm so sorry."

"Don't be. We're going to save so many people."

"Can you ever forgive her? Forgive me?"

"There's nothing to forgive. This was the only way."

I kissed the top of her head. "You should have told me. That first day. Right away, you should have told me everything."

Rina pointed to the book. "Pages thirteen, twenty-eight, forty-nine, seventy-nine, eighty-eight, and the very last page. You forbid me or anyone else from ever telling you who I am."

"I was an idiot."

She leaned back and stared up at me. "You were and are a genius."

"I'm not a genius. I can barely mentally grasp any of this."

"Is it awkward for you?" she asked. "Knowing who I am?"

"Honestly?"

"Brutal honesty."

"Yes. I wish it weren't, but jeez, I'm still getting used to the fact that I have a boyfriend. Nathan is the first and only boyfriend I've ever had," I admitted sheepishly. "In less than a year I met him, fell in love with him—for the first time I can thoroughly remember—and found out he was my soul mate." My cheeks warmed. "My biggest worry has been whether or not I'm a good kisser." I laughed uncomfortably. "I've never even had sex, yet somehow I have a daughter."

Rina scrunched up her nose. "Congratulations. You've officially known about being my mother for less than a day, and you've already traumatized me by discussing my parents having sex."

A sad laugh slipped from my lips. "See, I'm not mom material. I'm so sorry."

"I forgive you."

I touched her swollen face, hating Dedrick for everything he had ever done to hurt her. "In the book, I told you the time would come when we had all the power we needed. Then we would escape."

She nodded.

"Do you have all the power you need?"

She nodded again.

"How is that possible? I don't understand what it means."

"Page thirty-two. You knew your starstone needed to be kept safe. But you also knew more about its abilities than anyone else because the akin trusted you with the knowledge of its potential. You knew it did more than just connect elemental powers."

"We think I hid the starstone in my ring."

Rina touched my thumb then squeezed. "One tiny part of Meru's star energy is all you need."

"Does Dedrick know I have it?"

"Dedrick is a fool. He never knew what he was searching for. That's why he needed you."

"Evelyn said she'd be back to help us escape. What happens after that?"

"We stop Dedrick, and the stones are returned to where they belong so the world can be safe again."

"We? You, me, and Evelyn are going to stop Dedrick and all his Nefariouns?"

"We as in the kindrily."

"*Our* kindrily," I corrected her.

She hugged me.

"They massacred us last time we encountered them," I said. "What if that happens again?"

"It won't. We have eighteen."

"Eighteen?"

"Eighteen members."

I counted off each member with my fingers. "Edgar, Helen, Anthony, Louise, Dylan, Amber, Nathan, Me, Gregory, Harmony, Faith, Shiloh, Krista, Carson, Mikey." I hesitated, but yes, she was official now even if she wasn't born yet. "Sheila. And you. That's only seventeen."

"Me, and Dakota."

"We're not sure about Dakota."

"I'm sure. Eighteen is the magic number, more members than any kindrily has ever attained. We had to wait until there were eighteen of us or it wouldn't work."

"Was that in the book?"

"All of it was in the book."

"Even Dakota?" I asked, amazed that my plan was so elaborate.

"He didn't have a name yet, but you knew he'd find his way to us."

"Why is eighteen so significant?"

"Let me show you." She took the book from my hands and opened to one of the last few pages. She licked her finger then rubbed it on the dirt floor beside us then drew the number 18 on the page. She pointed at the 1. "One." Then she pointed to the 8 and turned the book sideways so the eight became the infinity symbol. "Infinite source."

She fixed her gaze on me then traced her finger around my eyes in a figure eight. "One infinite source. It took a long time for you to get us here, but finally, we have eighteen."

"That means we're powerful enough?"

"That means we're invincible." She waved her fingers back and forth between the two of us. "Strings and glue. Now, let's practice, because time is not on our side."

FLYING BLIND

Nathaniel

The plane had taken off less than an hour ago. Anthony's specially designed air vents hissed as oxygen poured into the cabin.

Carson sat beside me. "Please stop fidgeting."

"I'm sorry, but we're moving unbearably slow."

He leaned forward, resting his elbows on his knees. "This plane is flying at Mach 3, three times faster than the speed of sound. We're traveling across the world in less than three hours." He pointed out the window where the blue layer of the stratosphere merged with the black of the mesosphere, a glowing ridge of orange separated the two. "Do you realize what lengths we've gone to make sure this cabin is correctly pressurized and protected from radiation exposure while we travel at this altitude at over 2,000 miles per hour?"

I ran my fingers along my soft leather armrest and inhaled without becoming lightheaded. "It is comfortable, but still unbearably slow."

Carson pulled ear buds from his pocket. "You, my friend, have become a traversing snob."

I tapped on the window, willing the plane to fly faster, even though Anthony had far surpassed all possible engineering enhancements for a private passenger plane. I would have given anything to instantly travel to Maryah. Add losing my ability to the long list of reasons I despised Dedrick.

I stood and walked to the back of the cabin, making eye contact with each member as I passed by them. Everyone was aboard except Faith, Amber, and Mikey. Thankfully, no one showed any signs of playing body host to Dedrick.

I slipped into the small lavatory and shut the door. Bracing my hands on the sink, I stared at myself in the mirror. Maryah said they had a plan. I prayed on every galaxy in the universe for that plan to succeed.

Through the mirror's reflection, an orb of light floated behind me. I spun around but only saw the door. I looked at the mirror again, and it was there, pulsing in shades of blue, green, and white. I reached back, trying to touch it but keeping my gaze on its reflection.

I was about to shout for Louise so she could tell me if it was someone's aura, but my skin began tingling. As I inhaled, I was transported.

I stood in a dirt tunnel staring into a carved-out cavern where Maryah sat with Rina. They sat crossed-legged facing each other, holding hands.

"Maryah?" I dropped to my knees beside them, but neither flinched.

I touched Maryah's arm, but my hand passed right through it. I stared in disbelief. I had assumed I traversed, that my ability had returned, but that wasn't the case at all. I was only present in soul form.

"It worked," Maryah said.

Rina smiled. "Told you."

Rina's book lay open beside them. I studied it to see if I could figure out what they were referring to. The blank pages provided no answers.

"He can't see it?" Maryah asked, her eyes still closed. Were they talking about me? Did they know I was there?

"No," Rina replied. "Only you and me."

"He should know what we're going to do. I have to tell him."

Rina's chin dipped. "Maybe now isn't the best time."

Maryah pulled her hands from Rina's, and they disappeared from my sight.

I swayed and fell into the wall of the plane's lavatory.

"Nathan?" Louise knocked as the doorknob jiggled. "Are you all right in there?"

I opened the door. "I have no idea what just happened, but I'm certain it was important."

ILLUSIONS OF GRANDEUR

Maryah

I was back in the same dark room where I had stabbed Dedrick with a syringe.

River and Rina's motionless bodies were in the same place they had been when Dedrick left River's body. Or if they weren't in the exact same spot, they were as close as we remembered.

I stared at the door, waiting.

Until finally, it opened.

I had planned on pretending to be startled, but my reaction was genuine. Even though we had been expecting him, Dedrick charging into the room made me jump.

I stepped back.

"Well, isn't this an unexpected surprise." He sneered. "Hello, Evelyn." Dedrick towered over her. She straightened and lifted her chin. Her chest rose.

"Out of everyone, I never would have guessed you would be a traitor." He slapped her so hard I covered my own face. She stumbled backward, but he grabbed her by the hair.

I wanted to attack him, but they had warned me something like this would happen. I couldn't interfere. They said I had to act scared and helpless, so I pressed myself against the wall and watched as Dedrick clasped her cheeks and forced her to drink from a vial in his other hand.

She fought back, thrashing as she tried moving her lips, but Dedrick persisted. "Drink it or your other option will be much more gruesome."

Through the palpable tension in the room, I heard her take one long, hard gulp. Dedrick pushed her against the wall, lifting her by her neck until her feet came off the ground. She coughed, barking and choking as she spit out the poison.

"How dare you betray me this way?" Dedrick's voice was sinister. "I trusted you for so long. I gave you everything you asked for. Even that wretched child."

She kicked and wheezed as drool ran down her chin. Her eyes closed then she went limp, and he released his grip. She fell into a heap on the floor.

He turned slowly. I swallowed hard.

"When I was in River's body, I was susceptible to your schoolgirl attack, but now that I'm me, I'm done playing nice."

I stuttered. "Is, is she d-dead?"

"I have never killed anyone. Future gods do not dirty their hands with a sin such as murder."

He really believed just because he didn't do the physical act of killing that he wasn't responsible for all the deaths he ordered his Nefariouns to carry out?

He snapped. "Where is the starstone?"

I didn't speak.

He pressed his fingertips together, thrusting them in my face. "Your only chance of escaping just collapsed into a coma right before your eyes. I imagine your fear has left you paralyzed, but tell me where the stone is or every last member of your kindrily will be tortured in ways worse than you can comprehend."

Evelyn needed two minutes. She said I had to keep him talking for two minutes, which shouldn't have been difficult considering he loved the sound of his own voice.

"Come now, Maryah. I know you have the starstone. Do you think I got where I am by being a fool? By not knowing what's going on at all times? I know everything now, and I knew everything then. I knew Rina freed your soul. I knew you were traveling back and forth, reporting to your meddling kindrily. I knew every time River visited you. I allowed it, all of it, because I knew no matter what you peons thought you could achieve, I would always be three steps ahead of you. True, at times it was difficult hearing only one side of the conversations that took place in Rina's room, but mostly the information was easy to figure out."

Moments raced through my mind. Did he really know everything? If he did, our plan would never work.

"You're no fool either," Dedrick continued. "I'm sure you suspected I knew many times. The time River hid behind that curtain as if I couldn't hear every annoying thought running through his mind? But you wanted to believe you were beating me. You wanted to believe that you and your clan of misfits could stop me."

He was so absorbed in his speech that he didn't notice the dirt wall silently forming behind him. As fascinated as I was by Evelyn's illusion-creating ability, I kept my eyes locked with Dedrick's so he wouldn't turn around.

"The beauty of it is that you still did what I needed you to do," he scoffed. "You brought them to me. They'll be here soon, and I will dispose of all of them. I'll shut down the portals into this world. There will be no way for your kindrily to return, and oh, what a lovely world that will be."

I inched sideways, pressing my ankle tighter against Rina's open hand. River was pretending to be passed out only a couple feet away, perfectly positioned to do his part.

"You're not as invincible as you think," I said.

He laughed. "Brave words coming from a girl with no memories and limited power, who's trapped in the belly of a mountain with no one to help her."

Me telling off Dedrick wasn't part of the plan, but I had to. "That's where you're wrong. *You* helped me. By keeping me trapped, by talking to me so much, you made me face my fears.

Now, I can look into your heartless evil eyes and not be scared. I can tell you to piss off. I'm not afraid of you, Dedrick."

He leaned closer. "You should be terrified of me."

I cocked my head, grinning. "You're the one who should be terrified. It's your turn to be caged."

Rina squeezed my ankle tight. Dedrick's black eyes widened and flitted around like two wasps searching for someone to sting but finding no target.

We were invisible, just like Evelyn.

River roundhouse kicked Dedrick in the back of the knees. He fell backward, then turned, seething and probably ready to kill his attacker, but a dirt wall formed between River and Dedrick. And then another wall shot up in front of us, blocking him from my view.

Rina sprang to her feet and grabbed my hand. "It worked."

"Come." Evelyn appeared in our newly formed dirt cavern, waving us toward the door with one hand while she manifested another dirt wall with her other. "Hurry."

"What about Vivian?" I asked, worrying about her twin sister who was drugged and passed out on the floor.

"She'll be fine. She played her role well. Now our focus is getting you to your kindrily."

We grabbed River then ran out the door and down the hallways. Evelyn waved her hand every few seconds to form another wall. She warned us that her plan of confining Dedrick in a dark maze wouldn't stop him, but it would buy us time to escape while he tried to dig his way out.

"Why can't you just bury him alive?" I asked as we rounded another bend.

"He can't be killed that way. He would just inhabit a new body."

"He can't be killed?" I asked.

"That's not what I said."

We came to a room much bigger than any of the others. A helicopter—the one I had seen Vivian flying—sat in the middle of the cave. Lexie sat in the pilot seat.

"Here." Evelyn reached inside and handed coats to me and Rina. "Put these on, it's bitter cold out there."

"What about me?" River asked.

"You're staying with me," Evelyn told him.

"No way. I'm getting the hell out of here."

"You have no powers, and this is going to be a battle of supernatural forces. You'll only be a liability."

"I can hold my own."

"Not against people using every force on this planet to kill you. This will be a war of energy and powers, and I'm sorry River, but you're only human." Evelyn cupped his face. "You will play an important role, but you can't go with them. That's not the path you're meant to travel."

"I can't just sit here and wait for them to come back and rescue me."

"As I said." Evelyn's tone grew sterner. "You have an important role, but traveling with Maryah and Rina is not part of it."

River glanced at me then nodded. "Fine. I'll stay." He nudged my shoulder. "Be careful."

Rina and I put on our coats and climbed into the helicopter. Lexie turned the key. Nothing happened. She flipped a few switches but still nothing.

"Shit." She pounded her hand against the roof. "He disabled it."

"Do you know how to fix it?" Evelyn asked.

Lexie shook her head then leapt out of the helicopter. "You'll have to go on foot."

"Go where?"

"Down the mountain to the beyul."

I glanced at Rina and she shrugged. "What is a beyul?"

"The hidden valley," Evelyn said. "That's where the two groups must meet."

"A hidden valley? That's the only direction you can give me?" Even though the huge torch lit room was cold and drafty, I was sweating. Dedrick could find us at any second. "I have no idea where to go."

"You've been there before," Evelyn told me. "Let your intuition guide you."

She opened a sliding door to the cave that was eerily similar to the one at our hangar in Sedona. Rina gasped and covered her eyes as if the bright light burned her.

"There's no time to wait," Evelyn warned. She handed sunglasses to me and Rina. "He'll be here soon."

Rina put on her sunglasses as we walked to the threshold. I stared out at monstrous snowcapped mountains. "You've got to be kidding me."

I stared at Evelyn, wondering if perhaps I was wrong to trust her. She couldn't believe we'd survive out in the snow, by ourselves, hiking mountains that looked to be thousands of feet high. "We'll freeze to death out there."

"You'll find a way. They'll help you."

"They who?"

"Your kindrily."

"They'll never find us out there."

Rina pulled up her furry hood then held my hand. "They will. Dakota made sure of it."

And with that long shot of hope, Rina and I stepped out of the hangar, into the snow.

DON'T CHUTE

Nathaniel

Shiloh sat in the copilot seat beside Anthony.

"Anything yet, Shiloh?" I asked.

His fingers pressed against his temples. "I'm searching, but so far all I see is one snowy mountain after another."

"Keep searching."

"Wait!" Shiloh leaned forward, squinting, as if he could see something just beyond the plane's windshield. "I see them! Bank right, Anthony. We'll pass three peaks and then a sharp left. Maryah is on foot with Rina."

My heart raced. "Hurry, Anthony."

The plane's engines roared as we made a hard right.

"How high up is she?" I asked Shiloh.

He was intently fixed on watching them in his mind's eye. "Close to the summit."

"That's over 20,000 feet. They won't last long at all." I felt my own lungs constrict due to my panic. "They'll be struggling to breathe and losing feeling in their limbs."

"We're almost there," Anthony assured me.

"About five degrees east." Shiloh directed Anthony as the plane followed the path of Shiloh's pointing finger. "We'll pass over them. They'll be on our right side."

I ran to a window. Gregory and Carson moved to the right side of the plane as well. We practically buzzed the mountain where Maryah and Rina were walking. They looked so small and far away. Two slow-moving specks in a sea of white. They were much too close to the summit.

"Dear god," I whispered. "They'll freeze to death."

"Dedrick isn't far behind," Shiloh shouted.

"What?"

"He's following them."

"I didn't see him." But then again I wasn't looking. I was too fixated on Maryah and Rina.

"Nathaniel," Gregory's voice sounded urgent. His hand was pressed against the window as he turned to look at me. "She said pack a chute."

"Maryah? You heard her thoughts?"

"Yes, and she said to hurry."

"I'll circle back around," Anthony said. "But I didn't see any possible landing spots close enough to them."

Gregory and I were still staring at each other. He repeated himself. "Pack a chute. That's what she told me to tell you."

I stiffened. I wasn't there to help load the plane. I hadn't packed a parachute, and no one else had probably thought to either.

Carson blurred to a stop in front of me. He held a packed parachute bag by its straps. "Put it on."

I grabbed his head and kissed the top of it. "Always prepared."

Grinning, Carson shoved me away. "I can't take credit. This was all Dakota."

"Dakota?"

He strutted up behind Carson. He took a break from breathing into an air-sickness bag long enough to say, "My ability needs a lot of work, but I did get this detail right."

"He drew it," Carson explained. "In the comic version of this scene, you parachuted off of a mountain to save Maryah."

I eyed both of them, so young and so talented. "Thank you, Dakota. You just saved two lives, maybe more considering the ripple effect."

Dakota's cheeks blushed bright pink before he raised the bag to his mouth again.

I slipped my arms into the straps and pulled the pack snug. "You're sure it's packed correctly?" I asked Carson.

"Like I'd send my brother jumping off a jet into the freezing Himalayan Mountains with a faulty chute?"

"Thanks, Car."

"We're almost there," Anthony announced. "Go below now or you won't get a chance to jump until I circle around again."

I lifted the hatch to go under the plane to the loading ramp.

"Nathan?" Carson grabbed my shoulder, and I paused. "Pull the main with enough time to still pull the safety. You know, just in case." He shrugged. "No one's perfect."

After one quick nod, I climbed into the belly of the plane. Carson stared down at me from the hatch door above. "Go save our girls!"

The cargo door lowered, offering a spanning view of the sky and mountains. The plane had slowed significantly, but it felt as if I was witnessing the scene below me in ultra-slow motion. Dedrick and two of his cronies were much too close to Maryah and Rina, and they neared closer with every step. Maryah and Rina had reached the furthest edge of the mountain.

Maryah turned, her head slightly lifted skyward. Too much sky separated us, but our eyes locked on each other as if we were only a breath apart.

I didn't need Gregory's ability to read her mind. I knew what she was planning and what she needed me to do.

Dakota had almost drawn it correctly. I gave one nod.

She threw something toward Dedrick. It sparkled for a brief second as it flew through the air, but it wasn't nearly close enough to hit him.

Dedrick ran toward the object.

Maryah wrapped her arms around Rina.
I took one last breath and put on my sunglasses.
It was now or never.

JUMPING TO A CONCLUSION

Maryah

"Nowhere to run, my pets!" Dedrick shouted. His voice was muffled by the howling wind, but he was close enough to hear—too close.

I made the mistake of licking my lips a few minutes earlier when I tried reassuring Rina that everything would be okay. Now I knew better than to open my mouth. My lips were two icicles plastered upon my frosted face.

I glanced up at the plane flying toward us again.

Had Gregory heard me, or were they too far away? What if Gregory didn't hear my directions? Rina's life and mine were on the line.

The plane flew over us. The ramp was lowering out of the back.

Nathan stood on it, staring down at me like the superhero I so desperately needed him to be.

My hands and feet were numb. I could barely feel my legs and arms. Could I really do this? Was my brain frozen to the point of insanity? There was no other choice. No other way to escape.

Shivering and shaking, my gaze locked with Nathan's. He knew my plan. I could see it written all over his face. Nathan nodded as Dedrick shouted my name.

But there was one part Nathan didn't know about.

Rina shivered and shook uncontrollably. I wrapped one arm around her and pulled her tightly against me. Her head pressed against my chest.

The snow crunched under Dedrick's boots. A few more steps and he'd be close enough to grab us. "Did you forget your precious Nathaniel can't use his traversing power?"

I hadn't forgotten. It's what made what I was about to do infinitely more scary.

"This is your last chance, Maryah," Dedrick shouted, "Where is the starstone?"

I squeezed my ring tight in my palm one last time. "Here it is!"

I threw it to the far left of him. He ran after it, and I used the distraction for the precious seconds I needed. The last bit of oxygen in my lungs was used to direct Rina. "Hold on tight."

She flung her arms around my neck. I hugged her until it felt like we were one person.

With all the strength I had left, I leapt off the mountain.

CATCHING FALLING STARS

Nathaniel

I ran as fast as I could down the steel ramp.

One, two, three, four, five strides then I launched myself into the cold thin air. I streamlined my body, locking my arms against my sides to fly like a bullet toward Maryah and Rina.

They tumbled through the sky, falling too fast and too far away.

I would reach them. If it was the last thing I ever did in this lifetime, I would force my body to fly fast enough to reach them.

The wind screamed in my ears. My face felt like ice. But I had done this enough times to stay focused.

I visualized the air around me conspiring to move me faster than humanly possible.

Something Mary said in our first life blew through my mind. *Imagine you could travel as fast as a shooting star, where would you go?*

My answer was the same then as it was today. *To you. I'll always be destined to collide with you.*

As if the universe heard me, I flew faster than ever before.

I slammed into them so hard it knocked the breath out of me.

I kept it together, wrapping my arms around both of them, but struggling for a tight grip. Maryah was yelling hysterically, but it was hard to make out her words over the freight train winds ripping all around us. We were tumbling over and over like a snowball racing down a slope, but sinking like a stone in an invisible arctic ocean.

"Pull the chute!" I yelled to Rina. She was closest to the ripcord, and she wasn't screaming like Maryah. "On the side of my pack. Pull the silver pin!"

Rina wriggled her arm free. We somersaulted end over end so fast that I couldn't tell which way was up or down. "Pull it!"

Rina's hand reached around me and then we were yanked upward. I looked up and found a full canopy opened perfectly. Silently, I thanked Carson and Dakota.

I looked down at Rina and Maryah, face to face, cold and paler than death, but alive, and safe in my arms. I forced myself to take a deep breath. The wind was calmer, but it was still so cold. Rina looked a little better than Maryah. Maryah still clung to Rina for dear life, and I had a death grip around both of them. "Maryah, you have to hold onto me."

Her voice cracked, still hysterical. "I can't let go of her."

"Slowly, you can. Move your right arm up around my neck and then your left."

"She'll fall!"

"She won't fall. I have her. I have both of you. But I need you to hang onto me so I can use one arm to steer us."

"I'm okay," Rina weakly told her as her teeth chattered.

"I can't let go of you," Maryah groaned. "I can't."

We didn't have much coasting distance left before we'd slam into the side of a mountain. "You can, Maryah. It's the only way we're going to survive this. You have to."

She trembled as she loosened one hand from Rina and wrapped it around me.

"Don't worry, I have her," I promised. "She weighs next to nothing. Now move your other hand."

"I can't."

"I know your arms are so cold you can barely feel them, but you're going to need both to hang onto me."

"Here," Rina said, wriggling her left arm free and wrapping it around my neck. She looked up at me, and there wasn't a trace of fear or worry on her face. "I'm holding onto you. You're holding onto her. She's holding onto me. We make a circle. Circles can't be broken."

Pride and love made my throat tighten. "You're so brave."

Rina tightened her hold on me then wrapped her legs around my waist. "Just like my parents."

I spoke fast because we were running out of time. "Maryah, can you move your legs?"

"I think so."

"Try to wrap them around me like Rina did."

She struggled to position herself as Rina climbed higher, like a fearless monkey. Maryah's legs were wrapped weakly around my upper legs, but both of them were attached to me, so I reached up and yanked on a toggle. We sharply sailed left, away from the unforgiving mountain.

Maryah pressed her icy face against my neck. "It's so cold."

"We'll be on the ground soon. The plane will be warm, and Krista will help your blood flow properly again."

Her voice was hoarse. "How will they find us?"

"The GPS tracker embedded in my vest."

I steered us toward a stretch of open land between two mountains. I hoped it was enough room for the plane to land. If not, Carson would arrive on foot quickly with something to warm us. He was always several steps ahead of everyone.

"That was heroic what you did back there," I told them, "both of you."

I assessed the horizon line and toggled left again to gain us a bit more distance to my target. Rina was smiling at me. What a contrast to the life she'd been living for so long. From solitary confinement in Dedrick's dreadful cell to leaping off a mountain and soaring like a bird to freedom.

"You're free," I told her.

"Because of you." She hugged me. "Just like the book said."

"The book?"

She nodded then turned and admired the view, her smile unwavering. Her explanation could wait. I had to concentrate on safely landing us in the snow-covered foothills. And it had been quite some time since I traditionally landed after a jump.

"Ladies, keep your arms and legs wrapped around me. High and tight to avoid injuries."

Maryah hugged me so hard, she almost choked me. I yanked both toggles and prepared my feet to hit the ground running. We touched down, but I failed to balance my weight and theirs, so I slid us feet first into the snow.

The three of us just lay there for a moment, limbs still tangled together. I breathed a sigh of relief as I'm sure Maryah and Rina did.

Rina let go and peeled herself off me, kneeling beside us. She giggled as if she'd just departed a carnival ride. "That was thrilling. I'd like to do it again sometime."

Maryah lifted her head but then collapsed on top of me again. "She's her father's daughter."

I beamed at the thought as I shimmied the parachute pack from my shoulders.

The sound of our plane's engines was music to my ears. "Come on, up we go. The last thing we need is a jet landing on top of us."

We scrambled to our feet and moved away from the area serving as a makeshift runway for Anthony to land.

"They're all on board, right?" Rina shouted over the roar of the engines as it dove between the mountains. She watched the plane with childlike wonder. I didn't know if its hovercraft landing abilities were causing her wide eyes, or if it was her first time seeing a plane. "All of our kindrily?"

"Everyone but Faith, Amber, and Mikey," I shouted in reply.

Rina spun on me. "No! They have to be here. Go get them."

"I can't traverse."

She laid her hands on my chest and closed her eyes. "You can." She stepped back and peered up at me. "It's weak, but focus with Air energy and you can do it."

I stared, flabbergasted. "How do you know that?"

"Go! We don't have much time."

"Mikey is too young to be put in harm's way," I argued, "and Faith is pregnant."

The plane touched down. Rina glanced back at it then yelled at me, stomping her feet. "They all need to be here. All of them. If they aren't here, it won't work!"

"What won't work?"

Maryah grabbed the neck of my jacket. "Just go get them! And hurry."

I opened myself up to connect with the light. One magnetic pulse traveled down my right arm, but nothing more.

"Air," Rina reminded me, "Connect with Air energy."

I closed my eyes and visualized my sign's essence. Light flares flickered in the corners of my vision, but I visualized clouds and wind. My fingertips felt weightless. The sensation traveled up my arms, and I inhaled the feeling until it traveled through my core and down into my toes.

I concentrated on the details of Faith's eyes. The connection felt completely different from usual, but it clicked. I traversed.

Faith stood on one foot, the other bent up against her thigh. Her hands were in prayer position at her chest.

"Faith, you have to be with us."

She lifted her arms above her head. "I'm in the middle of tree pose."

"My apologies, but yoga will have to wait."

"I'm pregnant." She planted both feet on her mat. "Who in their right mind asks a pregnant woman to go to battle and jeopardize her and her baby's life?"

"Maryah and Rina. They said you have to be there in order for it to work."

She huffed then turned and grabbed her pink tennis shoes from the foot of the bed. "It's bad enough you have Shiloh with you, now you want me to risk our lives too?"

"Apparently."

"The things I do for this family." She finished tying her laces with a hard yank. A fleece, gloves, and a pink beanie lay on her bed as if she already knew she'd be going.

"You should grab a heavier coat," I said.

"Nope. I need freedom of motion for my ninja skills." She stepped into my arms and protectively covered her belly with her hands. "I'm sorry Sheila, but buckle up."

I traversed Faith back to the inside of the plane. From outside, Dylan saw me through a window and called my name. He ran toward the plane's steps, but I vanished before he could order me to leave Amber and Mikey at home.

Amber was sitting at the roundtable bouncing Mikey in her arms as she looked up from one of Dakota's comic books. "About time."

She and Mikey were already dressed warmly. She pulled a hat onto his head. Eightball and Molokai were in the kitchen eating from overfilled bowls of dog food. She had poured them enough to last two, maybe three days.

"You knew I was coming," I said. "That's why Faith was ready too."

Amber stood. "Before you all left, Dakota told me to read it." She motioned to the comic. "It shows a battle with Dedrick. All of us are there." She glanced down at Mikey. "Even him."

"And you believe he drew what's really going to happen?"

"So far the story is accurate. Details are a bit skewed, but overall the big events are spot on. We should have believed him. We should have read his comics as soon as he told us to."

I stepped closer and opened my arms. "We have to hurry back. They need us."

"One question first. Did you just jump off a mountain and save Maryah and Rina from falling to their death?"

"No." I wrapped my arms around her and Mikey. "I jumped from the plane."

POINT OF RETURN

Maryah

The entire kindrily stood around us, awaiting directions.

"What now?" Nathan asked me as he finished tightening my bulletproof vest.

"I'm not sure. Evelyn said we had to find a beyul, some hidden valley. She said I had been there before." I clutched my Howlite, hoping it would spark a memory.

Nathan's head lifted, and he stared at something behind me. "It's there, through that narrow pass."

"What?" The temperature was much warmer now that we were in the foothills of the mountain, but I still put on my coat. "How do you know that?"

"I saw it when we landed." Nathan slid another vest over Rina's head. "I've been BASE jumping from these mountains for a decade. I know every lake, mountain, peak, and valley. The beyul is an area of flat land, circled by mountains. From above, it looks like a lotus flower. I've tried landing there many times, but whenever I'd get close, the wind would pick up and push me away." He helped Rina shrug her coat back on. "I tried traversing there so I could explore it, but I'd only end up somewhere nearby, then I'd hike toward it but lose all sense of direction and end up lost."

Rina held my hand. The Howlite warmed against my other palm. I stepped back as a memory struck me like lightning.

I was in a breathtaking temple. A light figure sat across from me. Her soul spoke to mine.

Existing in the center of eight mountains is a temple with four doorways, and at the top, a gateway to the stars, to our world, to any point in time, to any point in infinity. The bridge between us is narrow, vulnerable, yet almost impenetrable, unless the stones are used together as a key. Meru must be protected. We must thrive forever. If it were to be overtaken, tainted by darkness, the universe would weep in such a cosmic way that the stars would never shine again. Countless souls would be lost forever."

Nathan's hand touching mine snapped me out of the memory. "This entire lifetime, I've been drawn to these mountains, and I never understood why, but now it's clear." He smoothed down Rina's hair. "My soul knew she was here even though my mind didn't know she existed."

Rina flashed him a warming smile that only a daughter could give a father.

Nathan's finger rubbed against my naked thumb. "Where's your ring?"

"I used it to distract Dedrick so we could jump from the mountain."

Nathan's eyes narrowed. "Used it how? Where is it?"

"I threw it into the snow."

His jaw dropped. Carson lurched forward. "You threw away the starstone?"

"It was a decoy. The starstone wasn't in my ring."

"It wasn't?" Carson, Mister Wise Scion, looked stunned that he had finally—and much to my satisfaction—been wrong about something. "So where is it?"

"Helicopter," Nathan said, alerting us. "They're coming."

I couldn't hear it yet, but he always heard everything before anyone else.

"Come on," Rina said. "Let's get to the beyul before they do."

"Wait." I sat down and unlaced my boots.

"What are you doing?" Nathan asked.

"Switching shoes with Rina."

"Why?"

"Just trust me." I squeezed my feet into the hiking shoes Evelyn had given Rina. Rina pulled on Harmony's shin-high boots. I stood and waved my fingers at Carson. "Give us some guns."

His brows rose. "Do you even know how to shoot a gun?"

"Yes, just give me two of the lightest ones."

He pulled two black handguns from his backpack and gave them to me. They felt cold and heavy. I shivered as I thought about having to shoot them, but then I reminded myself some bullets do more good than harm.

I stuck the lighter of the two guns in the back of Rina's pants. I grabbed a dagger from Harmony's shoulder holster and slid that into Rina's boot. "Ready?"

She shook her head. "We need Mikey."

Amber pivoted, turning Mikey away from us. "Why?"

"I promise, he won't be hurt." I held out my hands, reaching for him. "We need his ability."

Amber pulled Mikey's hat further down his head, making sure his ears were protected from the cold, then she kissed his cheek and handed him to me.

Rina held his tiny hand. I focused on the new skill Rina had taught me.

Together, with the rest of the kindrily, we hiked to the battleground. All of us were cloaked with Mikey's gift of invisibility.

∞

No wind blew. No sun shined. The path between the mountains was eerily void of sound and color. Even our footsteps were quiet. So many shoes plodding through the snow should have made a lot of crunching noise, but it was as if we walked soundlessly on clouds.

"Do they know?" I whispered to Nathan. "About Rina?"

Judging from the way everyone had been staring at Rina, and glancing at me with pity and curiosity, I suspected they did.

"Yes. I told everyone on the flight here."

"What did they say?"

He grinned and lowered his voice. "Mixed reactions. Harmony is suspicious. She says Gregory would have remembered an event that significant."

I peered down at Rina between us. She undoubtedly heard him, but she kept focused straight ahead, marching toward the enemy. We had lost our sunglasses during the fall. I worried Rina's eyes might be overly sensitive to daylight. "Rina, can you see okay? Do you need to borrow sunglasses from someone?"

"Nope. I can see just fine."

Rounding a blind corner of sky-high rock, we reached our destination.

Mountains towered above us on all sides, but the beyul was a flat stretch of land with no snow. People stood around, their eyes focused on the mountains. Not people—Nefariouns, with their snakelike gazes awaiting their commander's arrival.

Nathan motioned for everyone behind us to stop.

"They're already here," Rina whispered.

"I see them."

Rina pulled me closer. "Not his soldiers. The stones."

My eyes darted to Dedrick's army scattering the land. "Where?"

She pointed to the mountain to the left of us. "South." Then at the mountain adjacent to it. "North." Across from us, about halfway up the mountain's base, a subtle glint of red winked at me as if the mountain itself were watching us. "West." Her thumb jerked over her shoulder. "And East. They've already placed them in their keyholes."

"That cannot be good," Nathan said.

We all watched as the helicopter landed in the beyul. Dedrick jumped out of the passenger seat before the engine shut down. He shouted directions to some of the Nefariouns as he proceeded to the center of the beyul. He kneeled, held my ring up to the sky, and then placed it on the ground. He joined his hands together in a prayer position and waited.

Rina lifted her face skyward. Her blue eyes gleamed like waves of the ocean at sunrise. "That's my cue."

A beam of pink light radiated down from the sky and lit up the ground in front of Dedrick. The ring levitated. Rina's powers continued to astound me.

I bent close to her ear. "Rina, are you sure about this?"

She nodded and pressed her finger to her lips.

The ring lifted, higher and higher until it rose above the mountains and clouds, and could no longer be seen.

Everyone except Dedrick stood, their chins lifted, eyes to the sky, waiting for something epic and magical to happen.

An explosion, like a firework that splayed rays of every possible color, parted the clouds and shook the ground. I spread my feet wider, trying to keep my balance.

A swirling flame shot out of the Firestone, the flame stretched long and wide across the valley until it melded with the pink beam shooting down from the sky. Blue light poured from the Waterstone like a wave of water. What looked like brown dust spiraled from the Earthstone. From the mountain behind us, one long white stream of fog billowed from the Airstone and met at the intersection of the center of the beyul.

When they all joined together, the elemental tunnels of light burned so brightly, I had to shield my eyes.

Each unique form of energy spread high and wide, forming towering walls of light that enclosed the beyul. Shimmering, pulsing, moving walls of red, blue, brown, and white surrounded us.

In the blue wall of the Waterstone's light, ghostly images of sea life swam as if it were a real ocean. In the Firestone's wall of red, a massive white sun wrapped its rays around orbiting planets. Silhouettes of plants, trees, people, and animals scrolled across the Earthstone's ethereal screen. Birds, butterflies, leaves, and a dozen other flying objects flew through the Airstone's skyscraping tower of clouds.

I could even smell different scents as I focused on each element. Saltwater, the musty smell of dirt and fresh grass, the burning of wood, winter air chilling my sinuses.

Rina had given me the Cliffs Notes version of what would happen, but just like in school, the summary had left me unprepared. Seeing the real thing left me slack-jawed and spellbound.

The elemental walls around us flexed and quivered.

Dedrick bowed forward, kissing the ground. A glowing orb fell from the sky, hurdling toward him, but then dipped just before it landed and flew directly at us.

I held out my hand like Rina had told me to do. The ring gently slid onto my finger, still shimmering and changing colors.

"They're here!" Dedrick shouted. "They're invisible!"

Rina released my hand, and our kindrily's veil of invisibility lifted.

"Thomas!" Dedrick jumped to his feet. "The shield!"

A bubble of translucent light formed around Dedrick's entire army.

Rina's explanation from our earlier training echoed in my mind. *No one can get through Thomas's shields. Unless he allows it.*

We expected a fight. Even though Dedrick and the Nefarious were shielded, we still planned that someone, with some terrible ability, would try to harm at least one, if not all of us. But instead, Dedrick shouted one word, one name, and we instantly froze.

Dedrick's paralyzer immobilized us.

Dedrick rushed forward, but he was burned by an unseen force. He leapt back, touching his face and arms as if making sure they were still there. He slowly reached forward, and his finger was burned again.

Star power will trump his magic, Rina had said.

Directly down the center of the valley, stretching tall and wide, separating us and the Nefariouns, stood a multicolored wall of starlight he couldn't cross.

Dedrick called to his flame-throwing servant and directed her to penetrate it. Fire burst from her fingers as she blowtorched the air, but it did nothing except make the barrier swirl with shades of yellow and orange. She tried crossing through, but she was also burned.

If I hadn't been paralyzed, I would have smiled.

Dedrick turned to his paralyzer. "Allow the one with the ring to speak, but nothing more."

My lips parted as I blinked my eyes.

"You think you're so clever, don't you?" Dedrick asked me. "How long do you suppose this parlor trick will last? And once this force field dissipates, then what? How will you protect your beloved cattle herd from being slaughtered right before your eyes?"

"Look at all the power I have at my disposal." He motioned to his Nefariouns. "Shall I burn your kindrily to death? Crush their skulls? Strip them of their skin with ancient tools? Which method of torture will you choose for them, dear, foolish Maryah?"

"That barrier is nothing I have created," I said. "No one can enter or cross that sacred space unless they have the starstone."

Dedrick cackled. "You don't honestly expect me to believe that."

"Believe what you want. It's the truth." I didn't feel bad lying to Dedrick. In fact, it felt good. Rina's wall of star energy was even more impressive than how she described it to me.

"Is that so?" Dedrick snapped his fingers. "Bring me Evelyn and River."

Two of the Nefariouns removed Evelyn and River from the back of the helicopter. They were both gagged with their arms tied behind their backs. Evelyn's knees gave out and her head fell forward—she was obviously drugged—but the Neanderthal continued to drag her.

"If I shove your friend River into the divider, he'll burn, correct?"

"Please don't!" I tried to sound worried, but Rina had assured me she could control who or what the wall hurt.

"This should be fun to witness." Dedrick grabbed River by the back of his neck. "Enjoy the blazing pain."

He shoved River forward so hard that River tripped and tumbled to the ground. River rolled into the starlight, passing through to our side. He groaned while tugging and pulling at his wrist restraints, but he couldn't break free. None of us could move to help him.

Dedrick's rage ignited. "Give me the starstone or I'll start this massacre with her!" Evelyn's eyelids were barely open as she lay at his feet, bound and gagged. He lifted her head by her hair.

"Don't touch her!" I snapped. This time my anger was genuine. River thrashed and grunted even harder.

"Would you like to do the honors?" Dedrick asked his flame thrower. Before I could utter another word, she splayed her fingers and shot fire at Evelyn's feet. Smoke rose, and the smell of burnt flesh choked me as I screamed. "Stop! I'll give it to you!"

Dedrick waved his hand, and the flames ceased. "Wise girl, but you've taken more from me than just the stone. I want Rina back."

"No," I growled.

"Ahh. Such a protective tone. You know who she is, don't you? You know she was yours and I took her from you, just as I will take her from you again." He motioned at the flame thrower.

This time, Evelyn's face was burned as she thrashed and screamed through the rag gagging her.

"Okay! Stop!" I yelled. We never meant for Evelyn to be tortured. We knew he'd hurt her, but we didn't think he'd burn her to death. "I'll give you the ring and Rina. Just promise not to hurt her."

"I have never hurt Rina." He placed his hands over his chest. "She's like my own daughter."

My blood boiled at the thought, but this is what we counted on. Dedrick would never give up his prized possession.

"Unparalyze Rina," Dedrick commanded.

Rina threw her arms around me, but I couldn't hug her back. I was still paralyzed from the neck down.

"I'm so sorry," I told her, loud enough for Dedrick to hear.

"Rina," Dedrick snarled. "Come to me now before Mommy Evelyn suffers to the point of death. And don't forget the ring."

"Remember," she whispered to me, "The shield then the paralyzer. After that, you'll have all the help you need."

She pulled away and slipped the ring from my stiff thumb. She stared into my eyes. My daughter. My friend. The glue to my strings. She was my rock, or more accurately, my *stone*.

Rina's soul was the part of Meru I brought back with me. *She* was the starstone.

She squeezed my hand three times—our secret signal.

"You're ready," she whispered. "I believe in you. I always have."

"Rina!" Dedrick shouted. "I won't ask again."

"Jupiter adsit." Her hand slipped out of mine. She took two steps backward. The first step shattered my heart, the second my soul.

I bowed my head so no one would see my teary eyes.

But also because that's the only way the plan would work.

FOILED

Nathaniel

I couldn't move. I couldn't even turn my head to look at them. I was trying so hard to part my lips so I could tell them no. Rina couldn't go to him.

How could Maryah give her up so easily?

I tried keeping a tight grip on Rina's tiny hand, but she slipped free.

No, don't go to him!

I tried traversing over and over as I desperately fought to do or say something, anything, but I failed.

We swore we would protect her, and now we were giving her back to the devil.

Rina took off Maryah's ring.

I stopped internally screaming in time to hear Rina whisper, "I believe in you. I always have."

Was this part of their plan?

Rina stepped away from us then turned and faced Dedrick.

She inched forward as if her feet were arguing with her head. I couldn't peel my eyes away from her as she walked away from us.

I wanted to scream. I wanted to traverse to him and rip out his throat with my bare hands. I tried again and again, but every time my energy hit a brick wall.

In my peripheral vision, Maryah stood to the side of me. Only an arm's length separated us, an empty space where just moments ago, Rina stood grasping both of our hands.

Rina paused at the energy barrier. Her legs visibly shook. She stepped into the wall of light, crossing from family and safety into monsters and peril.

The man who was acting as Dedrick's shield stepped forward. His hand glowed silver as he reached through the Nefariouns' protective force field. He offered Rina his hand, but she had her head bowed.

He grabbed her by the hair then yanked her inside.

A part of my soul was yanked away with her.

ONE INFINITE SOURCE

Maryah

Rina's skinny legs shook with every step forward. Whether it was fear or adrenaline that made her shake, I wasn't sure, but her legs carried her body to the shield protecting Dedrick and his goons.

Rina had suffered so much. I had to keep her safe. She trusted me. She believed in me. She had put her life in my hands, literally, and I wouldn't fail her. I had failed enough in the past. It was time for me to be the brave and powerful soul I had once been.

I had never felt a heart hammer so fast and loud.

I took a deep breath. This had to work.

Someone yanked me through the protective barrier. It was Thomas.

We were in.

I raised Rina's gaze enough to see the shield's snakelike glare—and his moment of panic when he realized it wasn't Rina's soul looking up at him.

It was mine.

Rina's words rang through my mind again. *Shatter the glass.*

In a flash, I reached into Rina's boot, grabbed the dagger, and drove it into Thomas's heart before he could yell to Dedrick.

"I'm sorry," I said to him. "I hope you return much less evil."

It was just as Rina said it would be. I felt each of the kindrily member's powers as if they were strings connected to my soul. I yanked on Anthony's first, but it was just as difficult as before. I couldn't stop time, but I slowed it down.

Time stretched out to infinity, slowing everything and everyone. Rina was right; it gave me an advantage. Dedrick's head was still turning. His hand, in slow motion, was still reaching for the gun at his belt.

Tugging at the thread connecting me to Carson, I used his speed and strength as my own. I moved like a bullet through water. No one would be able to anticipate my next move, forget about trying to catch me.

One shield down. One paralyzer to go.

I blurred past Dedrick to the paralyzer while grabbing the gun from my other boot. I aimed it at the side of his head. Rina's arms were stronger and steadier than I expected. I had complete control over her body as if it were my own.

I shot him in the temple, wincing at the guilt of ending a life. But the guilt vanished when I felt my kindrily unfreeze.

Dedrick still stared, mouth agape, at the empty space where I—in Rina's body—had just killed his shield.

It won't be easy, Rina had said while training me. *You haven't had enough practice to build up your endurance. Using one ability will make you tired. More than one will drain you fast.*

My core shook as my soul struggled to maintain use of Carson's and Anthony's powers. Like a fatigued muscle snapping from exertion, my hold on time snapped away from me.

Everyone, the kindrily and the Nefariouns, sprang into action.

All the Nefariouns swarmed Dedrick, circling him like a defensive barrier.

Amber cawed, and black birds dove out of the elemental walls, attacking only Nefariouns. Hands flailed every which way, trying to defend against scratching claws, pecking beaks, and flapping wings.

A flood of voices bombarded my mind. I pressed my hands to my ears, trying to disconnect myself from Gregory's ability.

Nathan appeared in front of me, throwing his arms around my torso as I felt heat engulf me. We traversed and reappeared to the side of the flame-throwing woman. Nathan threw a knife into her back without ever removing his other arm from my waist. He traversed twice more, pulling a knife or dagger from a holster each time, throwing with deadly accuracy.

I couldn't tune out the rumble of voices, but no matter how loud the noise was in my head, I had to stay focused on the battle.

Nathan disappeared without me. I saw him reappear by my body, shouting something. Rina took off running. I prayed my legs were fast enough to carry her to safety.

People scrambled all around us. Faith and Shiloh fought three of the Nefariouns surrounding Dedrick. They punched, kicked, and leapt through the air like ninjas. Shiloh swung nunchucks across the side of a Nefarioun's head, and blood went flying through the air.

A bald Nefarioun dashed out from behind some trees, running straight for Harmony, but she was clotheslining the redhead and wouldn't see him coming. I aimed my gun and fired, missing the first shot, but hitting him in the ribs on my second. He fell to the ground, grabbing Harmony's ankle on his way down, but she mule-kicked him in the face and ended whatever plan he had.

Carson was nothing but a white blur, leaving crumpled and broken bodies in his wake.

Even Louise and Helen had a gun in each hand, aimed and waiting, ready to fire at anyone who attempted to attack them or one of our kindrily.

I focused on my energy net and found the string connecting me to Mikey. It took immense concentration, but I visualized his energy spreading through me and into every connecting string.

The Nefariouns paused. Heads whipped in every direction as I made our entire kindrily invisible.

Something that looked like small saw blades sailed through the air and into the throats of the two gorilla-sized Nefariouns flanking Dedrick. They both crumpled to the ground, one almost falling on top of Dedrick in the process.

I could see Dylan's aura directly in front of Dedrick. I sorted through the remaining thoughts and voices, which had thankfully decreased as Nefariouns were taken down.

Dylan's power of persuasion came in crystal clear. *You will stop fighting. You will command any other hidden Nefariouns to surrender, and then you will release them from your spells. You will put your hands behind your head and kneel before us.*

I took a much-needed breath as Dedrick's eyes glossed over. He slowly put his hands behind his head and knelt down. I lifted the invisibility veil. No one remained standing but our kindrily.

My own voice screamed from somewhere behind me. "Krista! Come quickly!"

My body with Rina's soul occupying it was yards away, crouched over Dakota's body.

Krista and I bolted across the valley. Krista skidded to a stop on her knees, dropping her ear against Dakota's chest. "What happened?"

Rina's soul gazed up at me through my own pained face. A warm shiver rippled through me. I gasped as our souls swapped places again, each returning to its own body.

I was clutching Dakota's hand. Rina, back in her own body, dropped to his side across from me. "I don't know. Nathan gave me a gun and told me to hide so I ran and hid behind these rocks. I was watching Dakota until everyone became invisible. When I could see everyone again, Dakota was here on the ground, unconscious."

Krista's hands had been furiously scanning his body. She adjusted his head, arched his neck, and started pumping against his chest. "I think he had a heart attack."

I stared, not believing that Dakota could have a heart attack at such a young age.

"I'll bring him back," Krista said before breathing into his mouth. "Don't worry."

"Maryah!" Nathan called to me from the middle of the valley where he stood beside River. At their feet, clutching his chest, was Dedrick.

Even from a distance, I could see the pool of evil blood.

RIPPLE EFFECTS

Nathaniel

Rina ran toward Maryah. Or vice versa depending on whether you meant bodies or souls. I rushed toward Dedrick.

Anthony, Gregory, and Carson all braced themselves, preparing to hold me back. But River reached him first.

He plunged a blade of bone into Dedrick's chest.

I closed in on them, close enough to hear River say, "That was for ruining my life."

Dedrick clutched River's wrist, but River stabbed him again. "That was for making people believe I was a psycho murderer like you."

The third stab sent Dedrick's eyes rolling back in his head. "And that was for telling me my mother was dead."

Stunned, I called out for Maryah.

"Whoa," Carson said, staring down at River and Dedrick. "Didn't see that coming."

Dylan could have stopped River with one word, but he didn't. He watched River approach and attack, and he let it happen. Dedrick's blood wouldn't be on the hands of any of our kindrily.

In a way, it was a relief, but also very unsatisfying.

Maryah walked up on the other side of them. Our eyes met, and I could tell her adrenaline was still pumping, but relief had seeped in—relief that Dedrick was taking his last breaths and that we had truly defeated him.

River looked up at me. "Sorry to steal your thunder, guys, but I had to do the honors. He had to be killed by his own blood with a holy bone."

"His own blood?" Maryah squinted, scanning River from head to toe.

"Apparently, he's not my uncle. I'm the result of this bastard's fastest sperm."

I rubbed my hand over my mouth, shocked, but also sympathizing with the disgust River must have felt at learning he was the child of a monster.

Dedrick still quivered, staring at the sky with dilated pupils, trying to find air in his shredded lungs.

Carson leaned down and flicked the curved blade of bone in Dedrick's chest. "How'd you know about the bone stipulation?"

"I cast the spell to protect him from aging or dying." Evelyn's voice was scratchy as she rubbed her sore, recently freed wrists. "So I knew its stipulations."

She waved her hand in front of her eyes, erasing her gold slits. The same wise and compassionate soul I had known as Emily gazed down at Dedrick with sad hazel eyes. She knelt at his side.

"Emily?" He watched her as if he was staring at an angel. And in a way, he was. "This whole time it was you?"

She pulled a handkerchief from her pocket. It was neatly folded in a triangle. "I tried so hard, Dedrick." She dabbed each corner of his mouth, wiping away the blood he was coughing up. Until the very last moment, I tried to talk you out of it."

"We can be together again." Dedrick reached for her, almost blindly as if he was losing his vision. He was clinging to the last frayed bits of his wretched existence. "I always knew we would be."

Evelyn shook her head. "No, Dedrick. Where you're going, no one can follow."

The ground beneath us trembled. The center beam of pink light turned into black fog, spiraling so deep into the earth that we couldn't see the bottom.

Dedrick still gasped and struggled, begging for another chance, demanding to be forgiven.

"Rot in hell, old man." River rolled his body toward the bottomless black hole and shoved him in. Dedrick's tortured scream faded as he fell deeper into oblivion.

One tear ran down Emily's burnt cheek. "Goodbye, Dedrick."

The black hole closed in on itself, and the light returned to a calming pink.

River embraced Evelyn. I hadn't seen the mother-son resemblance until that moment, but now it was inarguable. How could River have such an ancient-souled, powerful mother, yet have no ability of his own?

"I thought Dedrick was castrated," Harmony said.

Evelyn nodded. "He was, but I knew someday I'd need our child to end this path of destruction, so I took the proper precautionary measures." She stood back and held River's face. "And I couldn't be more proud."

The burning in my lower back pulled me away from the moment of victory.

As my adrenaline rush subsided, an all familiar light-headed feeling took over. I rocked on my heels, swaying as my fingers searched my back, then I dropped to my knees.

Maryah rushed to my side.

"Nathan?" She scanned me with panicked eyes. "What's wrong?"

The world had gone fuzzy, and along with it so did my body and energy. I found my breath and spoke with tingling lips. "I believe I've been shot in the back."

"No!" Maryah rushed behind me, lifting my bulletproof vest. Although I couldn't see it, I could imagine the shock on her face at the sight of the wound. "Oh god, no. It hit you right beneath your vest."

She screamed Krista's name so loud the elemental walls around us shook.

UNTIL THE BITTER END

Maryah

"I can't feel my limbs," he muttered. "I've lost too much blood."

"Shh." I cradled his head in one hand while caressing his cheek. Krista would heal him. Krista would fix it. "It'll be all right."

"You don't remember." He placed his hand over mine and gasped for another breath. "But we've been through this many times. It's part of the process."

My lips trembled. I couldn't relate to *the process*. "No. You're not going to die."

His eyes floated aimlessly like he couldn't see me anymore. "We'll be together again."

"No, I need you here right now." We had overcome so much. I couldn't lose him so soon.

His hand grew cold against mine. I grabbed his fingers, squeezing them, willing his blood to flow and make them warm again. Death was knocking at my boyfriend's door, and it felt like he'd be ripped away from me forever.

"Nathan?"

The elemental walls closed in on us until I couldn't breathe. The physical world shrank into darkness as Nathan slipped further through the veil of life and death.

"I'm always with you." His last words were a whisper. "Then, now, and eternally."

"No!" I curled myself around him, trying to be a barrier between him and death. I screamed for Krista again.

His heart wasn't beating against my chest. His body went limp in my arms. I kept begging for it not to be true.

I felt the sky sigh and the mountains weep as his soul left his body.

Krista skidded to a stop above us. "No, not Nathan."

"Save him," I begged. "Save him! Hurry!"

Krista dropped to her knees. She placed one hand on his chest and the other on his forehead. Her nostrils flared, and she bit her bottom lip as she sucked in a breath.

"Do something!" I urged.

She stared into my eyes and held my face in her hands. Her lips moved mere inches from mine, but her voice sounded miles away. "He's gone, Maryah."

"No." It was the only word that would form. "No!" I wailed, hugging his limp body tighter as if I could squeeze life back into him.

Louise hugged me from behind as I rocked back and forth, clinging to him.

"Please," I begged to any gods, or magic stones, or supernatural beings in the worlds that could help, "Don't take him away from me."

I caressed his face and eyelids, willing them to open so I could see his shining eyes again. I ran my fingers through his hair and choked on another sob. I pressed my forehead against his. His head and body felt so heavy. How could there be no life inside?

The venom in my voice stung Krista. "What took you so long?"

Tears welled in her eyes. "I was trying to save Dakota." She touched my shoulder, but I shrugged her away. "We lost him too."

I cried harder.

I cried for Dakota, who couldn't cheat death a second time.

I cried for Krista, who I knew would always blame herself for being unable to save either of them.

And I cried for Nathan. I cried like I had never cried before. I cried because half of me—my soul mate, my hero, my first boyfriend and my last—was gone. I wept, and convulsed, and cursed the heavens.

Our kindrily stood staring down at us. Many of them were teary-eyed too. I looked away from them and back at Nathan's perfect face.

Without Nathan our circle was broken.

Sobs strangled me to the point that I was hiccupping.

Harmony crouched beside us. "Maryah—"

"No," I growled. "Don't you dare. You tell him he's not allowed to say goodbye. Tell him to get back in his body." My voice hitched with anguish. "Tell him he can't leave me."

Harmony's chin dropped to her chest. "He can hear you."

I frantically searched the empty space around us, begging his soul with everything I had. "Don't do this, Nathan. Fight. Fight to stay alive. Fight to stay with me. I just found you." My throat constricted as my tears fell onto Nathan's chin and neck. "I can't lose you too!"

Harmony embraced me. I tried wriggling out of her arms but she held tighter. "I know how bad it hurts, and I'm sorry."

"Let go of me," I whined the words but didn't mean them. My heart was imploding. Harmony's strong arms were the only thing keeping me from fracturing into broken, useless pieces. I gave in, collapsing against her, but still clutching Nathan's shirt. "I love him. I love him so much."

"I know." Harmony stroked my hair. "Death will never change that."

The world was spinning out of control and no matter who I held onto, or how hard, Nathan was slipping away from me.

Harmony loosened her grip on me as Rina squeezed in between Krista and me.

I glanced at Rina's sad face staring down at Nathan. I hated how easily the truth slipped from my lips. "He's gone."

More tears fell. I was sure they'd never stop falling.

Rina lifted my chin. She wiped my cheeks several times before realizing there was no controlling the dam that had broken inside of me. Her hand fell away, but she stared at me so intently, it stifled my breath. Around her dark blue irises was the ring of green that matched Nathan's. In her peacock feather gaze, I saw so much sadness, but then she smiled. "We did it. We stopped Dedrick."

Nathan was dead, and she was still focused on Dedrick? My snot-filled voice came out gargled. "I don't care."

"It's perfect," she said quietly. "Now everything can be perfect."

Anger rushed through me. "Nothing is perfect. Nathan is dead!"

"Death is temporary."

"I need him with me now."

She swayed forward then back again. "I know."

In my grief and shock, I hadn't noticed she was holding Krista's and Nathan's hands. For a few seconds, I just stared, and then it hit me. "Rina, no!"

The color was draining from her face, but her eyes seemed to be brightening. "It's perfect."

I tried prying her hand apart from Nathan's. "No! You'll die if you use Krista's healing power to bring him back."

"I know."

I shrieked, "Then stop!"

My hand was closed around her entire wrist. She was so tiny and fragile, I was afraid I'd break her if I pulled any harder. She maintained her literal death grip. "You need him. And I need him. Trust me, it's perfect."

"How can you say that? You'll die!"

"I'll return. And you can be my mother again. But this time you'll remember me, and it will be the way it should be." Her voice was weakening. "I'll know what it's like to have a real family."

"You can't do this. I can't lose you!" Tears poured down my cheeks, but in some twisted way, my heart felt as if it were filling up.

The muscles in her wrist went slack. "It's already done."

Nathan arched his back and coughed. My heart leapt into my throat. His eyes opened. Rina toppled forward against Nathan's chest. He sat up, cradling her head in his arms.

He and Rina stared at each other as the last of Rina's life force drained out of her.

"Marina," he whispered. "No."

I couldn't speak.

The pink beam of light pulsed blindingly bright then retracted up into the sky until it disappeared. The pulsing walls of Air, Earth, Fire, and Water fell around us in colorful crashing waves then receded back into the mountains and into their originating stones.

My tears did not recede.

I hugged Rina for so long that eventually Carson and Krista had to pry my hands free.

Rina—the beautiful, fearless, heroic, lionhearted starstone—had returned to the heavens.

WITH THIS RING

Maryah

The stones were returned to their keepers.

The Nefariouns who were captured instead of killed had snapped free from Dedrick's mind control the instant he died. They were returning to whatever semblance of life they had left. The bodies that could be identified were respectfully returned to their families. Those who were unidentifiable, or had no family, were buried at sea as we prayed for the tides to wash away their involuntary sins.

I stared at the koi swimming around my feet. Drops of water dripped onto my arm from the tail of Eightball's toy alligator as he sat panting beside me.

Nathan whistled, and Eightball took off running, the tags on his collar jingling with each carefree gallop. In my next life, I wanted to be a dog. Their lives seemed so simple.

Nathan sat behind me, his legs stretched out on either side of me. He pushed my hair over one shoulder and kissed my neck.

His kisses soothed me and excited me all at the same time. I relaxed back against his chest, and he wrapped his arms around me.

"I miss her so much," I said.

"I know. So do I. And it's been only two days."

"It feels like forever."

"Death always has that effect on the hearts left behind." He laced his fingers with mine and pressed his cheek against the side of my head. "Will you come on a journey with me?"

"Where?"

"It's a surprise."

"Are we traversing?"

"Yes."

I pulled his arms tighter around me. His biceps flexed, and then we traversed.

When I pulled away from him, we were standing in the foothills of a desert mountain. Two hot air balloons were lifting off the ground, and two more were floating high above them.

"Nineteen," Nathan said. "Balloon Fiesta."

My grin lifted higher than the balloons. "Albuquerque. Where we first met."

"I took you up in a hot air balloon. You were wearing a green dress, and your curls were piled on top of your head with a jeweled clip that I didn't care for very much."

"What?" I thought back to our road trip for Nathan's birthday. I had never worn a dress. And I didn't curl my hair. "I don't understand."

"The clip had rhinestones glued to the plastic. It was gaudy, and it distracted from your beautiful eyes." He leaned in and kissed me, picking me up and slowly spinning us in a circle. His kiss was so intoxicating that the world seemed to turn with us.

When I opened my eyes, the world had turned. We had traversed to somewhere that was the complete opposite of the desert. Rolling greens hills and lush trees framed an elegant but old stone bridge. The sun had almost set, but even in twilight, I could see the detailed architecture in the ceiling and pillars. "Are we in England?"

Nathan nodded. "Eighteen. Palladian Bridge. It looked a bit different because I lined every wall, ledge, and pathway with candles, but you loved these gardens. You said Mr. Darcy would have proposed to Elizabeth in a place such as this."

"Proposed." I clapped my hands to my chest. "These are the places you proposed to me?"

"Yes."

I looked around, trying to take it all in. I ran my hands along the stone. "I love it. What a wonderful way to try jogging some memories." Wait. My fingernails dug into the stone as a thought jolted my nerves. Was Nathan taking me on this tour because he was about to propose? I glanced down at my raggedy yoga pants and T-shirt. No, he would have warned me to dress for such a special occasion. Right?

I was stuck in place, staring at the water beneath the bridge. My heart raced at the idea that today, or tonight, depending where we ended up in the world, might be the moment that Nathan proposed to me.

He wrapped his arms around me and pried my finger free from my nail-splitting grip. He whispered into my ear, "Shall we continue?"

My world spun for a whole new reason.

"Seventeen," he said before I opened my eyes.

I yearned to remember every location and every detail that he described, but I was useless. All I kept thinking was, *oh-my-freaking-god Nathan is going to ask me to marry him!*

Every new place gave me déjà vu. Every word he said made me giddy. Every kiss made my stomach drop until I was so jittery with excitement and nerves I thought I might pass out.

He had counted down from nineteen. We traversed to every location of every proposal, until we ended up at number one. Our first lifetime together.

We stood on the roof of a building, gazing out at white-capped waves as they crashed below us in the dark. Around us, hundreds of candles burned, their flames flickering in the wind, but never blowing out. I didn't know if it was luck or if someone had cast a spell to make sure they stayed lit. The glowing candles set a romantic vibe that left me shivering in a good way.

Nathan wrapped a blanket around me. "One. Isle of Man. This building wasn't here yet, but we used to picnic on the hill where it was built. I can't put into words how nervous I was."

I giggled, trying to imagine him that way. He was so confident and sexy, and always in control of himself and every situation. I still couldn't believe he was all mine. "I kind of remember this place."

"You do?"

"I think so." I walked to the edge and stared down. "It's like a Post-It note in my memory that's so faded I can barely read it, but it's there."

"Sheila lived here for decades. She loved the island's energy."

My eyes darted left and right. "Sheila."

The Post-It note came into view as I backslid into a memory. I spun around. Nathan watched me silently. A pain slithered up my neck and into my head, but I welcomed it. I was remembering something.

My ring had sat upon my finger as I scrawled words onto a page. "A letter."

Nathan's brow rose, but he stayed quiet. Was I remembering more about writing in the book to Rina? I shook my head. No, it wasn't the book. It was one piece of paper. A notecard.

"I wrote something here," I said, "something important."

Nathan encouraged me with his smile.

My eyes darted around the cement rooftop. "I put it in a box."

He nodded. "A letterbox."

"A mail box?"

"Not exactly. Letterboxing was a favorite hobby of Sheila's. It's like treasure hunting using notes."

"I left a note for her. I hid it here on the island."

He nodded again. "And as always, she found it. In return, she set up her own message for you to find. She gave the initial card to me not long before she passed. I was here, one floor below us, visiting her. The hunt led me all over the world, but the final message was here, full circle to where I started, hidden on this rooftop."

"What was it?"

He held my hand and guided me to the lip of the roof made of old stones. He ran his hand across a section of them, pressing as he went, and then one stone slightly shifted. He pried it loose and stepped back.

I squatted down, reaching in and pulling out a rectangular box. "Have you opened it?"

He pursed his lips, trying to conceal his guilty grin. "I wasn't completely honest about why I suspected your ring contained the starstone. I revealed as much as I could, but when you open that box you'll understand why I couldn't tell you the whole truth."

I lifted the lid and found a single card stamped with an elaborate gold star.

Nathaniel,

Do not give it to her until the time is right. You will know without a doubt.

Love Always, Sheila

I lifted it. Another card sat beneath it bearing the same gold stamp.

Sheila, my little star sweeper:

Keep it safe for me. When the time is right, give it to no one but Nathaniel. To me, it is more powerful and magical than its spurious replica.

My eternal love, Mary

Besides those two cards, the box was empty. I turned to ask Nathan what my note meant. He was on one knee, holding a ring in his hand.

"Maryah, we've been through a lot in a very short period of time. We've endured exponentially more throughout the centuries, but through it all I loved you—and still love you—mind, body, and soul. If you'll have me, I would be honored to be your husband. Again. And for the first time that you'll remember. May I have the privilege of marrying you?"

A happy tear streamed down my cheek. "Yes! Yes times infinity."

He slid the ring onto my thumb. It looked just like the one we had put in Rina's folded hands when we buried her.

"I was going to have it resized," he said, "but the way you wore the other one on your thumb suited you. I thought you might prefer this one to fit the same way."

"It's perfect."

He cupped my face and kissed me. I squealed and danced in place. "We're engaged!"

He smiled against my lips. "Yes, we are."

"I have to tell Krista and Faith."

"I'm pretty sure they suspected this day would arrive sooner than later. But there's one more thing. We weren't entirely alone during my proposal."

A stairway door opened. Harmony stepped out onto the roof and joined us. "Hola, lovebirds."

"We're engaged!" While hopping in place, I held up my hand to show her my ring.

She shook her head, but a smile cracked her lips. "Congratulations."

I hugged her. I didn't care whether or not she'd want me to. I was too excited and needed to share it with someone. Surprisingly, she hugged me back and even rocked me side to side a little.

"Okay, okay, enough." She pulled away and smoothed away invisible wrinkles from her sweater. "I'm here to translate."

"Translate?" My heart fluttered with even more joy. "Rina? She's here? Did she see Nathan propose?"

"Yes and yes," Harmony said. "She's thrilled and says if you wed quickly, she could be there." Harmony wiggled two fingers. "Before she crosses over."

"She's waiting on us?" I hated imagining Rina in limbo like my parents were.

"She really wants to be at the wedding."

I turned to Nathan. "How soon can we do it?"

"As soon as you want."

"Tomorrow?"

He held my hand. "That doesn't give us much time to plan."

"We don't need a big fancy wedding. I just want it to be us with our kindrily, on our cliffs, at sunset."

Nathan kissed my thumb. My new engagement ring sparkled in the candlelight. "That would be brilliant."

BURN BRIGHT

Maryah

It was our wedding day, and I was terrified.

Not terrified of marrying Nathan—I loved him more than chocolate. And we had already been married many times throughout our existence. There was no doubt I wanted to marry him again—and remember it. The thing that terrified me was history repeating itself.

Dylan and Amber's wedding in their previous life had been the event where many of our kindrily had gathered and been killed.

I was ninety-nine percent sure Dedrick's soul had truly departed our world for good, but the one percent *What if?* still worried me.

What if he had somehow taken over River's body again? What if he sought revenge? Every member of our kindrily would be there today. What if today—the day that was supposed to be the happiest day of my life—turned out to be another massacre of our kindrily?

I shuddered. I didn't have memories of Dylan and Amber's wedding, but knowing I was there and so many of the people I loved were killed sent my heart writhing with pain.

"Stop sweating." Faith blotted my cheeks and forehead with a tissue.

"I can't help it."

"It is kind of warm in here," Krista said. She opened the balcony door then returned to my dresser mirror to finish braiding her hair.

I flopped back on my pillows and stared at the dream catcher swinging above my bed. I blew out a big breath, hoping to send my negative worries up into its wood, string, and feathers to magically be erased.

"This better not be about Dedrick again," Harmony growled.

I lowered my guilty eyes and fidgeted with my bedspread.

"Maryah." Faith finished smearing extra glitter on her eyelids then shook her finger at me. "Stop. Evelyn told us River is living with her in Ireland, and there is no possible way that Dedrick has taken over his body. Don't let that hellhound ruin your wedding day."

"Rina agrees," Harmony said. "She checked on River and Evelyn a couple times, and she says River is definitely himself."

I took a deep breath. "I know, I know. Okay. I'll stop." I sat up. "Where is Rina?"

Harmony pointed to Faith sitting cross-legged on the floor in front of the other mirror. "Next to Faith. She's fascinated with her makeup ritual."

"Aww, Rina." Faith held up her eye shadow brush and blew sparkling powder at the space beside her. "As soon as you come back here, I will be your personal beauty consultant. We will accentuate all of your star princess features."

I giggled at the thought of Faith applying lipstick and assorted glittery products to the future toddler version of Rina. My stomach swirled because whenever I thought about being pregnant so that Rina could return to us, it required me to also think about having sex with Nathan—for the first time.

Most girls wouldn't already know their daughter before they married their baby's father, but add that to the ever-growing list of stranger-than-fiction facts about my life. Bottom line was it was my wedding day. And everyone knows what happens on the wedding night. My palms were sweaty, so I rubbed them on my thighs.

I closed my eyes and pictured Nathan's lustful gleam that he could never hide. I pictured his hands and how slowly but confidently they touched my skin, how he could be so gentle one moment and so incredibly strong the next, the way he'd discreetly moisten his bottom lip right before he kissed me. Every inch of me tingled just thinking about it.

Tonight would be the best night *ever.*

Louise tapped on the door then stepped inside with a garment bag draped over her arm.

Krista rushed toward her. "The dress!"

The same wedding dress I wore last lifetime was unbelievably beautiful. Louise had it stored in her bedroom closet, but last night she and Helen made me try it on for alterations. Much to my dismay, I wasn't nearly as busty in my current body so the strapless top didn't have much to hold it up, and several inches had to be hemmed from the A-line skirt, but when I stepped into that dress, I felt like I had slipped into a fairy tale.

"Helen and I just finished," Louise said. "We added a few embellishments. I hope you like them."

She hung the garment bag from one of the posts on my bed and unzipped it. Two peacock feathers had been added beneath the bust where it cinched together at the high waist. The feathers were secured with one blue pearl.

Louise's lips pursed with a bittersweet smile. "The pearl was—"

"I know." Tears welled in my eyes. "My mother gave it to me the first time I ever played dress up and pretended to be a bride. She told me she wore it when she married my father and that I could wear it at my wedding. As my something borrowed and blue." I smiled at the happy memory and then wiped away a tear. I wanted my mom with me today more than anything. "They're perfect. Thank you."

Krista handed me a tissue and wrapped her arm around me.

"That's not all," Louise said with a wink. "Nathan made a request too. Turn around for a moment and don't look. I want you to get the full effect when you see it for the first time. Faith, will you assist me?"

I turned around, but I was giddy. The dress was already so pretty. What would Nathan have requested be done to it? The bag and fabric rustled behind me. Krista stood right beside me, so I watched her face, waiting to read her reaction.

She gasped so hard, she almost sucked in my hair.

"Ooooooh," Faith cooed.

"What?" I turned my head, but Krista stopped me. "Not yet."

"I'll admit," Harmony said, "even I like it."

I bounced on my toes. "You guys are killing me."

"That side needs to be spread out a little more," Louise directed. Fabric shook a couple more times as Krista and Faith not-so-quietly tried to contain their excitement.

"Okay." Louise's bracelets jingled. "Ready."

With her hands on my shoulders, Krista turned me around.

I gasped even deeper than Krista had. The back of my dress was breathtaking. The skirt fanned out along the floor with a train made of *white* peacock feathers. They started near where my hips would be. Hundreds of them, layer upon layer, overlapped in arched rows until the final row lined the curved edge of the train.

"It's..." I couldn't think of a word that meant super-duper, jaw-dropping amazing, more-than-I-ever-dreamed beautiful, so I opted for, "exquisite."

Louise petted the soft feathers near the waist. "Nathan said they'd represent your purity. Your soul's new beginning."

Faith giggled. "He's such a keeper."

"Wedding number twenty confirms that." Harmony elbowed me. "What are you waiting for? Put that thing on so we can get you to the chapel on time."

I shook out my hands, which had been clenched from a mixture of nerves, excitement, and a million other emotions, and I untied my robe. I was about to marry my soul mate.

What more could a girl ask for?

∞

Krista and Faith stood on either side of me, helping me gather my dress so I could climb into the Desoto.

"Where are your shoes?" Harmony asked, staring at my bare feet.

"I'm not wearing any. I like feeling the earth between my toes."

She rolled her eyes.

I assessed the backseat of the Desoto then looked over my shoulder at the train of perfectly arranged white feathers.

"For crying out loud." Carson strutted down the driveway in his best man's outfit of tan pants and a matching vest. Under it he wore a crisp white shirt, and his blue and green tie was perfectly knotted. Krista lit up at the sight of him. I had to admit he looked handsome. He stuck his hands in his pockets and chuckled. "You can't be serious. No matter how careful you are, your peacock tail will be ruined if you climb into that car."

"We already discussed this," I said. "Nathan can't traverse me there. It's bad luck to see the bride before the wedding. I've had more than my share of bad luck already."

Carson started rolling up his sleeves. "The cliffs are less than a mile from here."

"Walking that far will ruin the dress too," Faith argued. "I can't promise to carry this skirt that far without dragging it at some point."

"I'll carry you," Carson told me. "We'll be there in no time."

I laughed. "No way. The only man allowed to carry me today is my groom. Besides, you'd probably ruin more feathers than the backseat of the Desoto would."

"Rina has a suggestion," Harmony said. "We blindfold Nate and then he traverses you there."

Faith dropped my skirt and clapped. "Oooh, I love that idea."

I raised one brow at Carson. "How come you didn't think of that one first, Boy Genius?"

Carson's face contorted while he searched for a snappy comeback. "Just stay put, Sparky. I'll take the girls to the cliffs and tell your past and future husband to come get you."

"We can't leave her here alone," Krista argued.

"I'm not alone," I pointed out. "Rina's with me."

Carson nodded. "Besides, it takes all of two minutes to drive there."

They piled into the car. Krista, Faith, and Harmony were all careful with the skirts of their green dresses. The Desoto cranked to life, and I waved to them as Carson backed my car down the driveway.

"Oh, Rina." I sighed. "This is happening because of you. Thank you for saving him. But I'm brokenhearted that you can't physically be here."

Her warm, loving energy embraced me in a hug.

"This is it." I stared up at the cerulean Sedona sky. "My whole life is about to change. Again."

∞

"Don't peek," I warned Nathan.

"I would never."

I ran my fingers along the muscles in Nathan's forearms. His sleeves were rolled up like Carson's, and maybe I was biased, but Nathan looked infinitely sexier in his wedding attire. I was ready to skip all the hoopla and start the honeymoon.

I examined the silk sash tied around his head. "You really can't see?"

"I swear." He hugged me tight to him. "I've waited too long already. Let's go."

I giggled as we traversed to the cliffs.

"Can I take it off now?" He asked.

"Not until I start walking down the aisle."

"Fine." He grinned. "But could you ask Carson to guide me from here?"

I waved Carson over, and he escorted Nathan to his position.

There were no chairs, no altar or stage, just a makeshift aisle lined with huge gorgeous stones that I assumed were the handiwork of Helen. The path led to a large circle of more stones and white flowers which looked beautiful against the red rocks and the setting sun.

All of our kindrily members circled around the ring of flowers. Nathan stood in the middle, blindfolded.

Harmony approached me with a genuine full-blown smile. "You look beautiful."

"Thank you, so do you."

"Take a deep breath," she ordered.

I did, and before I had completely exhaled, she hit me with another emotional bomb.

"Your father asked me to tell you something when this day arrived. He said to tell you that he understands you have been Nate's for centuries, but you will always be his little girl."

I stared down into my bouquet of white Stargazer lilies, fighting back tears.

"He couldn't be happier that you're marrying such an amazing man." Harmony wiped a tear from my cheek. "See you in the circle, Bonita."

"Wait, Harmony?" She turned. "Rina and Dakota, where are they?"

"Dakota is in his place in our circle." Her focus drifted to the space beside me. "Rina is by your side, ready to walk the path in front of you." Harmony smirked. "She said to tell you she can't sprinkle flower petals, but she will be sprinkling stardust."

Gregory watched me, waiting for me to tell him I was ready. I nodded, and he started strumming a slow song on his Spanish guitar. Eightball, our ring bearer, sat at Carson's feet and chewed on his leash. Manny the mouse, Eightball's new best friend, was perched on the ring pillow secured to Eightball's back.

I turned to the seemingly empty space beside me and exhaled. "Shall we, Rina?"

I could feel her loving energy move in front of me. I stared at the path, imagining the back of her dark hair fanning out like black feathers as she strolled along sprinkling stardust.

Amazingly, I saw a faint blue light. I happily followed her lead.

Anthony and Helen stepped apart, creating an opening in the circle and motioned for me to walk through.

Nathan slid the sash from his head. His green eyes locked on me. My knees weakened as dragonflies started our first official wedding dance in my stomach.

That beautiful, charming, sexy, superhero of a man standing in the center of the circle was about to become my husband. I walked faster.

"Anthony?" Pausing beside him and Louise, I whispered, "Will you give me away?"

"Never. We all love you too much." He winked as his dark eyes gleamed with honor. "But I will escort you to the center and leave you in the hands of the man who loves you more than life itself."

I blushed and tucked my hand around Anthony's elbow. We walked forward, and I stopped in front of Nathan. The intensity of love in his gaze took my breath away.

"You're breathtaking," he said.

"I was just thinking the same thing about you." We both smiled as he held my hands.

Edgar bound our wrists together with the sash. Until that moment, the term "tie the knot" had never held such a wonderful meaning.

Edgar returned to his place in the circle then spoke in a way that seemed to hush the desert around us. "A wise soul once said,

'If you love someone, put them in a circle, because hearts can be broken but circles never end.'"

I had heard those words before. I was sure of it. Maybe my soul had stored away that saying from a previous wedding.

We repeated meaningful statements and made sacred vows, but it was all a blur of joy. I removed a ring from Eightball's pillow and slid it onto Nathan's finger.

"This is the best part," Nathan whispered. "I'm looking forward to seeing your reactions since technically, you haven't experienced it before."

"What's going to happen?"

"Watch and see."

Edgar cleared his throat and announced, "May your twin flames be united as one and forever burn bright."

Nathan bowed his head, and I raised my lips to meet his. He let out a slow, steady, warm breath and I inhaled it into my being—my calm before the magical storm. Then his lips caressed mine.

Human words couldn't adequately explain what happened next.

Each member radiated different colors, shades, and textures of light. It was the most beautiful thing I had ever seen. Then, it was like the world stopped spinning. Night and day occurred at the same time. The white moon shone against a purple sky, and a multicolored halo circled the blazing sun.

We were surrounded by stars. They weren't small and distant; they were huge and so close that I reached out to touch them. They were above us, under us, to the sides of us. It was like we were suspended in a gorgeous, fantasy painting of the cosmos. There was no black in the sky; colors were everywhere.

I stared in astonishment. Nathan studied my every move and facial expression. Everywhere my eyes went, his followed.

I was so in awe that I struggled to find my voice. "This happens every time we get married?"

"Every time."

"Let's get married every day."

He laughed. "Then it wouldn't be as wondrous."

I couldn't believe my eyes, but it wasn't just my eyes. Feelings danced inside of me that I had never experienced—a sensation of calm and elation all at the same time. I had never known such an overwhelming feeling of love. The pulsing ring of light still circled us, but the faces and bodies of our kindrily had disappeared.

I gasped. "Where did they go?"

"They're all there." He motioned to the celestial wonder around us. "They are holding the circle for us."

"Holding the circle?"

"Once they let go, it will all return to normal."

"Don't let go!" I shouted to them.

Nathan beamed so brightly that I had to squint. The light swirled and spiraled around us.

A noise that sounded like a freight train roared toward us. I wanted to put my hands over my ears, but Nathan's hands were still bound to mine with the sash. "I don't like this part!"

His eyes narrowed. "Which part?"

"The noise!"

"What noise?" He looked confused. How could he not hear it? He could usually hear a leaf rustle in the breeze from a mile away. His eyes grew wide as he stared over my head. I could barely hear over the intensifying whistling-screeching sound. "Is it possible?"

"Is what possible?" I yelled.

"Look!" Nathan pointed over my shoulder, not taking his attention away from whatever was happening behind me. I turned to see.

It was blinding, but also incredibly beautiful.

A massive star was rising from behind Bell Rock, and then it barreled toward us. The noise, its heat, and its glow intensified as it came closer. Just as the star looked like it was about to crash into our circle, it looped around us and hovered at the edge of our cliff.

"Does that happen every time too?" I shouted to Nathan.

"This has never happened. But why are you shouting?"

Could he really not hear the bone-rattling noise? Through my clenched jaw I asked, "What does it mean?"

The giant ball of light seemed to be inching its way upward. Nathan's eyes were wider than I'd ever seen as he stared, fascinated. "Maryah, stars burn out and fall from the heavens all the time." He squeezed my hands and pulled me closer to him. "But we are witnessing your star reigniting and rising again."

The noise was so loud it vibrated my teeth. My toes curled into the dirt. My knees threatened to give out.

Nathan smiled at me. "This is by far our best wedding yet."

Could we be experiencing the same thing? How could he smile through such a jarring, eardrum-blowing experience?

A sharp pain stabbed my head. My eyes burned like bees were stinging my sockets. I clutched Nathan's arms as I buckled over in pain.

"Maryah, what's wrong?"

Bursts of light exploded behind my scrunched lids. With each flash it felt like someone was chiseling through my head with an ice pick. It took so much strength to speak.

"My head," I groaned.

"Krista!" Nathan shouted. "Maryah's in pain."

The moon and sun vanished. So did all the stars, except for one. My star. The flaring tunnel of screaming light hovered just above the cliff as if waiting to swallow me and the whole town of Sedona.

It glowed brighter and brighter until I had to look away. I stared down at my white dress, so bold against the red ground that it burned my eyes. Eightball barked as bursts of pain continued rippling through me.

"Hang on!" I heard Krista, but I couldn't peel my seared eyelids open. Her hands braced either side of my head.

As if I were an animal acting on survival instincts, I roared ferociously then punched Krista fast and hard in her face. I didn't even feel my fist connect, but she dropped to the ground.

"Maryah!" Nathan's voice was so distant. Eightball kept barking, but I could barely hear him. The star's noise grew even louder. All I could see was a steady glow of bright white. But the pain didn't stop. It increased steadily, more powerful and more excruciating, building and layering until I wanted to crumble under the pressure.

Every muscle in my body tensed as my spine felt torn out of me.

"Nathan." My jaw locked in a spasm. I squeezed his forearms tighter. My body was shattering into a million pieces.

"You're hurting me." Nathan sounded like he was on the other side of the galaxy.

A wave that I can only describe as raging fire poured through me and did not subside. I convulsed and thrashed.

I squeezed tighter and tighter until Nathan's bones cracked beneath my grip.

He cried out in pain.

I wanted to let go, but I couldn't. My hands were locked shut.

I couldn't bear it any longer. I had never heard death described as so torturous, but so much unimaginable pain could only mean I was dying.

It was beyond any human threshold of suffering. I couldn't survive it.

Every bone, muscle, tendon, artery, vein, capillary, cell, molecule, and atom in my body burst into flames. I screamed so loud it was probably heard on the opposite side of the earth.

Then finally my world went black, and there was nothing. Not even pain.

∞

I awoke to his heartbeat pounding against my chest.

His heavy breathing warmed my ear. His shoulder bone pressed against my cheek. I turned my head, trying to alleviate my facial pain. I inhaled, and his intoxicating scent caused my eyes to open. He sucked in a breath through his teeth as if surprised by my movements.

I glimpsed the red slab of rock he was sitting on with me cradled in his lap. He was holding me like I was a baby—his baby. His arms tightened around me. Krista must have already healed the broken arms that were my home. How many other ways had I broken him? Could all the damage I had done ever be repaired?

"Maryah?" He tilted up my chin, and my head fell back like a newborn with no control of its neck muscles. My eyes fluttered closed as he lifted my head to a normal position.

"Maryah, please." There was a degree of sorrow in his voice I had never heard before.

I caused that grief. I put that agony there, and I cursed myself for it. I needed to begin mending the damage, so I forced my lids to open.

His face was only inches from mine. His angelic green eyes were even more soul-rousing than I remembered. The welcoming windows of his soul expanded wider and deeper. He looked shocked and mystified. His eyes turned glassy as he blinked back tears.

I was quite pleased with myself. It had been too long since I stirred his emotions so strongly.

"Look!" Faith's voice cried out from somewhere above us. "She's awake."

Grateful prayers filled the space around us, but all I could see was him. Nathaniel's jaw ticked, and his bottom lip quivered—his telltale signs. It rarely ever happened, maybe a dozen occasions throughout our entire existence together.

"Don't cry," I whispered, "I'm right here."

A single tear rolled down each of his cheeks. He hugged me, then pulled back to stare at me again.

He didn't need to speak. I knew what he was seeing and why he was seeing it—countless volumes of our history together.

I swallowed hard, trying to coat my painful throat. It felt like I had swallowed broken glass then washed it down with acid. I was disappointed in myself for screaming like a banshee and not maintaining my composure.

"Yes." My voice was raspy. Another tear fell, but his expression changed to elation.

"Really?"

"Yes," I said again.

I had gained enough strength to gather my thoughts and obtain some control over the muscles in my body. I turned my head and saw our kindrily gathered around us. The sight of them filled my heart with joy. Carson held back Eightball who was squirming and whimpering, trying to reach me. I turned back to Nathaniel.

"All of it," I whispered.

He shook as he choked in a breath.

"Nathan, please!" Faith begged. "What is she saying?"

Nathaniel didn't flinch. He kept his focus locked on me.

I caressed his face. "The first time we met, you had blond hair. You tripped over your own feet and—"

I didn't get to finish the story of how we first met.

He clenched me to his chest so tight we were one again.

His whole body trembled as he laughed yet cried at the same time, saying *thank you* over and over and over. His gratitude spilled out in a soft whisper as he kissed each of my eyelids then my forehead. "She remembers."

"Everything?" Faith knelt beside us and held my hand. I allowed her to feel my love, gratitude, and relief.

They had done it. It was a huge risk, and the orchestration was daunting at times, but I believed in them, all of them, even the ones whom I hadn't met yet.

I sat up, searching for the one I had moved mountains for and did the unthinkable in order to protect. "Marina?"

"She's right here." Harmony motioned to the space beside her.

I was confident of my newly strengthened ability, so I connected to the strands of energy circling me. Using my power and Rina's—strings and glue—I tapped into Harmony's ability to communicate with spirits, and then I extended that gift through our kindrily's ethereal net so that every member could see and hear our interaction.

I ignored the collective gasps and mutterings of *how* and *what.*

My breath caught as Rina's incandescent soul came into view.

"Hello again," I said to my daughter.

"Hi," Rina answered.

"I am so sorry for what I put you through. So, so sorry."

"Stop apologizing. It was the only way."

No one knew that truth as deeply as I did, but it didn't change the anguish in my heart that she had endured so much sadness and solitude.

From behind me, Nathaniel squeezed my shoulders.

I placed my hand over his. "I didn't tell you because I didn't want to jinx it. We had lost so many children, and I was only several weeks along."

He nodded. "It's all right."

"No, I need you to understand." I glanced between him and Rina. "I need both of you to understand."

My heart ached as if the nightmare from my previous life happened yesterday.

I told Rina, "During the massacre on the beach, I couldn't stop my thoughts from worrying about you. The akin had assured me you would live by gifting my soul and yours with the vital energy of Meru's stars. It's all I could think about. Even as I slit my own throat, I was hoping your soul would stay attached to mine. That we'd travel to the Higher Realm together and I would be able to protect you."

I turned to Nathaniel. "But Lexie, Dedrick's mind reader, she heard my thoughts. She told Dedrick I was pregnant, but thankfully, not about the power Rina possessed. That was my first clue that not every Nefarioun was what they seemed."

I rambled on as all of our kindrily listened.

"Dedrick's healer kept me alive. I was restrained to a bed, not even let up to use the bathroom. Evelyn was my caretaker. For weeks, Dedrick watched us like a grimy, bloodthirsty vulture, but as he grew more lenient and allowed Evelyn alone time with me, I found out who she really was. She showed me the capabilities of her illusions. She told me about her mission to stop Dedrick, and how she hadn't figured out a way to do that until I showed up carrying the answer who hadn't yet been born.

Evelyn and I plotted endlessly. She told me Dedrick's plan to use my daughter as a bargaining chip. He would torture her until I agreed to tell him the location of the starstone." I touched Rina's ghostly cheek and her energy warmed my fingertips. "He was oblivious that the star energy of Meru resided in Marina's soul.

Every night Evelyn brought me the book, and I would write to you," I explained to Rina. "Dedrick took you from me before it was time." My throat tightened, remembering the horror of Dedrick cutting me open and taking Rina months ahead of schedule. "I was so distraught and broken, so worried you wouldn't survive." Tears filled my eyes. Rina turned into a prism of blurry colors. "He wouldn't even let me see you."

"But Evelyn did," Rina said. "She told me the first time you looked into my eyes, you knew I had the ability to absorb other people's powers."

I nodded.

Rina glowed brighter. "She said you loved me so much. She knew you'd reveal the truth to Dedrick to stop him from hurting me. You would have told him that I was the starstone to prevent him from hurting me, but then he would have taken me away because I contained the power he needed."

Tears spilled down my face. "Either way, no matter what I chose, I lost. And you suffered."

Nathaniel squeezed my shoulders again.

I spun to face him. "I had to erase. I didn't want to, but if I remembered, if I knew Dedrick had our daughter, I would have tried to save her as soon as I could. I had a premonition of the future." I cringed at the powerful foretelling of what would have happened if I hadn't erased. "The older kindrily members helped us, but so many of us were too young. Rina was too young. Our powers weren't strong enough yet. We didn't have eighteen members. I wasn't able to connect to anyone's abilities." I glanced around at my beloved kindrily. "Dedrick would have killed so many of us." My hand trailed along Nathan's strong jaw. "Including you. He would have won. He would have ended up with Rina. He would have shut down the energy portals to this world, and our fallen members wouldn't have been able to return. You and I would have been separated forever."

Nathaniel's muscles tensed as he winced.

"So you devised an elaborate plan." Rina melded her radiant hand over mine. "To stop Dedrick and allow all of us to be together again as a real family in the future."

Nathaniel reached down, brushing his fingers over Rina's light.

"Much too far in the future." My heart ached at the thought of losing her all over again.

"It went by in the blink of an eye," she said. "I'll be back soon."

"What if my body fails us again?"

"You're as healthy as can be. Krista and I have made sure of that."

Krista's heartfelt grin told me she had forgiven me for my uncontrollable slug to her face. She had already healed herself.

"That day can't arrive soon enough," I told Rina. "You were incredibly brave, and I am so proud of you, more than words can express. Dedrick never stood a chance against you."

"Against us," she said.

"Against us." I held Nathaniel's hand and nodded at the rest of our kindrily. "All of us."

Dakota moved forward, hovering supportively behind his soul mate. "You and Dakota will be a force to be reckoned with."

Rina beamed. "Created from love."

"More love than you can fathom." I touched her cheek. "I have loved you for so very, very long." She was the daughter I had prayed for each and every lifetime. "Thank you for choosing me."

"We chose each other."

After wiping away my tears, I touched her ethereal light one more time. "Go, so you can hurry back. The stars are waiting for you."

Carson stepped forward. "I hate to break up the warm and fuzzy moment, but can I say something to Dakota before he goes?"

"Of course."

Carson tucked his hair behind his ears and stood in front of Dakota. "Dude, I'll miss you. And I can't wait for you to come back, but—" His tan cheeks blushed. "Don't choose me and Krista as your parents, okay? It would be too weird, and I'm just not ready for that kind of responsibility."

Laughter graced the cliffs and Carson blushed.

Dakota attempted to punch Carson's shoulder as his light pulsed. "I would never give you the satisfaction of being my father and telling me what I can and can't do."

Carson nodded happily. "Cool. Glad we agree."

"Thank you, Maryah," Dakota said. "I'm honored that you made me an Element."

"You did that all on your own." That wasn't entirely true. I did have some influence, but Dakota had more than earned his position.

He hugged Faith and Harmony. "Take care of Mom and Dad."

"We will," Faith said, wiping away a tear. "See you soon."

We all watched Rina and Dakota cross through the veil. My heart broke but overflowed all at the same time.

Nathaniel wrapped his arms around my waist. Amber released Eightball, and he galloped over to us then sat at my feet.

"You did it," Nathaniel said. "As always, you pulled off the impossible. You wrote us a different ending."

"*We* did." I turned around and traced a figure eight around my twin flame's green eyes. "I knew you and I couldn't be erased. A love as strong as ours will always burn bright."

Nathaniel silenced me with a soul-tingling kiss.

I pulled away and peered up at him with a coquettish grin. "Where are we going on our honeymoon?"

His strong hands slid down the back of my waist. "Anywhere and everywhere you desire."

My insides danced with anticipation. "Let me thank everyone and then we can be on our way."

He nodded and we made our rounds. I was grateful beyond words for each and every member of our kindrily, and all they had done, but I did my best to tell them so.

When we were finished, I looked at the sky, at mine and Nathaniel's stars twinkling side by side above Cathedral Rock. Just to the right of us were two younger stars. The other fourteen that represented each member of our kindrily pulsed around us, each with its own unique glow.

"Every soul is a story shelved away in an infinite library in the sky." I sighed happily, relieved that our stories would continue. We would all shine for eternity.

Nathaniel wrapped his arms around me, preparing to traverse. He smiled then pressed his forehead against mine. "Ready for our next chapter?"

"Always."

THE END...

For now.

ACKNOWLDEGMENTS

I keep hoping my Acknowledgments become easier to write with each book, but they don't. I feel like I can never adequately express my gratitude to all the amazing people who help make my books a reality. I'm also thanking the same people over and over. I wish I could come up with something original and clever each time, but I'm running out of ways to say, "Thank you. You're awesome. I love you."

With that being said:

Mom, Dad, John, Marie Jaskulka (editor), Michelle Argyle (cover designer), Megan McBride and Natalie Bahm (critique partners), Krista, April, and Andrea (dear friends and long-time supporters), every blogger/fan who has ever helped spread the word about any of my books, and each and every reader of The Kindrily series (yes, YOU!)...

Thank you. You're awesome. I love you.

ABOUT THE AUTHOR

Karen was born and bred in Baltimore, frolicked and froze in Colorado for a couple of years, and is currently sunning and splashing around Florida with her two beloved dogs. She's addicted to coffee, chocolate, and complicated happily-ever-afters.

Other novels by Karen:

Grasping at Eternity
Fighting for Infinity

Tangled Tides
Dangerous Depths
Sacred Seas

Virtual Arcana

Find Karen and her books online at
www.KarenAmandaHooper.com

42146020R00234

Made in the USA
San Bernardino, CA
07 July 2019